finding faith

DENISE HUNTER

finding faith

A NOVEL

THE NEW HEIGHTS SERIES - BOOK THREE

Howard Books

New York   London   Toronto   Sydney   New Delhi

An Imprint of Simon & Schuster, Inc.
1230 Avenue of the Americas
New York, NY 10020

First Howard Books paperback edition March 2019

HOWARD and colophon are trademarks of Simon & Schuster, Inc.

For information about special discounts for bulk purchases,
please contact Simon & Schuster Special Sales at 1-866-506-1949 or
business@simonandschuster.com.

The Simon & Schuster Speakers Bureau can bring authors to your
live event. For more information or to book an event, contact the Simon &
Schuster Speakers Bureau at 1-866-248-3049 or visit our website at
www.simonspeakers.com.

Edited by Ramona Richards
Interior design by John Mark Luke Designs

Manufactured in the United States of America

10 9 8 7 6 5 4 3 2 1

Library of Congress Control Number: 2003067766

ISBN 978-1-9821-0902-8

ACKNOWLEDGMENTS

All novels are the collaboration of many people, and this author is thankful to everyone who had a hand in this book's production. First of all, I'd like to thank God who, during my formation, added an extra dose of imagination. What a fun gift it has turned out to be!

Thanks to all the people at Howard Publishing, who work so hard getting my books and many others into readers' hands. Thanks especially to my editors, Philis Boultinghouse and Ramona Tucker, who made editing an enjoyable process.

I also wish to thank my dear friend and critique partner, Colleen Coble, who reads every word I write and isn't afraid to tell me when it's all wrong!

For particular details in this story, I relied on Thomas Smith and the entire Sinclair family: Mark, Gina, Mindy, and Tyler. Thanks, guys, for all your help! Last, but not least, thanks to Kevin for putting up with my wandering mind and my boring writer-talk. Love you, hon!

CHAPTER ONE

"I'm ready to go," Paula Landin-Cohen called to her husband, David, as she snapped the latches on her suitcase.

The house rang with a familiar silence.

She checked the bag for her boarding pass and driver's license, then hefted the suitcase down the curved staircase, eying the bank of windows on the front of the house.

December had blown into Jackson Hole, Wyoming, with cold, biting winds and at least a foot of snow. Chicago's weather would be no better, but just the thought of the big city left her feeling as though she could soar there without benefit of Delta. As she had the past few months, she pushed aside the bitter memory of her first visit there and focused on her future.

Setting her suitcase by the door, she checked her Movado. "David, we have to go." Her voice echoed up the vaulted ceiling and through the cavernous kitchen, but this time drew a reply.

"Fine," he called—from the office, she thought.

OK, not the tone she hoped for, but at least he was talking to her today.

She grabbed her Burberry coat from the closet and wondered if she should take her warmest one too. Fashion overruling practicality, she closed the door just in time to catch David's hand.

"Do you mind?" he said.

She backed away, ignoring his snippy tone. She wasn't going to let him ruin this for her. She checked her bag again for the boarding pass and license. She was being compulsive, but she couldn't let anything go wrong with this flight. She went through the list of things she'd need over the coming week. Had she packed her tape recorders? Before she could panic, she remembered sliding them into her briefcase.

David stepped around her in his charcoal, woolen coat, picked up her suitcase, and walked out the door. Paula turned on the threshold and gazed at her home. Sweeper marks striped the beige carpet, running parallel across the expanse of the great room like yard lines on a football field. Her socks from yesterday lay in two distinct balls by the sofa.

She turned the lock on the doorknob and shut the door behind her. David placed the suitcase in the rear compartment of the Cadillac Escalade and pushed his trendy glasses up on the bridge of his nose in a movement as familiar to her as the smell of her own home. So familiar that she rarely noticed it unless she was away for several days. She wouldn't see David push his glasses up, smell his spicy cologne, or watch him squint over the *Wall Street Journal* for six days.

He opened the car door for her, and she slipped inside before he clicked it shut. In spite of their problems, in spite of his relentless blaming and silent treatment, she didn't want to part this way. Not now, when she was about to do the most exciting thing of her life. She wanted someone to share it with. Someone to be happy for her. Someone to cheer her on back home. Heaven knew her family wasn't doing that.

David slid in behind the wheel and started the vehicle. His movements were sure and precise. Another man's motions would reveal his anger, but not David's.

"Well," she said, "at least you'll be able to keep the house clean this week." She delivered the line with a hint of humor, planted there in hopes of coaxing him from his disagreeable mood. She cocked her head the tiniest bit so she could watch him from her peripheral vision. When his face gave nothing away, she almost wondered if she'd spoken the words aloud at all.

Paula turned forward and stared out her window. It was fine with her if David wanted to leave things this way. She could do this alone. She was a grown woman.

They headed up Snow King Avenue toward the Snow King Resort. Already a few dedicated skiers swooped down the slopes on this lazy Sunday morning.

She consulted her watch again. Her parents would be getting up for church about now—her mom boiling water for that wretched cup of instant coffee. Hanna and Gram would be making breakfast for the guests of Higher Grounds Mountain Lodge while Micah shoveled the two inches of snow that had fallen overnight. Natalie would be scurrying to get breakfast ready for Taylor and Alex after an undoubtedly sleepless night with her adopted newborn, Grace. Her stomach tightened at that one.

She squinted out the front windshield, up Cache Street, the road that would take her out of there. They were making good time. All the tourists had evidently stayed out too late drinking to do anything more than loll in bed.

As they crossed the line that demarked the edge of Jackson Hole, Paula almost expected the raucous blowing of party horns. She'd waited all her life to exit this miserable little hole in the middle of nowhere, and today was the beginning of that dream. But there were no party horns. She wished the radio were on so she didn't feel as if she was about to choke on the silence. She struggled to think of something to say. She, whose words usually came easily and flawlessly.

"Your clothes should be ready at the cleaners by five tomorrow," she said. It was lame, unnecessary even, since David knew very well when his clothes would be ready. At least she was trying.

But he sat beside her as cold as a mountain glacier. Couldn't he at least grunt? Even when she'd come home two days earlier with her auburn hair straightened, he hadn't so much as glanced her direction. Of course, having her natural curls pulled straight would have bothered him at one time. Now the stiff set of his shoulders made her wonder if he was ever going to thaw.

This is Paula Landin-Cohen, reporting from inside an SUV, where a man is attempting to freeze his wife with the cold vapors emanating from his body. Join us at eleven, and we'll give you all the details on this story.

They passed the Elk Refuge, but all Paula saw was acres of snow behind the fence. She looked at her watch again.

"You've got plenty of time," David said.

She didn't know whether to be thankful for his first voluntary words or peeved at his tone. She decided on the latter. He'd done nothing but snub her for months, and for what? She was innocent, and he was too stubborn to believe it.

"You know, we're married, David. A little kindness wouldn't hurt."

His jaw twitched. "Married people don't live across the country from one another."

Like he cared.

"It's only temporary."

Her last word rang out in the car like an echo across Granite Canyon. At least they were talking. OK, arguing, but it was better than the silence.

"Not if you get your *dream job.*"

If words could wear a sneer, those two did. And it rankled. Heat prickled her skin under the coat, and she felt like her temperature had shot up ten degrees. "Why do you care, anyway? You've walked around for months, giving me your self-righteous silent treatment. Now I won't be in the way. Not me or my soggy bath towel or my dirty dishes. You can live in your sterile house and keep it just the way you like it."

He had no right to deny her this opportunity or to make her feel guilty about leaving. He made decisions without her approval. Why should she have to get his?

He turned the car into the airport, and she realized this was it. They were parting as enemies on the biggest week of her life. Why had she imagined calling him on Monday night from Chicago and sharing everything that had happened? There was no reason to call home. She would go back to her apartment after work tomorrow with nothing to greet her except silence.

David pulled the vehicle up to the building and got out. Paula waited on the curb as he lifted the suitcase out and set it at her feet. He straightened and looked her in the eye for the first time in weeks. Face-to-face, they stood closer than they had since that day when everything had changed. Was he regretting his harsh tone?

Their breaths expelled in cold puffs, mingling in a dance more intimate than anything they'd done together in a very long time. She had a sudden memory of their first kiss . . .

It was their third date. She was teaching him to ski at Snow King, teaching him how to snowplow to control his speed, when the tips of his skis crossed and he went down. She snowplowed to a stop, laughing. They spent the whole day laughing. But when she saw he wasn't moving, her laughter stopped.

"David?" She sidestepped up to him, kicked off her skis, and sank onto her knees.

Reaching for her, he suddenly pulled her down on top of him. Bundled in so much clothing, he felt like a big, cuddly, teddy bear under her. His eyes sparkled with laughter.

"That was not nice," she said.

"It worked, though." His glasses were slightly cockeyed.

The stirring in Paula's stomach felt right and wonderful.

As his grin melted away, the look in his eyes could have melted the snow around them.

She went warm all over in spite of the cold temperature. Their winter breath met and blended together. He cupped her face and pulled her toward him until their lips met.

"I'm sure you can get a porter to help you from here."

The cold tone yanked her from the memory.

"Or maybe you can charm some guy into carrying them for you."

The words cut deeply. He was so wrong about her. So wrong about all of it. When would he believe her? What did she have to do to prove it wasn't true? He made her feel somehow guilty, like a little girl sitting in a principal's office.

Yes, the words hurt, but she didn't allow a trace of it to show on her face. It wouldn't have mattered if she had, since David was walking away.

Walking toward his side of the SUV.

Getting in.

Driving away.

Paula picked up her suitcase and walked toward the airport door.

And that's a wrap.

CHAPTER TWO

"What can you tell us about the new trauma wing, Mr. Boccardi? How will its addition help the people of Chicago?"

Paula watched Darrick Wilmington as he placed the microphone in front of Chicago General Hospital's president. She wished she were anywhere else. Why, of all places, did she have to come here on her first day on the job? She tried to focus on the man's answer, but her heart picked up speed, and her breathing accelerated to keep up. Her heart *was* racing, wasn't it? She laid two fingers against her neck. Yes, racing. And pounding. What was wrong with her?

She had to get out of here.

She looked around the room. Steve, the cameraman, and Darrick were focused solely on Mr. Boccardi. Maybe she could just slip out.

A second later she realized, *No maybe about it.* She had to get out of there.

Backing out of the room, she strode down the long, sterile hall. Her heels clicked with each step. She drew in gulps of air, blowing them out through her mouth. A nurse passed, and Paula wondered if the woman could tell something was terribly wrong. At least it felt terribly wrong. Did she need help?

She stopped beside a coffee machine, tucking herself away on the other side of it.

Get a grip, Paula. Just breathe. Everything is going to be OK.

Was she having some kind of reaction to the bad memories this place was stirring up? A panic attack because of the stress associated with the new job?

Her hands trembled as she gripped them together. She willed herself to be calm. Finally her heart and breathing began to slow. Her mind stopped spinning. She closed her eyes and leaned against the wall. Whatever that was, she hoped it didn't happen again. She had to pull herself together before they went back to the station.

Reaching into her purse, she pulled out some coins and dropped them into the machine. After they clinked to a stop, she pushed the decaf button. A cup fell into place and began filling with what she hoped was drinkable coffee. She didn't need the caffeine. If anything, she needed a tranquilizer. Looking around, she supposed she was in the right place to get one.

She sipped from the cup while inhaling the strong brew. Tugging her bag back up on her shoulder, she walked back down the hall. When she reached the office where Darrick was conducting the interview, the door was closed. Rather than causing a disruption, she passed the door and rounded the corner to a small waiting area.

She took a seat across from a woman clad in khakis and a pale orange sweater that washed out her fair skin. Today had been an exciting, educational experience. Field reporting was a different bird than what she did at WKEV in Jackson Hole. There was actually real news to report every day. They covered an accident on the tollway that took two lives and a robbery at a convenience store. She was eager to learn and hoped she'd be ready next Monday, when she would be on her own.

"Do you have an appointment with Mr. Boccardi too?" The voice came from the woman across from her.

Paula cleared her throat. "I'm with the news crew that's interviewing him right now."

"Oh." The woman twisted the straps on her black purse. "My husband and I have an appointment with him, and I was just wondering if there was a line." Her lips tipped up on the sides. At least Paula thought it was a tip, but it may have been a quiver.

"Are you OK?" Paula didn't know what prompted her to ask. Maybe it was the blend of sadness and anxiety that darkened the woman's eyes. After her episode a few minutes ago, she was feeling prone to sympathy regarding anxiety.

The woman drew a shaky breath. "Just nervous. This is an important meeting. I hope it goes well."

"Mr. Boccardi is a nice man. I'm sure it'll go just fine."

The woman nodded. "You have such beautiful auburn hair."

"Thank you. It's a gift from my Irish ancestors." Paula was glad for the distraction of small talk. Besides, the woman seemed like she needed someone to distract her from her upcoming meeting.

"Did they pass on the legendary temper too?" The woman smiled.

"My husband would say yes." Paula returned the smile.

The office door opened, and Darrick exited with Steve.

Paula stood. "It was nice talking with you. Good luck on your meeting."

The woman thanked her before Paula joined the two men. They removed their coats from the chair where they'd been left and slipped into them.

"Ready to head back to the station?" Darrick asked.

Paula agreed and followed the men through the building. The antiseptic smell filled her nostrils, making her stomach churn. She never wanted to come back here. Some memories were better buried forever.

When the cold air hit her face, she breathed in deeply, as if it would wash the acrid smell from her lungs. Eager to forget her experience at the hospital, Paula plied Darrick with questions all the way back to the station. When they arrived, Miles Harding, the producer, called a meeting in the boardroom. Finally having a chance to talk privately with Miles, she thanked him for the potted African violet and the nice note of welcome that had been on her doorstep when she arrived the day before.

When they were finished talking, Paula took a seat at the long table that was not quite rectangular, but not quite oval either. Darrick introduced the woman and man across from her as Roxy and Jaron, the station's weekend anchors. Cindy, Miles's assistant, whom she met earlier, was also present.

On the wall across from her was a collage of black-and-white photos of Walter Cronkite, Edward R. Murrow, Charles Kuralt, and a couple of men Paula didn't recognize. Below the collage was a framed, matted quote, attributed to Cronkite:

> Our job is only to hold up a mirror—to tell and show the public what has happened, and then it is the job of the people to decide whether they have faith in their leaders or government. We are faithful to our profession of telling the truth.

Paula glanced at the people around the table and wondered what the meeting was about. Two field reporters and two anchors. Just then Max Pierson walked in with Miles.

"Thanks for coming, everyone." Miles took a seat at the head of the table, and Max sat beside him. "Paula, this is Max Pierson, our evening anchor. Max, Paula Landin-Cohen, our bright, new investigative reporter."

Paula took the hand Max offered, approving of his firm, steady handshake. He had more wrinkles than what showed on TV, but that was typical.

"Some of you might've guessed why you're here," Miles said, "but I have some news that affects all of you. Or will at least affect one of you quite dramatically. Max?"

Max rested his elbows on the table. His gaze swept each person. "Well, folks, I've been in this business a long time. Longer than some of you have been alive." He looked pointedly at Jaron, and everyone smiled as Jaron shrugged.

"News is in my blood, just as I know it's in yours," Max continued. "But the time has come, or at least my wife tells me it has, for me to bid farewell to my work."

It shouldn't have been a surprise. Max was past retirement age, and most stations would have given his spot to a younger, fresher face a long time ago. Even Paula had been concerned about her own youthful looks slipping away in a world where men grew "distinguished" and women "aged." But she couldn't help but be excited by the opportunity that was possibly being served up before her.

"Now I can see all your eyes lit up like children on Christmas morning," Miles said. "But obviously, we're talking about one position here. And Max is going to hang around with us until the end of March, so we've got some time yet."

Paula's thoughts careened wildly. Did she have a chance at the anchor job? She was only here as a temporary fill-in for a disabled reporter. But could Miles be considering her? He must, or she wouldn't be in this room.

"There are almost four months between now and then, and come March, I'm going to have a big decision to make. I have no doubt that each of you is capable of doing the job. The question is, who's the best person for the job? Who's the hungriest for the job? You have three months to show me."

Paula felt the stirrings of desire and drive. All the ambition that had seen her through to a journalism degree, into lead position at WKEV, and now to a temporary spot in Chicago. This was her shot at her dream job. She remembered the way David had snarled those two words the day before. Why couldn't he understand? He was already achieving his dreams. How could he deny her a chance at hers?

Everyone was standing, congratulating Max on his retirement. But Paula knew that four of the people in that room were thinking of only one thing: grabbing the prestigious anchor chair for themselves.

⚜

Linn Caldwell stared across the desk at Mrs. Lipinski, her thoughts jelling in her head.

"And so you see, dear, while I really hate to do it, there's just no help for it."

Outside the office door a customer was scolding her child in whispered tones for running through the bookstore.

"Maybe you can just give me fewer hours." Linn regretted her words when she saw the way Mrs. Lipinski's eyes pulled down at the corners. But this was the job she'd counted on when she moved to Chicago. And living here wasn't cheap, even when you shared an apartment.

"Honey, believe me, I've tried working the numbers, but I wouldn't be able to give you enough hours to keep you going." The woman put her wrinkly hand on Linn's arm. "I'm truly sorry, Linn. If I had known sooner, I would've let you know, but . . ." She shook her head, pulling her rounded shoulders up.

"I understand." She would not cry. She wouldn't. She'd been through much worse than this, and God would help her find another job, wouldn't He? Hadn't He worked out her scholarship, her apartment, and . . . Grace? Her hand went to her belly to rub away the cramp that was building.

"Mrs. Lipinski." An employee stuck her head in the office. "There's a customer asking about an order that I can't seem to find. The system's acting up again."

"Be right there." Mrs. Lipinski squeezed Linn's arm. "I need to go take care of this."

Linn grabbed her purse and coat and left the office, her thoughts spinning. As she exited Book Nook, the crisp December air hit her in the face, much like reality had moments ago.

Charlotte was going to flip if Linn couldn't pay her share of the rent. They'd barely have squeaked by on the salary she would have made at the Book Nook. Linn needed a part-time job, and quick. If only her scholarship had covered room and board, she'd be living easy at the dorm with most of the other students at Loyola University. But having to miss the first semester had ruined that.

She thought of what she had left behind in Jackson Hole and felt a tugging. No. She couldn't go back there. It wouldn't be fair to any of them. And there was no way she was giving up her scholarship, even if she had to live on the street. She shivered and huddled in her coat.

Even at night, Chicago seemed bright, glowing with fluorescent and neon store lights. She strolled down the sidewalk past the bus hut, knowing the bus wasn't due just yet. She wished Charlotte had stuck around for a few minutes after dropping her off. Of course, neither of them had known what a short meeting her appointment with Mrs. Lipinski would be.

Ahead, a Java Joe sign lit the sky. Impulsively she turned and entered. Warmth glided over her cold skin like a welcoming hug. The place was hopping with college students. Students whose parents were probably footing the bill for college, books, and dorm with a little spending money thrown in on the side. Her dad was lucky to pay his own bills this month, much less hers. And that was even if they were talking. Which they weren't.

Linn got in line and tried to think of where she could apply. There was a diner close to her apartment, but she didn't remember seeing any Help Wanted signs.

The line scooted forward, and she moved with it. Maybe the university was hiring for the cafeteria or something.

She sighed. Probably not. The first semester was almost over, and kids who needed jobs had taken them in September, just as she would have if she hadn't been—

She didn't need to be thinking about that right now. She had barely a month before she started her first college semester, and she needed a job quick.

She should get a paper tonight and search the employment section. Did the coffee shop have a newspaper stand outside? She turned and looked past the line forming behind her. There were three stands outside the door. Reaching into her purse, she dug around for her wallet. Tissues, lipstick, class schedule, pens . . . where was it? That's when she remembered taking it out at the apartment before she left for the Book Nook. She must've left it there.

"What can I get for you?"

Her head snapped up to see the guy behind the counter. A real cutie, with his brows raised in expectation.

"Uh . . ." She glanced over her shoulder, uncomfortably aware of the students in line behind her. "I left my wallet at home," she said as quietly as she could.

Not that she had much in there anyway.

The noisy den swallowed her words.

"What?" The guy still wore his pleasant, I-aim-to-please smile.

"Never mind. I forgot my money . . ."

She backed away, and the girl behind her nudged into first place.

"Wait." He crooked his finger.

She wasn't sure if it was the motion of his finger or the depth in his eyes that pulled her back to the counter. The girl who had taken her spot reluctantly slid back.

"Magenta over here mismade a drink." He gestured toward a girl with pink hair who was dumping a shot of espresso into a grande cup. "Do you like mochas?"

Linn's head bobbed up and down.

The girl behind her huffed.

"Look—it's OK. I should just leave." Linn turned and walked away. Her face felt hot, despite the chill of her skin. How could she have been so stupid as to leave her wallet behind? She didn't even have enough for a newspaper.

Another thought smacked her. How was she going to pay for the bus?

She exited the coffee shop and leaned against the brick facade. Her breath vaporized in front of her face. What a dope she was. How was she going to get home now? Charlotte was at her own job, and the only other person she'd met in the short few days she'd been in the city was Mrs. Lipinski. And she was working too. Should she try and walk home?

Fear stabbed Linn as she stared down the lighted sidewalk. This wasn't Jackson Hole; this was Chicago. And her apartment was at least four miles away . . . maybe more. She had never been good at judging distances. She held her watch up to the light shining out of the coffee shop's front window. It was going on nine. She calculated the time it would take for her to walk home. Should she do it? What choice did she have?

"Excuse me."

The cute guy from behind the counter stood half in and half out of the door. He extended a vasto cup.

She straightened, feeling her hair snag the brick behind her. "Hi."

"It's going to go to waste if you don't take it."

She couldn't resist the mocha any more than she could resist his smile. "Thanks." The cup was warm against her cold fingers.

"Want to come inside and warm up?"

She thought about the long walk ahead and the hour, growing later by the minute. "Nah, I've got to be going."

"Right. Well, come back and see us again." He was inside the shop before she could respond. Which was just as well, since she was pretty sure she didn't want to show her face around there anytime soon.

She shoved off the wall and started the long walk home. The mocha slid like warm comfort down her throat. She could get a paper in the morning and start setting up interviews. She was fortunate that she still had more than a month before school started so she could pour all her time into finding work. Of course, she already owed Charlotte for their first month's rent, and she only had fifty-four dollars left.

She should look for a waitressing job. She had experience from working at Bubba's Bar-B-Que in Jackson Hole, and restaurants were always busier on evenings and weekends, when she would be available.

She'd walked about two miles when she noticed there were hardly any lights lining the sidewalk. Was this even the right street? When Charlotte had driven her to the Book Nook, she hadn't been paying much attention. Was it this street or the next where she should turn?

She decided to walk to the next one. She didn't remember the area looking so residential. Hadn't there been a gas station or something on the corner? She waited for a car to go by, then crossed the street and continued on, taking the last sip from her now-cold mocha.

At the next corner she stopped and peered down the street. It was as residential as the last one had been. Residential and dark. Should she go that way or keep walking? Why hadn't she called Charlotte from the coffee shop to make sure of the directions?

Linn closed her eyes and let out a breath. Her nose had gone numb, and her fingers were even worse. Three days in Chicago and she was already lost. So much for her bright future.

People whizzed by in cars without so much as looking her way. She couldn't help but think how different it was from Jackson Hole, where you couldn't go anywhere without passing someone you knew.

She knew she had to make a decision. She couldn't just stand on this corner forever.

A car turned the corner slowly—a sleek sports model, filled with guys. One of them smiled at her as they passed, then must have put down the window. She could hear them shouting back to her as they drove away.

As she crossed the road, her feet kicked into a faster gear. Would those guys round the block and come back? She didn't want to be anywhere near if they did. The streetlamps were further apart now, and the buildings had given way to mostly apartments and closed retail stores. Her feet pounded the sidewalk in a rhythmic *thump*. What was she going to do? She needed to ask someone how to get to her street, but who?

Behind her a car slowed. She moved to the far side of the sidewalk and quickened her steps. Had those guys come back?

Help me, God.

The metro section of the newspaper had told her all she needed to know about how safe Chicago was.

The car eased up beside her, making soft popping sounds as its tires rolled over loose pebbles. Then she heard the mechanical hum of a window sliding down.

CHAPTER
THREE

Linn swallowed gulps of frosty air and tried to get her frozen legs to move faster. She didn't want to look next to her, to see who was stalking her in the dark. There was no one else around—not even a car passing by.

"Hi again."

The voice registered as familiar. Her head whipped around. It was the guy from the coffee shop. Her body nearly thawed with relief. She slowed her frantic pace and turned.

The car stopped beside her, idling.

"I thought that was you, but I wasn't sure," the guy said, smiling. "It's not safe to walk around by yourself at night."

"I was supposed to take the bus, but . . ." She shrugged, not wanting to repeat that she'd left her money at home.

"Ah." His head tipped back slightly as if he was remembering her cash problem. A car buzzed around him, honking for good measure. "Can I give you a lift?" He seemed hesitant to ask, as if he knew the fear and uncertainty that would automatically enter a girl's mind at such a question. "I don't feel good about leaving you out here all alone."

Weighing the threat of those guys returning and the unknown threats ahead against the seemingly nice guy in the car, Linn decided the offer was definitely the lesser of two evils. She nodded. "Thanks."

He opened the car door from inside, and she hopped in. The car's warmth encased her like a fleece blanket.

"Where to?"

"3702 Cermak."

He checked the traffic and made a U-turn in the middle of the street.

Great. I was going the wrong way. She put the mocha cup between her knees and rubbed her hands together.

He turned up the heat to full blast. "You must be new to the area."

"I've only been here three days."

"Here as in Cicero or here as in Chicago?"

"Chicago. I'm starting at Loyola in January."

"Good school. Where did you come from?"

He had a pleasant voice and a kind demeanor that made her feel more comfortable than she had in all the time since she left home. She realized only then how strange it felt to know only one person in the whole city.

"Jackson Hole, Wyoming."

"Ah. That's where the Tetons are, right?"

"Right."

He was making a left at the first street she'd questioned. She remembered Mrs. Geischen, her fifth-grade teacher, telling the class, "*Always go with your first impression on tests.*" Maybe that applied to real life too. She wiggled her toes inside her boots. Now that she was inside the car and sitting still, she realized they also were half-frozen.

"Warming up?" he asked.

"Yes, thanks." She peeked at him discreetly. He was such a cutie. Or maybe she should say he was *attractive*, since he seemed less like a guy and more like a man. His dark hair was clipped short, and he had a strong profile that reminded her of a movie star.

She blinked. What was she doing? The last thing she needed to be thinking about was men. After her nightmarish record on that account and her precarious future, she needed to focus on keeping a roof over her head.

Just then he turned onto her street, and everything looked familiar again.

"You wouldn't happen to know anyone looking for some part-time help, would you?" she asked.

"Are you looking?" He glanced at her sideways, and she quickly averted her eyes. He was way too distracting.

"I had a job lined up, but it fell through tonight." She pointed toward her apartment building. "It's right there."

"You've had a rough night, haven't you?" When he pulled up to the curb, the way his lips went crooked made her smile.

"What gave it away? The fact that I: a) left my money at home, b) had to walk home and got lost, or c) lost my job before I even started?"

"D. All of the above?"

"*Ding, ding, ding.* We have a lucky winner."

The sound of his laugh made warmth curl in her stomach in a place that had previously ached. It was such a pleasant sensation that she didn't have the strength to fight it.

He grinned. "I can tell you're a student. Even conversation is in the form of a test."

Linn reached for the handle. "Listen, I really appreciate the ride."

"Wait. You asked about a job."

She faced him, the tingling of her thawing extremities temporarily forgotten.

"There's nothing available at the coffee shop right now, but one of our new employees might not work out. Joe, the manager, has been talking about finding someone else. Interested?"

"Sure. I've waitressed, so I'm used to waiting on the public. And I'm a quick learner."

"Just not so good with the north and south thing?" His eyes played with her.

She whacked him on the arm, though he probably couldn't feel it under the layers of nylon and down.

He grabbed a three-ring notebook and pencil from the backseat floor. "Jot down your name and number if you want, and I'll pass it on to Joe." He flipped on the interior lights.

"I really appreciate that." She turned past a bunch of notes to a blank page. As she flipped through, she caught the phrases "divine truth" and "inerrancy of Scripture." Was this guy a preacher or something? He didn't look like one.

She wrote down her name and new phone number with the stubby pencil and handed it back to him.

"My name's Adam, by the way." He put his hand out.

She shook his hand, feeling suddenly shy. "Thanks again for the ride." She reached for the handle again and opened the door.

"Now, don't get in the habit of hitching rides around here. You're not in Kansas anymore, Dorothy."

She smiled. "I'll be careful." She waved him off, wondering why he even cared about a stranger like her.

<hr />

"What do you think?" David asked.

Natalie, one of Paula's sisters, and her soon-to-be husband, Kyle Keaton, strolled through the two-story home, eying the distressed wood floor and the freshly painted walls.

David had been as surprised as everyone else at Natalie and Kyle's whirlwind engagement. Even the wedding, planned for Christmas Eve, was coming at lightning speed, though the couple seemed confident in their plans and thoroughly in love.

"I love it." Natalie shifted the baby in her arms.

"Want me to take her?" Kyle asked.

Natalie handed little Gracie over, and Kyle cradled her in one arm like a football.

"The floor is beautiful," Natalie said. "And I like the way the master bedroom is downstairs and the other rooms are upstairs."

"Are we going to be able to hear Gracie from down here?" Kyle asked.

"We can use a nursery monitor."

David watched how the two of them communicated so kindly and felt a tightness in his gut that he recognized as jealousy. When was the last time he and Paula had spoken to each other so amicably? Of course, he reminded himself, these two weren't even married yet. And talk about full plates. Natalie had two boys from her first marriage, an ex-husband who'd betrayed her, and a newly adopted baby who just happened to be her ex-husband's love child. Maybe David's life wasn't so whacked after all.

"The house has only been on the market three weeks, but the owners are moving out of state, so I imagine they're eager to sell." David flipped to the disclosure page. "The furnace is original. The roof was replaced three years ago. Everything seems to be in good condition."

"Could we find out what the utilities run?" Kyle asked.

"Sure. Anything else you want to look at before we move on to the next house?"

Natalie and Kyle shook their heads no and stepped out the front door. David locked the door behind him, putting the key back in the lockbox before joining them in the vehicle. The baby was still asleep, nestled now in the infant seat like a caterpillar in a cocoon.

A yearning sprang up from someplace deep inside David. A yearning he'd pushed away for months. Why hadn't he and Paula—

"What time did Paula get in last night?" Natalie asked from the backseat.

He would have been glad to change the direction of his thoughts, but this was another subject he wanted to avoid. He wondered when Natalie was going to bring up her sister. She had steered clear of the topic . . . until now.

"She decided not to come home." He put the car in reverse and backed out of the drive.

He knew the silence didn't indicate that the subject would be dropped.

"Oh," Natalie said, sounding puzzled. "Nothing's wrong, is it?"

How would he know? "I don't think so."

The baby woke and gave a squeaky little cry, but whatever Natalie did calmed her down quickly.

"How did her first week go?" Natalie asked.

David wished she'd just drop the subject. If she wanted to know how her sister was, she should call herself. "I have no idea, Natalie."

"You haven't called her?"

"No, I have not." David picked up the listing on the next house and scanned the sheet for the street address.

"Not at all? How do we know she even made it safely to Chicago?"

In his peripheral vision, David saw Kyle slip his hand between the seats and set it on Natalie's knee.

"She e-mailed to let me know she wasn't coming home, so I'm sure she's fine."

Paula hadn't said that. Hadn't said anything except:

I'm going to need time to prepare for my first week solo, so I'm staying in Chicago this weekend.

Not one word about how her week went or a single question about how his work was going. He'd sold a ranch this week worth 5.4 million, but did she care?

David turned into the drive of the next house he was showing Natalie and Kyle. Maybe he could help this couple find a home where they, too, could experience the wonderful journey to wedded bliss.

CHAPTER
FOUR

"Great job, Paula." Constanzo, the cameraman, patted her on the shoulder, then flipped off the bright light. "The camera loves you."

It was her third day on the beat by herself, and everything had gone smoothly. She interviewed an owner of a new bagel shop, a boy who was single-handedly raising money for needy children, and workers on strike from a local potato-chip factory. Not exactly the cream-of-the-news stories, but she was getting experience. Darrick got the bigger stories, but that was to be expected. She had to prove herself, and she had a long way to go if she wanted to convince Miles she was the best candidate for the anchor chair.

When she walked into her cubicle, there was a message on a Post-it: *Call Deb Morgan. Urgent.* Immediately she thought of her family so far away in Jackson Hole. What if something was wrong with David?

But then she saw the phone number scrawled under the message. It had a Chicago area code. *Deb Morgan.* The name wasn't familiar.

She asked Cindy, the secretary, about the message.

"Yes, I remember this call. The woman—what was her name?"

"Deb Morgan."

"Yes, yes, that's it. Deb Morgan. She sounded distraught. She wasn't sure if she had the right phone number, but she was definitely looking for someone named Paula who was with our news crew. She had to be thinking of you."

Paula mumbled a thanks and went back to her desk to dial the number. Immediately the phone was answered.

"Hi, this is Paula Landin-Cohen from WMAQ. I have a message to return a phone call to a Deb Morgan."

"Oh hi, Paula. Thanks so much for returning my call."

The woman spoke as if she knew Paula, but from where?

"I don't know if you'll remember me, but we met at the hospital last week. I was sitting in the waiting area outside Mr. Boccardi's office."

Immediately the woman's image came to mind. Blond hair, fair skin, fragile looking.

"Yes, I remember very well. How can I help you, Mrs. Morgan?"

"Deb. Please, just call me Deb. My husband and I have a . . . situation. We'd hoped to get answers from Mr. Boccardi, but he wasn't any help at all."

"I'd be happy to help if I can. Why don't you start at the beginning?"

Paula couldn't help but wonder why Deb was calling her, a news reporter, with a personal problem. Maybe she wanted some kind of media coverage.

"I was hoping we could meet. I have a—a story you might be interested in as a newsperson. It's a long story, and a painful one for me and my husband." She paused as her words choked off. "I'm sorry. This is very hard on me."

"That's OK. And, of course, I'd be happy to meet with you. Just name the time and place."

Could this be a story that would make Miles sit up and take notice? Adrenaline surged through Paula's veins, and she welcomed the excitement it brought.

They decided to meet at the Morgans' house at nine the next morning. Paula hung up the phone, her veins throbbing with anticipation at what could be her first investigative story.

On Thursday morning Paula parked in front of a small, one-story home. On this street, only the numbers on the porch posts distinguished one house from another.

Moments later she knocked on the door. Deb Morgan answered and ushered Paula in, taking her coat. The house held the faint scent of popcorn, presumably from the night before, and something else—a cinnamon fragrance that could probably be traced to a dish of potpourri.

A man standing behind Deb held out his hand. "I'm Deb's husband, Steve. And this"—he picked up a little girl who looked about three—"is Faith. Say hi, sweetie."

Faith buried her face in her dad's neck, her fine, brown curls cascading over his shoulder. Then, turning her face toward Paula, she peeked out from her father's embrace.

"Hi there, Faith."

The child looked angelic with wide, striking green eyes and a pixie nose.

"Come on in, Paula, and have a seat," Deb said.

As Paula entered the living room, she noted that the furniture appeared to be well-cared-for castoffs. All the pieces had a certain charm, but not one matched any of the others. A woven basket on the table held copies of *Parenting* magazine and *Cerebral Palsy Magazine*. She sat on a recliner.

"Can I get you some coffee?" Deb asked.

Paula had already chugged down a Starbucks on the way over. "No thank you." She reached into her satchel for a tape recorder. "Do you mind if I tape our conversation?"

"Please do."

Steve Morgan set his daughter down. "Go finish your Cheerios, pumpkin." He swatted her affectionately on the behind as she walked away. She limped as she moved, favoring her right side.

Steve and Deb, holding hands, sat opposite Paula on the couch.

Paula pushed Record on the recorder and set it on the coffee table between them.

"First of all, I want to say that this media stuff is all new to us," Steve said. "Deb and I have debated what to do ever since our meeting with Mr. Boccardi."

"Honey, let's just tell the story, and let her decide if there's anything she can do, OK?" The woman's words were as gentle as a morning mist.

"You're right," Steve said. He rubbed his jaw. "It's hard to know where to start."

Deb squeezed his hand and took over. "When I was pregnant with Faith, I went into labor too early. We went to Chicago General Hospital, and the doctors did everything they knew to stop the labor, but they were unable to. We were told to expect the worst. Babies as premature as Faith usually don't live at all, and if they do, well, there are usually severe handicaps."

Paula's heart pounded. What was it about that hospital? It was only her second week in Chicago, and she was being taken down memory lane yet again. She tucked her auburn hair behind her ear and focused on what Deb was saying.

"The first hours were terribly trying. We prayed and prayed. Everyone we knew was praying for little Faith." Deb looked down and pinched her lips together.

Steve continued. "Even with all the prayers, I think we were surprised at how well Faith seemed to be doing. She was in the NICU—Neonatal Intensive Care Unit—for four and a half weeks, and then we were bringing her home. I think that was the happiest day of my life."

"We knew there would be developmental delays," Deb said. "And the doctors warned about the potential for cerebral palsy, hearing loss, retardation—the list was endless."

Steve let go of Deb's hand and put his arm around her. His dark skin and raven hair was a foil for Deb's fair complexion and pale blond hair. "We didn't care. We were so thrilled our baby was alive that we felt like the most blessed couple in the world."

There was silence as the couple seemed at a loss for where to go next. Paula heard a cartoon blaring from another room in the house.

Deb picked at her blunt-cut nails while she spoke. "As time went by, we discovered Faith did suffer from a mild case of cerebral palsy. We were distraught, of course, but it was not unexpected."

"I know this may sound melodramatic," Steve said. "But when you're facing the death of your child, anything else seems minor in comparison. We accepted the diagnosis and went on to find the best help we could. Faith's doing very well—as well as we could have hoped for."

But if Faith was doing so well, Paula wondered, why had the Morgans invited her to come? She tabled the question, knowing she needed to hear the story all the way through first.

"Several months ago Deb and I had blood drawn for a life insurance policy. Our results were fine, but one night when I was looking it over, I noticed something disturbing. I saw that Deb has Type A blood, and I have Type AB." The couple exchanged a look, as though reliving the moment.

Deb picked up from there. "We knew Faith's blood type because of all the blood she'd had drawn over the years. Hers is Type O, and we both knew that parents with our blood types couldn't have a child with blood Type O. We asked our family doctor to run some lab work. We thought it must've been a mistake. We never expected . . ." Deb blinked rapidly, then lowered her head.

Steve's hand cradled his wife's shoulder. "When we got the tests back, we were devastated."

Paula straightened her spine. She saw the way Deb's eyes almost drooped at the corners, the way her nose had reddened as they sat there telling their story. And Paula now knew why. This child of theirs was not theirs at all.

"We even had Faith's blood tested again, just to be sure." Steve shook his head. He stared off toward the kitchen, as if temporarily lost. Finally, his gaze returned to Paula. "But it was true. Faith isn't our biological child."

Paula looked from one to the other. "I'm so sorry. You must be devastated." Paula tried to remain objective—she had years of experience at that—but she also needed to put herself in the couple's place so she could ask the right questions. "What did you do next?"

"Well," Deb said, "we were terrified. On the one hand, we wanted to know what had happened. If Faith wasn't our biological child, where was the child I gave birth to?"

"But on the other hand," Steve added, "we have someone else's biological child. And we couldn't possibly risk losing her."

"Of course not." Paula tried to imagine David being the support that Steve was to Deb. When David found out the results of his infertility test, he didn't support her at all. Instead he'd accused her of being unfaithful.

"Not only is Faith our only child," Deb said, "she's the only child we'll ever have."

As Paula watched Deb swallow, she imagined there must be a lump in her throat the size of a golf ball.

"Deb had to have a hysterectomy immediately after Faith's"—Steve stopped himself, evidently realizing his mistake—"right after the birth."

Paula checked her recorder to make sure the wheels were still spinning. As easy as it was to get caught up in the tragic story, she had to keep her wits about her. If handled right, she could help this couple and boost her career at the same time.

"Have you made any effort to find out what happened to your birth child?" Paula asked.

The Morgans exchanged a glance. "We took a couple of months to think and pray about what to do," Steve said. "Above all else we didn't want to lose Faith."

Deb sighed. "But we couldn't discount the idea that our birth child could be out there somewhere."

"Even with that fact," Steve continued, "we still didn't want to risk losing Faith. Both of us were set against saying anything." His eyes teared up for the first time in their meeting.

"After spending a lot of time on our knees," Deb said, "begging God for wisdom, we both finally came to the conclusion that we had to find out the truth."

Paula had mixed emotions about the Morgans' decision. She was impressed with their courage but wondered if they'd thought this through. They were clearly terrified of losing Faith, and that was certainly a possibility. On the other hand, this was the story of her life. If she investigated this and found answers, she would crack a huge story that would put her career on the map. Possibly deliver her that anchor chair.

She stared into Deb's eyes—pale blue orbs that showcased a contradiction of vulnerability and strength. Deb was looking at Paula like she was the answer to all their problems. Paula's driving ambition slowly bled away, giving way to something less impressive but infinitely more human.

"I know you said you're convinced you need to find out the truth," Paula said. "But have you thought through all the ramifications? What if Faith's birth parents are raising your birth child? Have you considered that you could become embroiled in a custody battle? Once this story goes on camera, there's no turning back."

Steve leaned forward, knees on elbows. "We know there's a lot of risk involved. We have a lot to lose. And honestly, my brain says no, don't do it." He exchanged a look with Deb. "But as Christians we leave these things to God. And we both sense He's telling us to go forward with this. Whatever comes with the truth, we'll face it then and pray He'll give us the strength to handle it."

Paula was impressed with the Morgans' beliefs. They reminded her of her parents' commitment to their faith. She felt a brief stab of longing for something so significant in her own life. She took a deep breath and exhaled, then focused on Deb.

"I have to ask, why me? Surely you know this is a story that would have national interest. We only met briefly last week, Deb. What made you think you could trust me with this story?"

The corners of Deb's lips lifted in a slow, thoughtful smile. "Just the fact that you gave us a chance to back out shows me we picked the right person."

Something inside her softened and relaxed, like a sleeping-baby's fist. She eyed Deb and Steve once again and saw their determined commitment to see this through. "All right then. Let's get started."

CHAPTER
FIVE

When she told her boss about the story, Miles nodded approvingly, his eyebrows climbing higher on his forehead. Paula got an appointment with Mr. Boccardi the next day.

Stepping back into Chicago General Hospital was something she did with teeth gritted and chin jutted forward. She was going to have to put the memory behind her to move forward with this story.

She'd e-mailed David and given him a brief synopsis of the story she was working on. He hadn't e-mailed back, but it had only been a day. Tonight he would pick her up at the airport, and she would see if their relationship was still as strained as it had been when she left.

When she reached Mr. Boccardi's office, he escorted her in. "How are you, Ms. Landin-Cohen?"

Paula suspected from the initial conversation with his secretary that she never would have gotten Mr. Boccardi's time if she'd not been here for the interview the previous week. It was uncanny the way this was working out.

"Fine, thank you. Call me Paula, please." She took the chair he offered on the front side of his mahogany desk. "How's the new wing operating?"

"Is that a pun?" He smiled and brushed the few hairs he had across the top of his bald spot. He would have been an attractive man in his younger days with his strong jaw and clear green eyes.

She laughed. "It wasn't meant to be."

He steepled his hands across the stack of papers on his desk. "The wing is running like clockwork. I've had good feedback on the feature your station ran."

"Glad we could help."

She couldn't help but think he wouldn't be so happy when he learned why she was here now. Especially if he made her use the little ace in the hole.

He consulted his watch. "Now, what can I do for you, Paula?"

Right to the point. That wasn't a problem for her. "I'm working on a story you might be familiar with. I'm doing an investigation for Deb and Steve Morgan."

She watched his body straighten, as if drawn from the head by a string hanging from the ceiling. She imagined the string pulling Mr. Boccardi to his feet and sending him into a marionette dance. Judging by his initial reaction, she guessed she'd have to resort to a little coercion.

"I've already told the Morgans I would look into their case," he said. "I am looking. We are doing everything we can to get to the bottom of this."

It would do no good to anger him. "I'm sure you are, Mr. Boccardi. No one is questioning your resolve to find answers. The Morgans thought it would be helpful to have a professional look into it as well. Perhaps we can work together."

He stood, his lips pinched so tight they went pale. "I'm not naive, Ms. Landin-Cohen. Despite the nice coverage your station did of this hospital's wing, I know how reporters are. Bad as the paparazzi. Once you get the scent of a story that'll make headlines, you're like a bloodhound on the trail and you won't be happy until there's a dead body at the end."

Paula gave him her most charming smile, one that seemed most effective with men. "Mr. Boccardi. Please don't put me in a class with those crass tabloid reporters. I didn't sniff this story out. The Morgans came to me, and I'd like to help them find answers. They're terribly torn up over this whole—"

"Get out of my office." Mr. Boccardi towered over her now, his chest puffed out like Popeye after a spinach binge.

She sighed. He was going to make her play dirty, and she really didn't like playing dirty. She was a nice, small-town girl, but she did have big-city ambitions, and she wasn't going to let a stubborn hospital administrator stand between her and an anchor chair.

She remained seated, despite his threatening position. "I was thinking of interviewing some of your staff as I leave today."

"Do you need some help out, *Ms. Landin-Cohen*?" He could sneer words every bit as effortlessly as David. "And you can leave my staff alone."

"I was thinking Leann Webber might be a good place to start."

When she'd been at the hospital with the news crew, she'd overheard Leann talking to another nurse about her affair with Mr. Boccardi. Who knew the information would come in handy?

He wavered backward until his weight rested on his heels. His eyes widened ever so slightly, then narrowed. She'd hit her mark. He turned and walked slowly to the back side of his desk. He was collecting himself. Weighing his options. She almost felt sorry for him. She heard an announcement from somewhere in the hospital and a muted ambulance siren, probably delivering the latest victim of some violent act.

Finally Mr. Boccardi faced her.

She schooled her face in a mask of resolution.

"Very well." His face was as tight as a trampoline. "You have me where you want me, as I'm sure you're aware. What would you like to know?"

* * *

Linn placed the last plastic cup in the old '70s model dishwasher and poured the powder detergent into the dispenser. Before she could shut the door and start the cleaning cycle, Charlotte whirled into the apart-ment, slamming the door.

"Linn," she called from the living room.

"In here."

When Charlotte rounded the corner, Linn could see something was definitely up with her roomie. For someone self-conscious about the sliver of a gap between her front teeth, she sure was smiling awfully big.

"Sheesh," Linn said. "You look like a girl who just got proposed to."

"Shut up. This is way better." Charlotte tossed her glossy blond hair over her shoulder. "Remember how I was on a waiting list for a dorm? I got in!"

Linn's stomach knotted. "What do you mean you got in?"

"See, there's this sophomore who had to go home—family situation or something—so a slot opened up for next semester. Isn't that fab?" Charlotte did a little joy jig. "I just signed the papers, and I get to move in next week!"

Well, that was just swell for Charlotte, but what about Linn? If Charlotte left, the rent would completely be up to her. And she hadn't even found a job yet. Even if she did find a job, there was no part-time work that was going to pay rent and utilities anywhere around there.

Charlotte was still hopping on the floor, probably sounding like a herd of kangaroos to whoever lived below them. How could Charlotte have done this without checking with her? Linn never would've come to Chicago without a job and a place to live, and now she had neither.

"Hello? Did you even think about the mess this was going to leave me in?" Linn fired back.

Charlotte's face fell like a punctured balloon. Clearly, she hadn't given it any thought. Charlotte might make straight As, but she scored much lower on common sense.

"Oh man, Linn." Charlotte plopped on the tweed sofa in their min-iscule living room.

Linn followed. "I don't even have a job anymore, remember?"

The girl should remember well. The morning she told Charlotte about losing her job, her roommate had been a little short on sympathy and a little heavy on indignation.

"You can get another roommate." Charlotte hugged one of the sofa pillows. It was pink and fuzzy, a poor attempt at modernizing her ancient furniture.

It hit Linn then that even the furniture was Charlotte's. She had nothing of her own but her clothes and cosmetics. She imagined herself camping out again as she'd done in Jackson Hole when she had no place to live. If she thought it was cold then, in the fall, what would it be like in the middle of a Chicago winter? Impossible—that's what it would be.

At least she wasn't pregnant this time . . .

It was a good thing she left Jackson so soon after she gave birth. Otherwise she wouldn't have had any time to find a job and a new roommate by the time school started.

Where would she find a roommate, though?

"I don't even know anyone in town," Linn said.

Charlotte's shoulders drew up slightly. "You can advertise."

Linn sagged into the recliner and closed her eyes.

God, where are You? I could use a break here. I haven't even started classes and already I'm jobless and nearly homeless. I don't know anyone here who can help me, and I haven't gotten a single call back from all the applications I've—

"Sorry, Linn. But I've waited so long for a chance to live in a dorm."

As much as it stunk, Linn knew she was right. Charlotte was a social bunny. They'd invented dorms for people like her. She was going to college as much for college experience as for the degree. Still, it was unfair to give Linn so little warning.

"You knew I was on the waiting list," Charlotte said.

"You said you probably wouldn't get in until next year."

Charlotte's nostrils flared. "Well, that's what I thought. How was I to know someone was going to have a midyear crisis?"

"The same way I was supposed to know I was going to lose my job, I guess." OK, so she had a sarcastic streak. But it was true. Charlotte had jumped all over her when she lost her job. As if it were her fault.

"Look, this isn't my fault." Charlotte wagged her head with attitude. "You could just be happy for me, you know."

Linn wanted to grab Charlotte's shoulders and shake her until some common sense knocked loose in that Barbie-doll head.

Silence hung between them until the phone rang. Linn got up and went to her room, letting Charlotte get the phone. It was always for her anyway. Linn didn't have any friends yet in Chicago, and no one from back home—except Natalie, one time—had called. When Linn thought of Grace, her insides got all tight and hot. The baby was in good hands . . . the best. And Linn was getting on with her life, just like she wanted.

She rolled her eyes. So much for her life. No job, no place to live, no friends.

She flung herself on the bed, ready for a good pity party.

"It's for you," Charlotte called from the living room.

Linn's mind flipped through the file of potential callers. Probably not Natalie, since she'd just called a few days ago. Maybe it was about one of the applications she'd filled out.

She jumped off the bed, more energized than she'd been in days. Opening her door, she took the receiver from Charlotte, covering the mouthpiece. "Did they say who it was?" she whispered.

Charlotte, obviously still ticked, flipped on the TV. "Adam something."

It didn't take long to place the name. If Linn were honest with herself, his name had popped into her head too frequently to attribute to a mere job possibility. Now, as she put the phone to her ear, she wondered which she hoped for more: that he was calling about a job or that he was calling just to talk to her.

"Hello?" She used her most professional voice, just in case.

"Hi, Linn, this is Adam Stoever. We met a couple of weeks ago at the coffee shop. I gave you a lift home."

Like she could forget.

"Hi, Adam." She hoped she sounded casual. "What can I do for you?"

"I was wondering if you were still looking for a job. The girl I was telling you about didn't work out, and we have a position open if you're interested."

Boy, was she interested.

"I do still need a job. What would my responsibilities be?"

He explained that she would be waiting on customers, same as he, making espresso, keeping the workspace clean, et cetera. "You'd need to come in for an interview with Joe first. I can set that up if you want."

"I'd love to. Just name the day and time." She had nowhere to go.

They agreed on a day early the next week and hung up the phone.

Linn felt optimistic for the first time in days. Now, if only she had a place to live.

CHAPTER
SIX

Paula applauded and laughed with all the other women when her sister unwrapped the lacy, red negligee. She couldn't remember the last time she'd slipped into something like that for David. Couldn't remember the last time he would have wanted her to. She shoved aside her negative thoughts and determined to focus on Natalie's bridal shower.

They were all squeezed into their parents' house, and her other sister, Hanna, was making a list of who gave what as Natalie opened gifts. The Christmas Eve wedding was a little over a week away, and Natalie seemed almost giddy.

Natalie picked up the last package, Paula's gift. She removed the elegant bow and tore off the glossy paper. When she pulled off the lid, she gasped. After exchanging smiles with Paula, she pulled out the plush, white robe.

"Oh, Paula, I love it!" Natalie fingered the Turkish cotton that Paula knew was soft as a hug.

"You can wear that negligee underneath it," said one of Natalie's friends.

"Or nothing at all," said another.

Everyone laughed as they passed the robe around, admiring it.

Paula's mother stuffed the last of the wrapping paper in the trash bag while Hanna shooed everyone into the kitchen for strawberry cheese-cake, Natalie's favorite.

Paula helped her mother tidy up the living room. They'd had a few minutes before the shower to catch up, and Paula had told her about the Morgans' story.

"It's so good to have you home, Paula," her mom was saying now. "It just doesn't seem right when you're gone. Like a piece of our family puzzle is missing."

"You know I've always wanted to live in a big city, Mom." Paula set the pillows in their respective places.

"I just always assumed you'd be taking your husband with you." The tone was gentle, but it poked nonetheless.

"It's David's choice to stay here, Mom. You know that. Besides, if I don't get the anchor job, I'll be coming back home anyway."

Her mom straightened from stuffing a box in the trash bag and pelted Paula with a look only a mom could master. "And what will you be coming home to, dear?"

Irritation wiggled its way under Paula's skin. Why did everyone lay the fault of her decaying marriage at her feet? Even her own family took David's side at every turn. For a moment she wanted to tell her mom exactly what happened between her and David. How her husband accused her of having an affair. How he refused to believe she was innocent.

Just as quickly, she dismissed the idea. It was between her and David. She was never one to tell Mommy everything, and she wasn't going to start now. Not to defend herself against something that wasn't true.

"I'm sorry if I'm prying," her mom said. "I don't mean to. I just want to say that problems don't get better with time or distance. Things have a way of getting worse and worse until neither of you cares anymore. I don't want to see that happen with you and David."

Paula sighed. She couldn't argue with anything her mom had said. "I don't either, Mom."

Her mother ran her fingers through Paula's hair. "Then work it out. Do whatever it takes. Confront him, talk it out, agree to disagree, something. Just work it out."

An ache welled inside Paula. She did want things to work out with

David. She remembered the way they used to be. They'd had a great relationship in the beginning. She wanted it to be that way again, but the thought of approaching David, of making herself vulnerable to him again, was scary.

Her mom seemed to sense her feelings. "The Paula I know can do anything she sets her mind to. Apply a little of that ambition and drive to the success of your marriage, dear. It's the most important partnership you'll ever have."

❦

Paula spent the afternoon with her sisters and mom, slipping in a last-minute final fitting for her bridesmaid dress. David was busy with a couple from out of town who was in the market for a ranch. She did take a minute to slip away and call the Rendezvous Bistro for reservations. Her mother was right. This argument between her and David was silly. They needed to stop running away from confrontation and find a way to work through it. She did want that anchor chair in Chicago, but she wanted the man she'd married back too.

Later that night, as she and David took seats in the crowded bistro, Paula second-guessed herself. While David agreed to go out with her, he was obviously reluctant to be there. He was colder than a mountain spring, and she wondered if she'd be able to get through to him at all.

The instant he sat down, he picked up the menu, holding it between them like a shield. The restaurant tried for elegance with dimmed lighting and starched white linens, but Paula couldn't help but compare it to the restaurants she ate at in Chicago with her coworkers.

Nonetheless, this place held a few memories at least. David had brought her here when she got the job at WKEV. He ordered the most expensive glass of wine in the house and lifted a glass to her.

"*To my amazing wife, who can achieve anything she sets her mind to. And to her husband, who is the luckiest man in the world,*" he had said.

The tenderness in his eyes had made her own sting as she clinked glasses with him and sipped the fruity blend. They made passionate love that night, and Paula was on top of the world in every way.

How was it that they were now sitting across from each other in the same restaurant, in better career positions, with a mountain of heartache between them? When had it started? What started that downward spiral?

"What?" David's menu had come down.

Paula realized she was staring at him. She spread the white napkin across her lap. "I was thinking about the last time we were here."

Did he remember? Did he remember how it used to be?

The aproned waiter came and took their drink orders, then left. The muted chatter from other tables drifted over to theirs. A familiar woman across the room caught Paula's eye and waved. Paula smiled and waved back before looking away. In Jackson Hole, even in tourist season, you couldn't go anywhere without running into someone you knew.

She focused her attention on David. He leaned back against the wooden chair, as if he couldn't get far enough away from her. There was so much emotional distance between them that she may as well still be in Chicago. Tomorrow she was going back, and more than anything, she wanted to be on better terms with him.

"How were the showings today? Did that couple find anything they liked?"

His gaze bounced off her. "They showed some interest in one of the ranches. They're thinking about it."

"Where are they from?" Her heart kept tempo with the eclectic music whispering from the speakers.

"California." He dipped his index finger in the wine, probably removing some tiny speck from the liquid, then wiped his finger on the dinner napkin.

Should she ask how JH Realty was going? He was now the owner of the company, and he was surely proud of that. However, David had bought it without Paula's agreement since ownership held him in Jackson Hole indefinitely. It was a bad subject between them.

She hadn't even told him about the Morgan story, but then he hadn't asked about her job. Despite his concurrence to have dinner together, he was not going to ease into this conversation as she had hoped.

After the waiter took their orders, she inhaled a weighty breath and began. "David . . ." She waited until she had eye contact, hoping for a softening there but not finding it. "I can't stand for things to be like this anymore. We're supposed to be husband and wife, and we're barely speaking."

Her pause was supposed to give him a chance to speak, but he didn't seem to have anything to say.

She went on. "This isn't healthy, and it's not doing either of us any good. We need to talk it out."

He pushed his trendy glasses up and crossed his arms. "I think we've said everything that needs to be said, don't you?"

She bit her tongue. Hard. Then she took another breath, letting it out through her nose before meeting his steely gaze. "Perhaps *you've* said everything you want to say, but I haven't." She shouldn't have to do this. She shouldn't have to defend herself for something he should know she'd never do. It felt degrading. And unjust. Like begging for a scrap of bread that was hers to begin with.

You can do this, Paula.

If she applied all her business acumen and determination, there was no reason she couldn't articulate herself in a way that would persuade David to believe her. It was stubborn of her not to have tried earlier.

"Back when you took the infertility test, you told me the doctor had said it was unlikely you could father a child in the normal way, right?"

"She said 'almost impossible.'"

Paula tried to see deep into his eyes, but she couldn't get past the frosty exterior. "Did you ever talk to her again? Did you ever ask her if your condition was something that might be more recent?"

When he averted his eyes, she wished she could climb inside his mind and know what he was thinking.

"David, it was you who got me pregnant." She steered the conversation a different direction. "I have never had an affair with anyone.

I've not let another man lay his hands on me since the day we met. I swear."

He looked at her then, and she allowed everything she was feeling to show on her face. All her devotion. All her candor. All her vulnerability. She hadn't given him so much, shown him so much in months. She was putting it all on the line tonight, because she had nothing to lose.

Then she thought of the baby they'd conceived together, and her insides twisted. The lie, the betrayal of that one wretched day, would never leave her.

Shadows danced across his face as his jaw clenched. "Very convincing, Paula. I almost believed you."

CHAPTER
SEVEN

David let his gaze swing across the crowded restaurant toward the other patrons. Toward the mustard-colored walls. Toward anything but the woman across from him who seemed bent on deceiving him. He'd almost believed her when her eyes softened.

But then those same eyes darkened with guilt, and she looked down at her hands folded demurely across the table for just a second. It was enough. After observing her for years, he knew when she was lying.

And it hurt. Man, it hurt so much, even now when he put a wall as thick as a sequoia between them. He sipped his wine to mask the pain that might be revealed in his expression. It was bad enough she still had the power to hurt him. She didn't have to know about it too. He clamped his jaw and stared at the art deco hanging on the wall.

"Please, David."

The pleading tone tugged his attention. She was a beautiful woman, her auburn hair framing a face that turned heads wherever she went. She handled it well, he'd give her that. He never caught her snatching looks at herself in rearview mirrors or windows the way some attractive women did. He'd been impressed with that when he met her.

"What can I do? What can I say to make you believe me?"

And her eyes. Moss green with flecks of caramel that danced in the candlelight. The way she looked at him now reminded him of another time . . .

❦

She was in her senior year of college when he came to Jackson Hole for winter break with his buddies. He noticed her when he visited a local church. In fact, he had trouble concentrating on the sermon because she was sitting across the aisle, four rows in front of him, and he had a perfect view of her profile.

Two days later, when his friends dragged him to the Million Dollar Cowboy, she was there. Their eyes met across the room, and he looked away. He had dated attractive women before, and he'd had enough of the egos that went with beauty. He wanted a nice, average girl—not some princess who expected too much, then left for a better catch.

She's probably just like Melanie, he thought.

When he turned around again, the tall and leggy redhead was standing beside his stool, leaning against the bar. He got lost in her eyes the moment they locked with his.

"You're not from here," she said, keeping eye contact as she sipped from the straw in her glass.

"I'm David. Just here for a few weeks with my buddies."

She introduced herself as Paula, and he introduced his friends, suddenly hoping they'd get lost.

He reined in his thoughts. A flirtation was tempting, but where could it go? Three weeks wasn't long enough to establish anything real, and his life was miles away in Warsaw, Indiana. His friends might jump at whatever she might offer physically, but David had been trying very hard to avoid physical temptation. And this woman was temptation with a capital *T*.

The music switched to an '80s love song.

"Would you like to dance?" Her voice, almost swallowed by the music, reached his ears.

He opened his mouth to decline, but something changed when his

45

eyes again met hers. Despite her bold invitation and incredible beauty, there was vulnerability in her eyes. As if something important depended on his answer, and she was desperately afraid he'd say no.

"Sure." The word slipped out of his mouth before he could stop it, and seconds later he was putting his hands at her waist. She surprised him by keeping her distance. Somehow he'd expected her to crush her body up against his and make this one dance agonizingly difficult.

"I saw you at church Sunday," she was saying.

He felt his lips pull up in a smile. "Meaning, what's a nice guy like you doing in a place like this?"

She shrugged. "I'm here, too, after all."

The top of her head was just at eye level, and she looked up at him as she spoke.

"This doesn't seem like your kind of place," David said. Frankly, Jackson Hole didn't look like her kind of place. She was like a fine, rare wine, and this town was more like a can of cream soda.

"Honestly, I'm here to review the place for the paper. Now what's your excuse?" She flirted with her eyes, and he liked it. A lot.

"Three friends with money and time to kill."

"Ah."

Her head tipped back, exposing her delicate throat. The song swelled into the chorus.

"Are you here to ski?" she asked.

"Not if I can help it."

She had a great laugh, and her eyes seem to catch fire when she did.

Just then a man laid his hand on David's shoulder. "Cut in?" The man didn't look at David. His eyes were for Paula only, and David wondered if he was her boyfriend.

David started to back away, but Paula grabbed his arm and held it there. "No thanks." She tipped her chin up and leveled a look that would have made Godzilla back off. Fortunately, this guy did too.

For all her bravado, her hand was clamped around his forearm like she was hanging on for dear life.

"Boyfriend?" He was suddenly hoping not, especially since the guy was taller and a good forty pounds stouter.

She gave a derisive laugh. "Not hardly." Her hand trailed back up to his shoulders, and he could feel her relaxing. "Sorry about that. He's actually my friend's boyfriend."

David watched the guy settle on a barstool, keeping his eyes on Paula the whole time. "He seems kind of taken with you."

Was it his imagination or did she step a little closer?

"I don't go for cheaters."

"Here we are." The waiter set David's dinner plate down in front of him, pulling him back from the memory.

Across from him, Paula was eying him strangely. The words she said all those years ago reverberated in his head: *I don't go for cheaters.*

Maybe she didn't go for cheaters, but had she cheated on him? Or had he accused her unfairly, and was he willing to give her another chance?

On Monday Linn walked out of the little office, her legs wobbly from nerves over the interview. As she passed the counter, Adam stopped her.

She leaned against the counter while he put a lid on a drink and handed it to the customer.

"Well? How did it go?"

His brown eyes were as warm as a cup of hot cocoa. Did he have to be so cute?

"I start tomorrow." Linn's excitement was replaced by a jolt of anxiety. What if this job didn't work out any better for her than for the other girl who'd gotten fired? What if she couldn't get the hang of making espresso? She knew how picky people were about their coffee.

"Hey, that's great. Looks like we'll be working together." The smile he tossed her way was all friendly.

Her heart kicked into high gear. "Looks like."

"You'll be great. What hours will you be here?"

"Mostly same as yours, I guess. Joe said you'd be training me." She slipped her coat on and then her purse over her shoulder, noting the small space behind the counter. She'd never worked so closely with a man, especially not one who looked like Adam.

"Don't worry. I'll be gentle."

Linn glanced at him, expecting the words to have a double meaning, but there was nothing except kindness in his eyes.

She checked her watch, wanting to be sure she didn't miss the bus. "I gotta go." She tapped the counter once. "See you tomorrow then."

He said good-bye, then she set out for the bus hut. Now she had a job. She allowed herself a moment's relief before she plunged ahead to worry number two: a roof over her head. She'd placed an ad in the newspaper but had no real takers yet. It wasn't a good time to find a roommate—what with all the college students going home for winter break.

At least she could spend a little of her money to buy Grace a Christmas present now that she had a paycheck coming. She would take the bus to the hobby store and have enough time to get the gift to Jackson Hole by Christmas.

Thank you, God.

She didn't have enough to buy Natalie anything, but Linn knew she'd understand. And anyway, Linn didn't know if she was supposed to buy Natalie anything. Would it make things more awkward?

Linn sat on the bus bench and watched all the cars speeding by. All the people on their way to or from work or Christmas shopping. A woman walked by loaded down with handled shopping bags. *She must have a lot of people on her Christmas list. A big family and lots of friends.*

It struck Linn that she had only one person to buy for. And that person didn't even know who she was.

CHAPTER
EIGHT

As Paula drove to the WMAQ station on Wednesday, she glanced over her notes from the interview with Mr. Boccardi.

His information was very helpful—if slightly coerced. He'd given her the names and contact information of all the staff during the time of Mrs. Morgan's stay in the hospital. She interviewed the doctor who delivered the Morgans' baby and the three nurses who were in the delivery room at the time. She interviewed all the nurses, except for two, who were in the Neonatal Intensive Care Unit during the first two days following the birth. Of the remaining two nurses, one had died in a car accident the year before and a second nurse was severely ill and unable to conduct an interview. Paula taped all the interviews, but so far she'd turned up nothing that explained why the Morgans now had someone else's birth child.

She wracked her brain trying to figure out what happened to the baby, but now she was at the end of the trail with no answers.

Mr. Boccardi was adamant about keeping the patients' records private. No amount of threats could cajole him into telling her the names and addresses of the other mothers who gave birth that day. He said he had contacted them himself, but Paula wasn't sure she believed him.

Keeping up with the scope of this story while still covering the daily news stories was a task. She did most of the interviews for the Morgans in her free evening hours since her return from Jackson. She called Deb and Steve the night before and assured them she was doing everything possible to get to the bottom of the story. Staying busy at night was actually a blessing, since during that time she was prone to think of David.

The previous weekend had been an odd one. After their dinner together on Saturday, David's mood changed. The anger and coldness thawed into some kind of somber mood on Sunday before she left for Chicago, but Paula wasn't sure if it was for the better or not.

She pulled up to the station and exited the leased Volvo.

Miles surprised her by meeting her at the door. After greeting her he put a hand on her shoulder and guided her toward his office. Once there, he shut the door and took a seat opposite her, behind his desk.

"How'd the interviews go?"

He wastes no time getting down to business, Paula thought.

"Not as well as I hoped," she said. "There's nothing significant at first glance. I still want to read through my notes and give some thought to where everyone was at any given time. Maybe a time line would help me put the pieces in order and we can—"

"That would be fine if we had weeks, Paula, but this is news. Big news. We can't take the risk that someone else will jump on the story. It's time to go to press with this."

Tension crept into her shoulders. She wanted answers before they taped the story. Once it was out, it wasn't her story anymore, and some other news reporter could pounce on it.

"I understand the need for expediency," she said. "But I'd like to have at least a day to put all these facts together. I haven't even located the other parents who gave birth that same day. We may find the answers we need there."

"Or the Morgans might leak this to another reporter."

"They won't do that. They trust me."

Strangely enough, they really did. Although Paula wasn't stupid. She knew that if they grew weary of waiting for her to find answers, they would probably do whatever they had to.

"You know how this works, Paula. The more people you talk to, the greater likelihood that this will slip out, and you'll lose the story to someone else."

Paula knew he was right. It was always a tough act to balance: trying to get the story out first but getting it out accurately.

"I want this on tomorrow night's news."

She hid her disappointment behind a confident smile. "You got it." She hated to air the story before she had answers. On top of that, other reporters would jump all over the story, and she wouldn't have the weekend to work more on it because Sunday evening, Christmas Eve, was Natalie and Kyle's wedding. Then she was scheduled to take the red-eye back to Chicago, where she would arrive exhausted and hardly ready for work on Monday morning. She'd just have to make the best of it. There was no way she could miss her sister's wedding.

Later that night Paula was feeling much less optimistic. She had all her notes, the tape recorder, and a time line spread out on her bed.

According to her notes, the Morgans' child was born at 1:52 p.m. on June 12, and was immediately rushed to the NICU, where the doctor hooked the baby up to a respirator and monitors. One of the nurses would have put the ID bracelet on the baby already. All the NICU workers agreed that this would have happened, though none of the nurses specifically remembered doing it for this particular child. But that was to be expected, since so much time had gone by.

Paula skimmed her notes from the Morgans' interview. Due to the hemorrhaging that had happened at birth and the doctor's inability to stop it, Deb Morgan had a hysterectomy immediately after the birth. While his wife was in surgery, Steve went to the NICU and checked on the baby. He was told there was little chance for her survival.

Paula's heart caught at the thought of what Steve must have felt. His only child was a tiny preemie whose chances of living were very slim. His wife was in serious danger herself. And at that moment she was having surgery that would take away any chances of conceiving and birthing another child.

Paula's heart ached for the couple. She knew what it was like to be denied children. But her circumstances were her own choice. She had once had a chance at motherhood, and she had given it up.

Paula closed her eyes against the pain. This story was stirring up things that were better left dead and buried. That part of her life was behind her, and she needed to focus on today and this story. But if she could find the Morgans' child, maybe it would, in some small way, make up for what she'd done.

She consulted her time line. At somewhere around three o'clock, Steve Morgan left the NICU and went to wait for his wife to get out of surgery. Shortly after that, the surgeon told him everything had gone fine.

Steve sat by Deb as she came out from under the anesthesia. She was crying and hysterical and insisted on knowing about the baby. Steve told her there was little chance of survival. When Deb wanted to see the child, the doctor told her she could go to the NICU. The nurses wheeled Deb down to the NICU, where she saw the baby for the first time.

Paula scanned her notes from the NICU nurses. Two of them had been on shift until three o'clock. She interviewed only one of them as the other nurse was the one who'd died. She clicked her tongue and shook her head. Could that be the missing piece of the puzzle? Had that nurse known something that no one else knew?

Two nurses had come on their shift at three o'clock, but one of them was running late and was stopped for a speeding ticket. The nurse remembered this because it was her birthday, and she was coming from a luncheon with her parents. The second nurse was the one who was ill and unable to be interviewed.

Shortly after that, by the time Deb went down to the NICU, the baby seemed to be holding her own. At that time, Deb and Steve decided on the name Faith. When the doctor reexamined Faith, he said there'd been a marked improvement.

Looking at the notes from the doctor's interview, Paula saw that he had expressed surprise that the baby turned around so quickly. But he also stated that sometimes things happen in medicine that are unexplainable except as a miracle, and he attributed the quick turnaround to exactly that.

Paula's feet began to prickle, so she flipped over to lie on her stomach. At what point was the baby switched? Sometime after the first doctor pronounced her chances for survival poor but before Faith improved? That made sense, but it was also theoretically possible that the baby simply improved on her own and then the switch happened.

Paula needed to find out who the other premature babies in the hospital were that day. The nurse said there were always several babies at least, most of them premature. But she also pointed out that most of the babies had been in the NICU for a period of time and that the parents would recognize their own babies.

Squinting at the clock, Paula saw it was after midnight. She had a long day coming, and she'd need to be fresh if she was going to try and get to the bottom of this. Either way, tomorrow night she would go on the air with a story that might change more lives than just her own.

"I'm so nervous," Deb Morgan said. She sat beside Steve on the couple's living-room sofa, twisting the afghan that covered the cushions. The Morgans had decided not to include Faith in the interview since she was so young and because they'd only described to her vaguely what was happening.

"You'll be fine," Paula said. "It's not live, so we'll tape a short interview, then edit it. If you mess up, don't sweat it. We'll edit it out."

"When will this air?" Steve was the picture of calm.

"On the six o'clock news. They'll probably rerun it at eleven."

Paula strove to keep a steady voice, but inside, her frazzled thoughts tugged at her nerves. She had tried all morning to track down the other parents who'd given birth the same day Deb had but ran into one dead end after another.

"Ready?" Her cameraman positioned a picture of the family on the sofa table, within view of the camera.

"Let's do it," Deb said.

The bright camera light went on. Paula glanced at her notes. She would make preliminary comments before the segment, so now she only needed to get answers to some questions to plug in at various points.

"Deb and Steve, how did you find out that the child you are raising isn't the child you gave birth to?"

Steve answered the question, and Paula admired the way he stuck to the facts. He noted that Faith had been premature and mentioned the date and year Deb had given birth.

The next question she directed to Deb. The viewers would relate to this mother, and Paula wanted them to feel the family's pain.

"Deb, how did you feel when you found out you were raising someone else's birth child?"

Deb shook her head slowly. "I just . . . I couldn't believe it. I *didn't* believe it at first." She looked to Steve. "We thought it was a mistake, as my husband said. But when we found out it was true . . . nothing can prepare you for learning that the child you thought was yours by blood isn't yours at all. Even though we couldn't love her any more than we do, blood-related or not."

Deb was holding up very well, though Paula saw the lines of strain around her eyes and mouth.

"Once you knew the truth," Paula asked, "what did you do?"

Steve folded his hands in his lap. "At first we wanted to do nothing. Faith is the most precious thing in our lives. We were terrified if we went forward with this, her birth parents would want her."

"That's the worst part of all this for us," Deb said. "We don't care if Faith isn't our birth child. She means everything to us. To us she is our child, and the thought of losing her is almost more than we can bear."

Paula asked a few more questions to detail the Morgans' effort to get information from the hospital. Steve handled those questions nicely.

Then Paula continued, "This was a difficult decision for you. Why go forward with this information at all? Why not just keep it your little secret?"

It was the question all her viewers would want to know.

There was a poignant pause.

Steve took the question. "Somewhere out there is another set of parents just like us. They may be raising our birth child, or they may think they lost their baby shortly after she was born. Either way, they deserve to know the truth. 'The truth shall set you free.' We believe that."

"Don't you worry that this 'truth' will bring a custody battle? That Faith could become the next Kimberly Mays-Weeks?"

Deb leaned forward. "We're aware it could happen, but we're prepared to do anything necessary to protect our little girl. And we know God will help us through it."

Steve put his arm around his wife. "If our birth child is out there somewhere, we owe it to her to find her."

Deb's chin rumpled up like a wrinkled sheet. "And if our child . . . died, we owe it to her to honor her with a proper burial."

"What would you like to say to anyone who might have information about the switched babies?"

Steve looked directly at the camera for the first time. His brows pulled tight, and two dashes formed between them. "If you were at Chicago General Hospital at the same time, or if you have any information that might be helpful, please call the station."

Deb turned toward the camera, too, and Paula noticed the cameraman zooming in.

"We need to know what happened to our birth child." Deb's eyes filled with tears. "And somewhere out there is another set of parents who may be wondering what happened to theirs."

Paula let the words hang for a moment as Deb blinked rapidly, then looked down.

When the cameraman flipped off the bright light, the room seemed suddenly dark. Paula gave the Morgans a minute to regroup. Steve took Deb in his arms and held her like she was his lifeline.

When they parted, Paula squeezed Deb's hand. "You both did great. Perfect."

"Do you think it'll do any good?" Deb asked.

Paula wished she could promise they'd get all the answers they wanted. "If someone out there knows anything and they see this, it may be just the break we need."

After Paula left the Morgans' house, she headed to the station to write the copy on the story. It wasn't every day a switched-at-birth story came along. She still couldn't believe the way it had fallen into her hands. Her mother would say it was God's doing, but God would have no reason for helping Paula's career along. After all, it wasn't as if she'd given Him anything lately.

Miles came to her cubicle as she was writing up the story. "Did you get everything you needed?"

There was a light in his eyes that Paula knew stemmed from the excitement of breaking a big story.

"The Morgans did great. I'm just putting it together now."

"I know you'll do a great job with the copy." He turned to go, then stopped. "You know, once this goes out to the AP, don't be surprised if it gets picked up nationally."

It was what Paula was hoping for.

"Let's hope and pray," she said, wondering a second later why she'd added the part about praying.

But Miles didn't seem to mind. He winked and walked away.

CHAPTER
NINE

Paula flicked on the small TV set in her studio apartment and crossed her legs, her foot ticking off the final minutes before the eleven o'clock news. The story had aired shortly after six o'clock that evening, but she was in front of the camera then. Now she would get to watch it as a viewer and see if Miles's assessment was correct. The whole news station was abuzz with the switched-at-birth story. The Morgans had called her earlier and told her how pleased they were with the way she'd handled the story.

Too anxious to sit still, she got up and paced the room. The African violet from the station sat on the living-room window sill, and Paula realized it was time for a watering. The directions had said to use a specially formulated plant food, but the store she'd gone to hadn't carried it, so she'd substituted a complete liquid food. Keeping a close eye on the clock, she put the plant food in the water and set the potted plant in it to feed from the bottom.

Leaving the plant to soak, she dried her hands and went back to the living room where the news jingle was playing on TV. Paula cranked up the volume. The anchor introduced himself and moved immediately to the head story: hers. She watched herself, standing in front of the Chicago General Hospital sign, introduce the story, then there was a cut directly to the Morgans' living room. Steve talked about the logistics of what had happened, then Paula was on the screen again, explaining the possible devastation this could ultimately cause.

Next there was a closeup of Deb. "We know finding answers may break our hearts. But my husband and I—we both have to know the truth. When we told Faith that I hadn't given birth to her, she said, 'But you're still my mommy and daddy, right?' She'll always be our daughter. No test can change that." The cameraman zoomed in while Deb blinked back tears.

Paula again. "While the Morgans fear losing their child, their biggest fear is that they will never know what happened to the child Deb gave birth to three years ago."

The final scene was Steve and Deb's final plea for anyone with information to come forward.

The shot switched to Paula. "While the true identification of this child remains a mystery, the Morgans have done everything they know to find answers to this switched-at-birth story. Now they wait. This is Paula Landin-Cohen, reporting from Chicago General Hospital."

The shot changed to the anchor, and Paula switched off the TV. Her heart was about to jump out of her chest, and her foot was still ticking off time. It was good. Her best ever, she thought. She'd spent a long time on that little bit of copy, and she was pleased with the final product.

She got up and paced across the wood floor toward the open dining area. Then she turned and paced back to the living room. Over and over she traced her steps. What would happen now? Would someone respond to their plea? Would Paula get to follow up the story and be the one who solved the mystery for the Morgans? She hoped for that. Not only would it benefit the couple, it sure wouldn't hurt her career, either. The anchor chair was looking closer every minute.

Darrick had been distant all day, undoubtedly unhappy that things were going so well for the new reporter. To say nothing of her being a woman. She was the underdog for the chair, and they both knew it. But now she had a fighting chance.

Linn rang up the customer's Americano and handed him his change. "Thank you."

The middle-aged man greeted Adam and propped an elbow on the counter while Adam started the three shots of espresso.

"How ya doing, Ken?" Adam asked while Linn took the next order.

Mornings were so busy they hardly had time to visit the rest room when nature called.

"Aw, I'm OK. Got a long day ahead with appointments way past dark."

"Business must be going good then," Adam said.

"Can't complain about that. My youngest is sick with the flu bug, though. Sure hope the rest of the family doesn't get it, with Christmas coming up. Speaking of kids, did you hear that story on the news last night? The one about those babies that got switched at birth here in Chicago?"

"It's been the talk of the shop this morning. I didn't see the clip though."

Linn hadn't seen it, either. She rarely watched the news except to see what the weather was going to be. She had enough bad news of her own without having to hear someone else's. Charlotte was moving out today. When Linn got home, there'd be next to no furniture left in the little apartment. The only person who'd responded to her ad for a roommate was a guy, and there was no way she was sharing space with a guy. Besides, he'd creeped her out even across the phone lines. Which reminded her— she was not going to have a phone when Charlotte moved out. Great.

Linn handed the girl her change and passed the mocha order across the counter to Adam.

His smile made her insides heat up like a Bunsen burner. They'd been so busy while he trained her that they hardly shared any personal details. But sometimes seeing a guy react to others was the best education of all. He was kind to everyone, even the persnickety customers who complained every time they came in. Linn just wanted to tell them if they were that unhappy with their drinks every day, they should go somewhere else. But Adam handled them with ease.

Only once had he shown any sign of irritation. It had been on her second day . . .

Linn was trying to ring up an order for someone who had an account at the shop. It was a first for her, and Adam was in the back making a smoothie for someone who didn't seem to think it was cold enough outside. There was a line a mile long, and this man kept glancing at his watch as though he needed to be someplace five minutes ago. Maybe he should have skipped the latte this morning.

Linn couldn't figure out how to find the customer's existing account, and she didn't know how to start his shots of espresso since Adam had only trained her on the register.

"Look, can't you just make my drink and charge me later? I'm in a hurry." The older man had a furrow between his brows that arched downward, mirroring the frown on his mouth.

"I'm sorry, sir, I haven't been trained to do drinks yet." She pushed another button, hoping it would pull up the accounts.

The man looked at his watch again. "Where's the other workers? Look, I can tell you what to do. I've seen them make it a thousand times."

Anxiety zipped through Linn like electricity. She glanced toward the back, wondering what was taking Adam so long.

Just then the phone rang. *Shoot.* "I'm sorry. Excuse me." She picked up the phone, watching the man cross his arms and huff.

She answered the caller's question about their closing time and hung up only to see she was still facing the same angry customer . . . with no Adam in sight.

"Do I have to come back there and make it myself?" He swore.

Linn felt her face go hot as all the customers in line got quiet and stared at her. "Let me go get someone who can help, sir."

Before she could turn, Adam appeared at her side. His jaw was all tense, and his nostrils flared.

Oh, great, she was in trouble now. She should have figured this out by now. What if he thought she was as incompetent as the last girl who'd had this job?

But instead of addressing her, he put his hands on the edges of the countertop. "Is there a problem, sir?" His voice was quiet and intense.

"Look, I'm late, and this girl can't seem to do much of anything. She's worse than the last girl."

Linn wanted to crouch down behind the register and hide for a good twenty minutes. At least long enough for all these people to leave.

"She's been on the job for all of nine hours," Adam was saying. His ever-present smile was gone, and he was squeezing the edge of the countertop so hard that three long bones fanned out on the backs of his hands. "She hasn't been trained to make drinks yet. And if you're running that late, maybe you shouldn't stop for coffee on the way."

The man's eyes narrowed as he gave Adam a look that would have melted Linn into a puddle. "Your boss will be hearing about this."

When he turned and stormed out the door, Linn sighed. The next customer slid forward as Adam squeezed her arm, then pushed the smoothie across the counter to the teenager who'd been waiting for it.

Later Adam apologized for the guy. He assured her she was doing great and that Joe would understand even if the guy did complain. The scene played repeatedly in Linn's mind that night as she tried to fall asleep. But it wasn't the impatient man who stood out in her thoughts. It was Adam and the way he stood up for her. The way he protected her and made her feel cared for and cherished. And no man had ever made her feel that way before.

Even now Linn was reliving the scene, and she knew it was not good. She had to focus on finding a roommate. Soon school would be starting, and she'd really need to apply herself. She wasn't going to blow this scholarship and her chance at a future. Jackson Hole was in the past, and there was no going back now.

Linn shut the register drawer and passed the last order to Adam. As he made the espresso, his movements were sure and precise, his hands strong and capable.

There I go again. I have got to stop this.

What she really needed right now were friends, and Adam would make a great friend. If he even wanted to be a friend, that is.

Linn grabbed the dishrag from the sink and ran it over the counter where a few drops had spilled during their rush. It looked like there was going to be a lull. Too bad she didn't have to go to the rest room. Adam said this past week had been busier than usual since it was nearly Christmas. Apparently the holiday hadn't put a crimp in anyone else's budget. But her own wallet was so thin that a kindergartner could count its contents.

Adam pushed the latte across the counter. "Skinny vanilla latte," he called.

The last customer took the drink, throwing a flirtatious smile toward Adam, even though she was at least ten years too old for him. "Thank you, sweetie."

Linn wanted to whack the woman with the wet rag. Instead, she closed her eyes and shook her head. She needed to snap out of this. Was she getting some kind of silly crush on this guy? No way. She was just looking out after a friend, that's all.

"Ready to learn the fine art of espresso making?" Adam asked.

Linn tossed the rag in the sink. "Sure." She walked to the machine, where he showed her how to remove the portafilter that held the grounds. After he filled the portafilter with ground beans, he showed her how to use the tamper to press the grounds down and put the portafilter back in.

She'd watched him do it a hundred times before, but this time she was standing close enough to see exactly what he was doing. And he wasn't going so fast that she couldn't take in every detail.

Soon the robust, dark liquid was ready, and he poured it into the bottom of a cup. "If the customer wants a flavor"—he gestured to the Torani bottles lining the wall—"you can pour it in first while you're waiting on the espresso. In fact, when we're busy, if you're working the register, you can go ahead and pour the flavoring."

"I should've been doing that for you all along."

"One thing at a time. You can't learn it all in one day, you know."

His patience was a gift.

When she'd trained at Bubba's, she had a veteran waitress who was all snippy with her, as if she expected Linn to know everything the first day. But her dad had always been that way, too, so Linn was used to it.

Adam showed her how to measure out the Torani, then poured it in the espresso he'd made a few minutes before. "Got it so far?"

"I think so. Now the steamed milk?"

"Exactly." He demonstrated slowly the way the milk was steamed and explained how to read the thermometer. When it was ready, he poured the steamed milk into the cup and stirred. After he placed a lid on the drink, he held it up. "And voilá! The perfect latte."

"Too bad that one lady isn't here, then, since we can't seem to make hers perfect."

"This one's for Joe. And I have a theory about people like that—people who complain all the time about the little stuff."

He leaned against the counter, something Linn had never seen him do. Normally he made himself busy even when they were slow.

"I think they have no control over other things in their lives, and they're frustrated with their inability to change things. So they harp over the little things. Maybe it makes them feel as if they have some say in their lives."

"That's really intuitive. I hope to learn—"

The ringing phone cut off her words.

Adam reached for it before she could move. "Java Joe . . . Oh, hi." He turned away from Linn.

She grabbed the drink and took it to Joe, who was more than happy to see her bearing a cup of caffeine.

When she returned to the front, there were still no customers, and Adam was getting off the phone.

"OK, I'll see you then, hon. Bye."

As he hung up, something heavy settled in Linn's middle. She couldn't miss the way he'd said "hon." Some people used the word casually with just about anyone, but she hadn't heard him call any of the customers by pet names.

"Sorry about that," he said. "My fiancée couldn't remember what time we were meeting tonight."

The smile Linn placed on her lips felt wooden and unnatural, but Adam didn't seem to notice as he showed her how to clean the steamer. She hardly heard a word he said. Instead, her mind wrapped around one thought. If she really thought of Adam as a friend, why was her stomach suddenly as heavy as a bag of rocks?

CHAPTER
TEN

The room was bright—so bright that Paula could hardly open her eyes.

"Turn off the lights," she said. But no one listened.

She lifted her head from the table and scanned the sterile room. Uniformed people buzzed around, but no one looked her way. Didn't they know she was the patient?

She laid her head back against the metal table and closed her eyes against the light. She wished they would just hurry. She had to get back to work. Didn't they know that? She didn't have all day.

When she opened her eyes, a man stood over her, wielding a pair of scissors . . . the pointy, haircutting kind. He was silhouetted against the fluorescent light, but she recognized him as her old boss at WKEV. What was Donald doing here?

To her right was a stack of papers on the table. It was work she'd brought home and was supposed to have finished. She would have to do it afterward.

Beside her, Donald spoke, but it was someone else's voice. A deep, soothing voice that almost hypnotized. "It won't take very long, Paula. Once we cut all the arteries"—he held up the shiny scissors—"we just lift out the heart and it's over. Everything's going to be just fine."

Yes, everything would be fine. They did this kind of thing all the time. Once it was done, she could get back to work.

Then she heard him snort. Her head jerked toward him, but it wasn't

Donald standing above her anymore. It was David. He shook his head at her.

There was another snort, but it wasn't coming from him. She looked around the room. What was that?

It kept getting louder and louder . . .

Paula's eyes flew open, and she stared, wide-eyed, into the dark. Moonlight shone through a large window.

The bed she was lying on was not metal, but a soft mattress. Beside her, David's body was a lump under the covers. His snores echoed across the master suite. She was home, in Jackson Hole, not in some hospital.

She turned over, burrowing into the pillow. What a bizarre dream. They were taking out her heart, and she was nothing but calm and docile.

A chill spread through her. She wrapped the comforter tightly around her, but nothing warded off the coldness that had settled inside her bones. As abstract as the dream had been, she knew what it was about.

She couldn't even say the word. Yes, she could. It was an *abortion*. There, she said it. She'd had an abortion, but that was all behind her. She just needed to shove it back down in its place. In the past, where it belonged.

There was nothing she could do about it now but forget it. Her breaths came in gasps, and her teeth began to chatter. She remembered the way the day had really gone. There'd been no doctor wielding a pair of scissors or a stack of paperwork. It was all some crazy concoction of her subconscious.

But her work had been involved in her decision. She'd been working toward a promotion and knew her career was about to take off. Her boss had a thing against working mothers. He was always complaining about how much time off they took for sick kids and snow days.

David had been working insane hours trying to build a clientele. It was a terrible time to get pregnant. They'd agreed to wait to have children until they were both more established.

When she found out, she was devastated. She'd been faithful about birth control. How could this be happening?

But David surprised her. She told him the news, thinking he'd be as disheartened as she, but a smile had spread across his unshaven face, and he swallowed her in a hug. To say she was stunned would be an understatement.

After his reaction she didn't have the nerve to tell him what she was thinking. A week after he found out, he brought home a miniature plastic hockey stick. His cheeks were flushed when he told her he bought it for their baby.

She knew then she had to keep the pregnancy. David wanted this child. But they agreed to keep the news quiet until later, after the promotion had been announced. Paula knew she would never get the anchor chair at WKEV if her boss knew she was pregnant. So she wore suit coats that disguised the little belly she was getting.

When she got the job, she was giddy for days. But then reality began to sink in. Donald would have a fit when he found out she was pregnant. And he would never recommend her for a better job, not the way he looked down on working mothers. Paula found herself resenting the pregnancy. It wasn't her fault she'd gotten pregnant. She hadn't been irresponsible or careless. Why did she have to risk her career while David got to experience all the benefits of fatherhood without jeopardizing his?

When her boss asked her to go to Chicago for a convention, a plan began to form. At first she was shocked that she thought such a terrible thing. But in the weeks it took to plan the trip, the idea grew on her like a hardy vine, wrapping around her every thought.

David would never agree to an abortion, she knew that. But if she miscarried, what could he do about it? And if it happened in Chicago, no one in Jackson Hole would have to know the truth.

Paula's skin prickled into goose flesh while the dream echoed through her mind like shouts across Dead Canyon.

They hadn't taken her heart that day—only a bunch of tissue.

She tugged the covers off and sat up, feeling the ache behind her eyes that usually preceded a good cry. She had to stop thinking about this. It wasn't doing any good at all. But the ache changed to a sting, and her vision grew blurry. She slipped off the bed carefully, so as not to awaken David.

Her feet took the stairs quickly, and she put her hand over her mouth to smother the wail that begged to escape. She made it to the downstairs bathroom before she closed the door, sank onto the marble tile, and let it go.

Later that day Paula watched her mom cut Natalie's hair. All the details were arranged for the wedding the next night, but tonight the family would celebrate Christmas together since Paula was flying back to Chicago on Christmas Day.

From a quilt on the floor, Grace began stirring and let out a tiny squeak. Paula picked her up and cradled her. She stared down into the squinting blue eyes and her heart squeezed. Oh, how she and David had wanted a child. They'd tried for over a year before the tests, David's test, had begun tearing them apart. Then the dream of a baby was put on the back burner as their marriage seemed to go up in flames.

Her mom handed Natalie a mirror. The same faded sterling one that had hung on the bathroom wall for as long as Paula could remember. "How's that?"

Natalie turned from side to side, studying her naturally dark hair. "Perfect. Are you sure my roots don't need to be done?"

"Honey, if there's any gray in there, I sure can't see it."

"You look gorgeous, Nat," Paula said. "I like the layers around your face."

Natalie handed the mirror back to their mom. "Thanks, Mom. You always do such a great job. The thought of going to a stranger makes me nervous."

Their mom was a licensed hair stylist, but she'd never worked in a salon. When the girls were growing up, women had come over regularly to their home to have their hair cut or colored. It was a little extra income for the family.

"Hey, Nat," Paula said, "do you remember when Mrs. Paxton used to come over to get her hair done?"

"The beehive lady, you mean?"

Her mom had always fixed the woman's jet black hair up in a style so tall an eagle could've nested in it. "She always used to bring her son . . . what was his name?"

Natalie laid both hands on her heart and sighed the name. "Lenny."

"Ah, yes, the elusive Lenny," Paula said.

"You girls had a crush on that boy?" Her mom swept up the cut hair with a broom. "He was a lot older than you."

"Did we ever," Natalie said. "We used to hide behind the sofa and spy on him while you fixed Mrs. Paxton's hair."

"I still think he liked me best," Paula joked.

"Ha! He didn't give you the time of day."

"Like he did you."

"He used to wink at me when you weren't looking."

"He did not."

"Girls, girls." Their mom playfully swiped both their feet with the broom. "You're too old for this."

"You're right, Mother." Paula stood, still cradling Grace, and pecked her mom's cheek. She turned toward the living room, and as she passed Natalie, she whispered, "He did like me best."

"I heard that!" her mom called after her.

⋆❖⋆

Later that afternoon the whole family gathered in the small home around the stone fireplace. Chairs were set up to accommodate their growing family, and the fragrance of pine and burning wood stirred up memories of Christmases past.

Paula checked her watch. She'd hardly seen David all day. The rest of the family was there and waiting for her dad to read the Christmas story from the Bible.

"Where's David?" Hanna, her other sister, asked. She wore a rose-colored maternity sweater that draped over her rounded tummy.

Paula shrugged. "He had showings today. I guess it's taking longer than he thought."

"On the weekend before Christmas?" Micah asked. "Who's looking for property this time of year?"

"Apparently, some wealthy client from out of state." Paula looked across the room at her dad. His wingtip shoes stuck out from a pair of Dockers. He had no taste whatsoever in shoes. "Dad, you might as well go ahead and start."

He opened his mouth to reply, but a couple of knocks sounded at the door before it opened. David appeared, looking sheepish. "Merry Christmas, everyone. Sorry I'm late."

Her mom took his coat and fussed over him for a minute before everyone settled around the room. Her dad read the Christmas story while Nat's two boys squirmed and Grace, cradled in her grandma's arms, let out a few cries.

Dinner was a flurry of activity. Paula and Natalie helped their mom and Gram get food on the table while Micah and Kyle guarded the presents from Alex and Taylor's eager hands. With all the noise and talking, Paula wondered if her family noticed that David hadn't said a word to her all evening. Her ponderings were answered, though, when she caught her mom studying her over pecan pie and an assortment of candies Hanna had made. Paula looked away before she could say anything.

When all their bellies were crying out for mercy, they returned to the living room and began opening gifts. They opened them one at a time, savoring the moments they spent together.

When David opened Paula's gift, he held up the leather coat, his eyes shining briefly. It was exactly like the one he'd worn when they'd been dating. But shortly after they'd gotten married, it had been stolen from the coatrack of a restaurant where they'd been eating. She'd seen it at Banana Republic in downtown Chicago and had known he would love it.

She watched him closely as he ran his fingers over the fine leather. Her heart betrayed her angst. She so wanted him to like the gift, to like her. To look at her the way he used to.

Finally he turned toward her, his lips curved in a small smile. "Thanks. I love it." He grabbed the wrapping paper and wadded it up in a ball before stuffing it in the garbage bag in the middle of the floor.

She didn't know whether to be grateful for the concession of a smile or disappointed that he hadn't said more. Surely he recognized this replica of his old coat as the peace offering it was. Her thoughts were swallowed in the mass chaos of gift opening.

She looked beside her, where Nat was opening a small box. Next to her, Kyle held little Grace.

"Who's it from?" Paula asked.

"It's to Gracie from Linn." From the amount of time it took Nat to open the box, it was apparent that the baby's birth mother was fond of tape.

Finally Nat pulled the box top off and clicked her tongue. "Oh, look, isn't it precious?" She held up a tiny pink-and-white beaded bracelet with *Grace* spelled out with letter beads.

"It's so little," Paula said.

"Look, it stretches." Natalie gently expanded the bracelet. "What a nice keepsake." She held it up to Grace, and the baby's eyes focused on it. "Look, precious. Look what your birth mommy sent you."

"When did it come?" Kyle asked.

"Today. Just in time." She looked at Paula. "That reminds me. I need to talk to you later, OK?"

"Sure." Before Paula could give it another thought, someone handed her a gift. She saw from the tag that it was from David. It was about the size of a book. She tore off the paper and saw from the box what it was: a PDA. Not a cheap gift by any means, but she couldn't deny that her spirits sank quicker than a boulder in Jenny Lake.

"Thanks, David." She tried for a smile and told herself that at least he'd thought of her. But deep inside she wished for a gift whose box didn't read "batteries not included." Was it so wrong to want something more personal from her husband?

"I thought you could use it to keep track of all your appointments."

"Good idea." She smiled again, glad when someone handed him another gift. The PDA would have been a good idea if she was a planner like David. But she was one who flew by the seat of her pants. Didn't he know even that much about her by now? Or was he just bent on making her into a clone of himself?

Despite their mother's chiding, Paula and Nat stayed to help clean up while the men watched football in the other room. Hanna and Micah had been firmly sent home since Hanna looked like she was about to fall asleep standing up.

Grace had fallen asleep in her grandpa's arms, and Alex and Taylor were playing with their new Game Boy on the living-room floor.

Paula washed a glass and handed it to Natalie to dry. "Mom said you and Kyle have decided on a house."

"I'm surprised David didn't tell you."

Paula picked up a coffee mug. "So, after the wedding, you two will live in your old place?"

"Nice change of subject." Natalie grinned. "It'll only be for three weeks, then we get possession of the new house."

They talked about the details of the house, then the subject changed to the wedding.

"Are you nervous?" Paula asked.

"Not one iota. I'm just eager, you know? I want to be married to him already."

"It's not like you've dated that long."

Natalie slid the mug into the cupboard and closed the door. "I know. But sometimes you just know when it's right. And when it is, what's the point of waiting?"

At Nat's dreamy expression, Paula had the stirrings of envy. She had felt the same way about David. Their wedding had been perfect in every way. "It's too bad you can't take a honeymoon."

Nat sighed. "Yeah, but I just can't see leaving the kids, you know?" Nat bit the corner of her lip, as if realizing, after she'd said it, that Paula didn't know. How could she when she had no children?

Sadness welled up in Paula, but she pushed it firmly down. "Mom's keeping them for a couple of nights?"

"Just one night." Nat leaned over close to Paula. "And don't tell Kyle, but I'm almost looking forward to a whole night's sleep as much as I'm looking forward to spending it with him."

"Did I hear my name?" Kyle appeared in the doorway and approached Nat, slipping his arms around her.

She leaned back into his chest. "I was telling Paula how much I was looking forward to our first night together." Nat winked at Paula.

Kyle stepped back. "Whoa. This sounds like a sister thing to me." He pecked Nat on the cheek. "I'll just be in there watching the game with your dad."

Natalie chuckled. "Chicken."

"*Bak-bak.*" Kyle ducked into the living room.

Nat smiled and shook her head.

After he left, Natalie picked up their conversation from earlier. "Wasn't that a sweet bracelet Linn sent Grace?"

"I'll bet she made it herself." Paula felt the stirrings of envy again. As badly as she and David had wanted a child, it seemed unfair the way Linn's baby had just fallen into Nat's lap. Paula sighed quietly and chided herself. She should be happy for Nat, not envious. It wasn't her sister's fault that Linn offered her the baby. In fact, it took a great deal of courage to do what her sister did. Not very many pregnancy center directors would have agreed to adopt a client's baby. And, in fact, Paula was proud of her sister for doing so. Still . . .

"And I was wondering if that would be a possibility." Nat set the dried fork on the counter and eyed Paula with expectation.

Paula realized her sister had been telling her something about Linn, but she hadn't heard a word of it.

"You weren't paying attention, were you?" Nat said.

Paula cringed. "Sorry. Try again. I'll pay better attention this time."

"I was telling you about Linn's letter. Her roommate got a dorm, and now Linn can't afford the apartment."

Paula really cringed now. She knew Linn lived in Chicago, too, and wasn't sure she liked the direction of the conversation.

"She's looking for a roommate, but if she can't find one and things get desperate, do you think . . . ?"

When Nat's nose wrinkled up, Paula could tell she hated asking the favor of her sister.

The feeling was mutual. Paula picked up another fork and scrubbed, noticing a flake of red polish had come off the tip of her pinky nail. So much for her manicure.

"I know it's asking a lot, but it would only be temporary until she found another situation. She has a part-time job in a coffee shop, so she'd be able to pitch in."

Paula hated the situation Nat was putting her in. She liked her space, and the studio apartment wasn't that big. She worked at home, and she liked it quiet when she did so. She didn't want to have to entertain some-one when she walked through the door. A dozen other reasons marched through her mind.

"I know you're thinking it would be inconvenient, and I hate even asking. But I can tell you when Linn lived with us, she was very helpful. She often had dinner on the table when I got home, and she picked up after herself."

"That's the last thing I'm worried about."

"Well, maybe she'll pick up after you, and you'll be able to see the floor again." Nat's mouth curved.

"It's not that bad."

"Without David there, I'll bet it is." The joke fell flat.

The truth was, her apartment was a mess. She didn't have time to clean it, and David wasn't there to complain about it.

"I won't mention it to Linn, but will you at least think about it? She has another couple of weeks before things get desperate."

Desperate. Now there was a word Paula understood. "I'll think about it."

CHAPTER
ELEVEN

David sat at one of the round tables in the small reception room of their church and set his Coke down in front of him. Across the room Paula stood talking with one of her distant relatives, looking beautiful in a hunter green silky dress.

The Christmas Eve wedding was simple and small, with only family and the closest of friends. Paula and Hanna stood up for Natalie, while Kyle's best friend stood up for him. He watched his wife through the ceremony, remembering their own wedding and the strong feelings he'd had for Paula. When Kyle said his vows, Paula turned and looked at him. Their eyes met and clung for a poignant moment. Was she thinking about their wedding too? About the love they'd felt for each other and the passion they'd stirred in each other? Ever since he'd opened her gift of the leather jacket, he couldn't stop thinking about when they'd dated.

Now Paula tossed her head back in laughter, her long, elegant neck drawing his attention. There was a ticklish spot in the crook between her neck and shoulder that made her laugh and scrunch up her shoulders whenever he kissed it. When was the last time he'd done that?

Christmas music played lightly from the sound system, and Natalie and Kyle took a spin around the open space. They were so focused on each other, he thought a bomb could go off and it wouldn't disrupt them. He was glad Natalie had found happiness again after the mess her ex-husband had put her through with the affair and the way he'd tried to sabotage Gram's lodge.

Paula's mom was trying to get her husband to the dance floor, but he was fighting her every inch of the way. From the nearest table, Gram called out encouragement. The Alzheimer's was taking its toll, but it was good to see her having such a clearheaded day for Natalie's wedding.

"They look pretty good out there, don't they?" Micah sank into a chair opposite David, his gaze following Natalie and Kyle across the floor.

"Why aren't you and Hanna dancing?"

Micah tugged his necktie loose. "Between my two left feet and her . . . uh . . . pregnant condition, we figured we were safer on the sidelines." He took off his jacket and draped it over the back of the chair next to him. "I feel sorry for people who have to wear these things every day."

"It's not so bad."

"Sorry. Forgot you were a suit."

David shrugged. To each his own. He would die if he had to spend days climbing mountains and nights sleeping on canyon floors, like Micah did.

"Where's Hanna?" David glanced around the room, where about thirty people mingled in clusters.

"Want to dance?"

Paula had approached the table. She towered over him in her high heels. His gaze swept down her figure and back up before he realized what he was doing. She was tall and lean but just curvy enough to stir his blood. After all the tension between them, it was a passion he didn't want to encourage. But with Micah as their audience, he could hardly turn his wife down.

He stood and walked with her toward the other couples who swayed to a jazzy rendition of "Silent Night." Turning, he put his hands at Paula's waist while she wrapped her hands around his neck.

He looked over her head toward her parents, feeling his heart kick into gear. They moved as if one. Always had. David thought it strange, because he'd danced with many women over the years and it never felt the way it did with Paula. Many nights after they married, they put on a jazz CD and turned their living-room into a private dance floor.

Even now, with so much between them, they moved so well together. As Paula's fingers toyed with the hair at his neckline, his throat constricted.

His eyes found hers and locked. Hers held a look he'd never seen before. There was such a depth of emotion it made him catch his breath. Was it sorrow or regret? Desperation or hunger? He couldn't pinpoint any one emotion, or maybe it was an intricate cocktail of them all. Whatever it was, it pulled him in like a black hole, sucking up everything in him. And he wanted to give in to it more than anything.

Before he could reason away the feeling, he drew her closer, his hand winding up her back and into her hair. Her eyes questioned, and he saw vulnerability there. A rarity with Paula. The last traces of inhibition drained away, and he leaned toward her. His lips found hers, soft and pliable, and his legs went weak at her response. She still wanted him. It was something, wasn't it?

The spark she lit fanned into a raging fire as she responded to him as she hadn't in years. It reminded him of when they dated. But this was more than physical. It was the desperate wanting of time turned back. The regret of words spoken in anger. The longing for the wall to come down.

He deepened the kiss. Regardless of the dim lighting, he struggled to keep it PG in a room full of friends and family. One of Paula's hands trailed down to his chest before she pulled away.

For an instant he feared he'd lost the moment and that she was regretting the slip in her carefully framed facade. But when he opened his eyes, he saw that she hadn't distanced herself. A film of tears covered her eyes, and she was drinking him in like a woman who hadn't seen water in days.

"I love you, David." She whispered the words so quietly, the music swallowed them. But he saw them on her lips.

His heart squeezed so tightly he felt pain. He wanted this woman back more than anything. More than his career. More than air. His mind fought for him to be reasonable. To think about the issue between them. But he shut it all off. He didn't want to think about any of that. He only wanted the woman who was in his arms to stay there. For the look on her face to last forever.

He gathered her close until her head rested on his shoulder. Then he whispered the words she needed to hear.

As Linn buttoned her coat and slipped on her gloves, Adam locked up the coffee shop. It was Christmas Eve, and Joe had said they should close early to allow employees time to be with their families.

Presuming we had families, Linn thought.

Linn hitched her purse on her shoulder and turned just as Adam did. The cold wind slammed into her face, and she figured her nose was already turning red.

"Where you headed?" he asked. "You have plans, don't you?"

"Sure. I'll need to take the bus, though." She didn't add that she was taking it straight home and that her plans consisted of a can of SpaghettiOs and a book.

"Need a lift?" He pulled the collar of his leather jacket up around his neck.

"Nope, it'll be here soon."

He seemed to scan the darkness that had already gathered around them in the short days of winter. "I'll walk you there."

She started to argue but knew it was futile. He probably wouldn't leave her until the bus picked her up. He was a real gentleman, an enigma to her way of thinking.

They began walking.

"Won't you be late somewhere?" she asked.

He shrugged. "It's Elizabeth's family dinner."

At the mention of his fiancée, Linn's stomach went all hollow. Which was just silly since she and Adam were only friends. And everything she heard about Elizabeth made her think she and Adam were a match made in heaven. Literally. Adam was working his way through college with his sights set on being a pastor. He already had a bachelor's and was now in his second year at a seminary. Elizabeth was also attending the seminary to be some kind of missionary.

"You know the drill," he went on. "Ham and turkey, sibling rivalry, and polite jabs, followed by a chaotic round of what'd-I-get-for-Christmas."

"Sure." She wished she had something clever to say, but it had been a long time since she experienced any semblance of the holiday he just described. Christmas had been something close to that before her mother died of cancer and before Jillian, her sister, died in the car accident. But even then, they never had the money for the big dinner, and her father always drank a little too much. In recent years her dad hadn't celebrated Christmas at all. Unless you count perching on the barstool at Sidewinders as celebrating.

What would Adam think if he knew more about her life? He'd probably feel sorry for her. She didn't need or want his pity. She blew out a frosty breath, feeling almost relieved when they neared the bus hut.

He followed her inside the Plexiglas shelter and sat beside her on the cold bench. Even though he sat a few inches away, she could feel the heat radiating off him.

"You don't have to stay. The bus will be here any minute."

He buried his hands in the pockets of his coat. "I don't mind." He gazed at her, then looked away, almost sheepishly.

She wondered what was on his mind. Normally he was self-assured. But tonight he was acting a little odd.

"Look, I . . . uh . . . got you something." He extracted a little package from his pocket. "I hope you don't think it's weird or anything, but I just saw it and thought of you. Merry Christmas." As he held it out, she could swear a flush climbed from under his thin scarf that had nothing to do with the cold.

Linn took the small, lumpy package in hand and smiled. Adam had rolled up the odd-shaped gift in wrapping paper and folded up the edges. "Sorry it's so sloppy. Believe it or not, that's the best I can do."

She chuckled, meeting his gaze, loving the way his brown eyes softened like a melting fudge pop.

She looked down at the gift. "I didn't get you anything."

He nudged her shoulder. "I didn't expect you to. Go on; open it."

Her fingers worked the tape and paper until she pulled out a Christmas-tree ornament. It was a figurine of a little girl with dark hair, like hers. The girl held a stack of textbooks that was nearly as big as she. The one on top said Biology.

Linn remembered when Adam had caught her sitting right here in the bus hut, reading her biology textbook. She had been embarrassed since school hadn't even started, but she'd wanted to get a jump on her classes by reading the first couple of chapters in all her books. Instead of poking fun at her eagerness, he'd cocked his head and given her that smile that made her feel all warm inside. "You are something else, Linn Caldwell."

She ran her fingers over the painted figurine. "Thanks, Adam. It was really sweet of you."

The sound of the approaching bus smothered her words. She stood and Adam stood with her.

"You have a Merry Christmas," he said.

She gathered her purse and tucked the ornament in her pocket. "You too."

The bus doors opened, and she stepped up into the vehicle. On the first step she turned. The wind tousled his hair, and she had the urge to flip his scarf up and tuck it around his bare neck. "Thanks again. For the gift."

He shrugged. "It wasn't much."

The doors closed behind her as Linn made her way to the third seat and sank down.

Adam may not think the gift was much, but when it was the only one you got, it felt like everything.

CHAPTER
TWELVE

Paula signaled a left turn and slipped into the right lane. After spending Christmas Day flying home from Jackson Hole and unpacking, she was eager to get back to work today and see what was transpiring regarding the switched-at-birth story. The night before, she'd gotten out her notes on the interview and made a game plan for the week, figuring which people she wanted to get another interview with.

But her mind kept returning to the night of Natalie and Kyle's wedding. The night that David was once again the man she'd married. When he'd kissed her, it was like a slice of heaven. Did he know she yearned for him through the entire wedding ceremony? And after the wedding they'd had a honeymoon of their own. Then they stayed up until two thirty in the morning, catching up on things that were going on in their lives. She told him about the Morgans' story she aired the previous week.

Their time together was so heartfelt and intimate that she hadn't wanted to leave David to come back to Chicago.

When she arrived at work on Tuesday, she immediately scheduled interviews with three of the key nurses and the doctor who had taken care of Faith in the NICU. After the last phone call, she turned her attention to the stack of mail on the corner of her desk.

One letter was from a viewer who saw her story on the news and wanted to tell a story about a friend of hers who'd been switched at birth thirty-four years ago. Then she rambled about her own life for a page and a half. Another letter was from a viewer who complimented her on her work. The last envelope had no return address. She tore it open and pulled out the single sheet of spiral-bound notebook paper. In heavy, black script it read:

> Roses are red
> Violets are blue
> Your very pretty
> I want to mete you

She wavered between chuckling and cringing. The simplicity of the words seemed childlike, but they gave her the creeps too.

"Fan letter?" Darrick asked as he walked by her desk.

"Something like that." She perused the words on the paper. "Actually, it's a little weird." She gave a little laugh as she handed it to him. "I think it came from a child."

He read the note, a thoughtful frown pulling at his eyebrows. "You think? The script is pretty small for a kid."

"But the words *you're* and *meet* are misspelled."

He hitched up his shoulder. "Lots of adults can't spell." He handed it back to her. "Probably just some lovesick fan. It's part of being in the public eye. Wait'll you get a marriage proposal."

"I can hardly wait."

A man Paula didn't recognize passed by with Cindy, and they stopped beside her desk.

"Hey, guys," Cindy said. "This is Stan. We've just hired him to work with information technology. Stan, these are two of our reporters, Paula and Darrick."

Stan smiled and shook their hands. "It's a pleasure to meet you."

When the phone at Paula's desk rang, Cindy, Darrick, and Stan moved along. She answered the phone, and Deb Morgan greeted her.

"Paula, you're not going to believe it, but guess who called this morning." Deb's voice was like three shots of espresso.

"I don't know, who?"

"*Good Morning America*! They want to interview us."

Paula sat up straight in her ergonomic chair. *Good Morning America.* "When?" Excitement buzzed through her like a jolt of electricity. Her story was going national.

"They're flying us out tomorrow, and we'll do the interview early the next morning. I can hardly believe it. I'm so nervous. What if this is a mistake? What if we start getting hounded by the media? What if some kooks start calling? And what if I mess up the interview and say something—"

"Deb, calm down. It's going to be fine. You're doing the right thing. This is just the thing that can help us solve your problem. The answer to this mystery may very well be beyond the scope of Chicago. If someone out there knows something, this will help us find them."

"Oh, I know you're right. I'm just so nervous. The *Tribune* called, too, and set up an interview with us."

"That's good. All the media coverage is just what you want if you want to find out what happened to your birth child. I'm not finding any clues in my notes, but I'm going to interview the nurses again."

"Thanks, Paula; we really appreciate everything you've done. We're grateful that you've treated it as more than just another news story."

After Paula hung up, she went to Miles's office and told him the good news. When his eyes lit up, Paula knew the anchor chair and her dream career were getting closer all the time.

Paula spent her free time the next two days interviewing the nurses and doctor about the Morgans' story. She was still unable to get an interview with one of the nurses, Louise Garner. Her son insisted she was too ill to conduct an interview.

On the morning of the big *Good Morning America* program, she paced the apartment like she was on a sugar high, glancing at the TV set and wishing they'd hurry up and get to the Morgans. They announced the story would be coming on later and showed the Morgans sitting in the studio before cutting away to a medical researcher who claimed a study he'd done proved that sugar improves memory retention.

As she walked by her cell phone, she had an urge to call David. This was a big moment, and she didn't want to spend it alone. They'd been e-mailing back and forth, and she knew he'd be watching the program, but she wanted to watch it *with* him.

He answered on the first ring. "Hi, honey."

"I'm so nervous. I just wish they'd get on with it already. I'm about to chew up my manicure."

"Stop pacing and sit down."

A smile pulled at her lips. "How did you know I was pacing?"

"Same way I knew you'd call."

She savored the words in the silence. No one knew her like David. She didn't realize how much she missed him until the night of Nat's wedding. Memories of their loving replayed in her mind, making her long for his presence.

"I miss you, David. I wish you were here with me." Did she really just say that? When had she let herself be that vulnerable to him lately? A prickle of fear poked at her. What if he didn't feel the same?

"I miss you too."

His words held her captive.

"I'll be home tomorrow night," she said. "I guess that's not so long."

"And we have the long weekend because of New Year's Day."

"That's true."

The network went to commercial, and Paula muted the TV.

They discussed plans for New Year's Eve before Diane Sawyer appeared on the screen. Paula turned up the volume.

". . . next story is a mystery that has one family tied in knots."

"This is it," David said.

Paula cranked up the volume.

Diane continued. "Three years ago Deb Morgan checked into Chicago General Hospital to deliver a premature baby girl. The child, which they named Faith, was not expected to live, but miraculously pulled through. Only weeks ago, though, the Morgans found out through a series of tests that the child they brought home from the hospital is not the child Deb Morgan gave birth to. The Morgans are here in our studio to talk about this switched-at-birth mystery."

The screen flashed to Deb and Steve, who looked relatively at ease. "Good morning," Diane said.

The Morgans returned the greeting.

"Your discovery must have been a very painful one. Can you tell us how you found out that Faith is not the same child you gave birth to?"

Steve fielded the question, answering succinctly, yet thoroughly. He repeated much the same thing he had said in Paula's interview.

"Given that Faith is not your birth child," Dianne said, "weren't you worried about coming forward? What if someone out there today gave birth at Chicago General Hospital during the same time that you did? What if Faith is her birth child?"

Deb clasped Steve's hand. "We realize we could be opening Pandora's box here. But if Faith is someone else's birth child, the other parents deserve to know, just as we deserve to know what happened to ours."

Diane switched focus. "Has Chicago General Hospital been helping you figure all this out? Figure out what mothers gave birth during the time you were in the hospital?"

Steve leaned forward. "Chicago General has supposedly contacted all the parents who were there at the same time. However, the hospital has not been very open with us, nor have they given us any helpful information. A local reporter in Chicago has been able to recover some information for us, and she's still helping us discover what happened."

"That's you," David said.

Paula hadn't expected the Morgans would say anything about her involvement, though she supposed it didn't matter since her name hadn't been mentioned.

"How have you explained this to Faith?" Diane asked.

Deb spoke. "We've told her in a very simple way that she's not our birth child. However, we've made it clear to her that we will always be her mommy and daddy and that we love her no matter what."

"What do you hope to accomplish by telling your story?"

"We just want to know the truth," Steve said. "If our birth child is out there somewhere, we deserve to know about her. 'The truth will set you free.' We believe that."

"Thank you for being with us today."

The Morgans thanked Diane.

"What an interesting story," Diane said. "Now we'll turn it back over to Charlie who has, shall we say, a rather interesting guest." The screen switched to Charlie Gibson, who had a chimpanzee sitting in the chair beside him.

Paula flicked off the TV.

"What did you think?" she asked David.

"I thought it went well. The Morgans seem like an average American family, and I think the viewers will be able to relate well to them."

"I think so too. Now I guess we wait to see what happens next. I still want to get an interview with that nurse, Louise Garner, but her son is saying she's too ill. And there's also a possibility that the nurse who died is the one who held all the answers."

"Are you worried another reporter is going to solve the mystery before you?"

"I'd love to be the one to figure it out. I really think that anchor chair would be mine if I did."

Silence crowded through the phone lines until David said he had to go. After they hung up, Paula kicked herself for bringing up the anchor position. The job would have her moving to Chicago full-time. What would become of their marriage then?

CHAPTER
THIRTEEN

Paula sank into her recliner, punched in Louise's phone number, and waited for an answer. The other interviews had turned up nothing new, and she was desperate to talk to this last NICU nurse. Paula had gotten pats on the back from most of the newsroom staff, though she sensed a little tenseness when Darrick had congratulated her.

"Hello?" The scratchy voice was female, presumably Louise.

"Mrs. Garner? This is Paula Landin-Cohen from Channel 12 News. How are you today?"

A second's silence ballooned like rising dough between them until the woman said, "Oh, yes. You're the one who interviewed that family here locally. I saw the news this morning."

Paula was relieved to be talking to Louise at last. She hoped the woman's son was nowhere nearby. "I've tried to schedule a time to chat with you about that, but I hear you're not feeling well."

"No, I'm not doing so good. I probably shouldn't be talking to you."

The finality in her voice set off an alarm in Paula. "Please, Mrs. Garner, can I ask you a couple of questions? Over the phone?"

She heard a throaty sigh.

"I don't think I'm going to have any information that can help you," the scratchy voice replied.

"That's OK. If you could just tell me if you remember this particular baby, Faith Morgan, who was born at—"

A male voice interrupted. "Leave her alone. She's sick, lady!"

The phone disconnected.

Frustration welled up in her, and she sighed hard. If she could just get Louise alone, she thought the lady would cooperate. She didn't seem too ill to talk over the phone.

For the remainder of the evening, she turned her attention toward tracking down the other women who'd given birth the same week as Deb Morgan. She'd gotten names from the birth section in the newspaper, but tracking them down after three years was time consuming. She had received two phone calls after her story ran from women who'd given birth to babies at the same time as Deb, but both of those babies had been full-term. She was looking for babies who'd been in the NICU at the same time as Faith. Chicago General had hired a team of lawyers and a media rep, and getting any information from them was like trying to run through a brick wall.

Taking out her notes from all the previous interviews, she determined to copy them into her computer. Maybe if she had it all organized, she would see something amiss.

Linn knocked on her landlord's door and stuffed her hands into her coat pockets. After nearly two weeks of advertising for a roommate, she was still looking. She wished Mr. Oliani would be flexible, though her interactions with him in the past left her feeling less than hopeful.

The door swung open. The little Italian man was no taller than Linn, with a head of black hair that would make a young man jealous. "Hello, uh . . ."

"Linn. I rent an apartment with Charlotte. Or I did, at least."

"Right. What's up?" He leaned against the doorframe and crossed his arms, as if guarding his apartment from entry.

Linn wished he'd invite her in so she could make a little small talk before she had to ask such a big favor. "I was wondering if we could talk a minute."

"Shoot."

So much for hospitality. "You know Charlotte moved out and that I'm looking for a roommate. I wondered if I might have a short extension on my rent."

There. It was out.

"Sorry, can't do that."

"But Mr. Oliani, I'm sure I can find a roommate soon, and I can give you a portion of the rent on the first, just not the whole amount."

He tipped his chin down. "Look, I don't like being mean. It's not my nature. But I got a payment to make myself, see? If I let you be late, I'll have to let everyone be late, and I just can't do that, OK? I'm sorry." He moved to shut the door.

Linn reached out and held the door open. "It's just this once, I promise. And I won't tell the other renters."

"That's what they all say." He pushed the door.

She stuck her foot in between the door and the frame. "I don't have anywhere to go. I don't have any family or anything, Mr. Oliani."

He eyed her foot, a scowl forming on his face. "Listen, kid, I feel bad for you. I do. But I gotta look out for myself, see? First of the month. Rent in full." He looked at her foot again.

She pulled it away and let the door shut in her face. There was no way she could come up with the rent in three days' time. Not unless she asked for money in advance from Joe. And how could she do that when she'd only been working there just over a week? She didn't want to risk her job by imposing on him like that.

If only she could find a cheaper place to stay. But she'd already scoured the apartment section in the paper. There wasn't anything cheaper than what she had now. And a week and a half from now, she'd have to go to part-time at the coffee shop so she could go to school. There might be some kind of government help she was eligible for, but she'd always sworn she would never resort to that. Anyway, it would take weeks to get the ball rolling on that, and she didn't have weeks.

The next morning, when Linn got to work, Adam greeted her with a kind smile. She tossed her purse down under the counter and wrapped an apron around her. Outside the streetlights still lit the dark sky.

"You look exhausted." Adam asked.

"Thanks. Just what every girl longs to hear." What could she expect when she'd tossed all night trying to figure out what to do?

"Just an observation. You OK?"

Well, I'm about to lose my apartment, it's the dead of winter, and I have no place to live. Other than that, I'm just peachy.

"Sure." Linn saw they were low on cups and went to the closet for another stack. She stepped inside the walk-in closet and looked around for the cups, wishing the closet was lit.

"Adam, do you know where the extra cups are?" She saw some old cups, the kind that weren't insulated, but not the kind she'd been using since she'd started working.

Adam approached. "We're out. Joe's going to get some this morning, but he said to use the old ones for now."

Linn retrieved the packages of cardboard cups from the shelf. "Do we have any sleeves to insulate them?"

The customers wouldn't be happy if the cups were too hot to hold.

"There should be some in the very back."

Linn rooted around, moving aside packages of sweetener, stir sticks, and straws. Everything but sleeves.

"Here." Adam stepped close behind her and leaned forward, almost pinning her to the shelves. He reached over her shoulder.

She could smell the faint scent of his spicy cologne and feel the heat of his skin. She didn't dare turn her face or she would have been staring into the crook of his neck. Time seemed frozen as he moved aside a box of straws and tugged the package of sleeves forward.

"Here they are." He pulled backward ever so slightly as he dragged the package to the edge of the shelf. Linn turned and faced him.

She could see by his expression that he hadn't realized how close he was standing until just then. And when he did, his face lost that casual, pleasant, everyday look. The corners of his mouth slacked, and his eyes changed somehow.

Linn forgot to breathe. If her heart wasn't an involuntary muscle, it would have stopped too. Instead, it thudded against her ribs like a warning alarm.

She wished she could read his eyes, wondered if they would give away any secrets if it weren't so dark. But there was only a dimness that transformed the closet into a cocoon.

"Sorry," he said softly. "I didn't mean to crowd you." He drew back, but only a little. Their eyes locked, like a missile on a target.

"That's OK." It was more than OK. He could crowd her any day, as far as she was concerned.

A jangle of keys at the register caught his attention, and he stepped out of the closet. Linn inhaled to feed her oxygen-deprived body. If she'd been alone, she would have grabbed a piece of cardboard and fanned her warm face.

Instead she joined Adam behind the counter and pumped hazelnut flavoring into a cup while he made espresso several feet away. She mentally reviewed their encounter in the closet, knowing it was only the first of many times she would relive that moment.

The same way she knew she wore her most flattering clothes to work.

The same way she knew Adam's Christmas gift would hang from her bedside lamp until well past New Year's.

And the same way she knew her heart would break when he married someone else.

CHAPTER
FOURTEEN

"Paula, honey, it's so good to see you." Gerdy Feldner, one of Gram's friends, crossed the church foyer and gave her a big, soft hug.

Paula leaned down to embrace the shorter woman who was wearing what David called "a granny dress." "Hi, Mrs. Feldner. It's so nice to see you."

"Honey, your mom has been talking about that story you broke in the big city. I watched it on the morning news and just had to come over and tell you congratulations." She tucked a strand of gray hair behind her ear and patted Paula on the shoulder.

Paula was surprised her mom told anyone about the story since she so obviously disapproved of Paula's leaving Jackson Hole. "Thank you. It's been a very exciting experience."

"I'm sure it has. Me and Mr. Feldner used to live in Los Angeles, you know."

"No, I didn't know."

"Yes, well, you get tired of the excitement after a while. At least we did."

Paula looked around for David and saw him across the foyer talking to Hanna and Micah. "Will you excuse me, Mrs. Feldner?"

When she approached David, he caught her off guard by taking her hand.

Hanna slipped an arm around Paula. "I was telling David you guys are welcome to come out to the lodge and bring in the New Year with us. We're putting on a movie night for our guests who want a quiet night. Of course, we'll tune in to watch the ball drop on TV when it gets close to midnight New York time."

Paula supposed it beat staying home. "Sure, that'd be—"

"Actually, we have other plans." David squeezed her hand.

She looked at her husband. He hadn't mentioned anything to her. In fact, she had specifically asked what they were going to do, and he'd seemed fresh out of ideas.

"I haven't told Paula about them yet," David said.

Paula had no idea what he was talking about, but they could talk about that later. "Oh, OK. Thanks for inviting us, though," she told Hanna and Micah.

When they got in the car, Paula slid off her gloves and laid them in her lap. David was gone a lot the day before, so they hadn't spent much time together since she came home. However, it was a three-day weekend, so there was still time. When she was flying home, she had worried he'd slip right back into his detached behavior . . . as if their intimate encounter the previous weekend had never happened. But that didn't happen.

"So, husband," she said flirtatiously. "What are these sudden plans we have for tonight?"

He pushed his glasses up on his nose but didn't meet her gaze as he pulled out of the church parking lot. "I thought you liked surprises."

This was sounding better and better. "You're surprising me?"

"You didn't know we had plans. Now you know we do." His lips twitched. "Surprise."

She whacked him on the arm. "David."

"You'll find out tonight. Where's your patience, Paula?"

"I don't have any."

A grin pulled at his lips. "You're like a kid who can't wait until Christmas morning."

She crossed her arms and gave a mock "Hummph." She had no idea what he could have planned or why. As far as she knew, their only options were the New Year's Eve service at church or a long wait at some restaurant since all the ones who took reservations would be booked already.

"I don't even know how to dress." She was pouting, but judging by his reaction, he didn't seem to mind.

"Wear layers."

Paula was still thinking about those words at eight o'clock that evening as they drove up to the base of Snow King. Didn't David know the ski slope was closed for the night? She hoped his surprise wasn't ruined. She turned and looked at him.

They exited the vehicle and, like magic, the lights flashed on, flooding the entire slope with light. The chairlift swung into operation, its empty chairs swaying at the abrupt start.

"What in the world?"

David just smiled. "Come on." He opened the back of the car and started unloading their ski gear.

"We're going skiing?" She hadn't been skiing since last winter, and she couldn't remember the last time David had skied. The thought of gliding down the slopes with nothing in her way but the wind made her blood stir with excitement.

"You don't even like to ski," she said.

He took the last of their gear from the trunk and shut it. "You do, though."

They put on their skis, and Paula added the ski coat he'd brought along for her.

Once they were on the chairlift, gliding up the mountainside, Paula turned and stared at her husband. His nose was already turning red, and she knew his glasses would start fogging up any minute.

He didn't like being out here on the slopes. He never had. She'd known it the first time she brought him here when they'd just met. They'd only returned one other time, right before they married. What had happened over the past few weeks that was changing him back into the man she used to know? She was afraid to ask him, afraid to break the mood.

His long legs hung down from the chair, the crossed skis angling out in a *V*. When they exited the chairlift, he guided her to the right, away from the slopes. She wondered where he was taking her, but he wasn't talking.

Finally they came to a stop at the Panorama House, a casual grill and a place for skiers to eat and warm up. They'd eaten lunch there on their third date.

The lights were on inside.

Her eyes widened. "David, what have you done?"

Instead of answering, he took off his skis on the stoop, and she followed suit. Inside, the lighting was much different than all the times Paula had visited. Candlelight bathed the walls, and in the center of the room, a table was swathed in white linen and set for two with sparkling crystal.

"Oh, David."

She stopped and took in all the details. White lights twinkled from the planters and the ceiling. A fire crackled and popped from the massive fireplace. And music. A sexy jazz instrumental played softly.

She was overwhelmed by the thoughtful gesture. Early in their relationship he'd planned dates for them. Once he'd even arranged a sleigh ride to celebrate their anniversary, but he'd never gone to these measures.

"David?" She gazed at him, and he met her eyes with an expression she couldn't recall seeing before. Not exactly the look he gave her the weekend before. This one held a seed of pride at his effort, but it was rooted in something else. Humility? He looked away before she could identify it.

"Come on. It's getting cold," he said. After they seated themselves at the table, David took her hand. "Grace first?"

"Sure."

David said a short prayer and squeezed her hand.

They lifted the sterling lids off their plates. The aroma of roasted duck wafted upward. Paula's stomach rumbled. It was perfectly roasted to a golden crisp and topped with an orange sauce. Sides of French-cut green beans and seasoned new potatoes filled out the plate.

"This smells divine." She glanced around the room. "How did you manage all this? The slopes, the food, the decorations . . ."

He sliced the roasted duck. "I helped Snow King's owner with a large real-estate transaction. He was inclined to do me a favor."

Must've been some transaction, Paula thought. "I guess so. Who did the food? And the decorations?"

"The food was catered, and I did the decorations."

"You?"

David didn't have a creative bone in his body. His idea of a decorated home was white walls and miniblinds.

"Well, I had some help," he admitted. "The manager of the Panorama made suggestions."

She savored her first bite of the roasted duck while she studied her husband. Who was this man, and what had happened to the one she'd been tiptoeing around for months? The one who accused her of having an affair? She remembered like yesterday the evening he came home after getting the results of his infertility test . . .

<hr/>

"It's very unlikely I can get you pregnant, Paula," David had told her.

He was upset over his low sperm count . . . and low motility. At first Paula thought he was feeling embarrassed or incapable. But it was more than that. He was so angry.

She'd never seen him that way. He flicked off the TV and tossed the remote onto the table. It clattered, then spun and plunked onto the carpet.

She stared at her husband, suddenly feeling like she didn't know him at all. "What is wrong? This is more than just a test result."

He swiveled the recliner toward her then, and she felt the full weight of his anger. "I can't get you pregnant, Paula." He spat out the words as if spewing some nasty food from his mouth.

Her heart pressed against her ribs; her blood gushed through her veins, but still, she couldn't figure out why—

Then a terrible thought occurred to her.

"Do you get it now? Yes, I see that you do." He blinked rapidly.

"You can't be serious."

Silence. So heavy and oppressing, it smothered her.

"You are," she said quietly. She couldn't believe he thought she'd—

"What am I supposed to think? The doctor told me it was highly unlikely I could father a child. 'Practically impossible,' she said."

"But you did. We did."

"Did we?"

The words hung in the air between them. Suspended like a poisonous cloud of gases, they sucked the air from her lungs. Her eyes stung. "Of course we did. Think what you're saying, David."

"I've had all afternoon to think. And you know what I thought about? I thought about the time I found a bunch of e-mails from Evan in your inbox—"

"He was just seeing how—"

"I thought about the time we had those mysterious hotel charges on our credit card—"

"That was—"

"And I thought about how you act around other men. How you flirt and act so coy, and how you and that . . . that *Dante* were acting two weeks ago when I walked in on you at the TV station." His voice escalated. "That's what I thought about, Paula."

He shoved in the footrest, got up, and left the room.

She felt as if some heavy boulder sat on her chest. Sure, she'd been attracted to Dante. And maybe she did act a little coy with men, but that was just her personality. Couldn't he see that?

Maybe he senses your guilt.

She shoved away the thought. That was a whole separate thing. He was accusing her of cheating on him.

She followed him on legs that felt uncharacteristically wobbly. When she reached the kitchen, he was making a pot of coffee.

She lounged against the counter. "I know I sometimes act a little flirtatious with other men, but I have never cheated on you."

He emptied the water into the reservoir and shoved the pot on the burner.

"That baby was yours, David," she said emphatically. Her heart turned flip-flops in her chest when he didn't respond. She'd told him the truth. Why wouldn't he believe her? She trembled but not from fear. "How could you even think it?"

He took a mug from the cabinet and turned to get the half-and-half from the fridge.

She grabbed his arm. "Why are you doing this? Talk to me!"

He flung the creamer across the counter, where it slid and toppled.

"The doctor said 'practically impossible,' Paula. Do you understand what that means?" He jerked his arm away, and her hand fell. "I grieved that baby. For weeks I grieved that baby. And it wasn't even mine."

Chills crawled up her spine. "Yes, it was." How could he think this? It was so unfair. She flicked away the tear that escaped.

"Whose was it, Paula? Have there been others?"

"There hasn't been anybody! Would you listen to yourself?" Her eye started twitching. "Maybe the test was wrong. Have you considered that? Did you even think about that before you started accusing me of adultery?"

He nailed her with a glare and left the room.

"Is everything OK?" David's voice pulled her from the past.

Paula realized she'd probably let emotions show on her face that didn't jive with their romantic interlude. "Everything is wonderful. The duck is amazing."

He smiled and popped a small chunk of potato into his mouth. She wished she could read his eyes, but a glare from the candlelight flickered on his glasses.

When they finished the meal, David cleared his throat. "I know you're wondering what all this is about. It's more than just a New Year's Eve surprise. I guess you've figured that out. The truth is, Paula, there's something I need to tell you."

Paula placed her napkin on her plate while her nerves drew taut. The last time David had something to tell her, it had ushered in months of bickering and hard feelings. Suddenly she wasn't sure she wanted to hear what David had to say.

CHAPTER
FIFTEEN

Paula stuffed down the feeling of dread and focused on David. The flickering light of the fire cast a warm glow on his skin. He was about to say something important. She could tell that much by the way his elbows balanced on the edge of the table.

He took her hand. "We've been through a rough time these past months. The worst of our marriage."

He looked at her then, and she wondered what was going on behind those eyes.

He squeezed her hand. "We tried to get pregnant for so long, and that was stressful, especially on you, I think. Then I got the results of the testing, and I . . . well, I went ballistic. I guess I was stressed too. About not getting pregnant, about the business, and . . . things weren't going so great between us either."

Paula nodded. She wished she had a fast-forward button so she could find out what David was getting at. Her biggest worry had always been that David would find out about the abortion. Every time there was conflict between them, she worried he would somehow find out. But tonight he seemed at peace. As if he wanted to put the past behind them. Was it possible?

He stared down at their hands, intertwined in the middle of the table. "What I'm trying to say, Paula, is that I owe you a huge apology.

The day I got those test results, I wasn't thinking clearly." He laughed derisively. "That much is as clear as glass."

When his gaze met hers, she felt it all the way down to her red toenails.

"I was so wrong to accuse you. I said despicable things and drove a wedge between us that has—"

"Stop, David."

He was finally saying the words she longed to hear. All these months of believing she'd been unfaithful, and now she was being exonerated.

Her eyes stung with relief. Or was it guilt? While David was repenting of his wrong, she was harboring her own. She had driven her own secret wedge between them, and she could never come clean about that.

Never.

David cradled her face in his palm. "I don't want to stop. What I did to you was indefensible. I accused you on so little evidence. Where was my trust?"

"We were already having problems. It's not so hard to see how you jumped to wrong conclusions."

"You're my wife." His eyes held hers captive. "I should have trusted you."

His words drove a spike into her heart. *I should have trusted you.* Was there anyone less worthy of trust than she? Yes, she'd been faithful to David. But she'd aborted the only child they'd conceived, then lied about it.

She broke eye contact, gazing at the fire across the room, unable to bear the guilt on her husband's face while she covered up a mountain of guilt inside herself.

"I know you're flirtatious by nature," he said. "I took a part of your personality, a part I happen to love, and used that as evidence against you."

"I do need to tone it down sometimes." She remembered how caring David had been after the "miscarriage." He tried to cater to her and comfort her, but she pushed him away. The guilt of what she'd done nearly swallowed her alive, but she buried it deep inside and plunged back into work to forget.

"Stop making excuses for me, hon. I was wrong, and we both know it. I've been going to this Bible-study thing the past couple of weeks. We've been studying this story about a man who was rebuilding walls, and it's really interesting how it pertains to the walls we build today."

"You're going to a Bible study?"

They used to attend church faithfully, but over the years their faith had taken a backseat to their careers.

"I know. Hard to believe. But this is different. I'm learning a lot."

Apparently. If it was having this kind of effect on him, who was she to complain?

He took both her hands. "I'm so sorry for falsely accusing you. And I'm sorry it took this long to see it. I miss you. I miss us. I want to get back what we lost."

"I want that, too, David." Was it even possible? Didn't he realize things hadn't been good between them even before his accusations? Things hadn't been right between them since . . .

No. It wouldn't do any good to think like that. What was done was done. David wanted to move on, and so did she. She would make it happen the same way she'd made her career happen. With hard work and determination.

As he stood and gathered her in his arms, she sealed the deal in her heart. She wouldn't let anything come between her and David. Not now or in the future. And she certainly wouldn't let the past tear them apart.

<hr>

Linn slid a drink across the counter. "Cappuccino," she called before starting two more shots of espresso for the next drink. Another employee, Tara, had been working the register all evening, and with midnight approaching shortly, the New Year's Eve clientele was slowly beginning to diminish.

Business had been hopping all evening, and Linn was ready to get off her feet and go to bed. A glance at the wall clock showed she had another seven minutes before midnight. They were open until twelve thirty because of the holiday, but at least she had New Year's Day off. She'd have the whole day to wonder how she could come up with the $384 she needed to complete her rent payment by midnight. As if that were even possible.

She poured the espresso into the cup and started steaming the milk for the latte. The bells above the door jingled, signaling another customer. She didn't notice who it was until he stepped up to the register. Her heart did a funny flip that felt good and bad all at the same time.

"Hey, Linn," Adam said, his smile making her insides heat up faster than the milk she was steaming. With his neatly combed hair and long overcoat, he looked every inch like the preacher he would someday be.

A petite woman slid up and nestled against his side. He put an arm around her waist.

"Tara, Linn, this is Elizabeth, my fiancée. Lizzy wanted to come in and meet you."

Elizabeth reached across the counter and shook Linn's hand. "I've heard so much about you guys; I wanted to put faces with names." Her honey-colored hair was clipped up on the sides except for a few wavy tendrils that framed her delicate face.

Tara extended a hand with long nails that were about as fake as the smile on Linn's face.

Linn poured the steamed milk into the cup, stirred, and placed a lid on top. "Snickers Latte," she called.

The customer, a tall guy who sometimes flirted with her, winked at her as he took the drink, his gaze lingering. "Thanks."

When she darted a glance at Adam, he was watching the tall guy walk away.

Tara took their orders, then Adam and Elizabeth slid down the counter to where Linn had started brewing shots of espresso. Elizabeth removed her coat, revealing a sweater and skirt set, both flattering and conservative. The black sweater had a draping collar that showed off her elegant neck, and the skirt flared out at the knees in a way that was flirty, yet innocent.

"Been busy tonight?" Adam asked.

"Yeah, pretty much." Linn didn't dare look at him as she answered. Her stomach had curdled up into a sour ball at the sight of Adam's fiancée. She was cute and petite and looked every bit like the perfect wife for Adam. Linn focused on the espresso machine, trying to keep her expression neutral. Could Adam tell she was bothered? She'd never been good at hiding her feelings.

She was relieved when Elizabeth struck up a conversation with a customer who was seated at a nearby table.

"It's almost midnight," Adam said.

Why did he have to have such a rich, deep voice?

"I know." *Duh. Could I sound more stupid?*

Catching a whiff of his musky cologne, she bit the inside of her mouth until it hurt while she poured the shots of espresso into the grande cup.

As she started more shots, she noticed that Elizabeth had found a seat by the window.

"Are you OK?" he asked. "I'm sorry you had to work tonight."

Adam had requested the night off so he could go to some event at the seminary with Elizabeth. When she glanced up at him to answer his question, she knew immediately it was a mistake. His brown eyes were injected with a dose of guilt that reminded her of a puppy dog that has just been caught chewing a shoe.

"It doesn't matter. I didn't have plans anyway." She would not look at him again. She wouldn't.

But her eyes darted helplessly toward him and stuck. Flecks of snow still clung to his hair, and already he had a five-o'clock shadow. Her gaze traveled down to the cleft in his chin, and she thought once again that he was way too handsome to be a preacher. Every woman in his church would be fighting temptation because he was everything a woman wanted in a man.

Except he was taken. Why did she always want the guys who were taken?

Linn cleared her throat and turned to pump the vanilla flavoring into Elizabeth's cup. She was glad to turn her heated face away from Adam. If she could just get these drinks made, maybe he'd take his fiancée and leave. Surely they had someplace else they wanted to be when the clock struck midnight . . . even though a glance at the clock told her there were only minutes to go.

She poured the steamed milk into the cups, and Adam put the lids on. "So you're not mad at me?"

For being so perfect? For making me fall for you? For throwing your fiancée in my face? "Why would I be mad?"

Out of the corner of her eyes, she saw him shrug.

"For sticking you with New Year's Eve."

"It's just another night to me, Adam." Her voice was more clipped than she'd intended. She threw a smile his way to soften it, but the smile felt as brittle as thin ice.

He had both drinks, so why wouldn't he just leave? Turn around and go back to Elizabeth, who was undoubtedly waiting to greet him with her friendly smile and missionary demeanor.

"Sugar-free raspberry granita," Tara told Linn, handing her the clear plastic cup.

She'd have to go to the back to make this one. Relief flooded through her at the chance to escape Adam.

"You guys have a good evening," she said without looking directly at him before she turned to go.

"Wait." He took hold of her wrist, and her pulse jumped even while his fingers slid away.

He paused until she glanced up at him. One look into his brown eyes, and she nearly melted into a puddle of chocolate. Adam was everything she'd ever wanted in a man. Kind, considerate, compassionate, protective.

Except he was taken.

Why did she keep forgetting that?

Worse, he was taken by a sweet, innocent, selfless woman whose past was undoubtedly as pure as the snow falling outside the window.

As opposed to Linn, who'd had an affair with a married man, broken up the marriage, and nearly aborted the child conceived by that relationship. If Elizabeth was as clean as the freshly fallen snow, Linn was as dirty as the slush lining the street curbs.

"Ten . . . nine . . . eight . . ." The patrons began counting down the last seconds of the year, their voices picking up momentum.

With Adam's eyes still locked on hers, Linn felt as frozen as the winter ground.

That is, until Elizabeth tugged him to her side, turning his face toward her.

The patrons continued their countdown, "Three . . . two . . . one . . . Happy New Year!"

Elizabeth cupped Adam's face and gave him a chaste kiss on the lips.

Linn hurried to the back of the shop with the plastic cup in hand. In the background, party horns went off, echoing the chaos in her heart.

CHAPTER
SIXTEEN

Paula slid into her desk chair and set her bag on the floor beside her. The newsroom was empty this time of night, but she'd been so busy reporting, she hadn't had time to keep up with things at the office. She needed to sort through the stack of mail that was mixed in with all her notes, business cards, and receipts she'd thrown down as she passed her desk. She was beginning to see she'd never have the time if she didn't forego sleep.

In the almost three weeks since her "Switched at Birth" story had aired on *Good Morning America*, the Morgans had appeared on the *Today Show*, and numerous newspaper articles had appeared around the country. The story was hot, and if Paula didn't get organized, some other reporter was going to beat her to the punch.

She pulled the chain on the little desk lamp she'd brought from home to illuminate her workspace. The office was quiet—eerily so when she was used to the noise of the newsroom during the daytime.

Oddly, she found the quiet more distracting than the noise. After opening the program on her computer that had all her findings on the Morgan story, she began typing in notes. She had three weeks' worth of information taken from interviews she did herself and tidbits she collected from the articles other reporters had written.

If she could only be the one to solve the mystery, her career would take off like a bottle rocket on the Fourth of July. Miles intimated that she'd be a shoo-in for the anchor chair, and who knows what else would follow once the national media got wind that she'd solved the mystery?

After she input all the information into the program, she saved the data, then tossed her notes into the trash and began sorting through her mail. Most of it was fan mail from viewers and thank-you notes from people she'd interviewed.

Her hands stopped when she unfolded a sheet of notebook paper. The familiarity of the dark handwriting sent shivers down her spine.

I hope you liked my poem.
We need to mete soon.
Your very pretty.

If the handwriting caused shivers, the words inflicted dread. She dropped the note on her desk and glanced around the darkened newsroom. The note wasn't in an envelope as if it had been mailed. How long had it been on her desk? She'd seen it yesterday, she thought, but it could have been there for a week, amid all her piles.

She caught sight of Darrick's desk several yards away. Could he be playing a prank on her? Maybe he was trying to psyche her out to distract her from the anchor job.

Well, she wouldn't let it happen. She wadded up the note and tossed it into the trash can. Even though Darrick put on a good face around her, she knew he had to be seething inside about the success of her story on the Morgans. Miles had taken her out for lunch at least once a week since Christmas, and she knew Darrick had to be feeling the sting of that setback. Not to mention the weekend anchors, Jaron and Roxy.

Paula had become well known very quickly as the Morgans' story was splashed across newspapers from Maine to California. Deb had phoned the previous day and told her that *Good Housekeeping* wanted to run the story in their magazine. The Morgans had been inundated with reporters and interviews.

Still, even after all those reporters had undoubtedly snooped into every possible angle of the story, it remained a mystery. What had happened to the Morgans' birth child, and whose birth child was Faith? Maybe they'd never find answers, but Paula wasn't about to give up.

A creak sounded from somewhere, and Paula jumped. Her eyes darted down the hallway while her blood zinged through her veins. Was someone here? Even the janitor was gone this time of night. Maybe a door was sliding shut or the furnace had creaked when it came on. She wasn't familiar with the little sounds the building made since they were covered with the chaos of a newsroom during the day.

She was ready to go home anyway. She gathered up her purse and coat and left the room, taking the opposite hallway. It was a longer route, but after the creepy love note and the mysterious noise, she wasn't taking any chances.

The building emptied into the parking garage, and as she entered the deserted garage, her heart could have substituted for a bass drum in a rock band. Her hands shook as she slid her key into the car door. Somewhere down at street level, a truck roared by.

She yanked open the door and got inside, shutting and locking the door. She breathed a sigh of relief and started the car with a turn of the key.

Suddenly she remembered when her sister Natalie had been attacked in her own car. She turned to make sure the backseat was empty.

You're being ridiculous, Paula. For heaven's sake, get a grip.

If only Darrick could see her now, he'd probably laugh his head off. She gave a wry laugh herself as she drove out of the parking garage and drove the short distance to her apartment.

As her anxiety drained away, she turned her thoughts to David. She missed talking to him today, but there would probably be an e-mail from him when she got home. Their relationship had come so far since New Year's. He was a different man, and she felt like a different woman when she was with him. They still had the major obstacle of where to live between them, but they decided to table that discussion for the time being. Although David had to know the anchor job was within reach.

When she got home, there was a message on her voice mail from

Natalie, asking her to call in the morning and saying it was important.

After getting into her pajamas, she went online and retrieved a sweet e-mail from David, telling her he missed her and was taking this coming Saturday off so they could spend it together. She sent a quick e-mail back. On her way to bed, she stopped at the living-room window where her African violet sat. She'd watered it regularly, taking care to keep the water off the leaves, kept it at seventy degrees, but even so, the flowers had faded and the leaves were turning pale yellow. Substituting the plant food couldn't make that much difference, could it? She'd never been much for houseplants, but surely she could keep a little plant alive.

Too weary to do anything about it, she decided to turn in for the night.

<hr />

When the buzz of her alarm woke Paula the next morning, she felt like she was coming out of a coma. Could it possibly be time to get up already? As she sat on the edge of the bed, snippets of a dream came back to her. She'd been in a dark building with David, and a doctor was telling him about the abortion.

She'd been lying on a hospital bed and couldn't talk. She tried to stop the doctor, but her mouth wouldn't open. She watched while the doctor told David everything, and that's all she remembered. The alarm must've gone off then.

She shook off the dream with a lingering, warm shower, then dressed in her favorite Anne Klein pantsuit. Over breakfast she remembered she was supposed to call Natalie, but a glance at the clock told her it was too early back home to call. She made a mental note to call later.

The morning flew by in a rush of interviews, phone calls, and note taking, and she was on her way back to the newsroom when her cell phone rang.

"This is Paula."

"Oh, good, I'm glad I was able to reach you."

Natalie.

Paula grimaced. "I meant to call you back. Sorry."

"Don't worry about it. Listen, I have a favor to ask. Remember what I told you over Christmas about Linn's apartment situation?"

Paula braked at a light. She remembered Natalie's telling her about Linn's roommate moving out and that she might have to find another place to live.

Paula closed her eyes. *No. This isn't happening.*

"Well, she's being evicted. I'm sorry for the late notice, but Linn didn't tell me until last night. Her landlord has already given her extra time, but he's found a new tenant, so she has to be out by tomorrow."

Paula wanted to do what she always did: hand over a check to smooth over the situation. She was always willing to help people. But between the house in Jackson, the apartment rental in Chicago, and plane trips home on weekends, she and David weren't exactly rolling in disposable income right now. David was already distressed about the extra expenditures, and she didn't want to ruin the rapport between them now.

"Paula? Are you there?"

"I'm here."

A car honked behind her, and she saw that the light had turned green. She accelerated.

"I'm really sorry to ask you this, but I don't know how else to help her. With the down payment on the new house, Kyle and I are tapped out."

Nat sounded sorry. Sorry that she couldn't help and sorry that she had to ask Paula for a favor. Well, Paula was sorry too. She worked hard all day, and when she came home, she didn't want to baby-sit a college girl.

"I know what you're thinking, but Linn is really easy to have around. When she lived with me, she made my life so much easier. And it would only be until she found something else."

Maybe it wouldn't be so bad, Paula thought. It wasn't like she was home all that much anyway. And Linn had college and a job to keep her busy too.

"She's a sweet kid who just needs a break."

Paula knew Linn's past—knew about her lazy, alcoholic father. Her mom had died of some disease, and her sister had been killed in a car accident. Linn had gotten pregnant out of wedlock and gave up her baby to Natalie for adoption. The kid had experienced enough tragedy in her short lifetime for two people. How could Paula not help?

"All right, all right. She can stay with me for a while." The words were out before Paula could stop them. She hoped she wouldn't regret her decision.

"You won't be sorry, I promise."

Famous last words.

Paula sighed quietly. "Give me her number, and I'll call her."

"She doesn't have a phone, but you could call her at the coffee shop. No—wait—I'll just call her and tell her to call you. I haven't said a word to Linn about this yet, so I'll need to explain what's going on. It'll be a complete surprise to her, and she's going to be so grateful and helpful. You'll see."

Three hours later Paula was sitting at her desk when her cell phone rang again.

"Is this Paula?"

She knew immediately the young-sounding voice had to be Linn's. She greeted the girl while opening the program that held all her notes on the Morgan story.

"Natalie told me you'd be willing to let me stay with you for a little while. I really appreciate that." The relief in the girl's voice came through loud and clear.

"Sure. No problem. I guess we need to arrange for your things to be moved to my place." Paula scanned the files for the Morgan document but didn't see it.

"Well, not really. I don't have much, and I can bring all of it with me on the bus if you give me your address. I need to be out by tomorrow, so maybe I could meet you there after work?"

Paula hardly heard a word. She kept scanning the short list of files in her program. She only had a dozen or so. Where was it? Where was the file that contained all her notes?

"Paula?"

"What?" She snapped the word . . . and immediately regretted it. "Sorry, I'm a little distracted. Listen, can I call you back? I'm right in the middle of something."

"Oh, I'm sorry. You can call me at the coffee shop anytime the rest of the day."

After Paula hung up, she closed the program and reopened it, hoping for some miracle. While the program logo flashed on the screen, she tapped her nails on the keyboard.

Come on. Be there.

The program opened, and she scanned the list of documents once, twice, three times. She hadn't backed them up. She'd always been negligent about that. Frustrated, she shoved the keyboard back and smacked the edge of her desk with her palm.

"Everything OK?" Darrick was passing by with a folder in his hands. For a second she wondered if he had something to do with the missing file. But when she saw nothing in his expression but concern, she realized she was being paranoid. Her computer probably had some virus or some fluke that happened when she'd tried to save the document the night before.

"Everything's fine."

They made small talk for a few minutes. When he left the room, Paula sank back into her chair. All her organized notes and her developing story were in that file, not to mention the time line she'd meticulously worked out.

She sprung upright. What did she do with the hard copy she wrote the story from? Her thoughts flew back to the night before. She'd tossed them into her trash can. She rolled her chair back and pulled the can forward.

Empty. She let her head fall back against the chair. Five weeks of material gone. Sure, she had the original tapes and could get a copy of the transcript, but she'd have to start all over with writing the actual story. How could she have been so stupid not to save it to disk? David was always telling her she'd regret it one day.

And today was the day. Now she had a virus or something. But weren't all the computers in the office linked? If hers had a virus, didn't they all?

She scanned the room, and her eyes landed on the new information-technology guy. He would know. She strode over to his desk. "Do you have a minute, Stan?"

He looked up from his computer. "Sure."

She perched on the side of his desk. "I have a technical question about computers."

"Fire away." He ran a hand through his short, brown hair. The man might be new to the station, but it was already obvious he had more computer know-how than everyone in the office combined.

"I lost a document in the Word program. I saved it last night, but when I got in this morning, it was gone. Is there any way to retrieve it?"

"Did you back it up?"

She could feel a flush spreading across her skin. "No."

"Well, let's have a look."

He followed her back to her station and searched for the document a few different ways. Finally he shrugged. "Sorry, it's not there."

"How can that be? I saved it last night."

"Could've accidentally hit the wrong key, I suppose."

"Could it be a virus?"

"If yours had a virus, all the computers in the office would have it. I keep the network updated against viruses, so it's unlikely. I can do a scan and check for sure."

"Would you please? I'd really appreciate it."

A while later Stan approached her desk. "I finished the scan. The system is clean. Must've just been a fluke."

Paula's eyes fell on Darrick, who was talking to Miles on the other side of the room, then trailed down to the empty desks of Jaron and Roxy. Yes, it could be a fluke.

Or a dirty trick played by a jealous competitor.

CHAPTER
SEVENTEEN

Paula exited the plane and hurried through the hallway to the airport. David would be waiting for her, and she'd missed him more in the last two and a half weeks than she cared to admit, even to herself. Between her being swamped at work and the out-of-town conference David had attended the weekend before, getting together had been impossible.

When she passed security, she saw him leaning against the tourist booth. She felt her mouth stretch into a smile as their eyes met.

When she neared, he folded her in his arms. "Hey, baby."

Paula let her bag drop to the floor and enjoyed the feel of his strong arms around her. "I'm so glad to see you." She'd almost said she was glad to be home, but that wasn't true. When it came to the location, she'd rather be in Chicago any day. It was her husband's presence she missed—not this town.

He grabbed her carry-on, and she followed him out to the Escalade. Darkness obscured the distant mountains, but lamps lit their way as they crunched through patches of snow. The parking lot was chalked by the salt they'd used to clear the snow and ice, and Paula guessed there were four or five inches of snow on the ground. Even so, the cold air was still stagnant, not gusting and tugging every which way on her hair the way it did in Chicago.

Once they were settled in the vehicle, David picked her hand up off her lap and drew it to his lips. He planted a tender kiss. "I missed you."

"Two weeks is too long." Phone calls and e-mails just weren't the same as being together. Especially when their marriage felt as new as newlyweds.

Feeling playful and slightly giddy in his presence, she widened her eyes in naiveté. "Whatever are we going to do with two whole days?"

She loved the way his eyes fell to her lips. "I'm pretty sure I can come up with a couple of hundred ideas."

"Do tell." She couldn't smother the smile if she tried. It was so good to be with David. She'd missed their banter.

"I'd rather show."

Paula laughed. Being with David now was just like old times, and she hoped it would stay this way forever. As hard as the times had been lately, the events had brought them closer together. She supposed she should be thankful for that.

David caught her up on his real-estate transactions and the goings-on at JH Realty, and then he turned the discussion toward her. "Is Linn all settled in at the apartment?"

When she'd told David the day before that she was letting Linn move in, David had been a little wary. But Paula had explained Linn's situation, and he seemed OK with the idea.

"She brought her stuff over today on my lunch hour, and I gave her a key. Nothing like getting a guest settled in, then leaving town."

"Are you sure you trust her?"

Paula shrugged. "I'm sure Nat wouldn't set me up with a convicted felon."

"I know. I just worry about you."

She squeezed his hand. "I'm a big girl. Oh, I didn't have time to tell you yesterday about losing my file."

"What file?" David guided the car out of the parking lot and toward Jackson.

"All my notes on the Morgan story disappeared from my program. I saved it Wednesday night, but when I tried to open it yesterday, it was gone."

"Do you have a backup?" He nudged his glasses up.

"Unfortunately, no. But you can bet I'll be backing up in the future."

"So what was it you lost exactly?"

When she reflected about the valuable information she'd lost, weight like a rock settled in her stomach. "Everything I had on the Morgan story. All the notes from all the interviews. All my questions about inconsistencies. In short, everything I need to help find answers for the Morgans." She shook her head. "Stupid. I can't believe I was so stupid."

"Are you going to drop the story, then?"

She sighed. "I can't. The Morgans want desperately to know the truth. Plus, if I can solve this, wow—talk about a career boost. It wouldn't just guarantee me the anchor chair; it might open other doors in the future. All the other reporters at WMAQ know their chances at the anchor spot are very narrow now."

When David didn't respond, she could almost feel the tension stacking up between them like cement blocks. It was the mention of the anchor chair. Why did she bring it up? That promotion would get her permanently planted in Chicago, and where would that leave her and David?

"But," she said quickly, "now that I've lost all my notes, I'm way behind a bunch of other reporters who've covered the story. Who knows how many of them are looking into this? It'll be a miracle if I can solve it first now."

When David remained quiet, Paula thought she'd better move on to another topic before she ruined their weekend.

But David spoke first. "Is it possible someone deleted that file, Paula?" He glanced at her as they drove into Jackson.

She didn't want to worry him, but she didn't want to lie either.

You mean lie again.

She pushed the thought away. "It occurred to me. But you know how I am with computers, hon. I'm an accident waiting to happen."

"What about the reporter, Darrick?"

"For that matter, there's the two weekend anchors, Roxy and Jaron, who are up for the same anchor spot. But I'm sure it's nothing like that.

They wouldn't have known I didn't have a backup file at the apartment or something."

Ahead the lights on the Snow King's slope brought back memories of New Year's Eve. She and David had skied for three hours, and she'd enjoyed every minute of it. The next day she'd paid for it with sore calves and thighs.

"You know," David said, "that makes me worried for your safety. What if one of your competitors did delete that file, and they think you have a copy of it at your apartment?"

Though the thought of it gave her goose bumps, Paula smiled. "Yeah, and they arranged for Linn to work her way into my apartment to sabotage my story." She laughed. "David, this isn't *CSI*, for heaven's sake."

"Didn't you say you got a wacky note from some guy?"

"I said 'kid.' It had to be a kid. His spelling was atrocious." She remembered the second note she found only a few days before. It also had a spelling error, and it, too, could have come from a kid.

"You haven't received any more, have you?" David's brow was knit with concern.

She bit the inside of her lip. The last thing she wanted was David worrying about her in Chicago. He already had half a dozen reasons why she shouldn't be there. Still, she wanted to be honest with him. "I did get one this week."

"And you weren't going to say anything?" His voice crescendoed.

Paula felt the prickling heat of guilt. She had wanted to hide it. "I didn't want to worry you unnecessarily, hon. It's just a kid."

"What did it say?" He turned up the winding street that led to their home.

She thought back to the note that she could remember word for word. "Not much. He referred to his poem and said I was pretty." She gave a shaky laugh. "I'm telling you, it's nothing. Darrick says this kind of thing happens all the time."

"Maybe so, but it seems weird to me. I don't want anything to happen to you."

The seriousness of his tone wiped the smile from her face. "Nothing's going to happen, David. You'll see."

⊰⋯⊱

Linn hurried as fast as she could down the icy sidewalk. She and Adam worked until closing, which always made catching the bus a close call. But tonight Adam had been talking with Joe in his office, and that left Linn to cover the register. Now she was going to miss the last bus to the apartment if she didn't hurry. She rounded the corner to see the bus pulling away from the curb. Smoke curled out of the tailpipe and disappeared like a vapor.

"No!" She stopped in her tracks and stomped a foot. She did it again for good measure. "This is not happening." She threw her head back and sighed. In the glow of the streetlights, tiny flurries wafted toward the ground.

How was she going to get home now? A taxi? She had about forty dollars in her bag, but that was supposed to get her through the next week.

She stuffed her hands into her pockets and hunched her shoulders against the cold. *Think, Linn. Think.*

She could call Paula, but she didn't want to. The woman had practically taken her in off the streets, and Linn was determined not to be a nuisance.

She couldn't go back to the shop and ask Adam. Just working with him was hard enough, without being alone in a dark car for twenty minutes. Her skin went warm all over at the thought of him, and she huffed, impatient with herself. She had to stop thinking about him all the time. This silly infatuation was getting her nowhere. Hiding her feelings from him was wearing her out. She'd been irritable with him the past few weeks, and she knew it was unfair. But she'd taken Natalie's husband away from her, and that had been so wrong. She wasn't going to stoop again to taking another woman's man.

Maybe she should look for another job. But where would she find the time for that? Her classes, job, and studying were taking up every minute of the day.

"Miss it?"

She spun at the voice. Her hands darted out of her pockets and clutched her purse.

At the sight of Adam, her body went limp and a thousand tingles shot down her arms as the adrenaline surge faded away. "You scared me." It was an accusation, and her words were sharper than she'd intended.

"Sorry," he said. His lips moved into a wry grin. "I didn't mean to sneak up on you."

How could she be angry at him when he looked so sincere? "That's OK."

His nose was already pink from the cold. "Did you miss the bus?"

She nodded. "I was just headed back to the shop to call someone." Yeah, like she had a whole slew of friends waiting in line to help her out. To confirm her story, she started walking toward the coffee shop. She'd have to call a taxi. If it cost too much, she'd have to call Paula after all.

"I can give you a lift." Adam shoved his hands into the pockets of his leather jacket.

Like she needed time alone with Adam. "That's OK." She quickened her steps.

"Really, it's no problem. Practically right on my way."

"I said no, Adam." She cringed at the harsh tone. Her heart was racing faster than her mind, and her mind was in a dizzying tailspin. It was driving her crazy working with him every evening. Having him reach around her and brush against her in the cramped workspace behind the counter. It was wreaking havoc with her peace of mind.

And he didn't even know it. But she could hardly tell him, either.

"Did I do something wrong?"

His words nearly broke her heart in two. She'd been snippy and crabby with him lately, and you'd think he'd have written her off.

Wouldn't most guys? Wouldn't they make some flip comment about the time of month and tell her to take a flying leap?

But not Adam. No, Adam had only given her space when she'd bristled and curious looks when she'd snapped at him.

"'Cause if I've done something wrong, I want to know," he was saying.

"You haven't done anything, Adam." Her feet couldn't move fast enough. If they could get back to the shop, he'd leave and she'd be safe from the feelings that were bubbling up in her.

He stopped her with a hand on her arm. She looked into his eyes. She couldn't help it.

"Then let me take you home," he said. "It's my fault you missed the bus. If I'd been out front where I should've been, you wouldn't have been late."

His eyes were squinted against the cold wind, and a few flurries had landed on his eyelashes. He was so good, inside and out. He didn't deserve her moody attitude. She could accept a simple car ride, couldn't she? For twenty minutes she could keep her mind occupied with something else and forget he was sitting eighteen inches away.

"All right." Anticipation stirred inside her in a way that both excited and frightened her. What was she doing? Why was her heart so rebellious, always falling for someone she couldn't have? She should have learned by now that this road only led to pain and heartache.

When they reached Adam's car, he opened the door for her and she slipped inside.

You can do this, Linn. Just make small talk all the way, and everything will be fine.

Then why did her mouth suddenly feel like it was stuffed with cotton?

Help me, God.

As Adam settled behind the wheel, the car filled with the musky scent of his cologne mixed with the faint smell of leather. It was like breathing in Adam. She wished she could plug her nose, or better yet, hang her head outside the window for the full ride. She imagined her brows and eyelashes turning white with frost, her face frozen in a smiling mask.

No, Adam, I'm fine. Just needed some fresh air.

She had to get a grip. Act nonchalant. This was no big deal.

Adam turned out of the parking lot and headed toward the apartment. She'd told him the week before that she was moving in with Paula, and he'd known exactly where the building was located.

There wasn't much traffic this time of night so they made record time. Why was a part of her disappointed at the thought? She closed her eyes and gritted her teeth.

Adam started talking about a story that was on the local news the day before, and Linn told him Paula was a news reporter. They talked about her living situation, and Linn described the apartment. Afterward Adam told her funny stories about the roommate he'd had in undergrad school. He had her laughing until her jaws were aching.

Just when she thought she'd get a side stitch, he changed the subject. "Remember the last time I took you home?"

She remembered. She'd been scared to death, walking down the sidewalk so late at night. Then those boys drove by, calling out to her. She decided to take her chances on Adam.

"I almost didn't stop because I figured you'd be afraid to hitch a ride with a stranger."

She smiled at him. "You looked trustworthy enough. Besides, if I hadn't taken the ride, I wouldn't have gotten the job at Java Joe."

"Still, you shouldn't hitch rides from strangers."

"Yes, Dad."

His hands twisted on the steering wheel, and he appeared to focus on the pavement in front of them. "I'm hardly old enough to be your dad."

Though his words were spoken lightly, she thought she detected a bit of sensitivity. "I was kidding. You can't be more than twenty-four."

"Twenty-six, actually."

She almost made a joke about old age but refrained since he seemed sensitive about it.

"What are you, all of eighteen?"

Was it her imagination, or did his words seem weighted? "Nineteen." She wondered why he cared. His tone made it seem like more than casual conversation. She suddenly wished she were five years older and a lifetime purer.

"Nineteen. Man, that seems forever ago. You're just starting out. Old enough to make choices and young enough to have no regrets."

Maybe he'd had no regrets when he was nineteen, but she had enough of them to fill Wrigley Field. And she still felt chained by them sometimes. No, not chained. More like they'd tinted her a different color. If they'd tinted her charcoal gray, Adam was tinted off-white. So was Elizabeth, no doubt.

She studied the tall buildings as they drove through town. She wondered if she'd ever be able to afford living in this section of town. Maybe someday—when she was a psychologist and had a great job in a nice office. She could see herself living in a studio apartment in the city.

"So you're glad you hitched a ride with me that day, huh?" He smiled at her, but she averted her eyes before his gaze caught her and trapped her.

"I thought you were a preacher or something."

He laughed. "Am I already giving off preacher signals? Was it something I said?"

"No, it was your notes. You took out your notebook to write down my number, and I saw some words that clued me in."

"And that didn't scare you off?"

She shrugged. "Maybe a little. I was desperate for a job, though."

"Aw, thanks."

She began to relax. Maybe she could survive this trip after all. "Well, you have to admit preachers can be a little intimidating."

"We're just regular people."

"I know that, but somehow a man of God is set apart from everyone else. At least in my mind."

When he paused, she wondered if she'd said something wrong. He was the first pastor she knew personally. Even if he wasn't quite a pastor yet.

Adam's face clouded. "I wish it wasn't like that. I can't live up to impossibly high standards any more than anyone else. I'm human; I'm going to fail. God is the only One who's perfect."

"I know that. I think everyone knows that, but still there's that high expectation."

He frowned. "It's a lot of pressure. More is expected of me than I feel like I can deliver sometimes."

"Adam, you're worrying for nothing. I've been totally impressed with you, and I've spent an awful lot of time with you the past five weeks. I've seen you stay cool when you've been provoked and think of others when it inconveniences you. You're going to make a great pastor."

When he didn't respond, she studied his profile. He stared out the front windshield, his mouth drawn into a straight line, his brows drawn together. He seemed unsure of himself, and that surprised her. Adam always seemed like he had it together. He was always protecting and picking up everyone's spirit.

"Are you worried you won't make a good pastor?"

Even as she asked the question, she was aware that this was their first serious conversation. They'd never talked about anything deeper than smoothies and lattes.

"Some," he said slowly. "Mostly I'm just confused about life in general."

Linn had never seen this serious, thoughtful side of Adam. He seemed almost vulnerable.

"What do you mean?" she asked.

He was drawing her in, and she wanted to get inside his head and know what he was thinking. What made worry lines spread across his face? What made him roar with laughter?

"How do we know what we're supposed to do? I mean, I know we're supposed to follow God's will for our lives, that's a given. But how do we know what that is?" Adam shook his head. "Sometimes I feel so sure I'm doing what God wants. Then something happens, and I think I've made the wrong decision."

It surprised her that Adam had these insecurities. He seemed like a steel tower all the time.

"I go through that confusion sometimes too," she admitted. "I thought it was because I'm kind of new at this Christian stuff."

He gave a wry laugh. "I don't know. I've been in church all my life and a Christian since the age of seven, but sometimes I feel like I don't know anything."

She wished he'd be more specific. He wanted answers but wasn't giving her anything to go on.

"You're not giving yourself enough credit," Linn said. "You probably knew more about the Bible at ten than I know now."

He parked the car by the curb, and Linn was surprised to see they were already at the apartment. Surprised and dismayed.

"I'm not talking about Scripture necessarily," Adam said. "I'm talking about knowing what God wants us to do. Sometimes there are two—or maybe even more—options. None of them are wrong or evil, just different. How do we know which one God wants for us?"

Linn rested her head against the back of the car seat. She couldn't believe a seminary student imagined for even a second that she might have answers. "I don't know, Adam."

He put the car in park and shifted toward her. "I mean, we can pray and look at circumstances and read the Bible and think it's all pointing one direction, then *boom*. Everything changes and we start thinking we made the wrong choice."

Linn turned to look at him. His coat collar was flipped up on one side and down on the other, and even in the shadowed car she could see the lines of distress between his brows.

She shrugged. "Maybe it's a matter of following your heart."

When his eyes swung toward hers, Linn's insides became as hot as a wood stove. His gaze lingered so long that the moment became intense and awkward. Why wasn't he saying anything? What did it mean? She searched for something to say to break the tension, but all coherent thought ground to a stop.

Finally he looked away. "Feelings can be misleading sometimes."

She started breathing again, only now aware she'd been holding her breath. Why did he stare at her for so long? People didn't do that unless it meant something. Or was he only gathering his thoughts and hadn't realized he was staring at all?

"*Feelings can be misleading sometimes*," he'd said.

Boy, was that ever true. She'd just made one little glance out to be something significant when he probably was unaware it had even happened. What an idiot she was.

She cleared her throat. "You're right. Feelings can be totally misleading." She remembered all too well feeling like it was so right for her and Keith to be together. Even though she knew he was married. He convinced her that his wife was horrible and his marriage was a farce. And she believed him. Believed those feelings he stirred up in her were right.

"Then what are we supposed to go on if not feelings?" Adam asked.

She was so new at Christianity. She wanted to give him answers, but what could she know that he didn't? Even as she asked the question, she remembered a story from her past that might apply.

"When I was little, maybe five or six, I wanted a dog really bad. But we had this tiny house and yard, and my mom kept telling me we couldn't have one. I'm sure I drove her nuts about it. One day she started talking about the pet gerbil she'd had as a child. She made it sound so neat, and before I knew it, I'd forgotten all about wanting a dog. I wanted a gerbil more than anything. When my birthday came, my mom and dad surprised me with one."

Linn stopped and looked out the window. "Only later did she tell me what she'd done." It had been when her mom was dying. They'd had great talks during those difficult months.

"She knew we couldn't have a dog," Linn said. "So she bought the gerbil the week before my birthday and kept it down in the basement. Then she proceeded to convince me that what I really wanted was a gerbil."

She caught Adam's expression. He was studying her, as if trying to read her thoughts.

"Maybe God's like that," she said. "He already has something special in our basement, and He's just waiting for us to want it."

"But how do we know what that is?"

She wanted to sink into the depths of his eyes. "Maybe we need to ask Him to help us crave whatever it is He already has for us."

Adam focused beyond the front windshield for a long moment. The car, still running, kept the inside nice and toasty, while the windows fogged up with their breath.

"If you've always felt the need to be a pastor," Linn said softly, "maybe God put that need there."

Adam closed his eyes. One of his gloved hands gripped the steering wheel, and his jaw worked. She wished she could read his mind.

"The thing is"—he smacked the steering wheel with his palm—"it's not my calling that I'm questioning."

At first the words were just words. But then she felt something. It was almost as if the air in the car became weighted with meaning. He wouldn't look at her, and she suddenly thought she might know why.

Yet it couldn't be. He wasn't questioning his feelings for Elizabeth, was he? It was only her own pathetic hopes that made her think so.

But when he finally raised his eyes to her, she knew she'd been right. And not only about Elizabeth. The way Adam was looking at her wasn't the way one friend regards another. It was the way a man looks at a woman he longs for.

She couldn't have moved, couldn't have looked away if she'd tried. There was enough heat in the car to fly a hot-air balloon, and it had nothing to do with the heat blowing through the vents.

His lips parted, as if he was about to say something. Then they clamped shut.

She wanted to drag the words from his mouth. But the ones that came next weren't the ones she longed to hear.

"It's getting late. You should probably be going in." He smiled gently to soften the blow.

She wanted to beg him to explain himself. She wanted to ask if she'd totally misunderstood. She wanted to reach over and smooth the creases between his brows with her fingers.

Instead she said good-bye and watched him drive away.

CHAPTER
EIGHTEEN

Paula finished the first-draft copy on a story about a local massage parlor that was found to have a hidden camera in one of their rooms. She'd gotten great bites from a regular client who was outraged at having been secretly taped. The story would air on the evening news. It was a story Darrick probably would have gotten if he hadn't been away on another assignment when the story broke. It gave her another chance to prove herself, and she was grateful for that.

She took the time to review the interview tapes for the "Switched at Birth" story and painstakingly tried to duplicate the lost file, but even so, she was reaching a dead end. The story had died down. Some of the other reporters who covered it suggested that the nurse who died was probably the one who held the key to the mystery.

Paula wondered if it was time for her to drop the story. It was taking a lot of thought and energy. Lately she'd sensed that Miles was ready for her to move on. The Morgans' story was taking time that could be spent on fresh news. So unless she came up with new information, she'd need to drop it. Even she was starting to feel like she was beating a dead horse.

Paula focused on her pad of paper and scratched out a verb, substituting it with a stronger one. She needed to forget the Morgans' story and focus on more productive work. She'd accomplished more in the short time she'd been at the station than she'd ever expected to. None of the other reporters at WMAQ had ever broken a story that went national. She should be content with that.

She read the last paragraph of the copy and marked a line through it. She could come up with a better wrap than that.

The phone at her desk rang, and she answered it absently.

"Paula, it's Deb. Deb Morgan."

Paula stiffened, feeling a twinge of guilt about the thoughts she just had.

"I was wondering if you'd come across any helpful information recently. Things have died down so quickly here," Deb said. "It's like someone turned on a faucet and deluged us, then turned it off just as suddenly."

"That's the way the news is, unfortunately," Paula told Deb. "In the media, stories like yours are a flash in the pan."

As Paula crossed her legs, she felt the silkiness of her hose glide across her skin.

"But this is our lives," Deb said. "I knew the media only cared about the story because it was something to fill airtime, something people would be interested in. But it's not finished. We raised a question to the public, but no one has answered it."

"I know. I know." Paula could only imagine Deb's frustration. All the hassles of going public, all the stress of coming out with the truth, and all seemingly for nothing.

"You're staying on the story, aren't you, Paula?"

Paula closed her eyes at the innocence in Deb's voice. The grieving mother thought way too much of this reporter.

"Deb, I know you're feeling desperate to know the truth, but maybe it's not meant to be. Maybe"—Paula searched for terms Deb might appreciate—"maybe God doesn't want it to go any further. Maybe He just wanted you to be willing."

"No." The adamancy in Deb's voice was something Paula hadn't heard before. "It doesn't end there. I know . . . Steve and I both know . . . we want the truth. We will scratch and snoop and beg and plead if we have to, but we will not stop until we know the truth."

Paula didn't know what to say. She admired Deb and Steve's fortitude. Was, in fact, surprised by it.

"I know you have a job to do, and you can't just drop everything," Deb explained. "But we believe you're the one who can find the truth, if anyone can."

Paula wanted to find the truth, too, but it seemed she'd already done everything she could. "Have you thought of hiring a private investigator?"

"Sure we have. We even called a few, but they're way out of our budget. We're scraping by as it is."

Paula tugged in frustration at her straight locks. Miles was going to get irritated if she kept following this story, and she couldn't afford that. Yet the Morgans wanted answers, and somehow Paula felt responsible to them.

"Please, Paula," Deb said. "I know it's asking a lot, and we'll help any way we can, but we just don't have the skills or the contacts you do."

Maybe she could work on the story only in her free time. She could even let Miles know that. Surely he'd be OK with that. He may even be impressed by her diligence and devotion. And if she found the answer to the mystery, it would be a win for the Morgans and for her.

"All right, Deb, I'll stay on it awhile longer."

"Oh, thank you, Paula." Deb's words rushed out in a gush of appreciation. "We're so grateful to you. Please let us know if you need anything."

When she got off the phone, Paula picked up her tablet of paper, but her eyes wouldn't focus on the words. She hoped she hadn't just bought more than she'd bargained for. Maybe the other reporters were right. Maybe the nurse who died held all the answers.

But there was still one nurse no one had been granted an interview with: Louise Garner, the woman who was too ill to see anyone. At least according to her son.

Before she could second-guess herself, Paula rummaged through her purse for the scrap of paper with Louise's phone number. She'd almost given up when she found it in the bottom of her purse. She picked up the phone and dialed, promising herself she wouldn't spend any more WMAQ time working on this story.

The phone was picked up on the third ring by a young woman.

"May I speak with Louise please?"

"Who's calling?" The young woman sounded wary. And no wonder—they'd probably had a hundred phone calls from reporters.

She was tempted to lie. "This is Paula."

"Paula who?"

The young woman wasn't letting her off easily. "Paula Landin-Cohen from WMAQ. I know Louise is ill, but I'd really like to speak with her for just a couple of minutes. Please."

"Look, Mrs. Garner is sick. I'm under strict instructions to prohibit calls and visits."

The phone clicked in Paula's ear. She set the phone back in the cradle and sighed. Maybe she should just leave the poor old woman alone. When she got home, she'd call her hospital contacts and some of the families who were in the hospital the same time as the Morgans. There were a couple of families who decided to have their children tested to see if they were the birth parents. Others had opted not to. Maybe she would find an answer that way.

◦──◦⟡◦──◦

Two days later Paula was on the couch, her head bent over her notes while Linn studied from a thick textbook at the small dining table. On the TV, David Letterman appeared to be giving his opening monologue, but the sound was muted so they could concentrate.

Having Linn at the apartment wasn't a problem. She was gone most of the time and quiet even when she was home. Plus, she picked up the studio apartment, leaving it tidy for when Paula returned home in the evenings.

Paula read through her second set of notes one more time. She'd talked to her contacts at the hospital, talked to everyone she could think of, and now she was officially at a dead end.

"Everything all right?"

Linn had turned in her chair, and Paula realized she'd just let out a frustrated sigh. "It's a story I'm working on. I can't seem to get anywhere on it."

Linn hugged her knees to her chest. "What's it about?" she asked.

Maybe it would help to talk it out. Paula couldn't talk to anyone at work about it. "It's a story about this family who found out the child they were raising wasn't their birth child. They didn't find out until recently, and the little girl is now three."

Linn's eyes widened a fraction. "I heard about that. Everyone at the coffee shop was talking about it last month."

"Really?"

It was always good to hear about viewer interest. The good stories were the ones employees chatted about over the water cooler at work.

"Adam said it was on *Good Morning America* too."

"Adam?"

Linn's head ducked down, as if she were studying the hands wrapped around her knees. "A guy I work with at the shop." She tucked her hair behind her ear, then rubbed the back of her neck.

Paula smiled. "Is this guy a boyfriend?"

Linn stilled for a split second, then her hands found their way back to her knees. "He's engaged." There was a world of disappointment in the young woman's words.

Paula wondered if it was a case of unrequited love. She felt sorry for Linn if that was the case. It would be hard to work with someone you had feelings for if he loved someone else. Hard enough for a grown woman, to say nothing of a girl barely out of high school.

"So are you stuck?" Linn was apparently eager to change the subject.

"You can say that again. I've interviewed everyone I can think of and gone over my notes until I have them memorized. I can't figure out what happened."

"You'd think the hospital would know something. Maybe they do, and they're just hiding it."

"Believe me, I've been working that angle." Paula had even tried to pull the affair trump card with Mr. Boccardi, but he wasn't budging. Maybe he didn't have anything to hide, or maybe he'd rather risk his personal reputation over his professional one. If the hospital was to blame, they could be in for a monstrous lawsuit from two families. No hospital wanted to be in the middle of all that controversy.

"Have you talked to all the nurses and doctors on duty?"

"All but two. One of them died, and one of them is too ill for an interview."

Linn wrinkled her nose, and for an instant, Paula could see a reflection of Natalie's baby, Grace. Sometimes it was hard to believe this young woman was the birth mother of her sister's baby.

"That stinks," Linn said.

"Tell me about it."

"What about the other babies who were in the hospital at the same time?"

"The Morgans' child was very premature, so that limits it to the premature babies who were in the NICU at the time. There were three children who were tested. All the preliminary tests were positive, meaning the parents were the birth parents of their children.

She'd been happy for those parents when she'd heard the relief and joy in their voices.

Yet the Morgans' questions went unanswered.

"What about the ones who weren't tested?" Linn asked.

Paula shrugged. "It's the parents' decision whether or not to have the child tested. I suppose the Morgans could take them all to court and try to make them, but I don't think Deb and Steve want to do that."

Linn's eyes seemed fixed on the framed Dali print on the wall. "Yeah.

I guess it would be hard to decide whether or not you wanted to know the truth."

Paula wished the other families would have their children tested. It would be a simple way of finding out the truth, but not so simple if one of the families had the Morgans' birth child. Then the mystery would be solved, but it would turn into a complicated web of rights. Would the Morgans keep Faith? Would they want visitation rights with the other child? And would the other family want custody of Faith or visitation rights with her?

Either way, the Morgans wanted answers, and Paula had promised to do her best to find them. Right now, though, her brain was mush from twisting around all the details.

"What are you studying?" she asked Linn, wanting to think about something else for a change.

"Communications 101. It's just an elective, but it's pretty interesting."

"Do you like Loyola? And living in Chicago in general? It's so different from Jackson Hole."

Linn grinned. "You aren't kidding. It's like major culture shock, but in a good way. Know what I like best? I like how I can go anywhere and never run into anyone I know."

Paula had begun to think she was the only one who felt that way. Her family thought she was crazy for wanting to escape what they called "a quaint little town." Paula exhaled. "It's nice to get away from the gossip too."

"No kidding. That 'everybody knows your name' stuff isn't all it's cracked up to be when they also know your business."

There were few secrets in the town of Jackson Hole, that much was true.

A yawn spilled out of Paula, and she decided to turn in for the night. She fell asleep with details of the Morgans' story floating around in disharmony. Maybe her subconscious would solve it in her sleep.

It was still dark when Paula was startled awake by a sharp, shattering sound. Glass breaking.

In an instant she was sitting upright, although she didn't remember doing so. The noise had come from the living room. Had Linn broken something? The clock read six fifteen. Linn would have left by now for her early class.

Paula crept out of bed, feeling her way through her bedroom, somehow afraid to turn on her light. When her hands grasped the softness of her robe hanging on a hook, she slipped it on.

As she opened the door of her bedroom, the light of a streetlamp filtered through the windows on the front side of the building. She stepped into the hallway and cold air smacked her bare legs. She shivered. Why was it so cold?

Her eyes went to the windows, and the sight made her feet go still. There was a gaping hole in the middle of one of the panes. The streetlight caught the jagged edges of the hole and glittered menacingly back at her. The African violet that had sat on the window sill now lay on the floor, spilled from the container, the dirt scattered around it.

Paula fumbled with the desk lamp and finally found the pull chain. Light flooded the room. Even while she blinked against its brightness, she scanned the room for what had come through the window. Surely not a bullet. The hole was too big, and she would've heard a gun go off. This was a nice neighborhood—not a slum where this kind of thing might be a regular occurrence.

Her eyes stopped on something in the shadowed corner by the entry closet. She walked toward the object, flipping on the overhead track lighting as she went. Her foot caught a piece of glass, and she bit her tongue.

After pulling the shard from the ball of her foot, she picked up the object. It looked like a ball of paper, but it was heavy, with a rubber band wadded around it.

A shiver crept over her flesh, and it had nothing to do with the cold air seeping through the gap in the window.

CHAPTER
NINETEEN

Paula removed the thick bands, and a rock the size of her fist fell with a *thwack* on the wood floor. She smoothed out the piece of notebook paper.

Drop the story.

Three words, typed in Courier New 12 point. She dropped the paper, not wanting to touch the thing. She looked at the window and followed the course the rock would have taken across the living room. It had knocked the plant off the sill, and her *Bon Appétit* magazine had slid off the table, so the rock had probably landed there before sliding across the floor.

She rose from her spot on the floor and pulled her robe tight. She should call 911. It took a few minutes to find the cordless phone, but once she did, she placed the call and was told to wait for the police.

Drop the story.

The words were beginning to sink in. They had to refer to the Morgan story. There was nothing else she'd worked on that would stir up such feeling.

Someone was threatened by the Morgan story. And that meant someone knew something.

Unless it was someone from the hospital trying to scare her off. Or someone from work trying to scare her off.

Her thoughts went back to the weird notes she'd received at work.

Was it some deranged fan? But why would he want her off the story? The police would want details. They'd want to know who could be responsible, but it could be any of a dozen different people. Was she safe here in her apartment?

Two hours later it was that very question that drew David's concern.

"I'm coming out there."

She'd heard this tone before and knew he'd be on her doorstep ASAP, the cost of the plane ticket notwithstanding. Even so, she argued. "David, I'm surrounded by neighbors, and there are three locks on the front door. I'm fine."

"I'm coming, Paula."

She wasn't due to go home over the weekend, so it would be a treat to see him. Besides, maybe it wouldn't hurt for him to get a taste of the Windy City. He might find that he liked it, and that would solve all kinds of problems.

"What did the police say?" She could hear him drumming his blunt fingers on the Corian countertop.

"Oh, you know. The usual 'We'll look into it.'" They hadn't been overly concerned—or very reassuring for that matter.

"You need to get the landlord to replace the window. What are you going to do in the meantime?"

"One of the cops got a piece of plywood and put it up for me."

"Macho cop meets damsel in distress?"

That's exactly what it was, or so the young policeman had seemed to think. "I already called Mr. Finley about the window, and he's going to get a replacement as soon as possible."

"Are you sure you can't pinpoint this incident to one or two people? Surely the stakes are highest for certain people on this story."

Paula pulled on her blazer, then slid her feet into a pair of navy heels. "Like I told the cops, David, it could be any number of people. The 'Switched at Birth' story involves a lot of people: parents, the hospital, the doctors and nurses. It could be anyone who feels threatened by it."

The tapping stopped, and she could almost see David rubbing the bridge of his nose where his glasses rested. "Maybe you should drop the story."

"I'm not giving in to a little threat." She couldn't believe he even suggested it.

He sighed into the mouthpiece. "That's what I thought you'd say."

She smiled at his quick capitulation. "I guess I can't blame the man for trying."

"Especially when he's the husband. And the one who's very much in love with his wife."

"When you put it like that, you're absolved of all blame whatsoever."

"I thought you'd see it my way."

He told her he'd arrange for a flight that evening. She tried half-heartedly to talk him out of coming, but he didn't budge. It wasn't as if he could do anything, and he couldn't stay in Chicago forever. But he seemed to feel a need to be there to protect her, so who was she to argue?

David tightened his scarf around his neck. He'd arrived at O'Hare an hour ago, and now he and Paula walked along Lake Shore Drive. Out on Lake Michigan, lights from a handful of boats twinkled like stars in the night sky. To the west the lights from the downtown buildings cast a glow in the sky that circled the city like a giant halo. Even in the cold darkness the city had a certain power.

"This is like a different world," David said.

"It's even better during the week. Of course, the traffic is something to get used to, but the energy . . . Man, I love the energy here."

"I'll bet it makes tourist season in Jackson seem lame." He'd been to big cities before, mostly for conventions and seminars. But he rarely left the huge hotels and convention centers long enough to get a taste of a city's culture. He evaluated the high rises along Lake Michigan and wondered what the condos sold for. A real-estate agent could make a killing here.

She took his cold hand and tucked it into the pocket of her coat.

"Everything here is driven. Everyone striding around with purpose." He watched her shake her head. "There's just something about it."

Her auburn hair shone under the streetlights. The wind picked up the straight strands and tossed them all around. The cold air had tipped her nose a delicate shade of pink, and he thought she looked more beautiful than ever. He wanted to stare at her for the next five days.

"What?" She was giving him that coquettish grin he loved.

"I'd forgotten how beautiful you are."

Her grin widened. "I'd forgotten how romantic you are."

"That settles it. We're just downright wonderful."

She laughed and nudged his shoulder. "I was telling Linn about you yesterday."

"What'd you say?"

"Fishing for compliments?"

"Am I using the right bait?" He loved playing with her. He'd missed it. They had lost months to make up for, and he didn't mind working a little overtime.

"Anyway, Linn has this project for her communications class. She's interviewing people about communication in marriage and asked if we'd participate. I told her yes. I hope you don't mind."

"Will I get to sit beside you?"

"The whole time."

"Deal." He reached over and pecked her on the lips.

The look she gave him made him want much more than a quick kiss. Suddenly he didn't want to be on Lake Shore Drive, surrounded by dozens of people. He wanted to be alone in her apartment. "What time did you say Linn would be getting home?"

She tugged him back the way they'd come. "Come on . . . we only have two hours."

***

The five days together passed in a blur, and as David shoved the last of his clothes into his suitcase, he found himself reluctant to leave

Paula. They'd eaten at fancy restaurants, taken a carriage ride through downtown, and cuddled on the couch. They had even visited a church together on Sunday. A lady there recognized Paula from the news.

The landlord replaced the broken window. David took a taxi to Kmart one day while Paula was at work and bought a bag of potting soil for the plant that had been overturned and a security latch for her door. He'd installed it before she returned home. Later that night Paula repotted her plant and set it back on the window sill. With the window fixed and the plant back in place, everything probably looked just as it had before the incident. But David couldn't help but wonder if there was more to come.

Now, as her arms wrapped around him from behind, he wished he could stay another five days.

"Don't go."

Though the tone was teasing, he knew she meant the words. It was unlike Paula to express her need of anything. Her self-sufficiency was one of the first things he'd been attracted to, but a man liked to be needed every now and then.

He turned in her arms. "I wish I didn't have to." But he had a business to run, and it wouldn't run itself. He'd already taken off more days for this trip than he'd ever taken off at JH Realty. There was no telling what kind of a mess he'd return to.

She sighed and snuggled against his chest. Her perfume teased his senses, conjuring thoughts that couldn't materialize in the time they had left.

"I wish I could drive you to the airport." Her fingers caressed his back, then trailed upward to play in his hair.

"It's OK." He should have timed his departing flight so it didn't coincide with her work. If he'd known how reluctant he'd be to leave her, he would have given it more thought.

"You'll remember to use all the locks at night?"

"David." She rolled her eyes.

Even though there'd been no additional threats, he worried about her. She tended to think she was invincible, and that could lead to carelessness.

"Linn's here too," Paula said.

"You're going to have some teenybopper protecting you? That'll be the day."

"Just trying to reassure you. I'll be fine, you know. I'm on the third floor, so what are they going to do? Kidnap me and haul me down three flights of stairs?"

His muscles tensed at the notion. "Don't even joke about that."

The thought of losing Paula now tore him in two. He didn't know he could love someone this much, and he wasn't sure he liked it.

"I'll be fine. Except for missing you like crazy."

"The feeling is mutual, baby." He pulled her to him and kissed her, letting his lips linger over hers for a fraction longer than he should have, given the direction of his thoughts.

When he ended the kiss, Paula turned her green eyes on him in a way that captured him.

"Did you mean what you said during Linn's interview on the tape?" she asked.

"Absolutely. You are definitely a messy."

She gave a mock glare and whacked him on the arm. "Not that part. You know, the part about love being a choice. And how you would choose to love me every day, regardless of what happens."

There it was in her eyes again. The vulnerability that was so unlike Paula. Maybe she'd never trusted him enough before to make herself vulnerable to him. That she did now made something stir inside of him.

He brought his hand to her face and let his fingers glide over her smooth skin. "I meant every word."

An emotion flickered in her eyes—relief perhaps?—then her lips curved and her cheek rested against the palm of his hand. "Oh, David, I love you so much it scares me."

Even though he'd had the same thought, he reassured her. "There's nothing to fear. This is good. Right." He punctuated each sentence with a kiss.

"I know. I'm being silly." She backed away and straightened her collar. Her suit fit her like a glove, and he couldn't help but admire her curves.

"Keep looking at me like that, and I'm going to make you miss your flight."

"Promises, promises."

She walked him to the door, and he kissed her quickly. He was cutting it too close. They said good-bye, and as he crossed over the threshold, she smacked him on the backside.

"I'll get you back for that," he said, taking the first step down.

"I'm counting on it." She leaned smugly against the doorframe.

David knew in that moment he'd rather spend the rest of his life in Chicago with Paula than in Jackson Hole alone.

CHAPTER
TWENTY

Linn had no more than taken off her coat and slid out of her boots when she realized she had left her book bag at work. It had all her books, all her notes, her schedule, and everything she needed for school the next day. She'd left the sociology book out on the break table where she was studying, and her book bag was sitting in the chair.

"Shoot!" She stood helpless by the front door, wondering what to do. Glancing at the clock, she saw that the coffee shop was closed by now. Her first class was at eight fifteen in the morning, and it took almost forty-five minutes to get there by bus.

But there was no way around it. She'd have to get up very early and take the bus to the coffee shop before school.

"What's wrong?" Paula poked her head outside the kitchen.

Linn noticed then that a delicious buttery scent filled the apartment. "I forgot my book bag at the shop. Oh well, I'll get it in the morning."

"I'd give you a ride, but I have an early appointment."

"No problem. Are you making popcorn?"

Paula spoke above the popping sound. "I made a special butter sauce to go with it. You'll have to let me know how it is."

"If I have to," Linn teased. Being on the tasting end of Paula's culinary skills was a real treat.

"It's almost done."

The popping stopped.

Linn approached the kitchen, where Paula scraped a buttery mixture over the top of a bowl of popcorn, then mixed it together with two rubber spatulas.

"Smells great," Linn said. "I'll get us some drinks."

The doorbell rang, and she met Paula's gaze.

"Are you expecting someone?" Paula asked.

"No." Ever since the rock came flying through the window, they'd been a little on edge.

Paula set the spatulas down. "Did you lock the door after you came in?"

Linn thought back. "No." How could she have been so careless?

"It's probably nothing," Paula said. She walked toward the door.

But it was late, and nobody stopped by to visit at this hour. It would be beyond rude to knock on a stranger's door so late on a weeknight.

Linn watched Paula peek through the peephole.

"It's a man," she whispered at the same time as she turned the main deadbolt. "I don't know him."

Linn's mouth went dry. Bad guys didn't knock on doors, though, did they? Especially if it was unlocked. The last thing she wanted to do was get closer to the door, but she had to. "Let me see."

Paula stepped aside, and Linn peeked through the hole. Her breath came out in a rush. "It's OK. I know him."

She started to unlock the door, but Paula put a hand on her arm. "Are you sure it's OK? How well do you know him?"

"It's fine. It's Adam. From work."

"Ahh, Adam."

Linn ignored the teasing smile that was beginning to curl Paula's lips. She released the lock and opened the door. "Hi."

She wanted to ask Adam what he was doing here but didn't know how to say it without sounding rude. Besides, he looked so handsome standing in the hallway with his scarf still wrapped around his chin that, for a moment, she wanted to pretend he was her boyfriend, just stopping over for a while.

"You forgot your book bag." He held up the bulky bag—no small feat since the thing weighed a ton with all her textbooks in it.

"Come in." Linn opened the door wider, and he stepped inside.

Paula had disappeared, probably back into the kitchen.

"I don't want to interrupt anything." He set the bag on the floor.

"Thanks for bringing it over. I didn't realize I'd left it until I got home."

He stuffed his hands into his pockets and avoided her gaze. Something he had done ever since he'd given her the ride home two weeks earlier. In fact, he'd been so distant toward her, she wondered if he was mad at her.

"No problem. I know you have an early class tomorrow."

"I was going to have to get up at the crack of dawn to go get it, so believe me, I appreciate it." She wiped her hands on her jeans, then tucked them in her pocket. Then she felt stupid because she was mirroring him, so she folded her arms over her chest.

"Well, guess I should take off."

She didn't want him to go, but his hand was already on the doorknob, as if he couldn't get out fast enough.

"Aren't you going to introduce me to your friend?" Paula entered the room, carrying a decorative metal bowl.

For a moment Linn saw her as Adam probably did. Her stylish auburn hair and model-like figure made Linn feel like a dowdy schoolgirl.

"Sorry. Paula, this is a coworker, Adam. Adam this is Paula, my roommate." She should have added something about Paula's generosity in taking her in, but she already felt like fish bait.

"Nice to meet you." Adam shook Paula's hand.

"Maybe you can help me out. I'm perfecting this popcorn recipe, and I need input. Can you stay a bit?"

Linn's eyes darted to Paula. What was she doing? But when Adam looked back toward the door, Paula winked at her.

"Well," Adam said, "I don't want to intrude."

"Nonsense. Linn was just unwinding, and I'm headed off to my room to munch and work. Sit down. I'll get you a bowl."

Paula handed the bowl to Linn, and she set it down on the coffee table.

"Let me take your coat," Linn said.

After he slid out of it, she put it on a hanger. The musky scent of his cologne wafted all around her. Cruel and unusual, that's what it was.

She hoped Adam didn't feel forced to stay. He hadn't put up much of a fight when Paula had insisted, but he hadn't exactly been friendly with Linn lately.

"I hope you don't mind." Linn shrugged. "Paula can be a little forceful." And her good looks probably got her everything she wanted, at least where men were concerned. She wondered if that's why Adam had agreed to stay.

Paula returned and set another bowl and two sodas down on the coffee table.

Adam grabbed a few popped kernels and put them in his mouth. "Mmm. Good. Unusual."

Linn tried it too. It was salty and had some kinds of herbs mixed in with the butter. "This is awesome, Paula."

"Not too salty?"

"Uh-uh." Adam took another handful. "I wouldn't change a thing."

Linn watched him from beneath the veil of her lashes, waiting to see if he gave Paula extra attention. But his smile was only polite.

"Well, I have to get some work done. It was nice meeting you, Adam," she said as she walked toward her room with her own bowl of popcorn.

"You too."

After Paula's door shut, Linn became aware that the only sound was the munching of popcorn.

It seemed almost surreal to be sitting here in the apartment with Adam. He'd only stopped by with her book bag, but she wanted it to be so much more.

"So how's school going for you?" he asked.

The first few weeks had been stressful, and Linn felt like a fish out of water among all the others, but her grades so far were good. "OK."

She knew she should say something else, but for the life of her, she couldn't think of a thing. Her eyes focused on the TV, a late rerun of *The Odd Couple*.

"I used to watch these reruns when I was younger," Adam said. "This show is a classic."

Linn had only seen snippets of it. The sound on the TV was so low, she couldn't hear what Felix was saying, but he was pitching a fit.

"So which are you more like—Oscar or Felix?" Adam asked.

Linn finished chewing a bite of popcorn. "Well, I like things picked up, but I'm not neurotic about it like Felix. What about you?"

She made the mistake of looking at him. The glow of the floor lamp cast a golden glow on his skin, and she thought he'd never looked more handsome. She looked away.

"I think I'm in between. Although my mom always said my room looked like a disaster, I did get around to cleaning it up eventually. And I always know where everything's at, you know? It might be in a pile, but I know where it's at."

"Paula's husband visited this past week, and he was just like Felix. It was hysterical to watch him go behind Paula and pick up after her. I don't even think he realized he was doing it."

Adam went quiet for a minute as Linn put the last few popped kernels in her mouth, sorry it was gone. What was she going to do to occupy her hands now? She wiped her greasy fingers on one of the napkins Paula had set on the coffee table.

"Why didn't you tell me about the rock through the window?"

Startled by his concerned tone, she almost caught his eye. But she stopped herself in time. Joe must've told him about it.

She shrugged. "Never came up, I guess." That, and he'd been as distant as Australia since he drove her home. She wasn't sure why, but it hurt that he didn't tease her or talk to her anymore. Maybe not telling him had been a childish way of getting back at him.

"You should have told me."

Her eyes swung to his face. She couldn't help it. He looked as hurt as he sounded, but she didn't know why. He was the one who'd put up walls between them. True, she hadn't exactly been Miss Congeniality before, but after he drove her home that day, she thought things would be different between them. They were different all right. But not in a way she could have guessed.

"What do you want from me, Adam?" The words spilled out before she could stop them. Suddenly she wasn't sure if she wanted to know. If he said he wanted her to be his friend, she was dead meat. She wanted so much more than that.

As he considered her now, his eyes were like chocolate melting in the sun. Soft and warm.

His lips parted as if he had an answer, but no words came out. His jaw line was all covered in stubble, giving him a bad-boy look. The thought almost made her laugh. Adam was as far from a bad boy as you could get. Her fingers itched to run across his roughened jaw line. She tucked her hands between her knees before she acted on the impulse.

"I don't know," he said.

She'd almost forgotten the question. Wanted to forget about everything else in the world with Adam staring into her eyes the way he was.

"*I don't know.*" Such an honest answer. Maybe that was what had taken him so long to answer. He took his time because he wanted to be honest, but he didn't really know what he wanted from her. Was that good? What did she want him to say?

He was searching her eyes. The moment had gone tense as if they were rock climbers, hanging on the edge of a cliff and trying to decide whether it was safe to let go or not.

"I think I have feelings for you, Linn," he whispered.

Something swelled in her.

Relief. Joy. Confusion.

There was so much she could say right now, and some of it involved his engaged status, but she pushed those things from her mind. It had been so long since a man had looked at her the way Adam was. She wanted to drown in his eyes.

"You're killing me here." His voice was barely audible. Worry lines stretched across his forehead.

Oh, Adam, I have feelings for you too. I think about you constantly. "I don't know what to say."

His eyes flickered downward, and she feared she'd blown it. She should have just said it all. What held her back?

He looked at her again, and a small sigh left her body. She drank him in.

"Your eyes say everything."

Could he read all her thoughts? Did he know she'd wanted him for weeks? Did he know that the way he looked at her now made her shiver? He leaned toward her until they were a breath apart. How did they come to be sitting so close? She felt his breath on her face, then his lips touched hers, so tenderly it made her ache.

CHAPTER
TWENTY-ONE

At first Adam's kiss was soft and searching. He moved as if he was afraid he'd hurt her, treating her as the most delicate, precious porcelain. Then he deepened the kiss, and her whole world spun. Her hands found his jaw line and relished the manly roughness of his skin. Her heart kicked as though it might punch right through her ribs, but she didn't care. Didn't care about anything but this man who treated her with such gentleness that she ached with it.

Then he was pulling back from her, and she didn't want to open her eyes. His arms held her firmly away.

And she knew.

"Oh, God," he said. It wasn't the casual slang tossed about by people today. It was a petition.

She opened her eyes and wished she hadn't. He'd turned away. She couldn't see his face because it was covered by his hands. She didn't need to see it to know he regretted the kiss.

"I'm sorry." The words seemed squeezed from him, but she didn't know if he was talking to her or God.

Instinctively she knew he was thinking of Elizabeth and how he'd betrayed her. He was taking every inch of blame when Linn was just as much at fault. She hurt for him. She hurt for herself and for want of him.

"I've got to go." He stood and was putting his coat on by the time she was at the door. "I'm sorry," he said again.

This time the words were for her, but she didn't want to hear them. She didn't want him to be sorry, even though he wouldn't be the man he was if he could act so recklessly without regret.

She wanted to take responsibility, if only to soothe his conscience. She wanted to tell him she wouldn't take back the kiss if she could. Instead she only nodded, knowing that when he left, he would take her heart with him.

⋯⋯

Paula stabbed her fork into the house salad and listened as Miles asked his assistant, Cindy, about a phone call he received earlier. Darrick had been on a roll past couple of weeks, breaking stories that viewers were responding to. It seemed like Miles was sitting up and taking notice, so when he invited Paula to lunch, she wasn't about to pass up the opportunity.

Bin 36 was a restaurant that made Jackson Hole seem as if it were on the other side of the planet. With its elegant, eclectic atmosphere and gourmet cuisine, it drew her like a skier to a warm, cozy fire. She put the bite of salad into her mouth, appreciating the delicate flavors of toasted almond and Riesling vinaigrette.

Miles waved at someone across the open room. "Excuse me, ladies. I see a boating friend I need to catch up with." He laid the napkin beside his plate and left the table.

Cindy tucked her chestnut hair behind her ear and took a bite of her smoked salmon.

"That looks really good," Paula said.

Even though Miles's assistant was just about her opposite in every way, Paula couldn't help but like Cindy. The woman was just a shade younger than Paula and had been married recently. She had a formal photo of her and her husband taped to her work station.

"Mmm. Much better than the chicken nuggets and macaroni we had for dinner last night."

Paula smiled. If she ate dinners like that, she'd have hips as wide as the El.

Cindy tugged the blouse she wore, trying to banish the little gap that seemed to plague her. "Have you gotten any more of those weird letters?"

Paula wondered where Cindy had heard about them, then remembered mentioning it to her several weeks ago. "No. I'm hoping Romeo has given up."

"So you don't really think it's a kid?"

Paula realized that even though she'd told others it must be a child, she was thinking of the person as a man. She shrugged. "I'm sure it's nothing to worry about."

"After the rock incident, I wouldn't be too sure. That had to be kind of scary."

"I hadn't thought of the two as being related."

"Maybe they're not, but it's possible."

"It doesn't matter anyway. I'm not going to let someone scare me off or determine my decisions. What about your own Romeo? How is married life treating you?"

Cindy looked down at her plate. "Not so good actually." She wiped her mouth with the linen napkin. "I guess I may as well tell you. I'm sure it won't be long before it's on the office grapevine anyway. We're separated. Cal moved out into a place of his own."

Hadn't Cindy and Cal only been married four or five months? Paula couldn't help but think. But who was she to talk? She and David had certainly been through their share of rough times. "I'm sorry," she said softly. "I didn't know."

Cindy shrugged. "I haven't exactly been telling everyone. Miles knows, but—" She took a sip from her glass. "Let me give you a little tip that I've learned the hard way: don't ever lie to a man. They're not very forgiving."

Paula's mind tripped over Cindy's words. It was a little late for that tip. "I hope you can work it out."

Cindy nodded, then changed the topic. "Are you still working on that 'Switched at Birth' story?"

Paula took a sip of her Diet Pepsi and watched across the room as Miles imitated a golf swing while the other man laughed.

"I'm working on it off hours." Paula was aware anything she said might get back to Miles. "There has to be an answer. It's just a matter of finding it."

Cindy rubbed at a water spot on the glass. "Just between you and me, I'm rooting for you for the anchor job."

"Thanks. I'll take all the rooters I can get."

"I guess you've noticed that Miles is fawning all over Darrick right now."

Paula kept her expression bland, though her spirits sank to floor level. She didn't realize it was so obvious that Darrick was pulling ahead of her. And Cindy certainly had the inside track with Miles . . . though, if she were Cindy, she'd be a lot more careful what she said.

"Well," Paula said, "it's not over yet, and I intend to give him and the others a run for their money."

"You'd make the better anchor. Hopefully Miles will see that."

"Darrick's very good, though," Paula said. "He connects with the audience, and he's easy on the eyes."

"Only if you like the tall, dark, and handsome type. I still say you should get it." Cindy held up her glass of Pepsi. "Power to the women."

Paula smiled as they clinked glasses.

Paula saw Miles approaching and took a sip.

"Sorry about that, ladies," he said as he reached the table. "I haven't seen Greg in almost a year. Glad I ran into him. Gave us a chance to plan a weekend out on the lake."

"Miles has a yacht to die for," Cindy said. "It's so big, you could practically live on it."

"Does David boat?" Miles took a bite of his quesadilla, though Paula knew it must be cold by now.

"He's not much of an outdoorsman, though I've gotten him out on Jenny Lake a time or two."

Miles had met David a few days ago when he'd visited. He'd taken her and David to Gibson's one night. She was a nervous wreck, but the men hit it off.

"In his defense, though," Paula said, "he more than makes up for lack of adventure with his expertise in the stocks, bonds, and real-estate department."

"I thought he seemed like a very intelligent man. Savvy and business minded. The two of you are a good match."

"We think so."

"He seemed to like Chicago," Miles said.

"Oh, he did. He didn't want to leave." It was true, though the real reason was that he hated leaving her.

"I'm assuming if you were offered the anchor job, he would move here."

"Of course." The words stuck like a brick in her throat.

She was relieved when Cindy struck up a conversation with Miles.

There was nothing "of course" about David moving to Chicago. They hadn't even discussed it, and Paula had no idea what would happen if she were offered the job.

David had worked for years to build a clientele and reputation in Jackson. And now that he owned JH Realty, he was as rooted there as a hundred-year-old oak tree. Could she ask him to give that up for her?

Suddenly she wondered what in the world she was doing. She was chasing her own dream, but it was a dream that could take her further than ever from the man she loved. If she got the job, one of them would have to be sacrificed, and Paula wondered which one that would be. Of course, the way things stood right now, it was a decision she may never have to make.

Later that night as Paula lay across her bed scanning her notes on the Morgan story, she felt like she needed her head examined. Why was she beating this story to death? All the other media had realized the story suffered from lead fatigue and dropped it. She'd never clung to a dead horse before. What was so different about this one?

Was it fear of disappointing the Morgans? Was it the need to see the story she'd broken brought to a conclusion? Or was it the deep, underlying need to atone for the abortion?

Maybe it was time to put this story to bed and move on with her life. There were other stories to be told, and this one seemed to have no ending, happy or not. Maybe she should be pouring her extra time into finding new stories.

She closed the notebook and slid her tape recorder aside, then rolled over onto her back. Miles had been thrilled when the story had broken, but now Darrick was in the limelight with his stories on the Cubs player who was caught using steroids and a man who was using his business as a money-laundering operation. Darrick was breaking all the big stories, and there didn't seem to be a thing she could do about it.

Maybe Miles was one of those people who constantly expected to be surprised and impressed. He'd certainly been both when she broke the Morgan story, but those feelings had faded.

She was still working the beat, but her assignments were lame most of the time. Darrick was getting all the big stuff, and there was only so much she could do with a ribbon cutting or a neighborhood house fire.

Maybe it was time to give it up. Not just the Morgan story, but the whole notion that she had a chance at the anchor position. Darrick and the others had been there longer. Paula was new at investigative reporting, and her only anchoring experience was in a town smaller than the smallest Chicago suburb.

She knew she did a good job with the stories she was given, but how could she compete with Darrick when he was assigned the big stuff? Maybe she should just finish her temporary assignment and prepare to pack it up at the end. She could move back to Jackson Hole and live happily ever after with David.

She rolled over and buried her face in the cradle of her arms. Being with David would be wonderful. But the thought of living in Jackson was so stifling, she felt claustrophobic. How could she go back to the town walled in on all sides by tall buttes? Back to the place where everybody knew her name . . . and her business? Back to the place where she would watch tourists come and go and wish she could go with them?

No. She didn't want to go back there. She was made for the city. Coming to Chicago had proved that to her. Back in Jackson she was a misfit, but here in Chicago she was surrounded by people just like her. People with energy and purpose. People who wanted to go somewhere in life, and today wasn't soon enough.

She sat up and smoothed her rumpled clothes. She wasn't a quitter. She couldn't believe she'd been ready to give up. If David knew, he'd be as shocked as she was.

There was a way to get that anchor chair, and she would find it. She consulted her notebook and the index cards lined up at the bottom of the bed. Had she exhausted every possible lead?

Yes. Except for the nurse who'd passed away. And the nurse who was terminally ill. Maybe there was a way to reach Louise Garner without having a run-in with her protective son. The one time Paula had talked to the woman on the phone, she'd seemed cooperative.

Maybe Louise didn't have any answers at all, but Paula had to try again. She retrieved her purse and located the scrap of paper with Louise's number.

Paula checked the clock and saw it was just past eight. Not too late to call. She picked up the bedroom extension and dialed the number. Before she knew what she was doing, she said a quick prayer that the woman's son wouldn't answer.

It rang three times before it was picked up. The voice sounded like an older woman but was too energetic to be Louise.

"May I speak with Louise, please?" Paula held her breath, hoping the woman wouldn't ask who she was.

"Just a minute."

Ah, progress. Maybe the son wasn't home. She heard the rustling sound of the phone being handled, then felt a moment's panic. She hadn't even prepared questions for Mrs. Garner. It wasn't like her to be so unprepared, but now she was getting the woman on the phone, and it may be her last chance to get an interview.

Where were the questions for the NICU nurses? She shuffled through her notebook, hoping to find them fast.

"Hello?"

She recognized the feeble voice from the last time she talked to Louise on the phone. "Hello, Mrs. Garner. This is Paula Landin-Cohen from WMAQ. We spoke on the phone just after Christmas."

Paula thought she heard a soft sigh and feared she was about to lose Mrs. Garner. "I'm very sorry to bother you with this when you're so ill. But the story I'm covering is about a very special family who needs answers. I was hoping you'd be willing to help. I won't take much of your time."

Her fingers rifled frantically through the notebook. Where were those questions? She reached the end of the notebook and started back through. If only she had her detailed notes from the computer. But those files were long gone.

Mrs. Garner had been quiet too long. "Mrs. Garner? Are you there?"

The woman cleared her throat. "I'm here."

There was some quality in her voice that Paula couldn't quite peg. Sadness? Resolve? "Would you be willing to answer a few questions, Mrs. Garner? The Morgan family would really appreciate your cooperation."

"I've wanted to talk long before now, but my son . . . well, he's just trying to look out for me."

Excitement stirred in Paula's blood. Did this mean Louise Garner knew something? Or was she just saying she'd been willing all along to cooperate with an interview?

"I understand. He only loves you and wants the best for you. But I promise I won't be a bother. I just want to ask some questions." Paula's hands were shaking, and she was nearly ready to rip out the pages of her notebook. Where were those questions?

"My son is away right now at a work thing. It's a good time."

Ah, thank you! Paula wasn't sure who the gratitude went to, but she was thrilled she had called at the perfect time. She spied a set of questions and nearly sent up a whoop of relief when she saw they were the right ones.

"He's out of town and won't be back until Monday," the weak voice continued. "Can you come over tomorrow morning? Say, around nine o'clock?"

Part of Paula was thrilled that she wanted to interview in person, but another part was afraid something would go wrong or Mrs. Garner would change her mind. "Would you rather just talk now, over the phone? I know you must not be feeling up to company."

"No, dear, I think it would be best if you came here."

The woman's tone was strong.

So the emotional quality I heard before was resolve, Paula thought. Did it mean anything significant?

"And please," Mrs. Garner was saying, "no cameras."

"Of course. Is it OK if I tape-record?"

A pause. "That would be fine. I'll see you in the morning then."

After Paula hung up, she felt like jumping on the bed. Maybe her instincts were wrong, but there was something in Mrs. Garner's voice that hinted the ill nurse knew something.

CHAPTER
TWENTY-TWO

Paula hitched her bag higher on her shoulder as she climbed the uneven porch steps. A heavy-duty railing, the kind disabled people use, had been installed along the steps. When she reached the top of the steps, she knocked on the edge of the aluminum screen door.

The door opened and a young woman held it open to her. She looked barely old enough to be out of college, and her orange-brown hair looked like a Sun-In mishap from the '80s.

"You're the reporter here to see Louise, right?"

"Yes. Paula Landin-Cohen."

"Come on in. She's waiting for you in her room."

Paula followed the girl through a tiny living room that seemed even tinier with all the knickknacks that cluttered every surface. Pictures and plates competed for wall space with shelves that held more of the same. A closer look revealed a windmill theme throughout the room.

Paula smiled to herself. David would call this house a dusting nightmare.

Louise Garner's bedroom appeared to be an addition, or perhaps it had once been a back porch. It was located just off the kitchen, and its floor rolled slightly downhill toward a window.

The girl gestured for Paula to go in. "Louise, that reporter is here."

A woman lay as still as death on a hospital bed that took up half the room. Her short, gray hair was spiked out at odd angles, making Paula think no one had fixed it in days.

"Louise?" the girl called.

Paula moved toward the bed, wondering why the woman didn't wake. She didn't like the possible answer that sprung to her mind.

The girl stepped around her. "Louise?" She laid her hand gently on the woman's shoulder. "Louise, you asked me to wake you up when that reporter arrived."

Louise's head moved as her lashes fluttered open. Paula began breathing again.

"She's here?" Louise's eyes fell on Paula, and her lips turned upward. "Oh, dear, I'm sorry. I can't seem to stay awake these days." She looked at the girl. "Laurie, can you help me sit up?"

The girl did as asked, then turned to leave the room. "Let me know if you need anything else, Louise. Your water's fresh." She shut the door—an old, five-panel, white one—behind her.

Paula introduced herself to Louise. The woman was younger than Paula had imagined—perhaps only in her late fifties. Though her eyes were puffy and her face sunken at the cheekbones, her skin was almost devoid of wrinkles.

"I must look a mess." Louise tried to pat her disarrayed hair into a semblance of order, but it did no good.

"You know," Paula said, "short, choppy hair is all the rage right now anyway."

Louise laughed heartily, then coughed. Paula spied a thermos with a straw on the bedside table. She handed it to Louise, who took a sip before handing it back to Paula.

"Thank you," Louise said in a weak voice.

Paula wasn't sure what to say next. It seemed insensitive to plunge right into the interview when the woman was clearly very ill. So she said first, "I'm sorry about your illness."

Louise waved her hand. "I've lived a good life. Not quite as long as I would've liked, but those are the breaks."

Paula noted the photos that were scattered around the room on numerous surfaces. In them were younger versions of Louise and a man, presumably Louise's husband. "You seem to have traveled a lot."

"Oh, yes. When we were younger, my husband and I traveled all over the United States in a camper for a year. He was my second husband, and even though I had three children from my first, Lewis raised them as his own. He was a good man. Two of my children have moved away and are raising my grandchildren, so I only have the one son who lives here. He takes good care of me, that boy does." She tucked her lips downward. "That's the one you've spoken with on the phone." She bit her lip and looked away. "But you didn't come to talk about my family. You came to get answers."

Louise sounded as if she had answers, and that excited Paula more than anything. She reached into her bag and pulled out the tape recorder. "Here we go." She pushed Record and set the device on the bedside table where it would pick up both of their voices.

"I know you said you have questions for me," Louise said. "But would it be too much of a bother if I told my story straight out?"

Her story. So she must know what happened to the Morgans' child. A surge of excitement passed through Paula. "Whatever is most comfortable for you."

Louise nodded, then peered across the room to where a collage of pictures hung on the plaster wall.

"Three years ago, as you know, I was a nurse in the NICU at Chicago General. I loved my job, working with those babies, but sometimes it was more painful than I thought I could bear. When we'd lose an infant, I would often go home and cry my heart out. I think it would have been easier if I could have just detached from the babies. Provided for their care and no more. A supervisor once warned me I got too attached to the babies, but I suppose that's just the way I'm made."

Louise shifted, her gaze drifting past the gauzy, white curtains. "But I'm getting off the subject, aren't I?" She wet her lips. "Five years ago my son was involved in a car accident that left him severely injured.

Unfortunately he had no health insurance at the time and no way to pay for the surgeries and rehabilitation. My husband—he passed away two years ago—was on disability at the time, and we didn't have anything extra. So I took on a second job."

She stopped to cough, and Paula handed her the drink again.

Louise continued. "I needed to work someplace close to the hospital, and I was trying to stay in the field of nursing so I could make decent money. I finally got a job working for Dr. Miller, an ob-gyn who performed quite a few abortions." She swallowed hard. "It's not a job I would have taken if I'd had another opportunity. But it was so convenient and close to my other job. I figured it was only for a year or so until my son got on his feet again."

Paula checked to be sure the tape was running. She didn't want to miss any of this.

Louise shifted in bed and pulled the afghan up to her waist. "Everything went OK for the first couple of months—other than my being worn out, of course. I wasn't used to working two jobs. And I realized through the months that Dr. Miller often fudged a bit when it came to late-term abortions. Sometimes the 'medical necessity' was ambiguous, and I sometimes felt he performed late-term abortions when there was no anomaly with the fetus and the mother's life wasn't truly in jeopardy.

"Dr. Miller paid me well, though, and the people were nice to work with." She stared out the window for a minute. "There were times, though, that it felt so odd."

She paused for so long, seemingly lost in thought, that Paula asked, "What seemed odd, Mrs. Garner?"

"Oh, you can call me Louise, dear." Her eyes flitted by Paula before staring again out the window into the backyard. "When I say it felt odd, I'm talking about my purpose at each of the jobs. My role in the NICU was to assist in helping the babies live. My other job was to assist in stopping the life from growing."

Paula's stomach tightened painfully. Perhaps Louise believed an abortion took a life. If that were the case, she shouldn't have taken the job at all.

"Oh, I didn't have anything against the women I assisted. I knew they were doing what they thought was best, and I was glad to help them. I wouldn't say I felt guilty about what I did. I'd always felt abortion was a woman's choice." She spared a glance at Paula. "I'm sorry—I'm rambling again. If I do it again, just nudge me like a broken record."

Paula smiled, then watched Louise as she smoothed her hair again, tugging at the growth along the side of her neck.

"The day of June twelfth is one I remember very well."

It was a day Paula remembered well, too, though she wished she could abolish it from the calendar. She stuffed the thought deep inside and focused on Louise's words.

"It started out quite normally. The last procedure of the day was an abortion of a twenty-one-week pregnancy. After that I was scheduled to start the second shift in the NICU. I was feeling very tired as I often did that year, what with two jobs. My son was here at home recovering from surgery after surgery. It was a difficult time for us."

Paula wondered what all this had to do with the Morgans' baby. She was on edge and anxious and wished Louise didn't ramble so much. She eyed her bag and wished she could pull out the questions she'd planned to ask. But that was unfair to Louise. Maybe the woman was lonely and needed someone to listen.

"Anyway, the abortion seemed to be going normally at first. I went through it somewhat on autopilot until—something went terribly wrong."

Louise's sparse brows constricted. "As Dr. Miller extracted the fetus, he went still. I turned just in time to see it. Nancy, the other nurse, was checking the patient's vitals. Dr. Miller, his eyes the size of quarters, was staring, transfixed, at the fetus. I looked into his hands and saw what had frightened him so."

She looked at Paula, whose breath felt stuck in her throat.

"That fetus was breathing." Louise's hand covered her heart. "Her little chest was going up and down so fast. It was no twenty-one-week-old fetus." She clutched at the floral nightgown. "Then Dr. Miller turned to me and put the infant in my hands—and it *was* an infant to me at that moment. She looked no different to me than the tiny babies whose lives I fought so hard for in the NICU."

She coughed again, and Paula handed her the thermos. She was so eager for the rest of Louise's story, yet a seed of fear was germinating somewhere deep inside.

"Before I could say a word, Dr. Miller peeled off his gloves and said quietly, 'Get rid of it.' Those were his exact words. I remember because they echoed through my mind for weeks. I remember standing there, staring at this miniature human being. Her eyes were sealed shut, and I could see her heart's movement through her thin skin. I was frozen. I could feel Nancy staring from across the room and wished she'd been the one he'd handed the child to."

She closed her eyes. "Dr. Miller nudged me out of the room, telling me what to do. I could tell he was horrified too. He wouldn't look at the baby." She blinked rapidly, lost in memory. "I knew what he asked of me was wrong. This was a living, breathing human being I held in my hands, and every instinct I possessed told me to save her. But Dr. Miller told me to get rid of it. I was confused and scared. Scared of disobeying his orders and scared to murder the child in my hands, for surely that was what it would be! Oh, I was so scared!"

Paula's mouth went dry. She was too taken aback to ask anything and was glad she'd let Louise tell her story, for what a story it was.

"I ran to the women's lounge and locked myself in the stall. My heart was beating as fast as the infant's. I unbuttoned my scrubs and held the baby against me for warmth. I knew her chances of survival were miniscule, but to do nothing seemed cruel beyond words."

Louise dabbed at her eyes with shaking fingers. "I tried to collect my thoughts, but there were other nurses coming and going through the rest room because of the shift change. And I realized I was going to be late for my other job. That's when the idea occurred to me." She drew her shoulders up in a helpless shrug. "At first I thought it was crazy. No, I *knew* it was crazy. And I wondered how on earth I could smuggle this child downstairs to the NICU without anyone noticing."

A terrible thought winged through Paula's mind. Chills chased down her spine. She opened her mouth to ask a question, but nothing came out.

"I took off my scrub top and wrapped the baby in it, keeping it loose around the face but covered nonetheless. I took a moment to compose myself and tried to hold her casually in my arms as if she was just my dirty scrub top. I hoped Nancy wouldn't be around to ask questions. I wondered how I would answer to Dr. Miller the next day, but I just put all that out of my mind. One thing at a time, I told myself."

Louise pushed the afghan down, as though she'd grown too hot under the layers of bedding. "I made it out to the hallway with no trouble, and I knew I needed to make it to the elevator without seeing Dr. Miller or Nancy. Once I was inside the elevator, I wished I could push the stop button and think, but the baby needed help quickly if she had any chance at all." She shook her head. "I had no idea what I was going to do when I got downstairs to the NICU."

When she paused for a sip of water, Paula gathered her courage. "Did you say downstairs?"

"Yes, to the NICU floor."

"The—the abortion occurred in the hospital? Chicago General?"

She nodded. "Dr. Miller's practice was on the fifth floor."

Dr. Miller. Dr. Miller. Had that been the name of her doctor? Paula's heart was working so hard, she felt slightly faint. What floor had her abortion been on? She couldn't remember. She steadied her voice. "And what was the date again? The date the abortion occurred?"

"June twelfth, three years ago."

It was all coming together now. Coming painfully together. Though she didn't remember the doctor's name, Paula did remember she'd been twenty-one weeks, or so she'd thought. She was under anesthesia for the procedure, and when she awakened, she was told everything had gone just fine.

But had everything gone as she thought, or was Louise . . . was Louise talking about her baby?

No, it can't be. Her thoughts raced. It wasn't possible. These things didn't happen. Fetuses didn't survive abortion. Nurses didn't smuggle them to safety. Was Louise demented or hallucinating? What did she really know about this woman anyway? And besides, Paula's abortion wasn't the only one that day, she was sure. Still, fingers of dread curled around her stomach in a white-knuckled grip.

"Do you remember the patient's name?" Liquid fear pumped through Paula's veins, paralyzing her. She wanted to take the question back. To put her hands over her ears.

"Yes, yes, I do. It was O'Neil."

Paula's vision swam; her thoughts spun. She remembered the day like it was yesterday. Filling out forms and pausing over the patient information section. David thought she went to Chicago for the conference, but she went to have a "miscarriage." When it was all over, she'd go back to her hotel and call him, crying, saying it had all happened so fast. As she hunched over the forms, she knew she wouldn't have any trouble conjuring up tears.

But she had to be careful. If she listed her own name and information, it would have gone through their insurance. She planned to pay cash, but she used another name just to be safe. So on June twelfth she had lowered the pen to the paper and written the first name that had come to mind. Paula O'Neil.

Now Paula closed her eyes as heavy and dark emotions welled up in her like a summer storm cloud. Panic followed, shoving her heart into a rhythm too fast for her lungs to follow. She stood and walked across the room, her back to Louise.

Sweat broke out on the back of her neck. She wanted to shed the Anne Klein suit coat. No, she wanted to run from the room.

"Are you all right, dear?" Louise called.

She couldn't face the woman yet. Not even Paula was that good at disguising her feelings. She sucked in a breath full of air, almost choking on the smell of antiseptic and urine. "I'm fine. This is just so—wow, it's amazing." Her voice sounded false in her own ears. But then she was hearing everything as if through a tunnel of disbelief. She had to finish this. Louise was going to wonder what had upset her, and heaven forbid she should find out the truth. The woman must not recognize her. It had been three years, after all. She needed to collect herself.

Paula schooled her features and turned. "Please, continue."

She walked back toward the bed but remained standing. She watched the wheels on the recorder spinning, catching every word. She wanted to reach out and jab the Stop button.

"Well, like I said, I didn't have time to plan anything. When I reached the NICU, I was late. I was so worried about what I would do once I got there. There were two nurses on the shift before me and another coming on the same time as I was, so I knew I couldn't keep the infant a secret. All I could hope for was to convince them we needed to treat the baby.

"But when I got to the NICU, the two nurses were peeved with me for being late, and they were in a hurry to leave. I set the baby, still wrapped in my dirty scrub top, on the sink counter while I scrubbed in. One of the nurses caught me up to speed on the conditions of a couple of the babies. I kept looking at the wad of material, hoping the baby wouldn't move and betray her existence."

There was something unfathomable in Louise's eyes. "According to the nurse, one of the babies was expected to pass anytime. A very premature infant who'd been born that morning. Her condition had deteriorated, and the doctor gave her less than a 1 percent chance of survival. A sad story, especially because the mother had hemorrhaged badly during the delivery and had to have a hysterectomy to save her life. The other nurses said the father sat by the baby's side that afternoon while his wife was in surgery. He was not only about to lose his baby girl, but he and his wife wouldn't be able to conceive again. My heart broke for them.

"The other nurse scheduled to work with me, Evelyn Bernard, called in just before my arrival and said she'd been pulled over for speeding and would arrive as soon as she could."

Louise shook her head. "I couldn't believe my luck. As soon as the nurse left, I opened the wadded-up scrub top, half expecting to see that the infant had died. But the little miracle was still breathing. I picked up the child and put her in an incubator. I didn't know how I was going to explain this child's existence to anyone. I knew I would probably lose both jobs, but I couldn't just let this child die."

She looked at Paula, a question in her eyes. She wanted Paula to understand why she'd done it. More than that, she wanted Paula to approve what she'd done. Paula nodded. That was her baby. *Her child.* An ache welled up inside her.

There was one vital question remaining, and Paula wasn't sure she wanted an answer.

Louise continued. "I started an IV through the umbilical cord, hooked up the assisted ventilation, and injected fluids and antibiotics. It was the same treatment we'd used for the infant who lay dying in the next incubator. I stood and watched her rapid breaths. I guessed her to be about twenty-four or twenty-five weeks. She was holding up remarkably well for the terrible ordeal she'd survived."

Her eyes found Paula's. "Have you ever heard of botched abortions?"

Paula shook her head, her mouth too dry to speak.

"It's rare, but there are documented cases of it. If the child lives, he or she often suffers from cerebral palsy or some other malady."

Louise's eyes got a faraway look in them, and Paula knew she was revisiting the past again.

"After the infant was stabilized, I turned to the incubator, where the other preemie was, the one who was expected to die. I'd just checked the monitors a second before they went off. The baby's heart had stopped. I had known it would happen soon, but when it did . . ."

Louise blinked away tears. "This is going to be hard to understand, but you have to realize, this baby had no chance of survival. The monitor alarm would have alerted the doctor on call, who would have tried to resuscitate the infant, but her little body wasn't developed enough to live outside the womb. It was a horribly sad but foregone conclusion."

Paula knew then what Louise had done, but she had to hear it from her. "What—what did you do?" This was *her* child Louise was talking about.

My child. The words echoed through the darkened corners of Paula's mind.

Louise wet her lips. "The idea hit me so quickly, it almost knocked me off my feet. I remember looking at the dying infant, whom the parents desperately wanted, and then at the nearly aborted infant, whom nobody wanted or even knew about. See? Can you see what I mean? There was a set of parents who needed a child. Then there was a child who needed a set of parents."

"Go on," Paula said.

"You have to understand that all those thoughts ran through my head in a matter of seconds. I reacted, that's all. First I turned off the alarm so the doctor wouldn't come. Then I did it." Louise's eyes were shadowed with emotion. "I switched them. I put a bracelet on the living child that would identify her as the Morgan child."

What Louise had done was unthinkable. But it happened. Paula pictured the nurse frantically unhooking all the medical equipment from the dead child and switching the incubators. It was clear the woman had operated out of compassion, but still . . .

And yet the child Louise had saved was her own. *And David's.* The thought awed her and frightened her in ways she couldn't think about right now.

She watched Louise dab at her face with the corners of the afghan.

"What—what did you do with the . . ."

Louise looked out the window. "The Morgans' birth child? I brought her home with me. I cradled her and told her she was greatly loved, then

I buried her under a shade tree at the back of the property." She wept then, covering her face with hands that appeared older than she was.

Paula gazed out the window that faced the backyard and saw the tree Louise referred to. It was what the woman had stared at throughout her story.

"I didn't know what else to do," Louise said through her hands. "It tore me apart—the guilt. But what was I to do? The baby had died. I gave her a proper burial, and I gave the parents hope."

Faith.

Paula struggled to remember the girl's face. *Her daughter's face.* Even now it seemed incomprehensible. But Faith had cerebral palsy, didn't she? Just like Louise had said happens sometimes to botched-abortion survivors. Paula thought of the Morgans but pushed the thought away. It was all too much.

"Looking back now," Louise was saying, "I can see how my decision seems irresponsible, even cruel. I've had three years to second-guess myself. But if I could do it over, I would. I would give that little girl a chance at life. But I didn't have three years to make the decision, I had three seconds. And I've lived with guilt every day since then."

Louise had stopped crying. Her face now simply appeared old and weary.

Paula felt like she'd aged ten years in the time she'd been in this room.

Her baby was alive.

My baby is alive.

My baby is alive.

Maybe if she kept repeating it, she'd believe it. The ache that had sprouted inside grew until it nearly swallowed her whole as she realized the truth. Part of her didn't want to believe it. Because to believe her baby had lived would mean the abortion she'd tried to have was . . .

Murder.

CHAPTER
TWENTY-THREE

The bus hit a rut, and Linn grabbed the English textbook on her lap to keep it from spilling onto the dirty floor. She wasn't sure why she had it open anyway since she hadn't read more than two sentences since she stepped on the bus fifteen minutes ago.

No, her mind was only on one thing: Adam. She both dreaded and looked forward to seeing him at work today, and she wasn't sure which feeling was stronger. She hadn't seen him since the kiss and didn't know how he'd act when she did. Would he feel guilty and ignore her? Would there be only awkward silence between them?

Had he relived the kiss a hundred times like she had? She closed her eyes and leaned her head against the vinyl seat. She'd only been kissed by a handful of guys, but she knew one thing. The passion and feeling that had been stored up in that kiss had been enough to fill the Sears Tower to the rooftop.

She closed her English book, finally giving up the thought of studying. As she slipped the book into her book bag, she saw the letter she'd retrieved from the mailbox on the way out of the apartment.

She pulled it from the bag and tore it open. At least a dozen pictures were nestled inside, but she only took out the sheet of stationery. She would save the pictures for last . . . like a long-awaited dessert at the end of a meal.

She opened Natalie's letter, two small pages written on parchment-like paper that had moose and bears chasing each other around the border.

Hi, Linn!

I hope you had a nice Christmas and that it's not as cold in Chicago as what I hear on the news! As you know, Kyle and I were married on Christmas Eve, and we have moved into our new house. Little Grace has the best bedroom. It has a huge gable overlooking our backyard with a window bench and bookshelves. It's a little girl's dream room!

Thank you so much for sending her the precious bracelet. I will make sure it is well taken care of, and one day she will understand just how much her birth mommy thinks of her and loves her.

Linn stopped reading and looked out the bus window, her eyes stinging. She watched people exiting the bus and noted it wouldn't be long until her stop. As much as she wanted to hear about Grace and see pictures of her growing, it was hard. She wondered if it would always be this hard. She knew she'd done the right thing for her baby, but would it always feel like a part of her was missing?

Her eyes found the page again.

I hope things are going well for you in school. I know you are going to ace all your classes, and I can't wait to see the future God has in store for you!

Have you had any luck finding another place to stay, or are you going to be staying with Paula for a while? She can be a little intense, but she's a softie at heart. One day God will grab hold of her the way He did you, and she will be a shining light, just as you are.

Oh, Alex just walked by and asked me to tell you that he got the new Uno game for Christmas and wishes you were here to play it with him because he "rocks" at it. His words, not mine. Ha, ha.

We went over to Higher Grounds yesterday and had dinner with Hanna, Micah, and Grams. Hanna is due in four weeks, and she is bigger than you were at the very end of your pregnancy. Of course, I would never tell her that. ☺ They have converted the room next to theirs into a nursery, and Gram is just on the other side so they can take care of her as her Alzheimer's progresses. Micah thinks he's located his sister, Jenna. I told you about her back in November. She and Micah were sent to separate foster homes as children, and he's been looking for her.

We stopped by Bubba's for lunch last week, and one of your friends that you worked with, I think her name was Kayley (??), asked about you and said to tell you hello. I almost gave her your address but didn't know if you wanted her to have it, so I didn't. She made over Grace and said she has your eyes and coloring, which is totally true.

Linn flipped over the page, already looking forward to seeing the pictures of Grace.

Well, I've rambled long enough. Write or call when you get a chance, and let us know how you're doing.

Love,

Natalie, Kyle, Alex, Taylor, and Grace

Linn folded the letter and returned it to the envelope before taking out the bunch of photos. Her heart squeezed at the first one. It was her little Gracie, snuggled up in a yellow fleecy blanket, her eyes closed in sleep. All you could see of her was her head and her little fist tucked up against her ear. The photo was a bit fuzzy, as if Natalie had gotten too close to her subject. Linn reached out her finger and touched the photo, almost expecting to feel the softness of Grace's skin. The next two pictures were from the hospital, when Linn had given birth to Grace.

She flipped to the next picture and smiled. Alex wore a Santa hat and was holding Grace on his lap. The next photo widened her smile. Grace was snuggled up asleep inside a Christmas stocking. She stared at her baby, her heart hurting. She wished so badly she could reach into this picture and sweep Gracie up in her arms. She would plant butterfly kisses all over her baby-soft skin and whisper in her ear that her mommy loved her.

Linn swallowed over the achy lump in her throat. *I did what was best for Grace. It makes me hurt, but it was the best thing for Grace.*

It was what she always told herself when her heart started hurting the way it sometimes did. Even more, she knew it was the truth. Grace couldn't have a better family than she had now. Even though Natalie and Kyle weren't the birth parents, they loved Grace as if they were. And in all truth, Alex and Taylor *were* Grace's real half brothers, even though they didn't know that.

Her thoughts spun back to when she'd met Keith at the bank. The affair had started innocently enough, with his giving her a ride home. It wasn't like she'd plunged right into a relationship with a married man. But one thing had led to another, and before she knew it, she'd been swept up in a whirlwind of emotions she couldn't seem to escape—no matter how wrong it was.

Even though she didn't know Natalie at the time, she should have respected Keith's wedding vows enough to end the affair, even if he didn't. But it hadn't ended that way at all. Instead, Keith divorced his wife, leaving Natalie a single mother of two boys.

At the time Linn thought she had it made. She got her way, at least for a while. But then after the divorce, when she thought everything would end happily ever after, he broke it off.

That's when she found out she was pregnant.

Linn looked at the next photo Natalie had sent. Natalie, Grace, Alex, and Taylor were all squeezed into the recliner that used to be Linn's favorite place to sit. Taylor was making a fish face, and Natalie was looking at him, in the middle of saying something. Grace's eyes were open, and she was staring straight at Alex. Kyle had probably taken the photo.

They made a nice-looking family. But then, Natalie, Keith, and the boys had probably been a nice-looking family until Linn had stepped in and ruined everything.

Stop it. That's all in the past. Why are you ragging on yourself for something you can't change?

It was true. She couldn't go back and change it. If it were to happen today, she knew God would help her make the right decision. No, she would never even think of stealing another woman's—

The thought stopped her cold. She remembered the kiss she shared with Adam. The kiss she invited and enjoyed. The kiss she wanted to go on forever. She kissed Adam when he was engaged to another woman.

She tensed as reality hit her. No, it wasn't the same thing. Adam wasn't married.

But he's engaged.

It wasn't the same thing, was it? But no matter how she tried to justify it, she knew an engagement was a promise. One she helped Adam break. One he clearly felt guilty about breaking. But what had Linn been feeling other than the selfish desire to have things her own way? She was doing it again. She was making the same stupid mistake all over again.

Oh, God, why do I find myself in these messes?

She closed her eyes, feeling the sting of tears all the way down through the bridge of her nose. *What is wrong with me? Why can't I just find a nice single guy like everyone else? Why do I keep going after the taken ones?*

She opened her eyes and considered the next picture of Grace, cuddled up in her carrier. The last time she made the mistake of taking someone else's man, she broke up a family and ended up pregnant, with her heart thoroughly broken. All the pleasure in the world wasn't worth that pain.

But then there was Adam and the feelings that beckoned her like a tropical island during a winter blizzard in Chicago.

A thought hit with sudden intensity, like a thunderbolt, and she knew what she had to do. It wouldn't be easy, it might take awhile, and she knew God would have to do it. Because she wasn't strong enough to do it alone.

CHAPTER
TWENTY-FOUR

After Paula left Louise's house, she drove back to her apartment. But instead of going inside, she walked. Putting one foot in front of the other was all she could do.

Now, as she stared out over the frigid shoreline of Lake Michigan, she wasn't even sure how she had come to be there. If someone were to ask what route she took, she would have to shake her head and say, "I have no idea." She was struck now by the irony that the same philosophy applied to her life.

How had she come to this point? Where had she taken a wrong turn? All day her mind skirted the real issue. She thought about Louise's actions; she even thought of Faith. But she danced around the main issue like a moth flitting around a streetlight—close enough to investigate but far enough to avoid getting burned.

She wasn't sure it was safe to get any closer.

Her gaze traveled over the still lake that absorbed the wet snowflakes as if they'd never fallen. *Faith*. She kept thinking about Faith. She wished she could picture the child more clearly. All she could remember was the girl's fine, brown curls and striking green eyes.

Eyes the color of her own.

She leaned against the railing and closed her eyes, letting the cold air slap her in the face. Even now, after hours of dwelling on it, it still seemed surreal. Her thoughts were mush, like a sticky stack of old pancakes. For the first time she wished she was more like her mother and sisters. They would have been on the phone with their closest friend by now, talking out their problem and getting advice. Their friend would have offered to pray for them, and they would have gotten off the phone feeling better about everything.

But Paula had no one to call. Her closest friend was David, and she couldn't tell him this. Besides that, her mother and sisters would never be in this place because they never would have done what she did.

Her bangs whipped across her face, but she didn't move to tuck them back into place. It was pointless anyway, the way the wind swirled around her like a tornado.

David. She'd kept her secret from him, thinking it buried and gone forever. Now it had come back to haunt her, and what could she do? She couldn't tell David the truth now. He would never forgive her. It would only tear them apart again, and this time, Paula was sure, the breach would never be repaired.

She stood upright and began walking along the shoreline. Placing one foot in front of the other. She'd been thinking all day, and yet she knew she'd only skimmed the surface. She was self-aware enough to know she'd held back from going any deeper. She wasn't sure she could handle dredging all the way to the bottom of this mire. She was afraid of what she'd find. For the first time in her life, she didn't have a battle plan. Didn't want a battle plan and didn't even want a battle at all.

She wanted to go back to yesterday, before she knew. She wanted to go back to that day Deb had called her and asked her to investigate the story. She wanted to—

She wanted to go back three years ago and make a different decision.

She stopped, her Jimmy Choos scuffing to a halt on the wet pavement. Her breath felt as heavy as mercury in her lungs and every bit as poisonous.

The ache traveled upward and lodged in the middle of her throat.

The back of her eyes ached with an intensity she'd never felt. She couldn't see the shoreline anymore or the snow that blew around her. All she could see was the horror of her decision three years ago.

Like a nearsighted woman slipping on a pair of glasses, she could see the wrongness of that decision with sudden clarity. Glaring clarity. She wanted to take the glasses off and forget what she'd seen. She wanted to go back to the way she viewed things before.

It's my choice because it's my body. It's not a baby anyway, only a bunch of cells. Now is not a good time for me to get pregnant. It's not my fault I'm pregnant anyway, so why should I have to suffer the consequences? We'll have a baby later, when it's more convenient.

There were a dozen more arguments where those came from. But they all seemed like lies now. Paula reminded herself why she'd done it. Her job. Her promotion. Her career. They were important to her. Her career was the most important thing in her life.

The words rang empty in her mind. So empty and shallow. She had an abortion—she tried to take the life of her child for reasons so shallow? She remembered how David had wanted to come to Chicago to be with her after her "miscarriage" and how she insisted she'd be fine and would come home the next day anyway. She remembered the way he held her when she arrived home—how he wept into her hair.

It had hurt to see him that way. She'd never seen him cry. But even then, she stuffed the guilt away. She told herself she did what was best for them, but the truth was, she did it only for herself. She told herself it was only a mass of tissue, not a real baby. She convinced herself of that, regardless of what she was told growing up in church.

But her thoughts went back to what Louise said: "*The fetus was breathing. Her little chest was going up and down so fast. Then Dr. Miller turned to me and put the infant in my hands—and it* was *an infant to me at that moment. She looked no different to me than the tiny babies whose lives I fought so hard for in the NICU.*"

Paula's hand covered her mouth. She could deny it before. Deny that the abortion was wrong. Deny that she'd done anything other than make a choice. But how could she believe that when she'd birthed a *baby*?

A little girl who'd lived despite Paula's efforts to—

She closed her eyes and swallowed the bile that rose in the back of her throat.

"The fetus was breathing."

I didn't know. I didn't know.

"Her little chest was going up and down so fast."

Oh, God, what did I do? I'm so sorry! I'm so sorry.

"Get rid of it. Get rid of it. Get rid of it . . ."

No. No. Louise hadn't done it, but Paula had intended to. She had planned to get rid of it. But it wasn't an *it*. It was a child. A little girl. The Morgans' little girl.

"I remember standing there, staring at this miniature human being. Her eyes were sealed shut, and I could see her heart's movement through her thin skin." Paula couldn't get Louise's horrified expression out of her mind. The woman had had more compassion for Paula's child than she'd had!

Louise's words rang in her head, overlapping, mixing together, blending with the look of horror that would be etched in Paula's brain forever. She rubbed at her temples with frozen fingers, wishing she could scrub it all away. She was tired of thinking of this awful thing, and now she knew this was something she would never be free of.

Would she ever have peace again? Did she deserve to have peace?

"Get rid of it. Get rid of it . . ."

Such cruel, heartless words. But three years ago those same words had fluttered around her own mind. *I can't be pregnant right now. I've come too far in my career to let it stall. I'll lose the promotion if I don't just get rid of it. Get rid of it. Get rid of it . . .*

Paula's hands clapped over her ears, as if she could block out the words. But they were coming from inside her.

"The fetus was breathing. Her little chest was going up and down."

She closed her eyes, trying to shut it out. She didn't want to hear it.

Couldn't stand the thought of what she'd done. The thought of having to live with this knowledge for the rest of her life. Would Louise's words ring in her head forever?

She thought of the words she'd captured on tape that day, and her eyes flew open. Sliding the bag off her shoulder, she tore through the contents until she found the tape recorder. She ejected the tape from the machine. In one motion she grabbed the tape and flung it out into the lake as far as her arm could throw it. It disappeared into the dark abyss, just like the snowflakes. But the tape left ripples, ringing outward, growing in size as they traveled away from the epicenter.

Paula turned away from the shoreline and walked. She tried to think about something else, but like a low, wet fog, the thoughts smothered her, seeped into her. She crossed Lake Shore Drive and stumbled back toward her apartment. A street bum lay haphazardly in the corner of an apartment stoop, his blanket wrapped around him, a stocking cap pulled low on his face.

She studied the skyscrapers that would come alive on Monday morning. She thought of her career and how far she'd come. She'd always been a person things came easily to. Whatever she put her mind to do, she succeeded at. She'd even been voted Most Likely to Succeed.

She'd never felt more like a loser than she did now. She was as low as the street bum she just passed. He probably never did anything as awful as she.

Somehow she made it back to her apartment building. When the doorman's smile faltered as he bade her good evening, she realized she must look as distressed as she felt. She didn't care.

She took the elevator to her floor, looking forward to the peace and quiet of her apartment. Maybe it would calm her.

She slid the key into the lock and turned it, pushing the door open. The sound of a TV program drifted to her ears, then she saw Linn sitting on the sofa with a fat textbook open in her lap. Paula's spirits sank to a new low.

"Hi," Linn said cheerfully. Then her smile slid off her face like water off a metal roof. "What happened?"

Paula inwardly cursed the bright overhead lighting. She wanted to paste on her TV smile and pretend. But the tone of alarm in Linn's voice told her it was no use. And Paula didn't have the energy to fake anything tonight. Not even a smile.

"Rough day." Her words croaked out. It was the first time she'd spoken since she'd said good-bye to Louise. She cleared her throat. "Maybe I'm getting a cold."

Paula slid out of her coat and draped it across the back of the sofa. When she kicked off her heels, she realized for the first time that her toes were stiff and achy.

"Are you all right, Paula?"

She heard the whoosh of Linn's book closing and the creak of the sofa springs.

"Nothing to worry about," she said. "I think I'm coming down with something. I'm going to lie down." Maybe if she kept her back to Linn, she could hold it together. She could do it. If she could only make it to her room. Suddenly she was so tired she felt like she could sleep a week. The prospect sounded like bliss. Blissful oblivion.

"Can I get you something? Some ibuprofen or a glass of water?"

"No, but thanks." Paula fled to her room, where she slid under the duvet, clothes and all. Her pant legs rode up to her knees, sliding easily against her hose. She wrapped the covers around her like her own private cocoon, but she couldn't get warm. She wondered if she would ever be warm again.

CHAPTER
TWENTY-FIVE

Even in the darkness there was a certain peace. Paula knew she was about to do something big, but she couldn't quite remember what. Even still, she knew it was OK. It would all be OK.

She heard voices around her, soothing and caring. Was she drugged? Maybe she was because she couldn't remember ever feeling quite like this before. She was so relaxed, she was almost giddy. She put her hand over her mouth to stop the giggle. What would they think?

A bright light turned on, and she blinked at the intensity of it. It blinded her and made her eyes squint and ache.

"All right, Paula, we're about to get started." It was Donald, her old boss from WKEV in Jackson. She closed her eyes when she heard it. He was a competent man. She could trust him to do whatever needed to be done.

"We're starting the procedure now," he said. "Everything is going just fine."

In the quiet of the room, she could hear the sound of metal clinking. Another sound caught her ears, a humming. She nearly opened her eyes to see what it was, then remembered she had her tape recorder running. Good thing, because she couldn't take notes if she tried. Her limbs felt as heavy as tree trunks.

"Here it comes," Donald said, his calm tones washing over her like a gentle wave. "OK, I've got it."

Paula tried to look to see what was going on. There was a crowd of people at her feet. Two of them had notepads and were furiously scrawling away. No matter. Everything was fine.

Then Donald took something from her, and she suddenly knew it was the baby who had been inside her. Yes, she'd been pregnant, hadn't she?

"What are you doing?" she asked.

The tiny body in his hands was gray blue. Was the baby breathing?

"Please, you've got to help her!" The fog had worn off her brain, but her body was immobilized. "Help her!"

Donald didn't seem to hear her. He handed the baby to one of the reporters. "Get rid of it," he said in a soft, soothing voice.

The reporter started for the door, holding the baby away from his body as if it were contagious.

"Stop! Bring her back!" She tried to sit up, but her body felt as if it were Superglued to the bed. "Please! Bring my baby back!"

Everyone moved about the room as if not hearing her.

"Please! Come back!"

"Paula?" The voice was coming from the closet or someplace far away. But she couldn't think about that. She had to get her baby back.

"Come back! That's my baby!"

"Paula."

Someone was shaking her, but she resisted. *My baby. Is she alive?*

"Paula, wake up."

Her eyes opened to the darkness. Somewhere outside the window a truck accelerated. She recognized the form beside her as Linn.

A dream. It had only been a dream. Her hair was matted and wet against her cheek.

"You were having a nightmare."

And now she was awake, but not really. The nightmare continued, but it was real. Paula wiped her face dry with the sheet.

"Are you all right?" Linn asked.

Was she all right? Would she ever be?

Paula glanced at the alarm clock and saw by the red digital numbers it was the middle of the night. She must've been calling out to have awakened Linn at this hour. What did she say? It was the worst nightmare she'd ever had. There was just enough truth to make it haunting. She remembered the tiny gray-blue body. Was her baby the color of death when she was born?

"Are you all right?" Linn asked again.

Paula shook her head, her hair tangling on the pillow. She wasn't all right. She'd tried to murder her baby, then buried the secret from her husband and everyone else. She lied about it a hundred times. Pretended to grieve her child . . . all the while denying it had been a child to begin with.

She turned her face into the pillow, letting the material soak up her tears. She felt Linn's hand brushing her damp hair off her face, tucking it behind her ear.

"Do you want to talk about it?" Linn asked.

It wasn't a matter of wanting to. It was a matter of having to. The feelings were so volatile that they had to come out.

"I had an abortion." The word sounded harsh and cold. She was suddenly so ashamed. She wanted to go back to sleep, but there was no escape there, either.

"Oh, Paula, I'm so sorry."

The sympathy in Linn's voice was enough to make Paula want to wail. But she turned over on her back and wiped her face dry.

"I didn't realize you were pregnant. Did you have it yesterday?"

Paula shook her head, trying to understand. "No. Not yesterday. A long time ago. Three years ago."

"Oh." The city lights seeped through the curtains, providing only murky details of Linn's face, but Paula could hear from her tone that she was confused. Of course Linn thought the abortion must be recent to evoke this kind of emotion. But that was because she didn't know the full story. So Paula told the story, starting with the news of her pregnancy and ending with her meeting with Louise.

By the time she finished, a weight had lifted from her.

"Oh, man," Linn said. "So that baby, that other family's baby, is yours?"

Paula couldn't believe she'd told a nineteen-year-old kid her biggest secret. And yet, strangely, she wasn't worried.

"So you can see, my world is a little turned upside down right now," Paula said.

"No kidding." Linn shifted on the bed, her knee hitching up beside Paula. "You're in a real difficult spot."

"It's just so much; I don't know how to begin processing it. There's the fact that I had an abortion to begin with. The fact that I hid it from David. The reality that our child is alive. And the thought of what I did . . . I mean, I didn't see it as a child at the time, you know? I only saw it as a medical procedure. Or at least that's what I told myself."

"I know. I know."

The tone of Linn's voice made Paula pause. Then she remembered that Linn nearly had an abortion before she asked Natalie to adopt her baby. "That's right. I'd forgotten."

"I was really scared when I found out I was pregnant. When I went into the Hope Center, I was dead set on having an abortion if I was pregnant. Your sister changed all that."

Paula had never wanted to be more like Natalie than in that moment. Why hadn't someone pointed *her* in the right direction? Then Paula remembered how she hid her feelings about the pregnancy and how adamantly she felt about her promotion at the time. She wouldn't have listened. She had chosen long ago to put her career before anything else.

"I went through guilt and regret after Grace was born just because I'd planned to abort the pregnancy. I can only imagine what you must be feeling."

"I'm not even sure I felt guilt about it before now. I felt guilt about lying to David, but I'm not sure I did about the abortion. I'd convinced myself I hadn't done anything wrong. But yesterday was like having blinders removed." Paula closed her eyes. "I wish I could put them back on again."

"No, you don't. That might be easier, but it wouldn't be healthy."

Paula opened her eyes and stared at Linn. "You're pretty smart for a nineteen-year-old."

"Unfortunately, I've had to learn things the hard way."

Silence settled around them. The kind that settles slowly down on you like snow on the ground. Paula was wide awake now, as if it were the afternoon and she'd just awakened from a nap. The monumental size of her discovery hit her freshly.

What would she tell the Morgans? She'd found their child's birth parent, and it was her?

Oh, God, are You there? I know I've ignored You for a long time, but I need help. I need to know what to do.

Linn broke the silence. "How are you going to tell David?"

Paula stared at the girl through the darkness. "Tell David? I can't do that, Linn." David would never forgive her for this. It would be the end of their marriage if he found out she tried to abort the child he wanted and lied about it. Lied about it for three years. No, he'd never forgive her.

"Paula, you have to tell him. He has a child who's living, and he doesn't even know it."

Paula gave a dry laugh. "You don't understand. David and I just came through a rough time in our marriage. I know him. This would ruin us forever."

"You can't keep something like this from your husband. It's not fair." The words were spoken gently, but they grated on Paula.

"Well, in case you haven't figured it out yet, life isn't fair."

"Maybe not, but I know one thing. Honesty may be harder in the short run, but secrets always come out. And when they do, they cause more pain than ever."

Linn rushed through the door of Java Joe and made her way behind the counter. She'd been running late all morning, from the time she got up for church after only half a night's sleep to nearly missing the bus after church. Now she was ten minutes late for work.

Adam had a line of customers he was trying to serve on his own.

"Sorry I'm late."

Adam looked stressed, and his smile was nowhere in sight.

She felt awful.

"Americano, three shots." He handed her a cup.

Great, he was mad at her too. Between Adam and Paula, maybe she could just alienate everyone in her life so she could be friendless *and* homeless.

She started the espresso and peeked at Adam from the corner of her eyes. He was definitely mad. He wasn't smiling and making small talk with the customers like he usually did. Of course, the day before he hadn't quite been himself either. Their kiss two nights ago had left him distant and on guard. He clearly regretted it and that hurt.

You dope, you regret it too. Yes, she regretted it, but only because it had been wrong. *That's the same reason he regrets it, stupid.*

She poured the three shots into the cup and added the steaming water. After topping it with a lid, she pushed it across the counter. "Americano." She offered a smile to the middle-aged guy.

He smiled back. "Thanks."

Adam continued to slide cups toward her on the counter until there was only one customer remaining. As he rung up the woman's smoothie, Linn went to the back to make it. She poured a cupful of milk and ice into the blender, then added strawberries. She put on the lid and punched the button. The machine noisily ground up the ice. Joe's office door was shut, which meant he was probably on the phone. When the mixture was smooth, she turned off the blender.

Only when the machine whirred to a stop did she hear a scuffling beside her. She turned. Adam stood several feet away, feet planted shoulder distance apart, arms crossed. The stance looked odd on him.

She turned back to the blender, took off the lid, and poured the smoothie into the clear cup. Her hands shook.

"When were you going to tell me?" Adam asked.

"What?" Her heart caught a chill from his tone.

"You don't have to quit."

Oh. Joe had told him. "I didn't quit; I just told him I would be looking for another job." Her fingers fumbled to get the plastic lid on. In her rush, it ripped. She took it off and grabbed another one from the stack.

"You didn't have to do that."

His voice . . . was it anger or something else? She wasn't sure she wanted to know.

She picked up the smoothie and walked toward the front. She stopped when she reached him because he blocked her path. "Excuse me," she said, careful to keep her eyes down.

He stepped to the side and she passed. The woman took her smoothie, and Linn saw that another customer had arrived. She rang up the teenager's latte, and Adam returned from the back in time to make it. Linn found herself wishing another customer would come in before he finished the latte. But by the time Adam had slid the drink across the counter, the store was empty except for two customers sitting at tables on the far side of the room.

She picked up a rag and wiped the counter, taking care to stay far away from the spot where Adam was leaning. Leaning and staring. At her.

How would she get through the day like this? This was even worse than yesterday had been. Yes, it had been hurtful to be avoided and virtually ignored by the guy who'd kissed you the night before. But even that was better than feeling as though she'd done something wrong. What was he so mad about anyway?

"Why are you quitting?" His voice sounded less angry now, but she wouldn't look at him.

"You know why." She scrubbed at a spot by the register. Did she have to spell it out for him? She liked him. Way too much. And—newsflash—he was engaged to someone else.

"I don't want you to quit."

He sounded sad, and she definitely wasn't looking at him now. She turned and cleaned the counter by the syrups. How was she supposed to come to work and be with him, be so close to him, when it was painfully clear she couldn't have him? She'd made up her mind on the bus yesterday that she would remove herself from temptation. Who was he, a future pastor, no less, to discourage her from that? Did he want her to make all the same painful mistakes she had made in the past? Didn't he know she already had a lifetime of regrets, and she wasn't even twenty? But no, he didn't know that because she'd never told him.

"You're mad at me."

It was only then that Linn realized she was scrubbing a little zealously. She eased up. "No, I'm not."

It was the truth. She wasn't mad at him. She was mad at herself. Mad at the circumstances. Mad that every stinking time she really fell for a guy, he was already taken.

She tossed the rag into the sink and went to the back to rinse out the blender. She had to get away from him. Didn't he understand it was too hard to be around him? How could she continue to resist him if she was working side by side with him nearly every day?

She took the blender container off and held it under the faucet.

"We need to talk, Linn. We can't just keep acting like that kiss never happened."

Just the thought of the kiss made her melt. As if time had rewound, all the emotions she felt when he kissed her sprang up all over again. The way she felt treasured and precious by the way he touched her. Then, just as real, the pain she felt when he pulled away and apologized.

"Sure we can." Her flippant tone belied the ache behind her eyes.

Don't start blubbering, Linn. Don't.

"This isn't right. You need this job, and you know it."

Yeah, I also need my sanity, and you're robbing me of it.

She'd only just arrived for work, and she already wished she was done for the day. Where were those customers when she needed them?

"I can find something else." She dumped the water from the blender and rinsed it again.

"Just stay. We'll work it out."

"There's nothing to work out, Adam."

He leaned against the counter beside her. "There is, too, and you know it."

His eyes drew hers until they met. Big mistake. He had the same look on his face that time when he took her home. When he told her he was confused about what he wanted. And she figured out he meant Elizabeth. She'd lain in bed for hours wondering how he could doubt his relationship with her. Elizabeth was perfect for him in every way. Perfect for the job of minister's wife. That he was even having feelings for Linn had at first pleased her, then shocked her. Could there be anyone less suited or less deserving of a pastor? Linn should have started looking for another job right then.

She tore her eyes away. "It was just a kiss."

"Was it? It was a lot more than that to me."

Say it. Say it didn't mean that much to you. Say it, Linn. Her dry lips clung to her teeth.

His eyes narrowed. "I think it was more than that to you too. I know it was wrong of me to kiss you, but I've been doing a lot of soul-searching since Thursday night."

Hope kindled inside her. He was engaged, but he did care about her. She could see it in his eyes. Had felt it in his kiss.

Stupid. That's exactly the way you thought about Keith. "He's married, but he cares about me." And then you broke up a marriage, ripped a daddy away from two little boys, and got pregnant in the process. Smooth, Linn. Are you going to work your charm on Adam too?

"I know I was a jerk for kissing you. But just the fact that I did, or even the fact that I wanted to, sends up red flags all over the place, you know?"

Red flags. What was he talking about?

"What I'm trying to say is I've decided to break it off with Elizabeth."

A crazy mixture of joy and anguish flooded Linn. As much as she cared about Adam, she was all wrong for him. Couldn't he see that? He didn't even know the horrible things she'd done. He probably thought she was as naive as Elizabeth. She was too ashamed to tell him otherwise.

She forced herself to say the words. "You shouldn't do that."

"Why not?" His eyes searched hers.

She looked down at the blender she still held before he read the truth. "Elizabeth is perfect for you."

"If she's so perfect, why do I want you?" He reached out and touched her elbow.

Even through the sweater, her skin responded to his touch. She crossed her arms, making his hand fall away. This was so unfair. He wasn't making this easy.

"You don't want me," she said. "You're just confused. You said so before."

"An engaged man shouldn't be confused. He shouldn't be having the kinds of feelings—the kinds of feelings I'm having for you."

Her heart felt heavy, as if pressed down by the weight of the world, and there didn't seem to be room for the oxygen trying to enter her lungs. He was saying all the things she wanted to hear, but it was wrong. So wrong. She was all wrong for Adam. He just didn't know it.

"I know we don't know each other very well." He shrugged. "Shoot, I probably shouldn't even be saying these things to you yet." His gaze focused on hers with an intensity she felt all the way to the soles of her feet. "But I'd like the opportunity to get to know you."

Oh, God, help me. I need to do the right thing, but I don't want to.

She turned away and began picturing all the things she'd done that disqualified her from Adam's future. Like a stopwatch, they ticked off, one after another:

I had an affair with a married man.

I broke up his marriage.

I got pregnant out of wedlock.

I almost had an abortion.

I tried to trick my lover's ex-wife into adopting the baby—

"Did you hear me, Linn? I want to know you better. I want to know what you do when you're scared. I want to know what makes you laugh. I want to know everything about your past—what makes you who you are and what you hope to become."

No, he would never know about her past. She could only imagine the horror this pastor-in-the-making would feel if he knew everything she'd done. She steeled herself to say the words forming on her tongue. Steeled herself against the pain they would bring, both hers and his.

She tossed her head. "Like I'd have anything to do with a guy who'd betray his fiancée."

She knew the words had hit their mark by the deafening silence.

She couldn't look at him. If she saw the pain she'd caused, she would want to erase everything she just said. And she couldn't do that.

Think of what's best for Adam. Think of what's best for Adam.

Her words might hurt him for a moment, but in the long run they were what he needed to hear. Maybe if he knew there was no chance with Linn, he would rethink his plan to break up with Elizabeth.

He cleared his throat. "I guess that's fair." His words were basted in disappointment.

No, it wasn't fair. It wasn't fair at all. Not for Adam. If she hadn't made a royal mess of her life, she might have been good enough for him.

"I'm sorry, Linn, if I hurt you." His tone beckoned her, but she ignored the call. "And, regardless of what happens, I have to tell Elizabeth what I did."

Linn's eyes flew to his. The past was reliving itself. Now Elizabeth would think she was a tramp just like Natalie must have when she found out about the affair.

"I won't tell her who it was. But I can't keep this from her." His eyes were slick as ice but a whole lot warmer. "I hope you understand."

In the distance the bell over the door sounded. A customer. She set the blender in the base and dried her hands on a paper towel. When she turned, Adam was gone.

CHAPTER
TWENTY-SIX

The next morning Paula was in a fog. She wasn't sure she could fake her way through the week when she was torn to shreds on the inside.

When she arrived at her desk, following an interview for an evening story, she found a white envelope. It was a regular, business-size envelope, devoid of writing and sealed. She unsealed the corner of the flap, took out the white piece of paper, and unfolded it.

I know what you know.
If you air the story,
you'll be sorry.

Anger rolled in like dark clouds. She was tired of feeling threatened and wished she could air the story just to spite whoever it was. For a minute she considered turning the envelope in to the police. Maybe they could lift a fingerprint and catch this creep. But there would be questions for her to answer, and Miles would have to be made aware of the note. How would she explain it?

No, she didn't want or need questions like that right now. She wadded up the paper and envelope and tossed it into the trash can. Her tormentor was going to get exactly what he wanted, whether Paula liked it or not.

David sat at his kitchen table and opened his laptop. After he connected to the Internet, he pointed the cursor at his inbox where it showed he had one message. He clicked on it and disappointment flooded him. Why hadn't Paula responded to his last two e-mails? He checked his Sent box to make sure they'd gone out. They had.

Discomfort constricted his gut. He knew she was busy, but it had been four days since he'd heard from Paula. Maybe he should just call her. He checked the clock and saw that it was way too early for her to be in bed.

He fished his cell phone from his pocket and dialed her on her Jackson cell phone. It rang so long, he thought Paula must have it turned off.

"Hello?" she croaked.

"Paula? You sound sick."

There was a pause before she answered. "David? No, I just went to bed early."

Paula never retired early. She had too much energy for that.

As if reading his mind, she justified the answer. "I didn't sleep well last night, so I figured I'd catch up."

"That's not like you. Why didn't you sleep well?"

"Oh, I—was up talking to Linn. You know, some crisis that came up." Her voice sounded guarded, like the old Paula. Something had happened.

"Are you all right? Have you had another threat?"

"No." Her answer was quick. "No, everything's fine."

David checked the time. He regretted that he had to leave for Bible study in a few minutes. "I was starting to worry. You haven't answered my e-mails."

"Oh." He could almost hear her wincing. "I'm sorry, David; I haven't checked my e-mail in a couple of days. Just busy, you know?"

"Sure. Sure." The only thing he was sure of was that something wasn't right. Paula wasn't trading barbs or flirting like she had lately. Of course, he had just woken her up.

"Did I miss something important? I'll go check it right now." He could hear the rustling of bedding.

"No, you can read them later. It was nothing important. I was just starting to worry because I hadn't heard from you since Friday. I'm wishing we hadn't decided to leave you in Chicago this weekend." He remembered their phone conversation. "Hey, how did that interview go? The one for the Morgan story."

She paused so long he thought he'd lost his connection. "Paula?"

"Yeah. Yeah, it went fine." Her voice was cheerful. Overly so.

"But did you learn anything? You'd thought this woman knew something."

"Oh. Oh, right. Well, she remembered a lot, but I don't think it's anything that will be helpful to the Morgans. Did you just get home from work?"

"Yes, and unfortunately I have to leave in a minute. To go to Bible study."

"Really?" She sounded distracted.

"It's not boring like I thought it would be. I'm learning a lot."

"That's great, David."

"How about you? Have you gone back to that church we visited?"

As soon as he said it, he knew he sounded preachy. He wished he could take back the question. Paula always hated it when her family pressured her about church. David hated it too. But that was before he realized how much it helped him.

"It wasn't my style, really. Maybe I'll try and find another one." The words sounded thoughtful, as if she considered it a good idea. That gave him a bit of hope.

"That's a great idea."

"Maybe I'll try Linn's church."

"Hey, hon, I have to go, or I'm going to be late."

She said good-bye, and he punched the End button.

Paula closed the cell phone and lay back on the bed. How could she have forgotten to check her e-mail? Now David was suspicious. She could hear it in his voice. Maybe she'd set his fears, whatever they were, to rest. But one thing was certain: she needed to get it together by Friday. At the moment she felt like she was running on fumes. She didn't know how she'd make it through the workweek, much less how she'd face David and continue to act like everything was fine.

Work would hold its own challenges this week. Now that she'd found an answer for the Morgans, what would she do with it? Her plan to cover the story and reveal the truth couldn't happen now.

And what about the Morgans? Would she just keep them in the dark? Would she hide from them the one thing they wanted desperately to know?

Well, she was an expert at hiding things, wasn't she? She had years of practice. Feeling more trapped by the minute, Paula threw off the covers and worked her feet free of the tangle of bedclothes. She wished she could as easily untangle the mess she'd made.

It would be cruel to hide her findings from the Morgans, yet how could she tell them the truth? Not only had their birth baby died, but Faith was *Paula's* birth child. The product of a botched abortion. *Paula's abortion.*

She pictured Faith as best she could remember. Remembered Faith snuggling up against her father's neck. Limping out of the living room with her cerebral palsy gait.

The thought stopped her cold. CP could result from being born prematurely, couldn't it? The child had this disease because Paula hadn't carried her pregnancy to full term. More guilt slipped in.

Then another thought hit her like a wall of ice. Hadn't Louise said something about cerebral palsy? Something about babies who lived through the process were often left with deafness or CP? Maybe Paula wasn't remembering right. She almost wished she still had the tape.

The computer. She could find that information online. Paula jumped out of bed and headed toward the corner of the living area, grateful that Linn was at work. She sank into the high-backed leather chair and Googled the words *botched abortion* and *cerebral palsy*.

A page of links came up—the first one titled "Survivors of Abortion." She clicked on the link. It was the first-person account of a girl who had survived an abortion. Paula skimmed through the entry until she came to the words she was looking for.

"I was diagnosed with cerebral palsy as a result of the abortion."

The words blurred on the screen.

It was true, then. It was her fault. Not wanting to read any more, Paula closed out the screen. Her head thunked back against the high-backed leather chair while everything inside seemed to hollow out. Her body felt like a brittle shell wrapped around an empty space.

Oh, God, will the repercussions ever end? How could I have caused so much damage with one decision?

The abortion caused a rift between her and David, though he didn't know the cause of it.

It caused the cerebral palsy Faith now lived with. It caused Louise to carry a load of guilt and fear. It caused the Morgans untold pain when they found out Faith wasn't their birth child. What would it do to them if they found out their own birth child had died?

They wouldn't. Paula couldn't bear to tell them. To tell them their child had died alone, except for the concern of one nurse. Better that they never know.

Paula closed her eyes. Another secret. She was treading neck deep in secrets, and they were about to drown her.

<hr />

Paula was washing her hands two days later in the station's washroom when Cindy walked in. Cindy bent over and peeked under the three stalls before turning to meet Paula's eyes in the mirror.

"Did you hear about Darrick?" she said.

The only thing Paula had heard this week about Darrick was all the hoopla over his last story. "Please tell me it's good news."

Cindy smiled. "It is good, at least for you. You know that story he broke last week about the CEO of Edmonton's? Turns out that sexual harassment charge was bogus."

"Bogus? What do you mean?"

"All Darrick did was interview the woman. He didn't get the full story, and he didn't double check his facts. The woman who accused the CEO was recently denied a promotion. She cracked this morning and told the truth. To WANE."

It wasn't good for Darrick at all. To have another station correcting his inaccurate coverage wasn't good for the station either. "How's Miles taking it?"

"Oh, man, he's fit to be tied." Cindy's eyes shone as she grabbed Paula's sleeve. "This is great news for you."

"I see now why you looked under the stalls."

"Hey, I'm not stupid." Cindy turned to leave the room. "Play your cards right, lady, and you're a shoo-in."

Adrenaline accompanied Paula all the way to her desk. She got the tape from her most recent interview and began writing the copy for the story that would appear on the evening news: a local high-school basketball player who was expected to get a full-ride scholarship to Indiana University. His high-school coaches thought he might be good enough to go straight to the NBA, but his mother insisted he go to college first.

She was halfway through the copy when her phone rang. Still distracted by the story, she answered it.

"Hi, Paula. It's Deb."

She jerked back to reality. "Deb. Hello."

"I'm sorry to bother you, but I'm actually just outside the station."

Paula heard Faith in the background pleading for something. Her heart squeezed.

"Anyway, I wanted to talk. Do you have a few minutes where I can come up? I have Faith with me." Deb said it like an apology, but the words filled Paula with longing. She yearned to stare at Faith, into every feature of her face and see the resemblance that must be there. Did she have David's cowlick? Paula's smile?

"Paula? If it's not a good time, I understand. Maybe we can set up a time to talk on the phone."

"No, no. Now is fine. Come on up. I'll tell Cindy at the desk to send you back. We're on the fifth floor."

"Great. Thanks, Paula."

When she hung up, she called Cindy and told her Deb was coming. Paula took her compact out of her purse and used the puff to blot away the shine on her forehead. She straightened her hair, tucking it behind her ears.

"You're wasting your time."

She glanced up to see Stan, the information-technology guy, walking by, a sucker stick protruding from his mouth.

He smiled. "Can't improve upon perfection."

She grinned at him as he passed. Another man might say the same thing and be smarmy about it, but Stan was as harmless as a puppy.

She put her compact back in her bag and turned her thoughts to what Deb wanted to talk about. She would want to know if Paula had found out anything. As much as she wanted to see Faith, Paula hated to lie to Deb.

Oh what a tangled web we weave, when first we practice to deceive! The old proverb flashed in her mind like a beacon on the shore of Lake Michigan. She'd never felt the truth of it as she did now. But the lie had started three years ago, and there seemed no way to fix it now. Telling the truth would only cause untold pain and damage. *There should be a proverb explaining how to get out of the web once it was already woven.* But she felt like a fly trapped in the intricate and sticky pattern.

She would think of something to tell Deb. For now all she wanted to think about was seeing Faith again. She wanted to hold her and tell her how beautiful and special she was, but that would seem odd since Paula had barely even acknowledged the child before. She glanced around the office and spotted the jar of suckers on Stan's desk. Perfect.

She approached Stan and asked to borrow the candy jar. He was more than happy to accommodate. Her hands shook as she set the jar, filled with all flavors of Dum Dums, on the corner of her desk. She wanted Faith to like her, even if the little girl couldn't know who Paula was.

She heard a child in the lobby and looked expectantly at the doorway leading to the room. She saw Deb first, bundled in a coat that might have been in style ten years ago. Deb glanced around the room, looking for Paula.

Paula stood so she could easily be seen. In doing so she could now see Faith trailing behind like a baby duck. Except for the uneven gait.

Deb's face lit with a smile as she made her way back to Paula's desk. She surprised Paula by embracing her. Paula returned the hug, feeling warmer than ever toward this remarkable woman. She moved two chairs from around the corner, and they all sat down. Faith's feet dangled from the chair, her snow-covered boots dripping on the tile floor.

"Hi, Faith." Paula smiled into the eyes of her birth daughter, staring in wonder at her beautiful green eyes. Eyes the same color as her own. Faith's hat covered her head, but Paula could see two low pigtails that dangled nearly to her shoulders.

"Say hello to Miss Paula," Deb said.

"Hewo." Faith looked down shyly.

"She doesn't have her *L*'s yet," Deb said.

"It only makes her sound as cute as she looks." Paula lifted the jar from her desk, then realized she should ask Deb first. "Is it OK?"

"Sure."

"Would you like a sucker, sweetheart?" Paula asked. Her heart nearly exploded in joy when Faith smiled and nodded. She reached her little chubby fingers into the jar and rooted around for all of ten seconds before she came up with a root-beer sucker.

"You and root beer." Deb shook her head. "The girl would drink root beer for every meal if we let her."

Faith peeled the wrapper off the sucker and popped it into her mouth. Paula was amazed by the pleasure it gave her to satisfy Faith in such a small way. What would it have been like to meet her every need—the way a mother did?

"I'll try and make this short since we've popped in on you at the last minute."

Paula tore her gaze from Faith and smiled at Deb. "You're fine. I'm glad you came."

How could she explain what she was really thinking? *I'm thrilled to see the daughter I gave birth to. Amazed by her sweet baby cheeks. Humbled by her resemblance to David and me.*

"Have you been able to do much investigating since we talked last?"

Paula shifted. It struck her again how hard this was going to be. She would have to lie. Again. The thought of lying to these kind people was like a punch in the gut.

"I've done as much as time has allowed. My job here keeps me pretty busy, and of course, I go back to Jackson most weekends."

"I know. I've felt guilty about that."

Paula watched Faith pull the sucker from her mouth and stare at it before she licked it. As she drew the sucker toward her face, her eyes crossed. Paula felt a smile tug her lips upward.

"I shouldn't have put the burden of this story on you after it wasn't newsworthy anymore," Deb said. "I knew you were reluctant, and I kind of played the sympathy card. I'm sorry."

She sounded like she was going to tell Paula it was OK to drop the story. Could she be so lucky?

"I did it because I wanted to help, but it wasn't sympathy," Paula said. "And don't forget, there was something in it for me too."

"I take it you haven't found any helpful information lately?"

Here goes. Paula knew the question would come. "I'm sorry. I can't tell you anything helpful."

Her eyes found Faith's. The little girl was staring at her with her wide green eyes. Paula wanted a lifetime to examine every detail of Faith's face. To watch it change as the years carved maturity into the planes of her face. But that couldn't happen. Paula could think of a dozen reasons why.

"That's as much as we thought," Deb was saying. "And please, don't apologize. You've gone above and beyond." She pulled Faith's hat off her head. "Faith, hold your sucker by the stick. Your fingers are getting all sticky." She helped Faith shift her fingers to the stick.

Paula reached across her desk to grab a tissue. But before she grabbed one, Deb pulled a wet nap out of her purse with the ease of a mother who's done it a hundred times before. Paula let her hand fall into her lap. What had she been thinking? A tissue would only stick to Faith's fingers and leave the tissue in shreds. Her mothering skills were as lacking as her integrity. The thought made her inexplicably sad.

"Anyway," Deb said as she wiped Faith's fingers clean, "Steve and I talked last night and reached a decision. We've decided to hire a private investigator. We'll have to take out a loan to do it, but we both decided this is a do-or-die kind of thing. We're not willing to let it rest."

Anxiety tiptoed across Paula's skin. If they hired a private investigator, wouldn't they find out the truth?

Deb was waiting for her to respond.

Paula didn't know what to say except, "I understand your need to know."

Faith laid the sticky sucker on Paula's desk and reached for the mini-recorder.

"No no, honey," Deb said. She seemed to notice Paula's gaze on the sticky sucker. "Sorry about that."

"It's OK. And she can't hurt the recorder."

"It's hard for them to sit still at this age. I'm surprised she's not wandering around the room getting into everything by now."

Faith turned the recorder over in her hands and held it up to her ear.

Paula felt a dozen angry bees swarming around her belly. What was she going to do about the investigator? She needed time to figure it out. "When are you planning to hire someone?"

"We've set appointments with three different people for next week." Deb picked up her purse and set it on her lap. "I just wanted to drop by and thank you for everything you've done. We really appreciate it."

Faith was talking to herself, her sweet voice filling the background like a musical score.

"It's been a pleasure to meet you." Paula looked at Faith. "All of you."

"Wook, Mommy." Faith held up the minirecorder.

"Oh, honey, don't push the buttons." Deb punched the Stop button. "I'm sorry. I hope she didn't record over something important."

"It was at the end of an interview. No harm done." Paula smiled at Faith, whose eyes had been filled with apprehension. "You're pretty good at this taping stuff. Maybe you'll grow up to be on TV like me." The thought stuck in her throat, jamming her words like Lake Shore Drive traffic at rush hour.

She stood, looking nowhere but at her desk.

Deb stood, too, and slipped on her coat. Paula wanted to ask when she would see Faith again. She wanted to draw the girl into her arms and hold her. But the stinging of her eyes warned her that she needed to get her visitors out of there before she lost it.

Faith slid down from the chair and plopped the shrinking sucker back into her mouth.

Deb embraced Paula. "Thank you so much. We'll never forget what you did."

The words only sprouted more guilt from the seed that seemed wedged against her heart. The clog in her throat grew until she felt choked by it.

"Tell Miss Paula good-bye," Deb said.

"Bye." Faith waved her little-girl fingers, opening and closing them against her palm.

Paula watched Faith walk all the way down the corridor, her awkward gait a painful reminder of what she had done.

And then they were gone.

CHAPTER
TWENTY-SEVEN

Paula took a bite of the rack of lamb, savoring the sweet glaze. Across from her, David started on his garlic mashed potatoes. After he'd picked her up from the airport, he drove her straight to the Sweetwater Restaurant. Paula made small talk, but she was having difficulty putting from her mind everything she'd found out this past week. And the worst part was, she couldn't say a word about it to David.

The server refilled their drinks, then walked away, the rustic floorboards creaking with every step.

"Hanna invited us to stop over later if we want," David said. "She said it was movie night. I guess Jenna, Micah's sister, is supposed to fly here soon to stay with them."

"I hadn't heard that." Paula wasn't sure that was what Hanna needed right now with a baby on the way, but maybe it would work out for the best.

"From what Micah said, Jenna's had it pretty rough out in California, so they're trying to help her get on her feet." He took a sip from his glass. "So are you up for a movie?"

Normally she'd want to go nowhere but home to have precious time alone with David. But tonight the thought of escaping into a movie, of avoiding alone time with David, was the more inviting option.

"Sure, let's do." Before he could question her decision, she changed the topic. "Is Hanna huge yet?"

He held his palms out. "It wouldn't be gentlemanly to respond to that question."

"And if there's anything you are, David Cohen, it's a gentleman." There it was. Her old flirtatious manner. She smiled, relieved. Maybe she could put everything from her mind and just enjoy the weekend with him.

"How's your plant?" he asked.

It took her a moment to realize what he was talking about. "Better. The leaves aren't so yellow anymore. No flowers yet, but who knows? Maybe it's just the time of year they don't bloom."

David shoved his plate aside and began playing with the glass cup that held a flickering tea-light candle. "Gram would probably know. Or Hanna. Isn't she due soon?"

"Is that your way of saying she looks ready to pop?" She wiped her mouth and set her linen napkin on her nearly empty plate.

He stared into the light, his lips tipping up only a fraction of an inch.

Why am I talking about Hanna's pregnancy? Paula chided herself. It would only remind him of her own pregnancy and the sadness he'd experienced at its end. And it reminded her of something much worse. She focused on the Neil Diamond song playing faintly in the background.

"Paula, do you ever think about having a baby?"

Her eyes swung to David. "What?"

"I know we had problems conceiving last year. But it's not hopeless. Especially if we go to a fertility clinic. It might take a long time, but . . ." He let go of the glass candle cup and took her hand. "I love you so much. I still want us to have a baby together."

Emotions roiled inside her. Her stomach clamped down hard with a yearning she'd never felt before. They'd tried for a year to conceive, and that had been hard. She'd been impatient, and he'd been . . . almost casual about it. But she was now on the verge of getting her dream job. How did she feel about that?

"I know it might not be the best timing. But it may take a couple of years. If you get the anchor chair, you'll have had time to become established. How do you think Miles would handle it if you got pregnant?"

"Well, at least I'd be behind a desk." She breathed a laugh. "The viewers wouldn't have to know I was pregnant."

"What about the leave of absence? And would Miles see motherhood as a distraction from your work?"

Motherhood. Had any other word ever held the same beautiful thought? The change in her attitude surprised her. "I don't care."

David pushed up his glasses. A frown furrowed above the nosepiece. "What?"

"I said I don't care." And she realized suddenly that she didn't care. Didn't care what Miles would think. Didn't care what her viewers would think. All she cared about was that she would be the most blessed woman in the world if she could have David's baby.

David's eyes swam with bewilderment. He looked frozen in time. Even his hand on hers had gone still.

"I really don't, David. This is our life we're talking about. As much as I want to climb the corporate ladder, I'm not going to let it steal from us something so important. We're not getting any younger, you know."

"Speak for yourself."

"You're three years older than I, Mr. Cohen."

"And you're more beautiful than the day I met you."

Warm emotions wrapped around her stomach like gently curling fingers. She felt her lips relax into a smile. "Let's not go to Hanna's."

David's eyes gave off more heat than the Buck stove against the wall. He slowly put his hand in the air. "Check, please."

⚬

Linn sat down at the small break table and ripped open her honey-nut granola bar. She looked at her book bag, then at the newspaper she'd bought on her way in this afternoon. Should she study or comb the Help Wanted ads?

Searching for a part-time employer who would work around her classes was proving to be a nearly impossible task. Add that to the limited time she had between going to class, working, studying, and commuting on the bus, and she felt as if she faced a Mount Teton climb wearing a pair of slides.

Working with Adam hadn't been as bad as she'd expected since he was going out of his way to avoid her. They hadn't had another personal conversation since the last one that had ended so badly. She felt like a hypocrite after telling Paula to be honest with her husband when she was pretending she didn't care anything about Adam.

She'd wanted to apologize for her harsh words a hundred times, but doing so would only bring on more trouble. Nothing had changed. She was still unfit for a relationship with a man like Adam, and how was she to know if he'd broken it off with Elizabeth yet?

As much as Linn wanted to know what had happened, it wouldn't do any good. Even if he and Elizabeth went as far as breaking up, Adam was still way too good for Linn Caldwell.

She snapped open the paper and turned to the Help Wanted section. When she found it, she folded the paper over and took a bite of her granola bar.

Footsteps sounded nearby, and she looked up.

It was Adam. He was carrying a coffee cup and a plate with a cinnamon roll. He stopped quicker than an elk in the path of an oncoming car. And he had just about the same look on his face.

Her eyes found the ads again. Why was he on break now? That only left Alicia at the counter. They had a big party coming in twenty minutes. Maybe Joe wanted them to get their breaks before that.

She stiffened as he took the only other chair at the table. Right across from her.

Oh, God, I have got to find a new job. I can't keep doing this. It's too hard. Help me.

Keep breathing, Linn. Look at the ads.

Across from her, Adam's fork scraped across the plate.

Read the ads.

Adam shifted in his chair. Then he sipped from his coffee cup. All of this she could see from her peripheral vision. Her eyes were fixed on the newspaper, but she couldn't seem to remember how to read.

He broke the silence. "I guess Joe thought we'd better take our break while we can."

Her heart jumped as he spoke. "I guess."

She brought the paper closer, as if she'd just found something very interesting. She couldn't say what it was.

"Any luck finding a job?" His tone was soft but guarded.

She couldn't blame him after what she'd said to him.

"Not yet."

He took another bite of his cinnamon roll.

It was a lesson in self-control to keep her eyes on the paper. She took a small bite of her granola bar. It tasted like fresh sawdust. She forced herself to swallow and took a sip from her Evian bottle.

"You don't have to leave, Linn." His tone was like a lifeline, drawing her in.

She had to resist. Staying there with him wouldn't save her. It would be her downfall.

"We've already been through this," she said.

His words from before came unwanted to her mind. *"If she's so perfect for me, why do I want you?"*

Why do I want you?

Why do I want you?

Just the memory of the words made her heart kick into a heavy, irregular rhythm, like a bass drum in a funky '80s song.

"I get that you don't feel the same way about me as I feel about you," he said.

Yes, I do. You have no idea.

"But we can be friends, can't we?" His tone eroded her resistance.

Finally she dared to glance at him. He looked puppy-dog sad with his brown eyes dimmed, as if a light had gone off behind them. She longed to say yes. That they could be friends. It would be an excuse to be near him, and she totally wanted that.

But she knew, with certainty, that she couldn't handle his nearness. She hadn't been able to handle it since her feelings had grown for him. And if he ever did break up with Elizabeth, she would wind up doing the selfish thing. She would let the friendship grow into something bigger. And Adam deserved better than that.

How could she explain it to him, though? Maybe she could appeal to his sense of integrity. "Please, Adam, I'm trying to make a good decision here."

"How is it a good decision to end a friendship? You're doing a great job here. Joe will be hard-pressed to find a replacement for you."

If he was trying to send her on a guilt trip, it was working. He made it all sound so cut-and-dried. But feelings weren't like that. And she wasn't strong enough to resist what she wanted when it stared her in the face every day.

"If it's about Elizabeth, she and I talked and—"

"No." She held up the paper between them like a shield. "I don't want to hear it. This has nothing to do with Elizabeth." Truth was, she was afraid she'd cave if she found out things were over between Adam and his fiancée. Better to just not know.

When he looked confused, she realized she'd spoken harshly.

"So that's that, then? You're just going to quit." His shoulders raised in a helpless shrug.

"That's the plan."

He picked up his plate and cup and stood.

Please don't go, her heart begged. *Convince me I'm wrong. Tell me you love me and won't give up on me.*

Then an instant later, the accusation came: *You are so weak, Linn.* She closed her eyes against the truth.

She felt him leave the room, and the void he left seemed as vast as Leigh Canyon.

CHAPTER
TWENTY-EIGHT

Paula let herself into her apartment, pulling the rolling travel case with her. The scent of garlic and tomato permeated the room, teasing her taste buds. She always passed on the airline food, but now she found herself hoping that the leftovers of whatever had been cooked for dinner were sitting on a shelf in the fridge.

Linn rounded the corner of the kitchen, wiping her hands on a dishtowel. "Welcome home."

"Thanks. Dare I hope you have leftovers to share?"

Linn smiled. "I made plenty. It's only spaghetti, though, and I'm afraid Prego was involved."

"Believe me—my stomach doesn't feel very picky right now."

"I'll fix you a plate."

Linn disappeared into the kitchen before Paula could protest. She was so tired from the travel and stress; maybe she would just sit down and take it easy. She'd been fine in Jackson. She had managed to put the whole mess of Faith and the Morgans out of her mind, more or less, and focus on David and the thought of having a baby. But the moment he dropped her at the airport, her mind flew faster than a jet toward her precarious future.

She rolled her bag into the bedroom and sat on the edge of the bed.

She had to make a decision about the Morgans—and soon. Once

they hired a PI, it was only a matter of time before he found the truth. The whole truth. What should she do?

"Paula? It's ready."

She shoved her thoughts to the back of her mind and joined Linn in the kitchen. "Smells great."

Linn set the plate and a glass of fizzy soda on the dining-room table.

"Thanks, Linn."

"You'll have to teach me to make your fancy spaghetti sauce sometime," Linn said.

"Sure." Paula rolled the spaghetti around the fork tines and slid it into her mouth. Prego aside, this really hit the spot.

Sitting across from her, Linn set her elbow on the table and propped her chin on her palm.

"Didn't have to work today?" Paula asked.

"Just noon to seven."

"You had to miss church?"

Linn's shoulder hitched upward. "I went to Sunday school."

"Sunday school. Man, I haven't been there since I was a teenager."

"I don't know why they call it that. It's more like a small group that studies the Bible and has an open discussion. They have a college-age class at this church."

"Anyone with boyfriend potential?"

Linn's lips parted, then closed.

"Oh, that's right. I forgot about *Adam*." Paula drew out the name in a sultry tone.

Linn sat back in her chair. "There's nothing between me and Adam."

"Oh, right. That tension I felt in the room last week was electrical energy from the thunderstorm we weren't having."

"Adam is a dead end for me. Number one, he's engaged. At least, I think he still is. Number two, I couldn't be more wrong for him."

Paula didn't miss the flicker of sadness in Linn's eyes. "Didn't you say he was studying to be a pastor or something? That seems like a perfect fit to me. You're a Christian."

Linn stared out the window before responding. "I'm a Christian with the past of a harlot. Not exactly preacher's wife material."

Paula thought back on what she knew of Linn. The affair with her sister's ex-husband, the almost abortion. And then she'd kept her identity a secret while convincing Natalie to adopt the baby. "Does Adam know about your past?"

Linn played with the gold chain that hung around her neck. "So how was your weekend?"

Paula narrowed her eyes. "Very shrewd, young lady. My weekend went quite well, thank you very much."

"So you didn't tell him?"

"Same as you didn't tell Adam?"

"It's hardly the same thing."

"What—there are times to be honest and times to hide all your dark secrets? What do you think I was trying to do all those years ago? It's no different."

"Then you think honesty is the best policy?" Linn cocked her head.

"That's not what I said."

"What are you saying?"

Paula sighed and laid her fork in her plate, her appetite suddenly gone. "I don't know what I'm saying. I have no idea what to do about my own quandary, much less yours."

"Isn't there a difference between lying and just omitting information? I mean, why is it wrong that I haven't told Adam everything about my past?"

"So you haven't lied to him about anything?"

Linn looked down. Her fingers played with a loose thread on the tablecloth. "I did lie about something. I've felt guilty about it ever since."

When Linn bit the corner of her lip, Paula felt bad. "I'm sorry. I shouldn't have asked."

"No, you're right. And I know what I should do."

Paula studied Linn's face. The drooping corners of her mouth had resignation written all over them. "Just like that? You realize you've lied and you just go fix it?"

Linn shrugged. "It's the right thing to do."

"What about the repercussions? Will there be any for you?"

Linn gave a wry laugh. "Oh yeah."

"Then why do it? Wouldn't it be easier to let it slide?"

"Sure, in the short run." Linn wrapped the thread around her index finger. "But experience has taught me that lies come back to bite you later. And when they do, they bite hard."

Paula put David from her mind for the moment and remembered her meeting with Deb and Faith the week before. "I lied to the Morgans." Paula wiped her mouth with the napkin and set it down beside her glass. "I told Deb I hadn't found out anything new."

Linn nodded slowly. "You need to tell her the truth, you know."

"That's easy for you to say."

"No, it's not easy for me to say," Linn refuted. "I'm just telling you that these things come out eventually. And it ain't pretty when it happens."

It was true, especially in this case. Paula attempted to rub the tension out of her neck. "Sooner rather than later this time." She met Linn's frank gaze. "They're hiring a private investigator this week."

"You should tell them before they find out on their own."

"How can I tell them I knew who Faith was and kept it from them?" Even now Paula cringed to think of it. Deb and Steve respected her and thought the best of her. Yet she had the answer they longed for, and she was keeping it from them for her own selfish reasons.

"Maybe I could just talk to Louise and get her to promise not to talk about it with anyone."

Linn shook her head.

"You don't understand what's at stake." Paula shoved her chair back and took her plate to the sink. Linn was practically a child. She may have had a difficult life, but she couldn't understand all the repercussions of a situation like this. She wasn't willing to throw away her marriage for the sake of honesty. She loved David way too much for that.

She didn't want to think about this anymore. It was like a massive snarl of tangled yarn—hopeless and frustrating. She should finish the copy on the story she'd interviewed for last week. It was nothing particularly exciting. Just a local author who'd won a prestigious award. It would numb her mind to her own problems, and that was exactly what she needed.

When she got to her room, she fished her tape recorder, notebook, and a pencil from her bag. She pushed Play and jotted down the interesting blurbs she thought she'd use. When it reached the end, she started to push the Stop button. But before she could, another sound began. A click and then the sound of singing. A child's voice, all airy and sweet.

Faith.

In the background Paula could hear Deb and herself talking, but Faith's voice was loud and clear as if she held the recorder to her mouth. She wasn't chattering, as Paula had thought. She was singing "The Wheels on the Bus."

That was *her* child singing. Hers and David's. The little girl she'd carried inside her own womb.

And had tried to abort.

Paula punched the *Stop* button. Her hands were unsteady, as if she hadn't eaten all day. And her legs felt quivery and weak, like the cooked noodles from dinner.

What do I do, God?

She couldn't believe she was even asking, but who else could she ask? She knew God was there, at least. And He was listening. On the other hand, hadn't she brought this on herself? Didn't she deserve whatever she got? Why would God help her out of her own mess?

Do you care, God?

She had always thought worshiping God was for weak people who were incapable of handling life on their own. She'd always felt a certain disdain for those who needed a crutch to get through life. But now she'd take a crutch if she could get one. She was clearly limping through life.

"Forgive me, God. I'm sorry," she whispered. Tears streamed down her face. "I've needed You all my life and didn't see it." She remembered all the times she repeated the "sinner's prayer" silently in Sunday school and Vacation Bible School. But she hadn't meant it then. She only followed along because it's what the teachers thought she should do.

Oh, God, I do believe in You. I know Jesus Christ, Your Son, came to die in my place. I've known it since I was a little girl, and yet I've denied You. I'm sorry. Help me change. Help me.

Where had she gone so wrong? Why, when she'd practically been born in the church nursery, had she left the path her parents had tried to set for her? Her sisters had never strayed from the course.

She lay facedown on the bed. When had she decided she would take a different path? How had she gone so far from where she belonged?

It must have happened slowly, because she couldn't remember ever making the choice. Only one bad decision at a time. And now those decisions had stacked up like so many bags of garbage.

How do I fix it, God?

Linn had made it seem so simple, but was it really as simple as telling the truth no matter what?

Paula suddenly remembered a Vacation Bible School she attended when she was ten or eleven. The theme was camping or something, because she remembered the kids were all spread out in sleeping bags in the church yard with a fake campfire in the center. Mrs. Young had been talking about the Ten Commandments all week, and she compared them to the guardrail above Jackson Lake's dam. *"Those rules aren't there to cheat you out of fun. They're there to keep you safe,"* she said.

Why had it taken Paula so long to believe it? Lying about the abortion had only made a mess of things and caused tremendous pain. Yet the thought of telling David still scared her to the point of trembling.

Help me, God. I don't want to lose him. I love him so much, but I don't think he'll ever forgive me for what I've done.

She wished God would magically take her fears away. That He'd make her do what was right, just like Linn was doing. But maybe she wasn't half the person Linn was.

She knew now that she'd have to tell the Morgans too. They would find out eventually anyway, and she'd rather they hear it from her. She wiped her eyes and rested her head in the cradle of her arms. She didn't know how she was going to get through it or how she was going to say it, but they deserved to know the truth. At least most of it.

CHAPTER
TWENTY-NINE

Paula paused on the Morgans' doorstep, remembering the first time she'd come to their home. She'd been ready to get a big scoop, to put her name on the map at WMAQ. Now it hit her hard that there were people behind each scoop. Real people, real lives, real pain.

She was about to tell the Morgans what had happened to their birth daughter, and it was the hardest thing she'd ever had to do.

Making a fist, she knocked on the door. How could she say the words? How did someone tell a mother and father that their birth child had died without their knowledge? Would they want to talk to Louise? Would they hate the woman for what she'd done? Paula couldn't even guess how they'd react.

The door swung open, and Deb greeted her with a warm smile. It made Paula feel like Judas must have felt after betraying Jesus to the authorities.

Steve shook her hand and led her into the living room while Deb put a cartoon on for Faith in the other room. Paula barely caught a glimpse of Faith as she passed.

She and Steve made small talk until Deb returned to take a seat on the sofa beside her husband.

"You said you wanted to talk with us about something important," Steve said. "Did you find out what happened at the hospital?"

Paula wasn't ready to delve right in. First she had a confession to make. She crossed her legs and tucked her feet to the side. "Before we get into that, I want to apologize, Deb." She made herself meet Deb's eyes. "When you came to the office last week, I—I lied to you."

Deb shook her head. "About what?"

Paula was afraid to look at Steve. Looking at Deb wasn't much easier. "When you asked me if I'd found out anything new, I said I hadn't. But that wasn't true."

She saw hope flicker in Deb's eyes, but it was quickly replaced by something else: fear.

"What did you find out?" Steve clasped his wife's hand tightly.

Paula had started this, and she had to finish. But, oh, what she'd give to change it all. "I met last week with a woman who worked in the NICU at the time of your child's birth. She remembers everything quite well."

Deb clutched Steve's hand.

"She was working two jobs at the time to meet some financial obligations. Her second job was also at Chicago General. She assisted a doctor who performed abortions."

She expected to be interrupted, but the Morgans simply sat frozen, a horrible mixture of hope and dread stamped on their faces.

She wanted to ease their fears, but the truth was as bad as or worse than anything they were expecting. The most compassionate thing she could do was get to the point.

"Right before the nurse was scheduled to work in the NICU, there was a botched abortion. The nurse was instructed—"

"Wait," Steve said. "What's a botched abortion?"

"There are rare instances when babies survive an abortion," Paula explained. "I found some articles online about it. Anyway, the nurse was instructed to get rid of the baby, but she couldn't bring herself to do it."

"Get rid of it?" Deb asked.

Paula's heart started some kind of syncopated rhythm that interfered with her breathing. "The doctor wanted her to—to kill the baby."

Deb's fingers spread across her lips.

"The nurse was terribly torn. She couldn't afford to lose her job, yet what she held in her hands was so clearly a tiny baby. And the child was breathing on her own."

"What did she do?" Steve's voice was monotone and knowing.

"She sneaked the child downstairs to the NICU. She kept the baby wrapped in her scrub top so no one would see it. When she reached the NICU and the other nurses left, she placed the baby in an incubator and treated her as a patient. She didn't know what she was going to do. Eventually a doctor or nurse would come in and discover the baby, and she knew she'd lose one or both jobs. But she couldn't stand the thought of letting the infant die."

Deb's eyes glazed over.

Paula stared down at her own hands, laced together like an innocent schoolgirl's. This was *her* baby she was talking about. Her child, whom she'd nearly destroyed. She blinked the thought away. She had to focus on the Morgans. This would be the most difficult moment of their lives, and it was her job to somehow soften the blow. The thought was almost enough to make her choke. This blow would come down like a sledgehammer, no matter how she delivered it.

She forced herself to continue. "In another incubator your birth child lay struggling for her life. As you know, the doctors expected that she wouldn't make it. Deb, you were in surgery at the time."

Deb gave a short nod.

"The nurse stabilized the baby she smuggled down to the NICU."

Paula struggled to find the words. How could she explain to the Morgans that their baby had died that day? That they'd been cheated from holding her little body or telling her how much they loved her?

Paula again felt the sting of tears behind her eyes. "The rest of this is going to be very difficult to hear."

Steve nodded. "Go on."

Paula didn't want to go on. She wanted to run from the room and never come back. But she owed the Morgans the truth. She lifted her face and met their eyes, looking back and forth from one to the other to assess their preparedness for the news they were about to hear.

"Shortly after the nurse stabilized the secret infant, your birth child stopped breathing."

A soft moan tore from Deb's mouth, and Steve wrapped her in his arms. His own face took on the numbness of someone who has just come through a trauma.

Paula put her hand on Deb's arm. "I'm so sorry."

They sat together, saying nothing, a triangle of pain. "She died?" Steve asked.

"I'm afraid so."

Deb wept silently, and Steve held her like she was the most precious thing on earth.

Paula blinked until her vision cleared. "The nurse knew your birth child had no chance of survival. She knew you'd had a hysterectomy and wouldn't be able to have any more children."

"She switched the babies." Steve met her eyes over the top of Deb's head.

"Yes." Paula wanted to add so much more. She wanted to tell them about Louise's struggle to do the right thing. About her desperation to spare the Morgans from the pain of losing a child. But they weren't ready to hear that yet. They just needed to grieve.

Paula pulled two tissues from her bag and handed one of them to Deb.

"What—what happened to our child?" Steve asked.

Deb burrowed her head into Steve's chest, as if she didn't want to hear the answer.

Paula forced herself to reply. "The nurse is a compassionate woman. She buried her in her backyard under a big oak tree."

After a brief pause Deb wept openly. The sound of it raked Paula's heart, making her feel completely helpless. There was nothing she could say to comfort them.

Steve's eyes were fixed, his mouth set in a flat line. His numb horror was as bad as Deb's weeping.

"I'm so sorry," Paula said again.

Deb clutched Steve's shirt sleeve and dissolved into deep, raw sobs. Her naked pain tied knots inside Paula's stomach.

The Morgans needed to be alone. They needed to grieve in peace. Paula stood, grabbing her bag. She touched Steve's shoulder on her way out of the room and cast one last look at the couple before leaving.

She drove home in a fog as thick as Jell-O. Her heart was still at the Morgans' house. It was all her fault. All her fault that they were grieving. That Faith had cerebral palsy. That Louise had carried three years of guilt.

Yet Paula hadn't told the Morgans about her role in this nightmare. She braked at a red light and closed her eyes.

I've done it again. I'm hiding the truth. Why is telling the truth so hard for me? Why didn't I just tell them I was the one who had the abortion?

The answer came quickly and clearly: *Because you're afraid David will find out.* It was her greatest fear of all.

Do I have to go that far, God? Do I have to lose my husband because of one terrible choice?

She asked the question but didn't really want to know the answer.

What should she do? Did the Morgans really need to know who Faith's birth mother was?

You owe them the truth.

The thought was a punch in the stomach. And what about Faith? Paula had already denied the child once. Denied that she even was a child by trying to get rid of her. Now she'd denied Faith again by refusing to claim her.

What a failure she was. Paula, successful reporter and business-woman. Confident and competent. Was it only a facade? Who was she really? The self-assured woman who could handle anything—or the woman who cowered from truth in a dark corner?

God, I'm tired of living this way. I'm tired of hiding secrets.

The Morgans deserved the truth, and Faith deserved to be acknowledged as her child, even if the Morgans chose not to tell her.

The light turned green and Paula accelerated. She had to tell them who she was, but now wasn't the time. Not when they just found out about their birth child's death. She would give them time to recover from that blow before she dealt the next one.

She only hoped her courage didn't fail her in the meantime.

CHAPTER
THIRTY

Linn rang up the customer and handed her the change. After she marked the cup as a skinny, decaf latte, she slid it down toward Adam and picked up the rag to clean the counters.

She still hadn't told him she lied to him, and this was her second day working with him after she made the decision to tell him the truth. She'd chickened out, and that's all there was to it. Then today, when she promised herself she would do it, they had customer after customer file through the doors. Now it was nearly time to close, and she still hadn't apologized.

Should she ask to talk after work? She'd have a thirty-minute wait for the bus, but maybe he'd want to go home and sleep since he had an early class too.

"Something wrong?" Adam tossed the words over his shoulder as he set the milk to steam.

Linn scrubbed at a spot of sticky flavoring. "No."

Except I have to tell you I lied, and essentially have to own up to my feelings for you, all the while making sure you don't hold out any hope for me because I am so not right for you.

"You look like something's on your mind." He poured the milk into the cup and put a lid on it before passing it off to the woman.

Now's the time, Linn. Just say it.

The bell above the door jingled as two men walked through. Linn glanced at the clock, feeling a mixture of relief and dismay. Only two minutes until closing.

The men only wanted plain coffee, so she rang them up and handed them the cups. "Help yourselves."

Adam had already started the cleanup process, wiping down the steamer and espresso machines. The counters were clean, and she'd already cleaned the blender. She rinsed out the rag, wrung it out, and laid it on the faucet. When she eyed the clock again, she saw it was eleven o'clock. The store was empty of customers, so she went and flipped the lock on the front door and turned the sign to Closed.

Time was running out, and now she'd let two days go by.

Ask him. Just ask him and stop standing here like a lost little girl.

"Adam?"

He stopped wiping the steamer prong and looked at her from across the room. "Yeah?"

Her heart seemed to forget how to operate. "I was wondering if you had a few minutes when we're finished here."

He went back to wiping down the steamer. "What for?"

She bit the inside of her lip. Joe had already left, and she was acutely aware it was only the two of them. "I just—can we talk for a few minutes?"

One side of his lips turned up in a semblance of a smile. "Sure. I'm almost done."

Linn went to the back room and removed her apron. After grabbing her coat, purse, and book bag, she went out to the front where Adam had seated himself at a corner table, away from the cold windows. He'd turned off the front lights to indicate they were closed.

She joined him, hanging her coat and purse on the chair back, scrambling for what she'd say and how she'd say it. Why hadn't she given it more thought?

By the time she seated herself, Adam was staring at her. How was she supposed to think when his eyes were as warm as melted caramel and held just enough sadness to inflict her with guilt?

She hung her head. "I don't know where to begin."

"You know what they say."

Start at the beginning? That seemed too scary, but Adam was right.

She took a breath and caught his eye. "I wanted to apologize to you for what I said last week."

Even now the cruel words echoed in her mind. *Like I'd have anything to do with a guy who'd betray his fiancée.* What a hypocritical thing to say. She'd kissed him right back, and she'd known full well he had a fiancée. But he'd never thrown that back in her face.

His eyes flitted downward toward the table. She'd hurt him with what she said. He couldn't even look at her. "Don't worry about it." He shrugged as if it hadn't mattered, but it had.

"It was a mean thing to say. And it wasn't true."

"Yes it was. I deserved it." He still wasn't looking at her.

And worse yet, she was sure he didn't understand what she was saying. She was going to have to spell it out. She was breathing so shallowly, it would be a wonder if she didn't hyperventilate.

"That's not what I meant," she said. "But while we're on that subject, I did kiss you back, you know." Heat crept into her face and out to her ears. She hoped the dimness of the room hid the flush.

His eyes met hers then, and his lips gave that same sad, crooked smile. "I noticed."

If she were a Southern belle, she would pull out a dainty fan and cool her face. She already felt faint.

"Look, it's OK," he said. "You were upset, and you said something you regret. Let's just forget it, OK?"

Oh, how easy it would be to just let it drop. She'd apologized—didn't that count?

You haven't even told him what you lied about, Linn. Stop being such a chicken.

When he scooted his chair back to stand, she stopped him. "Wait. Wait; there's something else."

He lowered himself back into the chair.

Are You sure, God? Are You sure I should tell him when it may just get me into a whole mess of trouble?

"What is it?" He searched her eyes, and she knew she had to tell him. Not for any other reason but that God commanded honesty, and it was the right thing to do.

"I—I didn't say what I said because I was upset. I said it to mislead you. I lied to you."

His brows pulled down low, his eyes questioning. "I'm not following."

She broke away from his gaze. Now that the time had come, she didn't know what to say. How could she explain her feelings without giving him any hope of a future together? A future she wanted more than anything. But a future that couldn't happen.

"I guess I kind of said what I did to—to scare you off. You were talking like you wanted there to be something between us."

"Oh." That one word was weighted with disappointment.

She wished she could read his mind. He seemed uncomfortable. Embarrassed, even.

"I was trying to tell you how I was feeling, but I never meant to force myself on you or pressure you into something you didn't want." He wouldn't look at her.

Now she knew why. He thought she wasn't interested and was trying to get rid of him.

"Oh, Adam, you have it all wrong." She propped her elbow on the table and her forehead against her hand. How could she explain it without having to humiliate herself by telling her whole sordid past? She heard him breathe a laugh.

"Then what, Linn? I don't understand."

She rubbed her forehead. She was making such a mess of it. "I'm sorry. I really stink at this stuff. It's just—" She wished it were even darker, so she could hide in the shadows. "The reason I was trying to scare you off was that I felt you shouldn't break it off with Elizabeth."

"Why?"

"She's perfect for you, that's why." Linn ran her fingers through her bangs, keeping her head down.

"It might appear that way from the outside, but just the fact that I was having feelings for you was a clear indication that I had no business being engaged to her. Anyway, it's over now. I explained what happened, and I broke it off."

Linn's heart crumbled. It was all her fault. If she had kept him at arm's length, this wouldn't have happened. Why had she kissed him back? Why hadn't she been strong enough to push him away?

Adam took her wrist gently and pulled her hand down from her face. With nothing to hide behind, she felt exposed. Nevertheless, her eyes met his and clung. Why was it that everything she wanted was unattainable? As he drew her in with his eyes, her resolve slipped away.

"Why do you look at me like that?" he asked. "Why, when you wanted me to stay with Elizabeth?"

She focused on the tabletop. She wasn't good at hiding her feelings, and now her transparency was telling him more than she wanted him to know.

"Don't." He tipped her chin with his fingertips until she had to look at him. His touch was gentle and brought back memories of their kiss.

"Do you have feelings for me?" he asked.

He'd asked her straight out, knowing she wouldn't lie.

"I don't want to talk about this, Adam." She scooted her chair back. "I have a bus to catch."

"You have twenty more minutes, and you know it." His voice was firm, determined.

She froze in the wooden chair.

"Do you have a boyfriend back home? In Jackson Hole?"

The question caught her off guard. "No."

"Then what? Am I misreading you, Linn? Because I'm getting signals from you that tell me one thing, but your words say something else."

She was such a hypocrite. He was right. Everything he said was true.

"You never answered my question," he said.

It was the point of no return. She had to be truthful, but she had to be strong.

Adam deserves better than you. Just remember that.

"All right, Adam. Yes, I do have feelings for you. But they can't lead anywhere, OK? That's why I said what I did. That's why I've discouraged you."

"What do you mean? Why can't they lead anywhere?" Two vertical lines appeared between his brows.

She set both elbows on the table and pressed her forehead against her fingertips. "They just can't."

"That's not an answer."

It was an answer that wouldn't lead to more questions. But he was hanging on like a dog with his last bone.

"I'm not good for you, OK?" she tried. "There's stuff—stuff you don't know about me."

"What stuff? I don't care about that."

She gave a wry laugh. He would if he knew. He'd be the one standing and leaving if she sat there and told him everything she'd done. But she'd never give him that opportunity. She wouldn't shame herself that way.

"What was that for?"

He was asking about the laugh, she knew. She'd gotten herself in so deep, she wasn't sure how she'd dig out of the hole. She shook her head.

"Linn." He took her wrist and pulled her hand down again until it lay nestled in his.

His touch made shivers run up her arm. His hand looked so big over hers. His fingertips were squared off, not round like hers. Every tiny hair on her skin responded.

"I've worked with you for hours on end. I've seen the way you work hard and treat other people with kindness. I've seen you be compassionate and fair and honest. I've seen the way a smile lights up your eyes in a way that's contagious. And I've felt myself falling harder and harder for you."

"Don't, Adam." She stared down at the table.

"There's nothing you can say that's going to change my feelings for you."

She almost laughed again but stopped herself. His pastoral mind couldn't even imagine the kinds of things she'd done. Someday he would minister in a big church somewhere, and the last thing he needed was a wife with a shameful past. She had to get out of there before she became too weak to say no.

She withdrew her hand from his and stood abruptly. "I have to go."

"No, you don't."

She put her coat on quickly and slung her book bag and purse over her shoulder.

When she turned to leave, he was there. Standing right in front of her, his jaw set, his lips in a firm, straight line.

"Stay. We need to talk."

"I have to catch the bus."

"That's an excuse and you know it. I can take you home."

And wind up alone in his car, where he'd have all the time in the world to talk her into doing what she already wanted to do? No way.

His hands framed her face, their warmth seeping through her skin. His eyes softened with tenderness. They pled with her. "Give us a chance."

She was powerless to stop what she knew would happen next.

His lips took hers gently at first. But when he pulled her closer and she pressed up against him, the kiss took on a passion unlike any she'd ever felt. Her fingers dove into his hair as their hot breath mingled in a dance as old as time. She was unaware of anything but the feel of his lips on hers, of his hands wrapped around her shoulders and cradling the back of her head. A desperate need for more bubbled up inside her, filling her stomach with all kinds of wonderful feelings.

It was heaven.

Except it was wrong. She had done this before, and look where it had gotten her. Pregnant and shamed. Was she going to pull Adam down with her? Adam, who had a future in the ministry?

She yanked her fingers from his hair and pushed at his chest. He took a step back. Their breaths came at a pace more in line with a marathon than a kiss.

And Adam. His eyes had taken on a look of wonder, as if the passion had taken him by surprise.

Linn knew exactly how he felt. She rubbed her swollen lips. "That can't happen again," she whispered.

She hitched the book bag up onto her shoulder and turned. Her feet carried her quickly to the front door, hoping he wouldn't say anything to weaken her resolve. She twisted the lock and opened the door. Before she stepped outside, she heard a heavy *thwack* behind her. It took a moment to realize Adam had hit something. The wood table or the paneling on the wall. Without turning to look, she slipped out the front door.

CHAPTER
THIRTY-ONE

Paula let the week slide by without contacting the Morgans. The more days that passed, the easier it was to wait. She knew that once the Morgans knew the truth, she would have to tell David. That was enough to make a procrastinator out of her.

Somehow she managed to stay focused and do her job. Darrick had clearly fallen out of favor, and Roxy, one of the weekend anchors, had found out she was pregnant and decided she was going to stay home once the child was born. But instead of boosting Paula's morale, the news only made her feel hollow inside. Would she and David ever manage to get pregnant again, or had she blown their one and only shot at parenthood?

She couldn't help but be relieved that it wasn't her weekend to go home. She needed more time to process the information, and she was looking forward to a quiet weekend.

But around noon on Saturday her mom phoned to tell her Hanna had gone into labor, nearly two weeks early. She was at the hospital and dilated five centimeters already. Paula left a note for Linn and took the first flight she could get, arriving at St. John's after dark. She walked down the hall toward her waiting family. David was the first to see her, and he stood and embraced her.

"How's Hanna doing?" She directed the question at her parents.

"She's doing great," her mom said. "Micah came out a few minutes ago and told us it wouldn't be much longer."

Paula gave everyone hugs, including Gram, then sank into the chair between David and Natalie.

A young woman sat between Gram and her mother. "Paula," her mother said, "this is Micah's sister, Jenna."

Paula saw a resemblance around the eyes and in the young woman's skin tone. "It's nice to meet you, Jenna. I'm so glad you and Micah have been reunited."

"Thanks." The word, though nicely spoken, was hard around the edges, as though the girl had built a bricks-and-mortar wall around herself.

Paula wondered what had happened to the girl out in California to put such a jaded look in her eyes. She turned to Natalie. "Where's Kyle?"

"Home with the kids. We thought it'd be too much to have them here, and our baby-sitter is otherwise occupied." Natalie smiled at their mom.

"How long's Hanna been in labor?" Paula asked.

"Since around eight this morning," Natalie explained. "She's about squeezed the blood out of Micah's hand."

Paula thought of her baby sister in that room, struggling through the pain of childbirth, and felt overwhelmingly protective. "Well, haven't they given her anything?"

"Hanna wants to do it naturally," Gram said. "That's the old-fashioned way."

It was barbaric, if you asked Paula. She suddenly remembered the cramping she'd had after the abortion. Sharp, intense pain that made menstrual cramps seem like a day at the park.

Was David thinking about pregnancy? Was he thinking about the child he'd believed they'd lost to a miscarriage? She glanced at him, but his head was leaned back against the wall, his eyes closed.

She had to put her problems from her mind. Hanna was having her first baby, and Paula needed to focus on that. Even though she'd wanted a quiet weekend in Chicago, she was glad Hanna had gone into labor on the weekend so she could be there for the birth.

She felt David's hand wrapping around hers. She turned to study him. He'd opened his eyes and was smiling at her. His glasses had slid a fraction of an inch down his nose.

"I'm glad you're home."

His words were like soothing aloe on a raw burn, and her heart expanded with the love he radiated. She loved him more than she ever thought she'd love any man. The thought of losing him was like being ripped in half.

She leaned into his shoulder and kissed him, savoring the fresh cinnamon on his breath, the softness of his lips.

"It's a boy!" a jubilant voice called.

Paula drew away from David to see that Micah stood in the doorway that led to the delivery rooms.

The room erupted with excitement as everyone stood. Paula's mom hugged Micah while Natalie and Gram asked questions about Hanna.

"She's fine, just perfect," Micah said. "Well, maybe a little tired."

They laughed. Micah looked tired himself.

"He's twenty-one inches long and weighs eight pounds, two ounces."

"Oh, my word," Gram said. "And he's two weeks early."

"What did you name him?" Paula's mom asked.

Micah smiled. "You'll see. They're going to clean him up and stuff, then I'll come out and get you. Shouldn't be long."

Paula couldn't miss the way Micah's eyes smiled, or the way he seemed to bounce on the balls of his feet like mere gravity couldn't keep him down. Would David have been the same way if she'd carried out her pregnancy?

Micah went back to Hanna, and Paula's mom hugged Jenna and congratulated her on being an aunt. Paula noticed that Jenna accepted the hug but didn't move so much as a finger.

The family talked excitedly about everything from the baby's weight to what a new mother felt after having a baby. Paula retreated to a place deep inside. She hadn't known how much regret being there would bring. This could have been her three years ago, giving birth to her child. Her family would have been waiting in these straight-backed chairs while she delivered her daughter.

Her gaze sharpened, and she realized her mom was studying her. The smile was going lax, and something akin to compassion was slipping into place. Paula looked away.

In a short while, Micah took them back into the room with Hanna and the baby, keeping his sister in the circle of his arm. They all crowded around the bed, and Paula found herself closest to her sister. Hanna looked tired, and her face was slightly swollen from the pregnancy. But there was nothing but joy on her face. In her arms she cradled a tiny bundle. His face was pink, and a hospital cap covered his tiny head.

"Oh, wow. He's just beautiful. Congratulations, Sis."

"Thanks." Hanna gazed down into the baby's eyes. They seemed fixed on his momma. "And thanks for flying out for this."

"I wouldn't miss it." Paula touched the baby's cheek, relishing the new softness of his skin. "I'd better let Grandma through, or she's gonna trample me."

Hanna laughed.

"I heard that," her mom said, "and you're right. Move aside." She playfully nudged Paula out of the way.

"Do we finally get to hear what you've named him?" Gram asked.

Micah and Hanna exchanged a glance, then Hanna spoke. "We named him Thomas Paul Gallagher . . . after Grandpop."

Gram's eyes misted over. "He would have been so proud."

Paula stepped back to stand in front of David, who leaned on the wall next to a clear bassinet. Hanna handed the baby to Micah, and Natalie and her dad gathered close. Micah held the infant as though he were made of delicate glass.

Behind her, David wrapped his arms around Paula's waist and laid his head against hers. The warmth of his body against her comforted and soothed her.

He whispered into her ear. "Someday."

<hr />

The weekend passed in a flash. She and David returned from the hospital late, and they got up early for church the next morning. Her flight left midafternoon, so there wasn't much opportunity to talk. After church she rushed home to get her things together, stopped by the hospital for a brief visit, and headed to the airport to wait for her flight.

When she got back to her apartment, she realized she'd taken her Jackson cell phone instead of her Chicago one. The next day she was back to work, flying at the dizzying speed of a world where deadlines ruled. That afternoon she tried to focus on the wording of her story for the evening news. A mom and pop flower store had been robbed that afternoon, and the elderly owner had been held at gunpoint.

At the thought of flowers she was reminded of the previous week on Valentine's Day when she'd come into work to find a red rose on her desk. The tag said only: *Paula*. David had already sent a beautiful vase of calla lilies, so she knew it wasn't from him. She remembered the "Roses are red" poem her mystery admirer sent her and shivered.

She left the rose there and went to ask Cindy if she knew where it came from.

Cindy shrugged. "It was on my desk when I got back from lunch break. I figured it was from your hubby."

Paula muttered a thank-you and promptly tossed the flower into her trash can. The guy had been thirty feet from her desk. The thought coiled in her mind like a snake ready to strike. She hadn't told David about it over the weekend. There hadn't been enough time to really talk about anything.

Now she rubbed her eyes and told herself to focus on the story at hand. There were stories to tell, deadlines to meet, and she couldn't keep getting sidetracked this way. She worked until the story was succinct, the wording tight.

Her desk phone rang, and she picked it up, still distracted by the story. "Hello, Paula speaking."

"Hi, Paula, it's Deb."

Immediately every part of her mind redirected to the woman on the other end of the line. "Deb. How've you been doing? I've thought so much about you over the past week. I didn't want to bother you with a call."

"We're OK, at least as much as can be expected. And we both want you to know how much we appreciate your telling us what you found out. It's been—very difficult, but with God's help we're getting though it."

Relief assuaged her like a storm-driven wave on the shore of Lake Michigan. It was amazing they weren't angry with her for keeping the truth from them for several days. Instead, Deb had thanked her.

"I appreciate your understanding," Paula said. "And I'm very glad to hear you're both coping as well as can be expected."

Just tell her the rest of it. You know you need to.

"Deb, there's—"

"We were wondering—"

They spoke at the same time.

"I'm sorry," Deb said. "Go ahead."

Yes, Paula, go ahead. Go ahead and tell her what kind of woman you are. Go ahead and make this even worse for her.

"I was going to ask if we can get together again. There's something else I'd like to talk about." Paula closed her eyes, knowing she'd just started the ripple that would fan out and rock everything in its path.

"That's funny—I was going to say the same thing." Deb gave a short laugh. "How about if we meet somewhere other than our house? Steve's mom is coming tonight to stay with Faith. I know it's late notice."

"Tonight would be fine." But they couldn't meet in a public place.

Paula wasn't going to spill her darkest secret someplace where she might be overheard.

Darrick passed by her desk without even making eye contact. He'd been distant with her and everyone else since his error on the harassment story.

"How about my place?" Paula asked. Linn would still be working, and the thought of coming clean in her own territory sounded a lot safer than doing it anyplace else. When Deb agreed, Paula gave her the address and hung up.

She was still thinking about the phone call that evening when she brewed a pot of coffee and straightened up the living area. She tossed a pair of her socks through the bedroom door and straightened the pillows on the couch and love seat. Then she paced.

She hadn't been able to eat a thing for dinner. David e-mailed, and she back-burnered the response. It felt as if two worlds were about to collide, and she wasn't sure there'd be any survivors.

Help me, God. I don't know how to do this.

Three soft knocks sounded on the door, and Paula went to open it before she could weasel out of it. Deb clutched her purse in her crooked elbow, and Steve offered a smile, though his eyes seemed coated with sadness.

They said hello, and Paula took their coats and offered them a seat. When she offered them coffee, they declined.

Paula sat on the recliner across from them. She addressed Steve. "Deb said the two of you are doing OK under the circumstances."

"With God's help." He placed his elbows on his knees and laced his fingers.

"My thoughts have been in a whirlwind," Deb said. "There are so many aspects of this: the fact that our birth child died without our knowing, the realization that Faith was nearly aborted, that her cerebral palsy could have been avoided. It's taken a week to start sorting through it all, and I'm afraid we've only scratched the surface."

At the mention of the abortion, Paula's nerves frayed, like the stringy ends of an old rope.

"I suppose the one positive thing here," Steve said, "is that there's no other birth mom out there wondering what happened to her birth child. There's no worry about losing Faith now."

Paula cringed from her toes to the top of her head. Now she really didn't want to tell them the truth. How come it just kept getting harder? Maybe if she started with their questions, she could ease into it. "You said you'd wanted to talk again. Why don't we start there?"

Deb and Steve exchanged glances, then Deb spoke. "I hope you won't think we're picking on you for asking this, because we do appreciate that you told us the truth." She folded her hands in her lap. "That day I came into your office and asked if you'd found out anything—why didn't you tell me then? I know you already apologized for that, and we've forgiven you."

Beside her, Steve nodded.

"But I don't understand why," Deb said. "Were you afraid of hurting us? And what about your story? Steve and I thought that when you solved the mystery, you'd put it on the air. Not that we're in a big hurry to have that happen—we just wonder why you haven't."

Everything inside Paula seemed to seize up like car brakes on a glazed, icy pavement. Words, which normally slid neatly into place, seemed stuck in a frozen jumble.

Help. It was the only word she could think of, and it was sent up to God like a desperate plea from a dying woman. But she'd be the first to admit she didn't deserve His help at all.

Deb and Steve sat patiently waiting for her to collect her thoughts. He took his wife's hand and intertwined his fingers with hers.

"You're right. There is a reason I didn't tell you that day, Deb. And there's a reason I've not been in a rush to air the story. It's why I asked to meet with you." She took a deep breath, and the expansion of her lungs pulled on her tightened muscles. "Several years ago, just when my career was starting to take off, I got pregnant. As much as I wanted to have a child someday, I was unhappy with the timing. I'd just received a promotion and didn't want to jeopardize that." She cringed at how shallow that sounded. But that's the way it had been.

"I was surprised that my husband was happy about the pregnancy. I tried to go along with it. I tried to be happy about it, but the only thing I could think of was my career going down the tube. In TV you have a very limited amount of time to make it. Especially women. As you age, your chances become slimmer and slimmer. Not that it's any excuse. I see now how distorted my thinking was." She tucked her hair behind her ear. "To make a long story short, I decided to have an abortion."

When she looked at Deb, she was surprised to see compassion instead of condemnation. It gave her the courage to go on.

"I was scheduled to attend a conference, and I saw that as the perfect opportunity. I decided to have an abortion while I was out of town, then call my husband and tell him I had a miscarriage." She closed her eyes, knowing the compassion in Deb's eyes would be gone, and not wanting to know what had replaced it.

"Looking back, I know it was the biggest mistake of my life. It was wrong and stupid and selfish." Paula twisted the ends of her cashmere sweater. "And the repercussions—" She shook her head. "I had no idea."

"I'm so sorry, Paula," Deb said. "I can't imagine the pain that brings."

Paula wished it were only her own pain. But her decision would cause pain for others who didn't deserve it, and that's what hurt the most.

Steve cocked his head. "It makes sense. All of this about the aborted baby surviving has opened up old wounds."

If only that was all it was, she could nod, and they would pat her shoulder and express their sympathy and leave. She had to say it before she lost her courage. "I'm afraid it's more than that." Her mouth felt as dry as talcum powder.

"What do you mean?" Deb asked.

Paula was about to shatter their world all over again, and the guilt was overwhelming. "The city that held the conference I was supposed to go to—the one where I had the abortion—was Chicago. I had it right here in Chicago." She made herself meet Deb's gaze. "At Chicago General. On June twelfth."

The emotions that passed over Deb's face were like the stages of dusk. One blended right into the other—confusion, realization, and horror, without any clear distinction between them.

"What year?" Steve's voice was like a taut wire.

Paula's heart felt like it was being squeezed in a vise. She was afraid to look at Steve. "The same year Faith was born. The very same day."

"But—" Steve tugged at his collar. "But there must have been others. More than one abortion that day."

He was reaching to grab hold of any other possibility than the one they feared.

"I'm sure that's true," Paula went on. "But when I had the abortion, I used the name Paula O'Neil. I didn't want it to be traced back to me. The nurse who saved the baby—saved Faith—told me the patient's name was O'Neil. I didn't tell her it was me. No one knows."

Deb's eyes seemed to deflate of every emotion except horror. Paula looked away. Steve closed his eyes, and Paula wondered if he was praying or just trying to escape the truth.

Across the room the computer fan hummed. Outside the window, cars whizzed by. Inside Paula's body her heart cracked like an old, brittle stick.

She felt like a human tornado. *Have you broken everyone around you yet? Is there anyone whom you've left untouched? Perhaps you should go tell your mom and your sisters, and don't forget David. Yes, you're not finished with your search-and-destroy mission yet.*

Paula's eyes stung, but she wouldn't cry. This wasn't about her anymore, and crying wouldn't fix a thing. She finally looked at Deb. The woman's face was mottled red, and her eyes were glassy.

"What—what are you planning to do?" Steve's tone was as smooth as a shiny, steel lamppost and every bit as hard.

Paula touched the couple's clasped hands. "I'm not going to do anything. Look, you're Faith's parents. I tried to abort her, for heaven's sake. What right do I have to be a mother to her? Please, believe me, I won't try and take Faith away. She's right where God meant her to be all along."

Steve's eyes filled, and his Adam's apple darted down, then back up again.

Deb met her gaze as if to weigh Paula's sincerity.

"I promise you, Deb. I won't do anything. I do love that little girl—" Paula's throat closed up. "But Faith is your daughter, and she belongs with you." As painful as those words were to say, they were the truth.

"What about your husband?" Steve asked.

David. Maybe Paula didn't deserve a child she'd tried to abort. But what about David? He'd wanted that baby. How would he feel about losing the child he was just finding out about? She couldn't make a promise for David. She didn't know how he'd respond to her or how he would feel about Faith. She wanted to reassure them, to tell them that David wouldn't dare take their child away, but how could she know?

"I—I haven't told him yet." She shifted in her chair and forced herself to maintain eye contact.

"You haven't told him about Faith?" Deb asked.

Paula's lips trembled. "I haven't told him anything. He still thinks I had a miscarriage three years ago."

"Oh, Paula," Deb said.

She heard both compassion and frustration in Deb's voice. "I know I have to tell him. Maybe I should have told him before I told you. I don't know. I don't know anything anymore."

"How do you think he'll take it?" Steve asked.

Paula looked at Steve, remembering when David had thought she'd betrayed him. He'd become like a stranger—even though he had little proof. What would he do when he found out she had tried to abort the child he wanted and lied about it? What would he say when he realized they'd held each other as he cried, all the while knowing she was the cause of all his pain?

A tear slid down her face. "I don't know," Paula said.

Steve stood up and walked to the window. The streetlamp outside the window spotlighted the flurries that drifted to the ground. "Maybe she doesn't have to tell him everything."

"Steve." Deb nailed his back with a look. "You know that's not right."

Steve turned. "You want to risk our losing Faith to a man she doesn't even know?"

Deb clutched her purse with her hand. "When we decided to go forward with this, when we called Paula to tell her our story, we felt God was leading us. It can't be a coincidence that Paula and I ran into each other at the hospital that day. God is doing something here. I don't know where it's going to take us, but we have to do the right thing and trust Him to work it out."

"I'm not losing my daughter."

Deb stared at her hand, wrapped tightly around her purse.

Steve's harshly spoken words were followed by a silence that made Paula want to squirm. She'd managed to divide the Morgans with her news.

"When are you going to tell him?" Deb asked quietly, as though sheltering Steve from her words.

"I'm going home this weekend. I'll tell him then." Paula's spirit trembled at the thought. But there was no sense in dragging it out. She couldn't hide the truth anymore, and the Morgans needed to know what David's position was. It was only fair.

"I'll be praying for you."

Who was Deb to say those words for her? She didn't deserve Deb's thoughtfulness and concern. Paula had only recently become a praying woman herself, but she said the only words she could think of to comfort the woman. "I'll be praying too. For all of us."

CHAPTER
THIRTY-TWO

David set his Coke on the coffee table and snapped open the *Wall Street Journal*. Though his eyes focused on the page, his mind wandered to his own business. JH Realty was doing well, considering it was winter. Of course, with Paula gone to Chicago, it meant more time spent working. His extra effort was paying off, though, and if it became necessary to sell it and move to Chicago, he'd be able to get his money out of it and then some.

Paula hadn't said much about the anchor spot when she flew home for the baby's birth, but they'd been rushed. Rushed to get to the hospital, rushed to get home to sleep. Well, not too rushed for the sleep.

He smiled, remembering their lingering moments in bed before they set the alarm clock so they could make it to church. Paula hadn't said anything, but she had seemed different. Softer somehow. And later she hadn't made a single sarcastic remark about the people at church or the pastor's sermon. She'd even seemed to enjoy the service. Maybe something was happening in her heart. He'd been praying for it.

When the phone rang, he knew it was Paula. Who else would call after ten?

"Hi, baby," he said.

"How'd you know it was me?"

"I could tell by the ring."

"And how is my ring different from all the others?" He could hear the smile in her voice.

"It's low and sexy. It practically purrs."

She laughed and the sound of it endeared him. "You goofball."

"It's late. I'm slaphappy."

"It's ten fifteen. You're not a pumpkin quite yet."

"How's your week going?" he asked.

"Well, that's what I called about. Miles took me aside today and asked if you and I could join him and his wife on their boat this weekend."

A part of David was disappointed. He realized he'd been looking forward to some quiet time alone with his wife. "But you've got tickets to fly home."

"Well, normally, I'd put him off. But he said something else. He said, 'We've got some important things to discuss,' and he had this twinkle in his eyes. Hon, I think he's going to offer me the anchor chair."

Conflicting emotions churned up in him, but the foremost one was happiness. "Oh, babe, that's great. You think he's going to offer it to you this weekend? But I thought that other reporter was doing a bang-up job lately."

"We didn't have time to talk about it over the weekend, but Darrick suffered a major career setback. His coverage of that big story he broke a couple of weeks ago was incomplete. Irresponsible even. And one of our competing news channels got the full scoop. Darrick's been in hot water with Miles ever since."

"What about the other reporters? You don't think any of them are in the running?"

She huffed playfully. "Thanks for the vote of confidence."

"I didn't mean it that way. I know you're destined to be the next Diane Sawyer."

"That's more like it."

"I'm thrilled for you, really. I guess I'm just a little disappointed that we won't have time alone this week. I was looking forward to talking, you know?" The pause went on so long, he thought he'd lost the connection. "Paula? You there?"

"I'm here. I was looking forward—I wanted to talk with you too. Maybe I can come home the following weekend, and it'll be just you and me. OK?"

He thought he detected sadness in her voice and realized he'd just dragged her down when he should have been excited for her. "Sure, you're right. And it's not like we won't be seeing each other this weekend. I'm thrilled for you, Paula. You've worked hard, and you deserve the promotion."

"But—but what are we going to do if I get the job? I can't keep flying home on weekends."

Ah, that's why her voice was laced with sadness. He hadn't told her yet, but he couldn't think of a better time to do it than now. "I've been doing a lot of thinking about that. If you get the anchor chair, I'm coming to Chicago with you."

He heard her quivery gasp, then there was nothing but silence. He would've given anything to know what was going on inside her head.

"Oh, David." Her tone was choked with emotion.

"I love you, baby. I'd move anywhere on earth to be with you."

"But your business, your career—"

"I might keep JH Realty for a while and let Jack run it. If I decide to sell, it shouldn't be too much hassle. I might even turn a profit. And Chicago is a great market. It's ripe with real-estate opportunity."

She sniffed. "You've built a clientele there. You'd be starting all over. It's such a sacrifice, David." She sniffed again, and her voice wobbled. "I don't deserve it."

"Stop it. I've already made up my mind." He tried to lighten the moment. "Miles is about to give you a huge leap up the corporate ladder. It's a culmination of years of hard work, a dream come true, and quite frankly, you're ruining it for me."

She laughed and the sound of it made his heart expand.

"I'm really proud of you, Paula."

He heard her crying softly and wondered for a moment why his gesture had moved her so much. It wasn't like her to break down. She'd never been the sentimental, emotional type. That's one of the things he loved about her. If she was getting all teary over one loving gesture, maybe he hadn't been so good about expressing his love. He'd have to work on that.

"I should go." Paula sounded like she had a whopper of a head cold. "I still have some copy to work on for tomorrow."

"All right. Let me know what time I need to get out there Friday."

"I will," she said. "I love you, David."

"Love you too, baby."

❦

David was still thinking about the phone conversation the next night while he packed for Chicago. Paula had e-mailed to let him know he needed to be at the pier at six o'clock Friday evening. That meant taking off early the next day, but he'd gotten caught up on paperwork and had scheduled showings around the days he'd be gone.

He pulled his navy Dockers from the closet and carefully laid them in his roller bag along with the finely knit sweater Paula had ordered for him from Banana Republic. Though he'd normally wear jeans and a sweatshirt on a casual trip, he wanted to be an asset to Paula where Miles was concerned, and he knew Paula sure wouldn't be wearing jeans.

He looked up the weather on the Net and saw Chicago was in for decent weather for late February. Saturday was supposed to be in the high forties with plenty of sunshine.

The warmth of the sun would help keep the crisp air from feeling freezing cold. He'd definitely need his prescription sunglasses to deal with the glare of the sun on the water. They should still be in Paula's jewelry box, where he always kept them in the winter. He walked across the carpet to the dresser on the far side of the bedroom and opened the jewelry box. They were nestled down at the bottom, where he'd put them at the end of summer.

As he shut the box, his eye caught a cell phone that lay between the back corner of the box and the mirror. Paula's cell phone. Not her old one, but her Chicago one. She must have left it in their rush to get her back to the airport on Sunday. She was probably going nuts without it.

He wondered why she hadn't mentioned it to him, but maybe she thought she lost it somewhere. Maybe he should call her and let her know it was here. He glanced at the red, digital numbers on his alarm clock. It was almost eleven. He'd just bring it with him tomorrow.

But maybe there were some messages she needed to know about. He turned on the phone and saw she had five messages. He'd just listen to them, and if there was anything that sounded urgent, he'd call her first thing in the morning.

He sat on the down duvet, pushing his roller bag aside. It took him a minute to figure out how to retrieve the messages. While he listened to the first one, he grabbed a pen and pad of paper from Paula's nightstand drawer. He jotted down the name and number of someone from the station who had a question about a story, then saved the message. The second one was from Linn, calling from someplace noisy. She'd just gotten her grade back on the video project he and Paula had helped her on, and it was a 98 percent. He saved the message and advanced to the next one.

"Hi Paula, it's Deb. I just wanted to say thank you. I know how hard it must've been to tell Steve and me about your—abortion. And I hate to bring this up, but there'll be custody papers you'll need to sign. I'm sure you knew that was coming, but, well, anyway . . . Also, Steve and I would like to talk to the nurse you got your information from. I know you said her name was Louise Garner, but I'm not finding a number for her in the phone book. Well, we're praying for you, Paula. Talk to you later."

David's insides went stiff and brittle. Did she say *abortion*? He replayed the message. Paula had an abortion? When? Where? Was it a mistake? Did the caller misdial the number? He played the message again and caught the greeting. She'd specifically said, "Paula."

Paula had had an abortion. Could it have been before they were married? Wouldn't she have told him? And what was with the custody papers? He played the message for the fourth time.

"I hate to bring this up, but there'll be custody papers you'll need to sign."

Why would Paula need to sign custody papers? As a witness or something? None of it made any sense. What was the woman's name who'd called? Deb? He played the message again. Yes, it was Deb. The name sounded familiar. Then he remembered Paula had talked about a Deb back in December when she'd been working on the "Switched at Birth" story. Deb was the mother who'd found out her child wasn't the one she'd given birth to.

How did it relate to Paula? Why was Deb mentioning Paula's abortion and talking about custody?

Liquid fire burned through his veins, a warning that he might not want to know the answers to his questions. When had Paula had an abortion? His mind wrapped around the question until the thought was compacted into a hard ball.

Paula had only been pregnant once that he knew of, and she'd miscarried. She'd gone off to a convention or conference or something in Chicago and that's where—

His thoughts stopped with jarring suddenness. No. Just because she'd been in Chicago, just because she'd been away from him when the miscarriage happened didn't mean—

He replayed Deb's message, listening for any clues he'd missed before. The only new thing he picked up was a nurse's name. None of it made sense. If she'd had an abortion during that pregnancy, why was Deb talking about custody?

No, it had to be something else. He should just ask Paula. She would tell him the truth, wouldn't she?

On the other hand, she'd obviously had an abortion at some point and had kept it from him. Who was to say she'd be honest about it now? Had she ever been planning on telling him?

Louise Garner. The name came to him like a bolt of lightning against the darkened silhouette of the Tetons. The message had said something about Paula getting all her information from this nurse. He looked at the phone, ready to replay the message, but flipped the phone closed instead.

Maybe Deb couldn't find Louise's number, but David was going to. He had fifteen hours before he caught his plane, and he was going to know the truth before he left.

Even if it killed him.

CHAPTER
THIRTY-THREE

Linn hung up the phone and clasped her sweater around her. Talking to Natalie always gave her mixed feelings. On one hand, she was happy Grace had such a happy home with a great mom and dad. On the other hand, it made her lonely and sad to hear Natalie's excitement and Grace's little baby sounds. She picked up her purse off the floor and settled into the leather recliner. After fishing around the cavernous interior, she found the envelope of photos Natalie had sent after Christmas.

She studied Grace's chipmunk cheeks and thought again how much she'd filled out since her birth. Giving her up had been the hardest thing Linn had ever done. It still hurt, and she wondered when it would get easier to have a part of herself living hundreds of miles away.

You're making a new life for yourself. You're going to be OK.

As often as she said it to herself, it was getting harder and harder to believe. She'd had to give up Grace, and now she'd had to give up Adam, and she was weary of ushering people from her life.

Help me, God. I know it was the right thing to do in both situations, but it just hurts.

Ever since the kiss in the coffee shop, Adam had been painfully polite to her. His mouth was always set in a tight line, and he'd spoken to her only when necessary. When a donut shop where she interviewed called and offered her a job, she jumped on it. Three days after the kiss, she thanked Joe, said a stilted good-bye to Adam, and walked out the door. It had been a week ago, and she missed Adam more than she wanted to admit.

Not until she lost him for good did she realize that her feelings for him had grown beyond the fondness stage. She had a bad case of love, and there was no cure for it. Even absence seemed to make it stronger. While she bagged donuts for customers before the sun came up, she longed to have him there, saying something to make her laugh. Instead, she was stuck behind the counter with a middle-aged woman who seemed to detest either people or early mornings. She wasn't sure which, but the woman had a negative attitude that drove Linn crazy.

Linn set the pictures on the end table and leaned back in the chair. She'd looked forward to having a Friday evening off, and now she wondered why. There was nothing to do except sit there and get lost in memories that made her heart ache. To make it worse, Paula would be gone for a couple of days, so Linn didn't even have the distraction of company.

She curled her feet to her side and noted that she had the beginnings of a hole in the knee of her jeans. Great. Like she had money to go buy new clothes. She'd have to wait until garage-sale season.

She needed to find something to do other than sit there and stare at the hole in her jeans. Maybe there was a good movie or something on TV. As she reached for the remote control, a knock sounded at the door, making her jump. She set down the remote and got up, approaching the door timidly. If she looked out the peephole, would the person on the other side know she was looking out? Well, the door was bolted anyway, so she supposed she was safe.

Rising on her tiptoes, she peeked through . . . and went rigid with shock.

Adam stood on the other side of the door, shoulders hunched down in his winter coat, eyes turned toward the floor.

What should I do?

She took her hands off the door and cringed at the slight sound it made as it buckled in the doorframe. Had he heard it?

What was Adam doing here? Had she forgotten something from Java Joe? A scarf, a book, her heart? Yeah—maybe he'd brought her heart back, and now everything would be OK.

She stepped toward the door. She wanted to see him, longed to see him. Just to talk to him like old times and catch up on stuff.

Another knock startled her, and she took a step back. *Bad idea, girl. Don't do it.*

"I know you're in there, Linn." His voice seemed only inches away from her ear.

So he'd heard the stupid door thump as she'd stepped away from it. Now what should she do?

"Come on, I just want to talk."

She closed her eyes, savoring the sound of his voice. Her heart beat unsteadily.

"Please?"

Everything in her constricted into a knot. She stepped close to the door and slid the bolts from their slots. Lastly, she slid the chain aside and opened the door.

Adam's eyes locked on hers and didn't let go. "Hi."

She squeezed the cold metal doorknob in her clammy fist. "Hi."

"Did I catch you at a bad time?"

The best of times. And the worst of times. She hadn't realized she had something in common with Charles Dickens, she thought wryly. "Not really."

"Thanks for opening the door. I know you didn't want to."

It wasn't true. She wanted to see him more than anything. She craved him the way a dieting woman craves chocolate. "Want to come in?"

She regretted the words the minute they were out. Being alone with Adam was just plain dangerous. But he was already stepping across the threshold. She took his coat and hung it on the closet doorknob.

"Want something to drink? Coffee or tea?"

He didn't come for a tea party, Linn.

"No thanks."

She gestured toward the couch, and she sat opposite him on the recliner.

Distance is good.

"How've you been?"

"How's your new job?"

They spoke simultaneously, then laughed.

"You first," she said. Her feelings swam so close to the surface that the less she talked, the better.

"I was wondering how it's going at Dunkin's."

She shrugged. "It's pretty much a breeze. Bag the donuts, ring them up, and hand them over."

"How do you like getting up so early?"

She smiled. "It's the pits. But it's nice to get work over with early and then be able to focus on classes and homework the rest of the day."

He leaned back against the sofa and crossed his ankle over his knee. He'd hardly taken his eyes from her, and in the silence she could almost hear the channels changing in his mind.

"We've missed you at the shop."

What was she supposed to say to that? Did it mean he missed her, or that her old coworkers missed her?

"Your replacement is kind of lame. Well, she's OK at the register, but she hasn't gotten the hang of making drinks."

"She hasn't been there long." A part of her was jealous, imagining Adam standing behind another girl, teaching her how to use the steamer. Was she pretty? Did she have a crush on Adam?

Knock it off, Linn.

"You're right." He stared into her eyes. The glow of the lamp on the end table carved shadows into the other side of his face. "I guess the real problem is, she isn't you."

His words stirred up hope. How was it a guy like him cared about her?

I'll tell you how. It's because he doesn't know you. Not really know you. If he knew what you'd done, he wouldn't give you the time of day.

Adam's voice broke into her thoughts. "You haven't said much."

She shrugged. "I guess there's not much to say."

Please leave. Just go before I spill my heart out to you.

Her eyes pleaded, but he didn't pay any attention.

"That night at the coffee shop you said you have feelings for me."

She swallowed hard. Why was it suddenly so hard to breathe?

"You also said I didn't know everything about you."

She looked away, her spirit cringing. He wanted to know, and he wasn't going to let it go until she told him.

Please, God, don't make me tell him. I thought I left it all back in Jackson. I don't want to relive it all. Especially with Adam.

"Look, Linn. I'm not trying to force you to tell me anything. But I—I care about you. And you said you cared about me. And this thing from your past is like a big wall between us."

Just don't say anything, Linn. Let him have his say, and then he'll go.

Even if she did tell him everything and it didn't kill every feeling he had for her, it still wouldn't work. If the relationship got serious, they'd want to be married, and preacher's wives didn't have pasts like hers.

Her eyes skittered across the end table where her photos of Grace sat. On top was the one of Linn holding Grace in the hospital. Everything in her wanted to reach out and snap up the pictures, but to do so would only draw attention to them. Maybe he wouldn't see them. She looked away. She felt vulnerable having her secret baby's photos lying exposed on the table. She had to get him out of there.

"You're not saying anything."

"There's nothing to say."

His jaw clenched, and she was torn. Torn by the need to keep her secrets and the yearning to soothe Adam's hurt feelings.

"Maybe you should go, Adam." She spoke softly and hoped he hadn't heard the crack in her voice.

He stood, but instead of walking toward the door, he paced to the window and back, his hands stuffed in his pockets. "I don't get it, Linn. I mean, what could it be? Were you an alcoholic? A drug dealer? A prostitute?" His voice crescendoed. "Do you think I'm such a jerk I couldn't get beyond anything you may have done?"

Her heart rate accelerated. "That's not fair. And how can you know my past wouldn't matter when you don't know what I've done?"

His jaw worked. "Then tell me."

She shook her head. "I can't!"

"Why not? If I walk out of here tonight, we may never see each other again. We could lose any hope of ever—" He ran his hand through his hair. "What's worse than that, Linn? What do you have to lose?"

Her pride? Adam's affections? She would shrivel up and die if she told him and saw disgust on his face.

He was in front of her now, down on his haunches, his hands on the chair's arms. "Tell me. Just tell me." His knuckles were like white pebbles against the black leather.

She felt like a wild animal cornered by a hunter. Her eyes flickered over to the photos, only inches from Adam's hand. She honed in on Grace, whose eyes were wide open, her little fist clutched beside her jaw. Linn's blood pumped through her veins so fast she was almost dizzy with it. She tore her eyes from the photo.

But it was too late. He'd followed her gaze and was staring at the photo. The space between his brows puckered.

He looked at Linn, and she felt pinned to the chair. There was no mistaking that it was Linn in the photo, even without makeup and wearing a dorky hospital gown. And holding a newborn.

He reached toward the photo and picked it up.

She froze, watching him take in all the details of the photo. The baby cradled in her arms. The railing of the hospital bed. The thermal jug of water on the bedside table.

"Is this—is the baby yours?"

He knew.

Her lip quivered. She couldn't lie, and she wouldn't deny Grace. "Yes."

Oh, God. Oh, God, don't make me tell him everything.

"When?" He examined the photo, as if trying to determine her age. "It's recent."

She crossed her arms over her chest and clutched the material covering her ribs.

"You have a baby." He said it out loud, as if that would help him believe it.

Don't say a thing, Linn. Just because he knows about Grace doesn't mean he has to know everything.

"Where is she? He?"

"She." Linn clamped her lips down. So much for not saying anything.

"Where is she? What happened to her?" He searched her eyes with compassion.

"It doesn't matter."

He frowned. "I already know your secret, Linn, right? What's the point in not talking?"

She gave a wry laugh. "You don't know the half of it, Adam."

He set the photo down and placed his hands on her knees. "Then tell me."

He just wouldn't give up, would he? No matter how many times she pushed him away, he kept at it. Would the truth finally drive him away? Would he see that she was no good for him? Would she survive the hurt it would cause when he turned away from her?

"Tell me, Linn. It won't matter to me. Nothing is going to change the way I feel."

He was so naive! Anger expanded her chest until she thought she'd burst with it. "Nothing, Adam? So it wouldn't matter if I told you I had an affair with a married man? That I stole him away from his wife and kids? And it wouldn't matter if I told you that I found out I was pregnant with his baby after he dumped me? Or that I almost aborted the baby? And then there's the part about how I connived my way into his ex-wife's life and tried to trick her into adopting my baby. Yes, that's right. The baby was mine and her ex-husband's. I was the 'other woman'—only she didn't know it at the time. But I'm sure all this won't bother you at all."

Somehow she'd gotten up from her chair and pushed her way past Adam as her words had rushed out. Now she found herself across the room, looking out the window but not seeing anything. And whatever she did, she was *not* going to look at Adam. The silence was enough to tell her all she needed to know. Maybe Adam had read a story or two about people like her, but he'd never dated one. And he'd sure never marry one. She needed to get him out of there before she crumbled into a pathetic pile of emotion.

"Get out, Adam." Her voice was choked, squeezed through a throat that seemed to have shrunk nine sizes.

"Linn—"

"Just get out!" She dug her fingers into her hair at her temples, wishing she could bury herself in the folds of the drapes.

When she felt his hand on her shoulder, she shrugged away from him. It was so like him to act compassionately, but she knew what his next words would be. *It's OK, Linn. You've been forgiven for all that.* And then he would start to say it was all a long time ago, then remember that the photo had been taken recently. He would slowly ease out of her life because he would soon realize she wasn't fit for him. If he didn't realize it himself, his family would be sure to inform him of it.

She swallowed back the sob that was working its way up over the lump in her throat. She couldn't hold it back much longer. "Get out, Adam!" She crossed her arms, hugging herself around the waist. "Please."

He paused so long, she was afraid he'd touch her again and that she'd fall into his arms and sob like a baby.

But then the floor creaked, and he was moving away toward the door. She heard him taking his coat off the closet doorknob. Heard him opening the door.

She could feel him pausing on the threshold, as if the air in the room stood fixed, immobilized.

"Don't forget to lock up." His tone was soft and heavy at the same time.

She wanted to run to him and tell him she loved him. She wanted to beg him to stay. But before she could act on the notion, she heard the door click shut.

CHAPTER
THIRTY-FOUR

Paula stood on the boat deck, her mittened hands clutching the railing as Miles and Eleanor got the boat ready to sail. As the wind whipped her hair around her face, she was glad she'd dressed warmly. Eleanor had dinner cooking in their onboard oven, and when David arrived, they'd push out into Lake Michigan's cold waters and have a quiet dinner together.

She wondered when Miles was going to spring the news. Would he tell her tonight, or would he wait until tomorrow? She didn't know if she would sleep at all if he postponed it. She consulted her watch, the lights from inside the boat casting a glow on its face.

David should arrive any minute if his flight wasn't delayed. There had been no bad weather in Chicago or Jackson that day, so at least the airports were operating normally.

"Here's your coffee," Eleanor said from the cabin door. She held out the mug.

"Thank you. You have a beautiful boat. Or should I call it a yacht? I'm not much of a sailor."

"Technically it's a yacht, but you can call her *Daddy's Girl*. My father gave it to us as a wedding gift."

That was some wedding present. "Well, I'm thrilled you invited us to join you. I can't remember the last time I was on any body of water."

A strand of hair came loose from Eleanor's chignon, and she brushed it behind her ear. "Well, Miles is a sailor at heart. It's a lot more fun in the summer, but even in the winter he just can't stand being off the water for too long."

"I heard it was supposed to be mostly sunny tomorrow and unseasonably warm. We can put on our sunglasses and pretend it's summer."

"I vote we stay in the cabin and play rummy."

Paula laughed. "Oh, good, you have cards. But don't let David convince Miles to do a round of poker. He's a card shark." She glanced up the pier, expecting to see her husband any minute.

"It must be hard seeing him only on weekends." Eleanor's fingers toyed with the gold pendant that dangled from her earlobe.

"Sometimes every other weekend. And yes, it's been hard. I think it's made us even closer, though."

"They say absence makes the heart grow fonder."

"Well, it didn't become a cliché for nothing." When she glanced back up the pier, she saw David still on shore, pulling a roller suitcase and looking around as if he were lost. "There he is." She waved her arms. "David!"

He stopped, his head following the sound of her voice. He stood still so long she thought he didn't see her. She waved her arms again. "Over here."

He began walking slowly toward them. Dusk had settled around them like a darkened fog, but the lights on the pier lit the way for him.

Eleanor poked her head through the cabin door. "Miles, David's here." She closed the door to the cabin and stood by Paula, watching David approach.

As David neared, Paula offered him a big smile. Even though they couldn't be alone together, she was so glad to see him. David was looking at Eleanor, though, a business smile curving his lips.

"Hi, hon." Paula stepped forward to embrace him, but his body was as stiff as a lamppost, and she didn't feel his arms around her. She stepped back and saw one hand was on his rollaway, the other tucked in his coat pocket.

"Mrs. Harding, nice to see you again." David shook her hand.

"Eleanor, please. We're so glad you could come. Are you much of a sailor?"

Miles exited the cabin before David could answer the question.

Paula studied David while he greeted Miles. He was cordial enough to the Hardings, but he'd hardly looked at Paula, and his jaw appeared to be chiseled from the Grand Tetons. Something wasn't right, but she'd have to wait until they were alone to pry it from him.

Eleanor, Paula, and David went inside the cabin to warm up while Miles untied *Daddy's Girl*. Eleanor showed David to the room they'd bunk in so he could stow his bag, then he excused himself to the rest room, a small compartment in the lower level of the boat.

After being shooed away from the galley, Paula took a seat at the table, where Eleanor had a lovely setting of china and silver, minus the dinner plates. The candles in the center of the table were fastened down to avoid being toppled over, and the flames danced on the wicks, pushed by the heat that flowed through the cabin.

Paula wished she could follow David below and ask what was wrong. But it would be rude to abandon Eleanor while she was cooking for them. After several minutes Eleanor declared everything was ready and that they'd eat as soon as Miles had pulled away from shore and found a spot to anchor down for the night.

Just when Paula began wondering what was taking David so long, he came up the stairway.

"Something smells wonderful," he said.

"Oh, David, have a seat. Thank you, but I'm afraid it's only Cornish hens and rice. I've heard Paula is a culinary queen, and I'm afraid I can't compete with that."

Paula thought David would jump in and say something about her cooking, but when he didn't, she spoke. "I'm afraid I haven't had much time lately for the culinary arts, and anything home cooked is a treat."

Eleanor settled into a chair next to her. Across from her, David still wasn't acknowledging Paula. It was like he'd turned back into that man he'd been before she'd come to Chicago. Was he regretting that he'd agreed to move from Jackson? Was he angry with her that she was pulling him away from his home and his business? Was he hoping she'd been wrong and that Miles wasn't going to offer her the job? She would have to wait until they were alone to find out. She only hoped it wasn't painfully apparent to Miles and Eleanor that something was amiss between them.

A strange broken triangle of conversation ensued. Eleanor spoke with both David and Paula, Paula spoke with both Eleanor and David, but David spoke only with Eleanor. It seemed awkward and stilted that David never responded to anything Paula said. It was as if she were visible only to Eleanor.

When Miles finally came in, Paula felt only relief. Maybe the broken verbal chain would be less obvious with a fourth participant.

Paula insisted on helping Eleanor by carrying the dinner plates with golden Cornish hens to the table, and they settled into their seats.

"You have quite a boat here," David said to Miles.

"Thank you. She was given to us by Eleanor's parents as a wedding gift with the name *Daddy's Girl* already painted on. I think it was his way of warning me to treat her right." He laughed.

"Miles." Eleanor delicately dabbed her lips with the linen napkin and addressed Paula. "He always jokes that he'll never be able to sell the boat just because of her name."

"Well, how would that look?" Miles said. "My trading in *Daddy's Girl* for a newer model?"

"I see your point." Paula took a sip of wine. "I'm sure you'd never want to trade either of them in since they're both top of the line."

"Well said, Paula." Miles sliced the meat off the hen, his knife scraping against the plate. "David, how's that business of yours going?"

"Very well. We've had a busier than usual winter and are gearing up for the spring rush."

"Everyone always wants to house hunt in the spring, don't they? I'll bet you work a lot of hours through the warm months."

David responded that he did work a lot of overtime, and the subject changed from real estate to station talk, where Miles and Paula dominated the conversation. He raved about the job she'd done and how much potential he felt she had.

Finally Miles raised his glass of Pepsi in a toast. "To Paula, an ambitious woman, a thorough reporter, and WMAQ's newest evening anchor."

Paula froze, his words starting to sink in. Did he say "evening anchor"?

"Congratulations, Paula." Eleanor patted her hand.

She should say something, but she didn't seem to have any breath.

"Look, she's actually speechless," Miles said.

Paula looked at David, but his eyes were downcast.

She'd gotten it. She was the new evening anchor! "Miles, I don't know what to say. I'm just—just ecstatic."

"You deserve it. I knew from the minute I viewed your tape from Jackson Hole that you had something special. You've more than lived up to my expectations."

Eleanor held her glass up. "To Paula."

Paula raised hers and looked at David, who finally raised his glass.

"To Paula," David said. "It looks like all your sacrifices have paid off." He stared at her with cold, hollow eyes.

The slightest of pauses seemed to fill the cabin with a wave of frigid air.

"To Paula." Miles began clinking glasses, regarding Paula with the proud eyes of a father.

Paula kept her smile carefully in place and hoped it was convincing. Though she was thrilled she got the job, fingers of fear had wrapped around her joy, all but strangling the much-awaited elation.

She looked at David, whose eyes were blinking rapidly. She had to get him alone and find out what was going on, but first they had to get through the meal. She took a sip from her glass, trying to focus on what she needed to say to Miles.

"I just can't tell you how much this means to me, Miles. A year ago I was wondering if my career would ever lead anywhere and now—evening news anchor for WMAQ in Chicago." She shook her head. "I can hardly believe it."

"Well, believe it, because it's happening. I know we've made the right choice."

Paula took a bite of the seasoned rice and cast a sideways glance at David. If he didn't say something soon, the Hardings would know something was wrong even if they'd missed the sarcasm in his voice at his toast.

"So," Eleanor said, "have the two of you discussed what you would do about living arrangements if you got the job?" She looked between Paula and David.

"Yes, we have."

"Not really."

Paula and David spoke at the same time. The contradiction of their answers introduced another layer of awkwardness. What was going on? David had told her just this week he'd be happy to move to Chicago.

"Well," Paula said, trying to recover, "what we mean is that we have discussed it but haven't completely reached a solution."

"I have some good contacts in real estate," Miles said. "I'm sure you could have a very successful career here in the Windy City."

David swallowed a bite of bread. "Thank you. I'm sure Chicago is burgeoning with real-estate opportunities."

"Oh, it is." Eleanor added. "And my family has a lot of contacts with potential buyers."

David wiped his mouth. "Well. I appreciate your both wanting to help."

David always had such control, even when he was steaming inside. He rarely raised his voice even when he was angry. But Paula had been with him long enough to see the signs of hidden anger. His blinking eyes, his working jaw. Even the way he spoke to the Hardings in careful, measured tones, dropping each word in place like a Scrabble player setting down tiles.

Perhaps sensing the tension at the table, Eleanor changed the topic.

The rest of the meal was stilted and uncomfortable for Paula, who tried to follow the conversation while attempting to identify the source of David's anger. She was thrilled when the meal was done and Miles suggested they go out on deck to view the stars.

Eleanor insisted on leaving the dishes for later, so they bundled up in coats and went out on deck to sit in lounge chairs.

Above them, tiny white dots twinkled in the crisp air. Miles pointed out some of the constellations. David remained silent, even though Paula knew he could identify nearly every visible constellation.

Miles engaged David in a discussion about stocks while Eleanor gave Paula tips on the best places for a good haircut and manicure. But Paula couldn't fully focus on the conversation when David was sitting twelve inches away and hadn't touched her all night.

Finally, when Paula's skin felt stiff and cold, David stood and said it was time for him to turn in.

Paula took the opportunity to get David alone. "I hope you don't mind, but I think I'll turn in too."

"By all means," Eleanor said. "If you need anything, just holler—and please, make yourselves at home."

"Thank you for the wonderful meal, Eleanor. And Miles, I'm truly thrilled about the anchor chair."

"You deserve it," Miles said.

They said good night, then Paula made her way after David into their cabin. Silence followed them through the narrow doorway like a stalker. After unzipping her coat, Paula shut the door behind them.

The only sounds in the room were the *swooshes* of coats being removed. Paula laid hers across the dresser and watched David as he hung his in the tiny closet. Had he said a single word to her all night? What was his problem? The Hardings had to have noticed. She'd just gotten the biggest boost of her career, and her husband hadn't even congratulated her. Didn't he know what this meant to her? Couldn't he at least be happy for her, even if he was angry with her for some unknown offense?

She began changing her clothing. Even if he wasn't thrilled about moving to Chicago, couldn't he have shown a little joy? Maybe even been proud of how hard she'd worked?

She slipped her silky nightgown over her head, wishing she'd brought an old ratty pair of sweats instead. But David didn't notice anyway, as he was rooting through his travel case.

Feeling angrier by the minute, she went to the rest room and washed off her makeup with her three-step face-care method. After moisturizing she brushed her teeth, then returned to the bedroom.

David sat on the edge of the bed, setting his travel alarm, his roller bag tucked neatly by the nightstand. They needed to talk, but apparently he didn't think so. Did he think they could go through the whole weekend this way? Just the thought of it was enough to make acid stir in her stomach. She'd be snacking on Rolaids all weekend if they didn't resolve it.

David jerked the sheet loose from the edges of the bed with a hard, angry yank and got under the covers.

"What is your problem?" she asked.

Silence was his answer.

She tried again. "You haven't said a word to me all night, David. You haven't touched me. You've hardly looked at me. Can you *please* tell me what's going on?"

He lay down, punching his pillow up and turning away toward the window. "What could be wrong? You just got everything you wanted." The tone of his words was chipped from an ice block.

She tugged the covers back and sat on her side of the bed. Yes, she got what she wanted in her career, but why the silent treatment from David?

Her frustration with him grew. "We just talked two days ago, and everything was fine. You said you'd move to Chicago, and now you're saying you won't? I don't get you at all. I can't read your mind, and I'm not into telepathic messages, so maybe you can clue me in."

He reached over the side of the bed. "Messages. Ah yes, they can be quite enlightening." He tossed something to her side of the bed, and it landed on her bare leg. "You forgot something last weekend."

Her phone. She'd thought she'd lost it at the airport.

"Messages . . . they can be quite enlightening." His words rang back in her mind, making sense in a way that made her middle clamp up.

"Go ahead, Paula. You'd better get all the important messages you missed this week."

She was shaking now. The phone sat in her clammy palm. She didn't want to hear them. Just the thought of what might be on there made her want to go up on deck and toss the thing out into the frigid waters of Lake Michigan.

She made herself turn on the phone and push the buttons to retrieve her messages. She put the phone against her ear. Her heart pounded up into her throat. The first message began. It was Cindy calling on Miles's behalf with a question about the dry-cleaning story. The next message was from Linn. Paula listened to it, part of her wanting to skip ahead, the other part wanting to turn off the phone.

The bed was still except for the slight rocking of the boat. Back and forth. Back and forth. Beside her, David lay as tense and still as a coiled snake.

The next message began.

"Hi, Paula, it's Deb. I just wanted to say thank you. I know how hard it must've been to tell Steve and me about your—abortion."

Paula sucked in her breath.

"And I hate to bring this up, but there'll be custody papers you'll need to sign."

Oh, God, no.

"I'm sure you knew that was coming, but, well, anyway . . . Also, Steve and I would like to talk to the nurse you got your information from. I know you said her name was Louise Garner, but I'm not finding a number for her in the phone book. Well, we're praying for you, Paula. Talk to you later."

Paula closed the phone, and it dropped on the mattress beside her leg. Her breaths came in shallow puffs. Her heart beat like a frightened rabbit's, kicking frantically against her rib cage.

Oh, God, why did this have to happen? Think, Paula, think. He knows you had an abortion.

Deb also mentioned custody papers. Does he know Deb is the mother from the Morgan story? Maybe he's forgotten.

What did it matter? She had to tell him the whole truth now anyway. This wasn't the way she'd planned it. They were supposed to be in the privacy of their home when she explained it. She was supposed to tell him first, not have him find out on his own.

"I—I was going to tell you." It sounded lame, but it was the only thing she could think of.

"Right, Paula."

"I was! I was going to tell you this weekend when I went home, but then everything got messed up when Miles invited us here."

David turned then, but she wished he hadn't. His eyes were like cold death. "You lied to me all this time, and you think I'm going to believe you now?" His tone was as flat and icy as a frozen lake.

"I know it sounds implausible, but it's true, David. I swear it."

He ripped the covers back and went to stand in front of the window.

What was going through his mind? How could she fix it? Why hadn't she told him earlier? She should have told him before the Morgans. David was her husband, after all.

He turned and stabbed her with a look. The corner of his nose curled up in a snarl. "Why would I believe anything you tell me?"

She reared back at the hissed words. She didn't know this man. "Let me explain. Please."

"I don't need your sorry explanations, Paula. I already got them from Louise Garner."

Louise Garner. Oh please, no, God. He's heard it all. He knows it all, and he heard it from someone else.

Oh, God, he'll never forgive this.

"I'm so sorry, David."

Lame, lame, lame! What good would her apologies do now?

"Sorry? You're *sorry?*" He sneered the word.

She hugged her knees to her chest.

"You aborted our baby and told me you'd miscarried? *Miscarried*, Paula? I *wanted* that baby. I *grieved* that baby. I held you and tried to *comfort* you, and you lied about all of it!" His voice escalated, and she wondered if the Hardings could hear him. "And then you find out by some miracle that our baby, *our child*, survived—and you didn't tell me?"

David's image blurred through the tears that began pouring down her face.

"And you're—*sorry? Sorry*, Paula, is for someone who forgets an appointment or someone who says something in anger, or someone who betrays a confidence. Sorry is not for—for *this*."

She sniffled. "You're right. You're right, David. I don't deserve your forgiveness."

"That's right, you don't."

She stared down at the bedspread. His anger glared like the afternoon sun, and she couldn't bear to look at him.

"How could you do it? That's all I want to know. Did you sacrifice our baby on the altar of your career, Paula? Was the pregnancy just one little snag on the way up your precious corporate ladder?"

She closed her eyes and wiped her nose. If only she could deny it. But it was true. She *had* done it for her career. It was every bit as awful as he made it sound. She knew that now.

"I made a horrible mistake. I'd do anything to go back and change it, David. Anything."

"Did you plan the abortion before you went to Chicago, or was it a last-minute decision to end our baby's life?"

"I—"

"Were you just planning to brush it all under the rug and go your merry way?"

"David, I—"

"And our daughter. My *daughter*. Didn't you think I might like to know she was alive? Was I ever going to get to see her or hold her or tell her I love her?"

She realized then that she did have something to offer. She could tell him about Faith. He would want to know every detail. "Her name is Faith," she said through a constricted throat.

David went still.

"She's got eyes the color of mine, but they're shaped like yours, kind of almond-shaped but turned up at the corners a bit. When she smiles, they look like crescent moons. Her skin is dark for being in the middle of winter. I think, in the summer, she would tan, not burn like me. Her hair is dark, the color Mom's used to be, and she has these adorable curls . . ."

David's face wore a look she'd never seen. Part awe, part broken-heartedness.

She didn't know whether or not to continue, but plunged in anyway. "She's very curious and active and affectionate to—"

"Stop." The word seemed to grate across his throat. He turned the stiff line of his back toward her. Beyond the window the night was dark, a black, empty canvas.

Had she said too much? She'd only wanted to give him what little she had to offer. She noted the broadness of his shoulders and how they tapered down to a trim waist. She wanted to wrap her arms around him and beg his forgiveness again. But he'd already told her it was too little, too late. She drew her knees closer and laid her cheek against her folded arms.

"David," she whispered. "I love you so much. I don't want to lose you."

He was quiet so long, she wondered if he'd heard her. Tears ran down her temple and into her hairline. What was he thinking about? He'd gone from raging anger to a chilling calmness, and it frightened her.

"I know I don't deserve your forgiveness, but I'm sorrier than I can say for what I've done. I'm sorry I did it, and I'm sorry I've hurt you. You mean more to me than anything—"

"Stop it."

She smothered the sob that clogged her throat. There was nothing she could say now. She'd ruined everything that mattered . . . and all for *a career*.

"You cheated me out of fatherhood," David said, startling her. "I could've had a little girl who ran to meet me when I came home. Who called me Daddy and gazed at me with stars in her eyes. Now she belongs to someone else."

Paula closed her eyes against the truth. It was too harsh, too final. And it had been all her doing.

"There's nothing you can do now to fix that." He turned toward her.

She searched his eyes. They were bathed in regret and something else she couldn't quite define. Hope began to stir at his words. There wasn't any going back, only going forward. Maybe he saw that now.

"I fell head over heels for you when we met." His eyes narrowed as if he was examining the past. "And we've had our rough times. But lately I've grown to love you more than I ever thought possible."

"Me too, David." She let her love for him shine through her eyes. He had to know how much she loved him.

He paused. "But I don't know who you are. The woman I fell in love with would never do what you've done."

"David, I—"

"The woman I've been married to has a dark corner in her heart that I didn't know about. A dark corner that has undermined every thought, every feeling I have toward her. I can't love someone I don't know, and Paula"—he shook his head—"I don't know you at all."

"Yes, you do. You do. I'm not this—"

"I don't want to hear any more." He opened his case and grabbed a turtleneck, pulling it over his head. Next was a pair of Dockers.

She sat upright, letting her knees fall flat. What was he doing? They were stuck on a boat, and the Hardings were up on the deck. "Where are you going?"

David buttoned his pants and walked toward the door.

She clutched the pillow. "Where are you going?"

He stopped, his hand curled around the doorknob. "I can't stay in here with you. I'm not sleeping with a stranger."

Her breath caught in her throat.

He opened the door and stepped through it. Then the door clicked shut with a snap of finality.

CHAPTER
THIRTY-FIVE

David turned and waved good-bye to Miles as he stepped off the plank. Hints of light had only now begun to appear on the horizon. He lined up the roller bag beside him and started down the pier, where Miles had arranged for a taxi to meet him.

He'd slept on the padded bench that lined the windows on the lower deck across from Paula's room. When the heartburn had started, he'd sat upright against the hard-foam back. When he awakened, it was just past five and he knew what he had to do. When he heard someone stirring above, he stepped quietly into the cabin to gather his belongings. He hardly looked at Paula, who lay sleeping like their world hadn't just screeched to a halt.

Miles was gracious about taking him to shore when he learned there had been a "family emergency." He asked twice if Paula wanted to go with David, but little did Miles know that the family emergency was all Paula's doing.

The wheels on the suitcase thudded over the wooden planks. When he reached the end of the pier, he saw the cab waiting along the street. He hurried his steps. The further he got from Paula, the happier he'd be. Even as the thought formed in his mind, his gut refuted it by clenching down hard. It was just anger, he told himself. And he had every right to that emotion.

He stepped into the cab, stowing his suitcase on the seat beside him. "O'Hare Airport."

The driver grunted and pulled away from the curb. David called to check on flights and found out he'd be stuck at O'Hare until three thirty. He closed his phone and dropped it into his coat pocket.

Closing his eyes, he leaned back against the cold, vinyl seat. He could picture Paula crying the night before and pleading for forgiveness, her green eyes covered by a glassy layer of tears. He shook the image from his mind. He could count the times on one hand that he'd seen her cry.

He turned his head and watched the steel and concrete landscape whizzing by. Was this Paula's home now? Was she going to take the job and live here? Was their marriage over?

He didn't see any way it could be salvaged. There was more hurt and rage inside him than he knew what to do with. It seemed like it was a week ago that he'd talked to Louise Garner, when, in fact, it had only been yesterday morning. He'd told her he was Paula's assistant, calling for details on the story. It was a lie he hadn't stopped long enough to feel guilty for.

Louise had been all too willing to talk, though her words were slow in coming. David had fished carefully and had eventually gotten the full story.

Now he almost wished he hadn't. Would it have been better to confront Paula with the message on her cell phone? Would she have told him the truth? He would never know.

Her words from the night before whispered in his mind. *"I love you so much. I don't want to lose you."*

Then why, Paula? Why did you do this? It was our baby.

And she was alive. The thought smacked him like a gust of February wind. She was here somewhere in Chicago. The cab stopped at a light, and he watched a dozen people cross the road. She could be only miles away. He was closer to her now than he'd ever been, and he longed to see his little girl. His heart sped at the thought. He had hours before his flight left—almost a whole day. He opened his mouth to speak to the driver, then shut it again.

Was he ready for that? Was he ready to face the little girl who didn't even know he existed? Was he ready to see her and walk away again, as if nothing had happened? Were the Morgans even willing to let that happen?

He needed more time. Time for the red coal of anger burning in his gut to cool off. The reality deflated him, and his breath left in a *whoosh*. He wished he had a picture at least so he could look into her face and see if there was a resemblance to him as Paula had said. He remembered the tape he had of *Good Morning America*, when the Morgans had been on TV. But even then, Faith hadn't been present.

Then something else came to him. Faith had some kind of disability. Paula had mentioned it when she'd been covering the story. Was it muscular dystrophy? Cerebral palsy? David couldn't remember for certain, but now he wondered if the abortion had had something to do with his daughter's condition.

He ached inside at the thought. Was there no end to this nightmare? Not only had he been cheated of his daughter, but his daughter had been cheated of a healthy body.

Someone else was taking care of her, taking her to doctor appointments and showing her how to tie her shoelaces. Everything he knew about the Morgans was positive, and he knew they were Christians. He supposed he should take comfort in knowing Faith was being raised in a loving home.

But somehow the thought only made him long for her more.

On Monday morning Paula rolled her chair into the slot at her desk and moved the mouse to wake up the sleeping computer. She blinked a few times, trying to shake out of the daze she'd been in since David left her on the yacht. She'd been in a fog through the whole staff meeting when Miles announced her promotion. She barely heard the congratulations offered by nearly everyone at the station. Instead, her mind was on David.

For the hundredth time her mind flicked back to their horrible weekend. How could things have turned so bad so quickly? David's parting words rang in her mind until she wished she had a delete button. The night of the argument she'd lain in bed for hours, listening for David's return, wondering where he'd gone, and how they'd get through the rest of the weekend.

As it turned out, she needn't have worried about that. When she'd awakened late the next morning, after having fallen asleep in the wee hours of the night, she found out David was gone . . .

***

"I'm so sorry there's been an emergency in the family," Eleanor said. "I hope everything's OK."

Paula tried for a smile. "I'm sure it will be."

"Miles insisted it was OK for you to leave, too, but David said he could handle it on his own."

Paula peered out the cabin windows, wondering if David was gone already or if he was still aboard somewhere. She hadn't noticed if his suitcase was still beside the bed. "I'm sorry for the trouble."

"Oh, it was no trouble at all. Miles is an early riser anyway. I swear the man only needs five hours of sleep."

They made small talk while chopping up onions and green peppers for omelets.

Somehow Paula got through the remainder of the weekend without breaking down.

However, when she arrived back at her apartment on Sunday, she escaped to her room and cried until she was drained.

***

When the phone on her desk rang, Paula's first thought was of David. She'd hoped when she got back from the lake that he would have sent an e-mail. Now, as she picked up the extension, she felt the same hope bubble up inside her.

"Paula speaking."

"There's a young man out here to see you." It was Cindy from the front desk. "He's asking to meet you."

Paula's hopes settled like a deflated inner tube around her feet.

"Does he have an appointment? I'm a little busy right now."

Cindy lowered her voice. "Just for a minute? He's really sweet."

She sighed. "All right."

Paula hung up the phone and headed toward the entry. She couldn't imagine why someone would just stop in and think she could drop everything at their whim. And today she wasn't in a good frame of mind to appease whims.

She smoothed her suit and stepped out onto the slate-floored entry. A big guy, maybe in his late twenties, stood rocking back and forth from one foot to the other.

She pasted a smile on and put out her hand. "Hi, I'm Paula Landin-Cohen."

His grin was almost goofy, like a shy nine-year-old.

"I'm Gordon." His words slurred across his tongue.

Her eyes met Cindy's. She was beginning to understand why the assistant had wanted Paula to meet him.

"Hello, Gordon," she said "It is so nice to meet you. Do you watch our news on TV?"

He nodded vigorously. "Every night. You're the prettiest one."

"Gordon!" A woman stepped through the front door, breathing hard and making a beeline for the guy. "Don't you ever run off like that again. What were you thinking?" She took hold of Gordon's hand. "You scared me silly."

"I wanted to meet Miss Paula," he said simply.

"I'm so sorry to have disturbed you," the woman said. "We were just standing in line for a pretzel, and next thing you know, I turn around and he's gone."

"It's OK," Paula told her. "I'm glad he stopped by."

Gordon's grin could have lit Wrigley Field. "Did you like my poem, Miss Paula?"

"Your poem?"

"The one I sent you."

"Oh, honey, she might not even open her own mail," the woman said. She addressed Paula. "He's a big fan of yours. Stops and turns on the TV at six o'clock on the dot every night."

"Roses are red, violets are blue, you're very pretty, I want to meet you." Gordon grinned.

The words rang with familiarity. The letter she'd received, the one she'd stressed over, had been from this harmless guy. Not some weird stalker. Relief flowed through her. "It was a lovely poem, Gordon."

He beamed and gave the woman a told-ya-so smile. "I wrote it."

"It's the nicest poem anyone has written for me."

"Really?" he asked.

"Did you send that gorgeous red rose on Valentine's Day?"

He nodded, his face looking as sheepish as her nephew's did when she kissed him on the cheek.

Paula felt a twinge of guilt for tossing the flower into the trash.

"We'll get out of your way now," the woman said. She tugged Gordon toward the door.

"It was nice meeting you, Gordon," Paula said.

He waved his fingers. When they reached the door, the woman turned around and mouthed "thank you."

Paula smiled as the door shut behind them.

"Well, I guess there goes your mystery stalker," Cindy said.

Paula gave a wry laugh. "Some stalker. He's a six-foot teddy bear."

"I'm so thrilled about your promotion. I knew you'd get it."

"Thanks."

"Did you have a good time on the yacht?"

Paula could think of a dozen ways to describe the weekend, and none of them included "good time." "Wow, what a boat. The Hardings are very gracious people."

"Miles said David had to leave early for a family emergency. I hope everything's OK."

Paula twisted her earring and nodded. "How are things with you and Cal?"

Cindy scooped up a handful of papers and stapled them. "Actually, he's filed for divorce."

Paula was stunned. She remembered Cindy's confession about lying to her husband. The whole thing hit too close to home. "I'm so sorry, Cindy."

Cindy seemed relieved when her phone rang.

"I'll let you get back to work," Paula said quickly and headed toward her desk. Would David do the same thing that Cindy's husband had done? If ever there was a lie that deserved the ultimate punishment, it was hers. Her life was unraveling, and there was nothing she could do to stop it.

CHAPTER
THIRTY-SIX

Four days later Paula climbed the stairs that led to her apartment, feeling older than the nursing-home residents she'd just interviewed on the air. Her career couldn't be going better, but nothing mattered anymore but David. He hadn't called, hadn't e-mailed, and she was feeling desperate for him.

She'd tried calling twice, but when the phone rang into voice mail, she could have cursed the caller ID she had installed on the phone the year before. The long e-mail she sent him had gone unanswered, and she didn't know what else she could do but pray.

She slid her key into the doorknob and turned it, pushing it open with her shoulder.

Linn tore her gaze from the TV. "Hey. You're just in time."

Paula glanced at the TV. "For what?" After the long week she'd had, she only wanted to go to bed.

"It's my video project. The professor gave them back today, and I wanted you to see the final version."

She thought of the day Linn had taped her and David. They'd spent a day out walking Chicago, connected and always touching, stopping to kiss every so often. It seemed like a lifetime ago.

"Sit down and I'll start it." Linn picked up the remote and pushed a button.

Paula took off her coat and draped it across the back of the sofa. Did she want to watch it? Could she bear to see the way she and David were *before*? She kicked off her heels and hesitated.

But then the tape flickered to life and there they were. She and David—sitting right there on this very couch holding hands. Linn jacked up the volume, and Paula heard Linn asking a question.

They laughed, then David responded, looking at Paula as though she was his everything. Linn had gone in for a closeup, so Paula could see the crescent-shaped crease bracketing his smile. Then the camera panned out. Paula was talking now. She couldn't remember what she said and couldn't seem to focus on the words she was hearing. David's arm wrapped around her shoulder and gave her a squeeze.

Was this all she would have to remember him by? A tape of a moment in time, when everything had been perfect? Would he never hold her hand or draw her close or look at her as if he couldn't get enough of her?

Her legs crumbled and she sank onto the sofa.

"What's wrong?" Linn asked.

Paula stared at the TV, seeing all she'd lost and how little she'd gained by the terrible mistake she'd made three years ago.

The image of her and David froze.

"Paula?"

She stared at the screen. "I'm fine."

Linn sat beside her on the sofa. "You're crying."

Paula wished she could hit the Rewind button of life and go back to that day she'd done that interview. Better yet, she wished she could go back three years ago and do everything over. But life wasn't like that.

"David knows about Faith," Paula said. She hadn't told anyone, not even the Morgans. She evaded their phone calls twice because they would want to know what happened when she told David. They'd want to know if he would sign custody papers, and she couldn't bear to tell them how badly the conversation had gone.

Linn straightened. "When did you tell him?"

Paula shook her head. "I didn't. He found out on his own."

Linn shifted. "Oh, Paula."

"I was going to tell him, but it was too late. He already knew." She wiped her face with her fingers. "It happened last Friday on the boat. He had Miles take him ashore while I slept." A bitter laugh pushed through her throat. "But, hey, I got the anchor position, so woo-hoo." As if that meant anything now.

"Have you talked to him since then?" Linn asked.

"Strangely enough, he isn't returning my calls." Paula's eyes brushed by the African violet on the sill. She'd thought the plant was regaining its health, but instead, the leaves had darkened until they were brown. Now, despite her diligence, the whole plant had toppled over at the base.

"I'm sorry."

"I'm sorry, too, but you know what I've learned? Sorry doesn't mean squat. Sorry doesn't undo the past or bandage the hurt. It doesn't do anything."

"He probably just needs time," Linn said gently. "He might still be in shock over the fact that his daughter is alive. I'm sure he'll realize how much you regret it. He'll come around, don't you think? It's obvious he loves you."

Paula didn't think it was shock so much as anger toward her for trying to abort their baby and keeping it a secret all these years.

"The woman I've been married to has a dark corner in her heart that I didn't know about. A dark corner that has undermined every thought, every feeling I have toward her. I can't love someone I don't know, and Paula . . . I don't know you at all."

The words had haunted her all week, and now they were like a brand on her heart.

⁂

When Paula went to bed, Linn prayed for her. She prayed for David's heart to soften and that he would find it in his heart to forgive his wife. If Natalie could forgive Linn for what she'd done, maybe David could forgive Paula. It might take some time, but God was capable of changing hearts. Linn should know better than anyone.

It looked like Friday had been a bad night all the way around. Her conversation with Adam had played in her head a hundred times. She missed him, and it hurt to imagine what he must think of her now. She hadn't realized until after it was over, but she'd been hoping deep inside that her past wouldn't matter. Why else would she have been in a major depression all week? But he left, just as she told him to, and she hadn't heard from him again. She supposed that was all the answer she needed, but it hurt like nothing else to admit it was true.

It had been a whole week, and he would have called her or come over again if he hadn't been completely repelled by what she'd done. If he cared about her as much as he claimed to, would her past have kept him away?

You are such a dork, Linn. This is what you said you wanted. You knew it would happen this way, and how can you blame Adam for the way he feels?

Adam had a future to consider, and he couldn't just follow his heart's whim without considering the consequences.

She picked up the remote and flicked the TV off. No sense in watching the tape now. It was too depressing to see how a vibrant relationship like Paula and David's could implode in a matter of weeks. She should study for the tests that were coming up, but she was burned out on studying this week.

The knock on the door made her jump. She looked at her watch and saw it was only a little past eight. She walked to the door and peered out the peephole.

Adam.

Why was he here, a week after they'd parted so badly? She couldn't contain the hope that swelled up in her. She glanced in the tiny mirror beside the door.

Ugh! The hours had melted away the last of her makeup, and her hair resembled something a cat had coughed up. She ran her fingers through her hair, then wiped the area under her eyes with her fingertips.

Before she could second-guess herself, she undid the locks and opened the door.

Adam's lips parted, and his eyebrows raised a fraction. Maybe he'd thought she wouldn't answer. His hair was windblown, his cheeks ruddy from the night air.

"Adam." She couldn't seem to think of anything else to say.

"I was afraid you wouldn't answer."

She shrugged. Truth was, she missed him so badly that she almost thought she conjured him up by will alone. But he was here. Standing right in front of her. The hope that rose inside her terrified her, and she punched it firmly down.

"Can I come in?"

She opened the door wider, catching a whiff of leather and cologne. "Can I take your coat?"

"That's OK." He didn't even make a move to take it off.

She offered him a seat, realizing the hope she'd punched back had sunk even further. He was going to make this a quick visit. She sat across from him in the recliner, keeping her spine straight and her guard in place. Getting hurt all over again wasn't at the top of her wish list, and it was feeling more and more like a real possibility.

"I guess you're wondering why I'm here."

She lifted her lips but couldn't quite call it a smile.

He crossed his ankle over his knee. "I've been doing a lot of thinking this week and realized I owe you an apology."

Here it comes. He just came to apologize. Though for what, Linn couldn't imagine.

"I'm sorry about how I handled things last week. I pushed you to tell me something you didn't want to, and I was wrong to do that." He looked at her, pausing.

"It's OK." Disappointment sucked the moisture from her mouth. What did it matter now? He knew the truth, all of it, and that had changed everything. What good would an apology do?

"It's not OK." He paused again until she met his gaze. His dark eyes drew her in and held her there. "I said I wouldn't push, but I did. I'm sorry." He stared down at his intertwined fingers. "There's another reason I came too. Two more, actually."

She tore her eyes away from him and settled into the curve of the recliner, tucking her trembling fingers between her knees.

Stop it! Stop hoping, Linn. You are just going to get yourself hurt again.

"There are things I should've said to you that night, but I was just so—"

Shocked? Horrified? Disgusted?

He shook his head slowly. "I had no idea what you'd been through. It about broke my heart to hear it."

"I brought it all on myself, Adam, so you don't need to pity me."

"It's not pity. I just—" He propped his forearms on his knees. "Linn, I get the feeling you're holding all these things against yourself. Like you're dragging this burden with you everywhere you go. Have you asked God to forgive you?"

There was nothing but compassion in his eyes, but somehow the question bothered her. The conversation was not going in the direction she'd expected. He was asking her about God?

"Of course I have."

"Are you familiar with the passage in Psalms where it says 'As far as the east is from the west, so far has he removed our transgressions from us'?"

She watched him sitting there on the couch, hands clasped as if in prayer, head tilted. All that was missing from this pastoral counseling session was a Bible and a box of tissues. This is what he'd come for? To counsel her like she was a member of his future church? Was that all she was to him now?

"Sometimes the hardest part of forgiveness is forgiving ourselves."

She crossed her arms, hugging herself. He wasn't here as the man she'd fallen in love with. He was there as a pastor, and that hurt more than anything.

"Even after the people we've hurt have forgiven us, we often carry around a grudge against ourselves, sometimes for years."

She didn't want to hear anymore. She just wanted him to go. "Did you learn that in seminary, Adam?"

He blinked, caught off guard, she supposed, by her sarcasm. "What's wrong?"

What's wrong was that he was treating her like—like any other person. What was wrong was that he was there to counsel her for the sins of her past. What was wrong was that he wasn't there to tell her the things she wanted desperately to hear.

"I'm sorry," he said. "I'm not making my point very clearly."

She stood up. "Actually, you've been crystal clear." She walked toward the door, expecting him to follow.

He did. "Wait. I'm not finished."

She clenched her jaw. "Don't worry, Adam, you got an A for content and an A for delivery." Her voice rose and trembled.

He grabbed her shoulders, his face only an arm's length away. "I don't want a stinking grade, Linn." His fingers loosened their hold. His eyes shone with fervency. "I want *you*."

She stared at him, unwilling to let his words sink in any further, afraid she'd misunderstood.

"Did you hear me, Linn?" He squeezed her shoulders softly. "I want *you*. I don't care what you've done or who you used to be. I only know that the woman standing in front of me isn't the woman who did those things. You let Christ into your life, and you're different now." A crease formed between his brows. "You're the woman who made me see there was something missing in my life. You're the woman—"

He touched her cheek, and she felt it to the bottom of her feet.

"You're the woman I fell in love with."

Her breath caught somewhere between her lungs and throat. She could have drowned in the warmth of his eyes. She knew she should say something, but she couldn't seem to make her lips move.

"I love you, Linn. I love the way you laugh and the way you bite your nails when you're worried. I love that you're so brave, and I even love your little sarcastic streak."

But there was still her past. Even if he could get beyond that, what kind of a future could they have together if he was going to be a pastor? Would his family even accept her if they knew the truth?

"What? Tell me what's going on behind those worried eyes." He caressed her face, and the gentleness of the motion put tears in her eyes.

"What about—I mean, I know this is looking pretty far into the future—but, Adam, you're going to be a pastor." How could she even mention being his wife when they'd yet to have their first date? She felt her cheeks start to burn. "You can't have someone like me hanging around."

He understood what she was getting at. She could see it in the way the corner of his lips tucked in. "Pastors don't have perfect pasts, and neither do pastors' wives. No one would expect you to be perfect." He brushed away the tear that had fallen onto her cheek. "Any mistakes we make can be used by God to help others. Think of the young pregnant women you could advise. They'd listen to you because you've been there. Think of the women who might be considering an affair. They'd listen to you because you've been there."

"I hadn't thought of it that way." After everything she'd done, she had a whole arsenal of personal experience at her disposal. Maybe God *could* use it somehow.

"You could have a real ministry to young women. If you wanted to, that is."

His words from earlier came back and washed over her like a mountain spring. *I love you, Linn.* Did he really mean the words? She was afraid to believe it.

As if sensing her doubts, he cupped his hands around her face. "Did I mention I love you?"

Her knees trembled, and she drank in the love that poured from his eyes. She'd only said "I love you" to one other man, but she knew now she hadn't even known then what love was. Looking into Adam's eyes, she could say it now, with full understanding. "I love you, too, Adam. With all my heart."

He pulled her closer, and his lips met hers. Like a breath from heaven, it sent a shiver through her.

When they parted, she remembered what he said earlier. Breathless from the kiss, she asked the question. "You said you came for three reasons." His lips cocked up on one side, and she thought how absolutely adorable he looked.

"That's right. I have a quiz for you."

She groaned. "A quiz?"

"Patience, Miss Caldwell, I think you'll pass this one with flying colors. OK, here goes." He looped his arms around her waist and set his forehead against hers. "A man and woman are in love with each another but have never gone on a date. The man asks the woman out. Does she: a) tell him she has to wash her hair, b) tell him she doesn't like dates, or c) accept the offer and kiss his socks off?

Linn couldn't keep the grin off her face. "C?"

His eyes lit like a sparkler on the Fourth of July. "*Ding, ding, ding,* we have a winner."

Linn wrapped her arms around his neck. "Looks to me like we have two winners," she whispered before her lips met his.

CHAPTER THIRTY-SEVEN

Paula found a space alongside the rows of parallel-parked cars and squeezed her car in between two others. A few minutes later she was invited into Louise's house by a nurse and walked into the bedroom with the vase of flowers she'd picked up on the way. "Hello, Louise."

Louise's eyes opened, and her head rolled toward Paula. "Hello, dear. It's good to see you again." Her voice sounded scratchier than it had on the phone when Paula had asked if she could stop by.

Paula set the flowers on the bedside table and picked up the thermos of water. "Would you like a drink?"

When Louise nodded, Paula helped her sit up enough to sip, then put the thermos back on the table.

"Thank you for the flowers."

"You're welcome. I appreciate your letting me come over again."

"I was worried about you after you left last time. You seemed shaken."

Paula swallowed. "I really appreciate how honest you were with me. I've come to tell you I won't be running the follow-up story on Faith. I'm not even sure why you told me everything. You didn't seem eager to have the story broadcast, yet why else would you have told me?"

Louise got a faraway look in her eyes. "As I reach the end of my life, I'm finding that I view things differently. I was no longer afraid of being shamed or ridiculed or punished so much as I was afraid of dying with answers people needed. That's why I told you the truth."

"Are you disappointed I won't be doing the story?"

"Honey, I just did what I felt was right, and I've done my part now. Mr. and Mrs. Morgan were over awhile back and we talked. It was— hard. But now that they know, I feel it's as resolved as it can be. There's no need for any of this to go further."

"I think you're right about that."

In the other room she heard the front door open and close.

"Brought you something, Mom," a male voice called.

A man stepped into the room, holding a sack in his hand. But Paula could only focus on his face. Their eyes met at the same time.

"Stan," Paula said. What was the station's new information technologist doing here? Then she recalled what Stan had just called Louise. *Mom.*

Stan's hand fell as his eyes widened. "Hi, Paula." A pink tide swept up his neck.

"Here, Mom, your favorite bagels." He leaned over and kissed her.

Louise patted his cheek. "You're such a good boy. I'll have one after dinner." She cocked her head toward Paula. "I didn't realize the two of you had met."

Confused, Paula looked at Stan. Didn't his mother know he worked with her? Suddenly a string of suspicions marched through her mind. Stan was Louise's protective son who'd refused to let Paula interview her. Stan had recently been hired at WMAQ. She'd received threats concerning the story and had her notes disappear from her computer.

"Can I speak with you a moment?" Stan asked her.

Paula tore her eyes from Stan and tried to smile at Louise. "It's time for me to be going anyway. It was nice to see you again, Louise."

"Stop by anytime."

Paula exited the room, feeling Stan's presence behind her. When she heard the bedroom door click shut, she pivoted swiftly. "Would you like to tell me what's going on?"

"Look, Paula," he began nervously. "I swear I would never have hurt you. I was only trying to protect my mom."

Despite her anger she couldn't even look Stan in the eye and believe him capable of anything hurtful. "You threatened me."

"I know, I—I'm sorry. I hated to do it, but my mom. You don't know what she went through after burying that baby. She grieved like it was her own child. She planted flowers out back every spring . . . like she was trying to pay penance for what she'd done. But all she did was save a baby no one wanted. It wasn't her fault the other baby died."

"That doesn't give you the right to do what you did."

His shoulders fell two inches. "I know."

"You threw a rock through my window and scared the snot out of me."

His gaze fell to her feet. "I'm sorry. I'll pay you back."

She huffed. "The money is hardly the issue. You stole my file, too, didn't you?"

"Yes." He tugged at his shirt cuff. "Look—I can't take back what I did. All I can do is say I'm sorry."

The words were painfully familiar. She knew all too well about regret.

"I was only trying to protect my mom. She's been there for me every step of my life, and I'm going to be there for her until she takes her last breath."

His tone softened her.

"I could probably have you arrested, you know."

He put his hands in his pockets. The light from the table lamp high-lighted the crow's feet at the corner of his eyes. "I know. But I'm asking that you don't. For Mom's sake."

"Is this the only reason you took a job at the station?"

"Yes."

"So you have no reason to stay there now."

"Are you ever going to air the story?" he asked boldly.

Paula gave a quiet laugh. "You have a lot of nerve. And not that I have to tell you, but no, I will never tell your mom's story."

"Then I have no reason to stay at the station."

Paula released her breath and narrowed her gaze on Stan. "I'm going to give you the benefit of the doubt and, for your mother's sake, not say anything about this. But if I ever hear another—"

"You won't." He lifted his hand in a pledge. "Not ever again. Promise."

She turned to go, but as she opened the door, he called to her.

"Thank you, Paula."

She looked at him over her shoulder and nodded before leaving.

⚜

David's legs wobbled like a rickety rail as he walked up the porch steps. Was he ready for this? Would seeing her be more than he could handle?

He lifted his hand and rapped his knuckles on the door. When it swung open, a dark-haired man gave a half smile and shook his hand. "I'm Steve Morgan. You must be David."

"Nice to meet you." David stepped inside, letting his gaze travel around the house. He could take three steps in any direction and be in a different room. If he listed this house, he'd use phrases like "cozy cottage" or "charming bungalow."

A woman rounded the corner. "Hi, I'm Deb." She wiped her hands on her jeans before shaking his hand. "Faith's having breakfast; I thought it would give us a chance to talk for a minute."

David pushed back his impatience. A few minutes wouldn't matter one way or another. They invited him to have a seat, and when he did, his eyes focused on three photos of Faith hanging on the wall. Her eyes stood out most of all. They were a familiar shade of green and almond shaped, just like Paula had said. They twinkled when she smiled.

"Is this the first time you've seen her photo?" Deb asked.

"Yes." David couldn't even identify the emotions that were spreading through him as he stared at his daughter. Though her eyes favored him, her lips were all Paula—full and pink and capable of a heartbreaking pout.

"We weren't sure how much you knew about Faith," Steve said. "You'd mentioned that you and Paula were—uh—weren't on speaking terms."

David tore his eyes from the photos and met Steve's eyes. They were guarded, and David couldn't blame him.

Steve continued. "Faith doesn't know exactly what's going on. She knows she's going to be meeting a friend of ours, but she doesn't know you're her—birth father."

A weight sunk to the bottom of David's stomach and anchored there.

"She's only three," Deb said. "And we feel it would be confusing for her."

"We will tell her the truth eventually," Steve added. "But we think it's best to wait awhile." Firmness framed his words.

"I understand." David was so eager to see Faith, he was willing to go along with about anything.

"This is awkward for all of us," Steve said. "We can't help but feel a little threatened by your appearance, and our attorney was against our having you over. But considering your position, we think we're doing the right thing."

David recognized the fear in Deb and Steve's eyes and saw that they were putting their hearts on the line by letting him meet Faith.

"Daddy, wook!" Faith sped into the room with an uneven gait, her legs carrying her as fast as they could. She climbed into Steve's embrace and held up a piece of Pop Tart. "It's a puppy. See the tail and the ears?"

David couldn't take his eyes off her. She was as cute as a button, with two curly pigtails and cheeks that gave her a baby-faced look.

"Did you make that?" Steve asked.

She nodded, her pigtails bobbing up and down.

"Honey," Deb said, "this is our friend Mr. David. Can you say hello?"

Faith tucked her head into the crook of Steve's neck, turning her face to peek at David. "Hewo."

He'd never cherished a word so much. "Hello, Faith." His throat almost closed up, but he forced himself to speak, not wanting to end the first conversation with his daughter. "I used to make shapes with my toast when I was a little boy. I'd bite off chunks until I made a boat or a fish."

"I have a fish." She slid the Pop Tart into her mouth and nibbled off a piece.

"You do? What kind is it?"

She leaned back and looked at Steve with questioning eyes. He answered for her. "It's a goldfish."

"His name is Jonah," Faith said.

David breathed a laugh. "Does he remind you of the Bible story?"

She nodded and finished off the last of her Pop Tart. "Can I show him Jonah?"

Deb's eyebrows darted up, and she looked at her husband.

"Sure, princess," Steve said.

Faith scooted off Steve's lap, and David followed her. The bedroom was tiny, but the lavender walls and frilly bedspread resembled a life-size dollhouse. The fishbowl sat atop the dresser.

"Wanna feed him?" She got a can of fish food from the bureau drawer and handed it to him.

"How much do I put in?"

She held her forefinger and thumb together. "Just a tiny pinch, see? If you feed him too much, he'll die." She lowered her voice to a whisper. "That's what happened to Fwipper."

"Flipper?"

"I put *all* the food in the water," she said gravely.

"The whole can?"

She nodded.

David heard movement behind him and knew both Steve and Deb were standing in the doorway. He gathered a pinch of the flakes and held it up for Faith to see. "Like this?"

"Just right."

He dropped the flakes into the bowl, and Jonah started feeding off them.

Faith saw her parents and walked to Steve, putting her arms up to be held. He swept her up, and she wrapped her arms around his neck, letting her legs dangle from her dad's grip.

Her dad.

David rejected the words mentally for the pain it caused him. Even though he couldn't dispute Steve was every definition of the word *dad* to Faith, it drove a stake in his heart to think of the man that way.

David closed the fish-food container and set it on the bureau. "Looks like you take good care of your fish, Faith. Jonah seems very happy."

When Faith didn't say anything, Deb answered for her. "We've only had him for a few weeks, but she feeds him every day without being told, don't you, honey?"

Faith leaned back in Steve's arms. "Can I watch cartoons?"

Steve traded a glance with Deb. "Sure, go ahead."

Faith wriggled down and limped away, her long, pink floral shirt swaying with the movement.

David took a deep breath. It was bittersweet, this first meeting with his little girl. Faith was everything he thought she'd be . . . and more. It felt as if a missing piece of his heart had been put into place, and now it was whole again.

She was bright and sweet and well-adjusted. She was being taught to live for God. She was being cared for and loved.

But she was not his.

"She likes you," Deb said.

Did she know he needed to hear that? How the father in him yearned to have his daughter's approval? His throat tightened, and he couldn't speak for fear he'd lose control.

"She doesn't just take to anyone like that," Deb said. "I couldn't believe when she asked to show you Jonah."

"Or let you feed him," Steve said. "That's the highlight of her day."

A strange mixture of joy and pain blended together in his heart. His emotions needed release. David walked toward the door, knowing he needed to leave *now*. He cleared his throat. "I really appreciate your letting me meet her," he said when they approached the front door. He wanted to tell them what a great job they were doing. He wanted to ask if he could see her again. But his throat had closed.

"You're welcome," Steve said.

"Faith," Deb called into the living room. "Say good-bye to Mr. David."

"Bye, Mr. David." Her sweet voice carried to his ears, and he wished he could catch it in his hands and tuck it into his pocket for later.

"Bye, Faith." David turned before the Morgans could see the dampness in his eyes. "Thank you again," he said over his shoulder.

Somehow David made it to the privacy of the car. He started the rental and backed out of the drive. He made it three blocks to a rundown shell of an old gas station before he pulled over and let the feelings out.

The padded Manila envelope sat on the coffee table where David put it when he reached home. He fixed himself a roast-beef sandwich with a side of deli potato salad and ate alone at the kitchen island while going through the stack of junk mail and bills. Now, sitting in his recliner, he opened the *Wall Street Journal* and tried to ignore the package.

But instead of focusing on the paper, his thoughts turned to Faith, as they had so often over the days since he met her. He wished now that he'd asked for a picture or two. So many times he toyed with the idea of getting custody. He teased himself with thoughts of raising her in Jackson, of taking her to see the Jackson Moose hockey team or to Music in the Hole on the Fourth of July.

But the fantasies always spun out in the end, and he knew deep in his soul why that was. The Morgans were good parents, the only parents Faith knew, and she belonged with them.

The thought made him ache a hundred different ways, but it didn't change the reality of the situation. He did want to be part of Faith's life, and he hoped the Morgans wouldn't have a problem with that. He knew he could probably win visitation rights, but didn't think he would have to resort to that. He wondered if Paula was having the same thoughts as he. Had she seen Faith since they argued? Had the Morgans told her he came by?

He received e-mails from her faithfully. The first few he deleted without reading, but slowly his anger faded away. In its place was a lonely depression. He'd been coming home to an empty house for over three months, but it was different now because his relationship with Paula was severed.

Her e-mails were eating away at his resolve to stay angry. When she e-mailed the weekend before, saying she'd like to come home, he responded *Don't.* It was all he wrote. He couldn't have told her he'd be in Chicago visiting their daughter. He hadn't even told the Morgans yet for fear they'd say no if they had too much time to consider it.

He should have known that the one rejection wouldn't stop Paula. The day before, he got the request from her again.

I want to come home this weekend. We really need to talk. I miss you, David.

He closed his mailbox after reading the message. It wasn't until he came home from work this night that he opened it again and responded.

I'm not ready.

He wasn't sure when he would be ready, but he knew he was putting off the inevitable. One way or another the impasse would have to be resolved. Was he ready to let Paula go? Was he even able? The anger enabled him to think he could give her up, but now that the anger had burned down to a slow simmer, he wasn't sure what he wanted.

He flipped the page, trying to focus on the newsprint in front of him. The Dow was up, and his stocks were holding their own. He checked his father-in-law's stock and saw it was up a bit.

The top half of the paper flopped forward, and David caught sight of the padded envelope. He snapped the paper upright and turned the page. He couldn't imagine what was in the package, but with a postmark of Chicago, he knew who it was from.

He didn't need to look again to know his own name and address were scrawled across the front. Judging by the messy writing, she must have waited until the package was full before addressing it or filled it out in the car on the way to the post office.

He folded the paper and set it on the table beside him. His heart sped as he lifted the envelope and set it in his lap. It was bulky but not heavy. He slid his finger under the tab and opened it. When he emptied the contents, a newspaper-wrapped item with a yellow Post-it note tumbled out. He read the note:

> *Thought you might like a copy of this.*
> *Thanks for all your help.*
> *Linn*

The speed at which his spirits sank left him shaking. It was from Linn. He hadn't known how much he'd wanted it to be from Paula until he'd seen Linn's name scrawled on the bottom of the note.

He almost laid the package aside, disappointed and angry at himself for hoping. But instead, his fingers found the end of the newspaper wrapping, and he pulled on it, letting the package flip-flop until the contents tumbled out.

A VCR tape. He read the label: *Communications 101: Video Project, Linn Caldwell.*

His thoughts made a quick jaunt back to almost two months ago, when Linn taped him and Paula talking about communication in marriage. The irony hit him like an openhanded smack. Paula was more qualified to give advice on *mis*communication. She had three years of practice to her credit.

He stuffed the newspaper back into the envelope and set it on the table. The tape rested in his lap, destination unknown. It was an unwanted gift, a dangerous look back in time. But time transport wasn't a reality, and the tape would only reopen a wound that had recently begun to heal. He picked up the tape.

He would go to the garage and dump it in the garbage can. He stood, tape clutched in his hand, and moved toward the kitchen.

His trip to Chicago was so clear in his mind. He and Paula had walked the streets of Chicago that first day, and he wasn't able to keep his hands off her. The cold wind brought a blush to her cheeks and tousled her hair into a just-out-of-bed look. They went back to her apartment and made love, and afterward he simply watched her. Stared at her wide green eyes and thought about how much he loved her. It hit him full force that she was the only one on the planet for him. That God made her especially with him in mind.

He hadn't told her his thoughts then, and now he wondered why. Was some part of him holding back? Some part of him that knew Paula was holding back from him?

He opened the garage door and stopped on the threshold, staring at the garbage can. The trash truck would come tomorrow, and if he threw the tape in the can, the tape would be gone forever. He'd never again see Paula and him together as they had been that week.

His fingers tightened on the tape. It felt as if he would be throwing away their relationship instead of a plastic tape. Did he really want to get rid of it, or was he acting blindly, on emotion?

Suddenly he remembered a remark Paula made during the interview. Linn asked them about resolving conflict, and Paula said something about how they both have a tendency to shut down when there's conflict. She said it was an obstacle they had to work at, and David agreed with her. When he'd accused her of having an affair, he shut her down completely. Then she'd gotten weary of defending herself and shut down too.

It took months to resolve that conflict because he was too stubborn to stop and consider he might be wrong. Being stubborn then was the biggest mistake he'd made in their marriage.

He remembered New Year's, when he apologized for his accusations. Paula forgave him easily, something that stunned him at the time and only served to deepen his feelings for her.

Which doesn't even come close to what Paula's done.

Let him who is without sin cast the first stone.

The thought came from nowhere and settled on him like a heavy woolen blanket.

He considered the tape, imagining Paula the way she looked that day, the way she elbowed him halfway through the interview when he made some joking comment.

He knew then he didn't want to get rid of the tape. He wanted to watch it.

He was standing in front the big-screen TV before he realized there was only a DVD player on top. The bedroom TV. Didn't it have a built-in VCR player?

He went up the stairs and into the room, straight to the TV on a high table in the corner of the room. Relief soothed him when he saw a VCR player. He popped in the tape, grabbed the remote, and hit Play. It seemed to take forever to get going. Linn was on the tape first explaining her project and what she hoped to accomplish. When she wrapped up her comments, suddenly there they were. David was sitting beside Paula on her living-room couch, his arm stretched across the sofa behind her.

Linn introduced David and Paula, then launched into her first question. "One of the top-cited reasons for discontent in marriage is lack of communication. Why do you think that is?"

David answered first, then Paula added some comments of her own. He watched the way she tucked her auburn hair behind her ear. He always teased her about having an Irish temper, but in reality, Paula was too controlled to let herself fly off the handle.

He jerked his attention back to the tape. Linn asked about conflict and communications, and that's where Paula commented that they both tended to run from conflict.

He'd lightened the tension by talking about his affinity for neatness and Paula's tendency to be somewhat of a "messy." That's when she elbowed him in the ribs.

His mind went back to the moment when he was packing to leave Chicago that week. He kissed Paula, then she stared into his eyes with a look he didn't quite understand.

"Did you mean what you said on the tape?" she asked.

"Absolutely. You are definitely a messy."

She gave a mock glare and smacked him on the arm. "Not that part. You know, the part about love being a choice. And how you would choose to love me every day, regardless of what happens."

Now he wondered. Was she thinking of what she had done three years ago? Was she thinking of the lie she'd kept from him?

"Would you choose to love me every day, regardless of what happens?"

Was it fear that made her ask? Did she doubt his love was strong enough to forgive her anything?

Haven't you proved her fears right?

The words stirred something deep in the pit of his stomach. He focused on the video again. They were laughing at something Paula said. Then everything turned serious.

David was speaking. "I think the biggest thing I've learned is that love isn't about the feelings you have when you're dating. They're a start, but true love is a choice. For me it's about choosing to love Paula, even when there's been a miscommunication or when we're too irritated with each other to talk. You just have to choose to love each other, regardless of what happens."

He was looking at Linn when he said the words. But now he looked at Paula. She watched him as he spoke, and tears filled her eyes before she looked down at her lap. He could see her blinking back tears, see her jaw stiffen as if trying to hold in her emotions.

Minutes later the interview ended, and she and David traded a smile before the screen changed to another couple Linn had interviewed.

David turned the video off.

Paula had taken those words to heart. It was obvious by her reaction to them and by the fact that she had asked him later if he'd meant it.

He said he had, but did he really? He had done nothing but run away the past few weeks. Not that he didn't have reason to be angry. What Paula had done was—

Let him who is without sin cast the first stone.

He stared at the blank TV screen, the scripture flooding him with guilt.

All right, all right. I get it.

It wasn't as if he was perfect either, but this . . . Could he forgive this, forgive her, and make their marriage work?

"You just have to choose to love each other, regardless of what happens."

It was easy-to-spout rhetoric, but to actually put it into action . . . that was another matter. And yet he did love Paula. He missed her. Having a chasm between them was like having his heart cut out. He missed bantering with her and holding her. He missed the way she made herself vulnerable only to him. To everyone else she might seem an ice princess, but with him she would sink into his embrace and become as vulnerable as a child.

Yes, he loved her even now. Even after the abortion. Even after the lies. Sometime over the past few weeks, Paula had confessed everything to her mom. The family had tried to offer their support, but David had shrugged it off. When his father-in-law had put his arm around him in the church vestibule, David had gritted his teeth through the advice.

"I know my daughter's caused a lot of hurt. What she did was terribly wrong, and her mother and I are devastated too. But eventually, love forgives, and when it does, it grows. That might be hard to believe right now, but just try and hang on to that, OK?"

David hadn't been ready to hear it at the time, but now the words gave comfort.

"Love forgives, and when it does, it grows."

When Paula forgave him for his accusations, it proved true. Their love had grown immeasurably. He was astounded at how quickly their relationship deepened. He just never attributed it to forgiveness.

Help me, God. I do want to forgive her. Is that enough to start with?

A sudden longing for Paula surged through him. He remembered the e-mails he'd skimmed through, and he had the urge to read them again. He went downstairs and opened his mail, then reread all her e-mails. She apologized over and over.

I would give anything on earth to go back and undo what I did. My selfishness hurt so many people. I'll have to live with my mistake the rest of my life, and worse . . . so will you. And that's the most terrible thing of all. When I think of how you must feel, my heart breaks. You deserved to be a father to our child, and I cheated you of that. Words can't express how sorry I am, David.

When he was finished reading all the e-mails, he wiped his face with the sleeve of his shirt. In all the days following his discovery, this was the first time he'd given any thought to what Paula might be feeling. He had been so caught up in the unfairness of the situation that he hadn't once considered the enormous regret she was carrying.

He was running again, and it was getting him nowhere.

Before he could change his mind, he logged on to a travel site and booked a ticket for the next day. He didn't know how they'd get through the aftermath, but somehow they would. And he prayed they'd come out the other side stronger for having weathered the storm.

CHAPTER
THIRTY-EIGHT

Paula entered her apartment and flipped on the table lamp. The room was quiet, and she knew Linn must've gone to bed. She brushed the snowflakes from her hair as she kicked off her heels. Flurries had begun to fall, the beginning of the snowstorm the station meteorologist had promised.

But Paula didn't care about the coming snowstorm or the interview that had kept her out too late. There was only one thing on her mind this evening, and that was getting home to check her e-mail. Maybe he was ready to talk now, and she could book a flight home for the weekend. It was what she wanted more than anything.

These past weeks put everything in perspective. Her job was only a job. Her career, only a career. The things that mattered most in life were not things one was paid for. And she'd let the most important person in her life take a backseat to her career goal.

She tossed her coat over the couch arm and settled in at the computer desk. Her fingers trembling on the mouse as she opened her mailbox. Eight e-mails. She skimmed the list looking for David's screen name. Her eyes stopped on the sixth e-mail.

She clicked on the message and tapped her nervous fingers on the desk edge, wishing she could retrieve the e-mail faster. When it opened, it took only a second to read the three words.

I'm not ready.

Disappointment washed over the hopes she'd built up since she'd sent the e-mail the day before.

Last time she asked to come home, he said, "*Don't.*" This time he said, "*I'm not ready.*" Did the change of phrase indicate a softening? Even a slight one? Just the phrasing indicated that there would come a point when he *was* ready.

She leaned back against the chair as the weeks of stress overcame her. But when would that point come—when would he be ready? Was he just going to sit by and let their marriage dwindle down to nothing?

A thought intruded, like an unwelcome guest. Was he simply stalling for time while he consulted with an attorney and filed divorce papers? A surge of adrenaline raced through her blood, sending tingling prickles down her arms. She sat upright.

David wouldn't do that. He loved her. He might be furious with her, and he had every right to be, but he did love her.

His words came back to haunt her again. "*I can't love someone I don't know, and Paula . . . I don't know you at all.*"

Oh, God, does he really feel that way? Does he still think I'm a stranger?

It wasn't true. She was still Paula, with all her faults and foibles. And the secret she kept was like an indomitable weed that she tried to stamp down into the soil. But the weed had a life of its own, and now it clawed its way to the surface and was strangling everything around it.

Would there be anything left of their marriage by the time the secret was finished wreaking its havoc?

Why hadn't she seen earlier that the lie needed to be pulled up by its roots? Now so much damage had been done, she didn't know if there was anything left to salvage.

She clicked on David's e-mail again. She wanted to talk to him. She wanted to hit Reply and pour her heart out.

But she'd already done that. What else could she do? Her gaze swung to the phone sitting on the coffee table atop a stack of magazines. Should she call, or would he only ignore it again?

It was late, after eleven, and too late to call even if he did pick up. Her eyes flickered over the computer screen and focused on the travel icon on her Favorites bar. Should she go home and confront him? What would she say that she hadn't said in a dozen e-mails already?

Her eyes fell to David's e-mail in the window below.

"*I'm not ready.*"

Well, *she* was ready. She was ready to take all the blame. She was ready to beg and plead. She was ready to earn back his trust for the next fifteen years if that's what it took to win David back. She would go to counseling; she would give up the anchor chair; she would move back to Jackson Hole.

If only David would have her.

She opened the travel site and found the familiar flight, relieved to see there was space available. Tomorrow she would fly home, and there wasn't anything that was going to get in her way.

⋯

David pulled his carry-on to the row of seats at the gate and sat between a middle-aged woman and a man talking on a cell phone. He had pushed it a little by arriving only forty-five minutes early, but his client's closing had run over. Besides, Jackson's airport was small, and security was a breeze compared to a place like Chicago.

An announcement came over the speakers calling for the boarding of a flight to Salt Lake City. He watched the middle-aged woman gather up all her belongings and wondered how she'd make it down the long hallway and across the tarmac to the plane without dropping it all.

Since he had decided to go to Paula the night before, his resolve had only strengthened, and he knew it was because it was the right thing to do. He'd run long enough. It was time to stop and listen.

"For those passengers flying on flight 738 to Chicago, there may be a slight delay. We hope to begin boarding soon."

David took his newspaper from the carry-on and opened it.

"You heading to Chicago?" the man beside him asked.

"Yes, I am." David wasn't in the mood to chat with talkative strangers. He hoped he wouldn't get seated beside someone who flapped his jaws constantly.

"I hope they don't cancel it." The man gestured to the phone in his hand. "My wife said they're in the middle of a snowstorm."

David had been so busy preparing for his weekend off work that he hadn't even checked Chicago's weather. "You're kidding." He hadn't realized how badly he wanted to see Paula until now.

"Started last night and has been snowing all day. She said they have eight inches, but it's starting to warm up."

Maybe it wouldn't be a problem after all. Chicago was used to dealing with snow. "Well, that's good."

"Not really. They're calling for an inch of sleet and ice."

Paula set the suitcase by her feet and looked out the wall of windows lining O'Hare's gate B10. The pavement, the planes, even the sky appeared to have been swallowed up by a great sea of white. It was a winter wonderland. But all Paula could wonder about was whether or not her flight was going to get off the ground.

She pulled out her Jackson cell phone and punched in Natalie's number. Kyle picked up and transferred it to her sister. In the background she heard Grace wailing.

"Hi, Paula." Her sister sounded frazzled, and Paula realized she probably didn't have time to chat.

"What's going on over there? It sounds like a zoo."

"It's family night," Natalie said. "We're playing Uno, and Alex is skunking everyone, which means Taylor has a handful of cards and wants to quit."

"Ah. And what's Grace's problem?"

"She's just hungry." The phone sounded like it was getting jostled around. "There we go. She's happy now. Sounds pretty noisy wherever you are too."

"I'm at the airport, getting ready to fly home. At least I hope so. There's a winter storm in full swing."

"I didn't know you were coming home this weekend. Is David ready to talk?"

Paula hefted her suitcase to an empty chair and sat down. "No, but I am. This isn't going to go away if we just ignore it."

"Do you think that's wise, hon? Some people just need more time to process things."

Her hand gripped the cell phone. "I can't stand it anymore. I miss him, and I want him back. I know what I did was unthinkable, but I don't care what it takes. I'm not giving up on our marriage." An announcement started over the intercom. "Hang on a sec, Natalie."

". . . give you an update shortly. Repeating, flight number 257 to Jackson Hole, Wyoming has been delayed. We will give you an update shortly. Thank you."

"Oh, great," Paula said. "We've got a delay now."

"Well, you might not get here until late, but at least you know you'll be seeing David soon. You should probably call him if you're going to be too late so he doesn't think you're a burglar when you come in."

A ruckus started in the background. She heard Alex cheering. "OK. I'll let you go."

After she disconnected, she carried her bag back to the window, unable to sit still. The snowflakes were thinning out and being replaced by rain or sleet. She didn't know whether it would hurt or help her cause. She turned and leaned against the cold windowpane. People rushed up and down the terminal, pulling suitcases behind them. Most seats at the gate were occupied, and Paula wondered if other flights were delayed too. She checked her Movado. They would be boarding now if the plane were running on schedule.

To pass time, she walked down to the nearest Starbucks and ordered an Americano. By the time she got back to the gate, she was wishing she'd brought her larger rolling suitcase. Her feet ached from the heels she'd been in all day, and carrying a fifty-pound bag didn't help matters any.

She sipped her drink and thought about David. What would she say to him when she saw him? Would he be angry she had come home after he asked her not to? Would he refuse to talk? How could she make him understand how deeply she regretted the things she'd done?

She was ready to tell him she'd move back home. Surely he'd see then how much he meant to her.

Unless he'd already decided it was over. He may have met with an attorney and started the divorce process for all she knew. The thought was a kick in the stomach. She set her drink under the chair, her hands shaking at the thought. Had she waited too long? Given him too much time alone?

What a fool she was. She should have gone home weeks ago, even if he didn't want her there. If he made up his mind it was over, it would be like uprooting an oak tree to change it now. Why hadn't she realized that before?

"Attention all passengers. We're sorry to inform you that due to the inclement weather, the airport is temporarily closing. All flights for this evening have been cancelled. Please see the attendant at your gate for further information regarding your flight. Thank you."

Paula quickly moved to the gate booth behind the one man who was already there. This couldn't be happening. She needed to get home to David this weekend. The urgency she felt could not be denied.

Another attendant stepped up to help, and Paula met her at the counter. "Do you have any idea when the airport will open again?"

"I'm sorry; I don't. Would you like to book the next flight to Jackson Hole?"

Paula smiled, trying to hide her frustration. "When is it?"

The woman punched keys on the computer and paused. "We have a flight tomorrow afternoon that goes through Salt Lake . . ."

Tomorrow wouldn't be so bad. It would give them all of Sunday together.

"However, it's full."

Disappointment and frustration twisted Paula's nerves.

"Oh, here we go," the attendant said. "We have a flight out Sunday evening. Would you like me to book it for you?" She smiled as though she was the one-woman neighborhood welcoming committee holding out a hot apple pie to the newcomer.

Sunday night. She would get home just in time for David to be going to work. Not to mention she had her own job to worry about.

"Is there any way I can get on standby for the Saturday flight?"

"Well, you can give it a try, but it looks like it's already over-booked."

The woman's carefree smile was tugging on Paula's last nerve.

"I'd like to try anyway," she said.

After Paula stepped away from the counter, she went back to her seat and picked up her coffee. She might as well go back to the apartment, but suddenly it seemed as if every drop of energy had drained out of her. She sank into the now-empty row of chairs. Everyone who'd been at the gate was now in line to reschedule flights.

God, this isn't the way it was supposed to work. Not only would she not see David tonight, she highly doubted she was going home this weekend, and that meant she wasn't going to see him for a week. She couldn't wait a whole week to talk to him. There was no telling what plans he was already making or what he was planning to do this very week. Every minute now seemed like precious seconds ticking away, like a countdown to the end of their marriage.

She wasn't going to wait. She had to talk to him now. She took out her cell phone and punched in their home number. Her limbs weakened as she tried to think of what she'd say. It didn't matter because the phone rang until the voice mail kicked in.

She disconnected and dialed his cell number. The phone began ringing. He normally left it off in the evenings, so it would probably kick over to—

"Hello?" She hadn't heard his voice in weeks, and it was like balm on her soul.

"David." It was all she could think to say. Her mind went blank.

He paused so long, Paula realized he didn't know it was her before he picked up. He must not have checked the screen to see who the incoming call was from. "Don't hang up, David. Please." She took an unsteady breath. "I was going to fly home so we could talk, but the airport just closed, and the flight for tomorrow is booked and another one doesn't go out until Sunday."

"Where are you?"

"O'Hare. David, we have to talk. I know you're angry, and you have every right to be, but this silence isn't fixing anything."

The cacophony of announcements and voices drove her to stand and move away to the window. She peered out into the darkening sky, wishing he would say something. Maybe he'd hung up, and she hadn't heard the click for all the noise.

"Are you still there?" *Please, God, don't let him hang up on me.* Not now, when she'd finally gotten on the phone with him.

"I'm here."

"Will you give me a few minutes, David? You don't have to say anything if you don't want, but would you just hear me out? Please?" She laid her forehead against the cold windowpane.

"I'm listening."

The relief was followed quickly by anxiety. What would she say, and how would she word it? When she reported a story, she wrote it out and edited it before presenting it. Now, when it was most important that she be clear and persuasive, she had nothing. No written speech, no audio track, no video. Just her, humbled and vulnerable, speaking straight from her broken heart.

"When I was a teenager, I remember having this emptiness inside me. This hole that I kept trying to fill with activities and friends. But somewhere on the way, I began filling that hole with my own ambition. By the time I was seventeen, I knew I wanted to be the next Diane Sawyer. I wanted to get out of Jackson Hole and climb the ladder until I stood at the very top. On my way up the ladder, it didn't seem to matter who I trampled. I only saw one thing: the goal, the prize."

Now that she'd started, the words tumbled out. "Even after we fell in love and married, the career was still my number one priority. I didn't see it then, but it's true." The hard part was coming, and she didn't know if she could find the words. But she had to try. "When I got pregnant, it was unexpected for both of us. I guess I saw it—and I'm really ashamed to say this—I saw it as an obstacle to my goals. The child I carried was one more thing to trample on my journey toward success." Her eyes stung, and she closed them.

"When I got the temporary job here in Chicago, once again I put my career first. I didn't care what you had to say or what you wanted. All I could see was the goal."

She wished he'd say something. She wondered if he was even on the line. "David, are you still there?"

"I'm here." The words were so soft she could barely hear him. But at least he was still listening.

She took a deep breath. "When I found out about Faith—my life just turned on end. I can't even begin to tell you all the emotions I've felt. I was shocked that she was alive, joyful that she'd survived, and—*ashamed*. Oh, David, I was so ashamed. When I turned to God, I began to see what had happened, what I had done to bring myself to this place. I had rejected God and set up another idol in His place. My career had come before everything. Before God, before you, and before the child we'd conceived.

"That one grave error led me to a string of tragic choices that have hurt a lot of people, especially you. And the worst part is . . . I can't go back and undo them. I can't change the consequences for any of us. All I can do is say I'm sorry, and as you said before, sorry isn't enough for this. I don't deserve your forgiveness."

She drew a shaky breath. "But I do love you, David. With all my heart. I'll do anything to earn your trust back. I'll quit my job and move back home. The anchor chair would be an empty place to be if you weren't in my life anymore." Tears blurred the darkening sky outside the window.

She let silence fall across the lines. It was up to him now. What would he do with it? Would he throw it all back in her face? She couldn't blame him if he did.

"You're beautiful," he whispered.

The words caught her off guard. A compliment like that was the last thing she expected, especially from three hundred miles away.

"Turn around," he said.

What? Why was he acting so strangely? She straightened and turned away from the window, though for what she didn't know.

Then her eyes fell on him. Across the sea of empty chairs, he stood holding his phone against his ear. Their eyes locked. The moment swirled around her like a surreal painting, everything in her periphery dancing in a hazy mosaic of colors. But there he was. He was here.

He walked toward her, pulling the phone from his ear and flipping it closed in one motion.

She let her own hand fall, her feet rooted to the floor as he neared. Her vision went blurry and she blinked, not wanting to lose sight of him for even a second.

He stopped an arm's length away.

"You're here," she whispered. She wanted to reach out and run her fingers down his jaw just to make sure. But she didn't know if he'd welcome her touch. Maybe he'd come to tell her it was over. Maybe he had divorce papers in his case.

"Why did you come?" Her muscles tightened as if they could block the blow his answer could inflict.

"Because I love you." His words were so quiet she nearly had to read his lips.

Her heart caught midbeat, then continued at a frantic pace. She didn't deserve his love after what she'd done. She deserved to be left alone with the career she'd chased so diligently. Tears flowed down her face in earnest now.

"Don't cry." He smoothed away her tears with the back of his hand. "It'll be OK." He drew her tenderly to him, and she buried her face in the softness of his sweater.

She thought of how David had lost the chance to be Faith's father. She thought of the lies she told and the pain she inflicted. "How can it ever be OK?"

His arms tightened around her. "I'm not going to lie to you, Paula. It's going to take a while. But I'm willing to try. We're going to make it work, and with God's help, it's going to be better than it ever was before."

She turned her face, hearing his heartbeat in her ear. "How can you know that?"

He leaned away and took her face in his hands.

She looked into his eyes, knowing she probably had black streaks of mascara running down her face, but she didn't care. All she cared about was David and the love that still shone in his eyes.

"I have it on good authority that when love forgives, it grows," he said, his own eyes filling with tears.

"How do you know you can forgive me?" Her lip quivered as she awaited his answer.

"Because I'm willing. And God is able."

He kissed her, and she tasted the salt of her tears. His lips were warm and soft, and she never wanted to part.

When he pulled away, his eyes held her captive. "Let's go home." They were sweet words, tugging at her in all the right places.

She withdrew her gaze from him and scanned the knots of frustrated travelers. "We can't. The airport's closed, remember?"

He grabbed the handle of his carry-on and picked up her suitcase. "I meant the apartment." He started walking and tossed her a look over his shoulder. "Maybe I'll have a chance to scope out the real-estate market over the weekend."

She followed him, speeding her steps until she was beside him. "Why would you do that?"

"You don't think I'm going to let my famous wife support me, do you?"

She stopped in her tracks and stared hard at him, not sure she was hearing what she thought she was.

He walked three steps before he seemed to realize he'd lost her. He turned. "What?"

She couldn't believe how blessed she was. After all her mistakes, all her bad choices, here was a man who was sticking by her regardless. "You want to move here?"

He set down her bag. "You belong here, Paula. And I want to be wherever you are. Always."

A lady jostled Paula as she rushed past. She hardly even noticed. She couldn't take her eyes off her husband. Even when she'd done nothing but drive him away with her secrets and lies and walls, he was there to pick her up again and give her another chance. She moved closer to him, drawn to him like never before, and stood face to face with him, so close that their breath mingled.

She thought of Faith and wondered how it would be for them, living in the same city as their daughter and having no right to her. And David— "You haven't even met Faith yet." His daughter was three years old, and he'd never met her.

"Actually, I met her last weekend."

"You did?"

He nodded. "I flew here, and the Morgans had me over." He gave a sad little smile. "She's a doll, just like you said with those green eyes and cute little curls."

Paula couldn't believe he had met her. The Morgans hadn't said a word.

"She reminds me of someone," he said.

"Yeah?"

"Yeah." He brushed a strand of hair behind her ear. "She reminds me of the little girl we're going to have someday."

A sweet fullness swelled up inside her as she framed his face in her hands. "Oh, David, I'd like that more than anything."

And then he kissed her again—a slow, sweet kiss that made her ache at its beauty.

Outside, snowflakes swirled around, but inside the warmth of their love rekindled a fire she knew would be burning for a long time to come.

The End

Dear Reader,

The main idea of *Finding Faith* came to me during a brainstorming session with my author friends Colleen Coble and Diann Hunt. The actual seed of the story came from Diann, and when she blurted out the idea, I gasped. It was a stunning twist, but did I want to explore the painful issue of abortion? And how would I get my characters—who were on various sides of the issue and thus experiencing vastly different emotions—to push past the pain enough to forgive? Mostly I wondered if I could do justice to such a difficult topic.

For some, the issues in this book were difficult to read about. My prayer is that the message of forgiveness and love for a special little girl will offer hope. Hope to those who are in that frantic place of deciding between aborting "a fetus" or letting a baby live. Hope to those who are in the long nine months of carrying a baby they will never see grow up. Hope to those who've been harmed through the lies that "everything will be fine" and will "return to normal" after an abortion.

The strength to forgive can always be found through Jesus Christ. It will not necessarily come quickly, and sometimes it's a long journey. But you, too, can "find faith"—that place of safety in the midst of a stormy world. God is always there, waiting for you.

Denise Hunter

As far as the east is from the west,
so far has he removed our transgressions from us.
—Psalm 103:12

DISCUSSION QUESTIONS

1. If you discovered that you (like Faith) were the "product" of a botched abortion, how would you feel? How would that news affect the way you see yourself and your role in this world? the way you feel about others (especially the woman who tried to abort you)? the way you think about God?

2. Paula found herself in a painful position—torn between her family and her career. Have you ever felt that kind of tug? If so, when? How did you handle the pressure? What decisions did you make as a result? Looking back, is there anything you would change about those decisions? Why or why not?

3. Natalie had two young sons and had suffered through a lot in the past year, including her ex-husband, Keith's, betrayal. Yet she chose to adopt Grace, the love child of her ex-husband and Linn Caldwell (the "other woman" who had broken up her marriage). If you were in the same situation, what would you choose to do? How would you respond to Keith? to Linn? to baby Grace? Why?

4. Have you (or someone you love) longed to have a baby—and yet been denied that dream through infertility or other circumstances? When you hear about others getting pregnant or adopting a child,

what is your first thought? your first emotion? As you wait for a child, what are you doing in the meantime to fill that longing?

5. The inability to conceive drove a wedge between Paula and David—a wedge that widened every day when they shut down and refused to talk about the problem. When your feelings are hurt, how do you respond (with angry words, the silent treatment, by removing yourself from the situation, or . . . you fill in the blank)? Why? From whom did you learn these patterns of communication?

6. Are there any "wedges" in your life right now—between you and a spouse, a friend, or other loved one? What could you do to remove the wedge and open the way to effective communication and healthier problem solving?

7. Have you, like Adam, ever wondered if you were doing the right thing? If you were following the path God intends for your life—whether in career, love, or something else? If so, when? Do you think it's possible to pinpoint God's will for any individual? Why or why not? In what ways could you explore God's will for you?

8. Even though Linn knows she did the right thing in giving Grace life and then allowing her to be adopted into a wonderful family (with half-biological brothers, no less!), she lives daily with a lot of regrets. She has caused so many people so much pain—not to mention the effects on her own relationships now and down the road. Do you live with any regrets for things that you have done? for things that have been done to you? How have these regrets impacted your relationships today? What first step can you take to break the cycle of regret?

9. Imagine for a moment that you are either Deb or Steve Morgan. You have just found out through a blood test that Faith, the sweet,

three-year-old girl you brought home from the hospital and have been raising, isn't your biological daughter as you thought. How would you respond to: the doctor who helped in the birthing? the hospital staff? your daughter? Would you have taken the same risks the Morgans did in trying to find out what happened that day? Why or why not?

10. In *Finding Faith* Paula has to own up to what she did three years ago and admit that one wrong, selfish decision has caused huge ripples of pain in her own and others' lives. David has to get past his shock and horror of his wife's betrayal before he can even think of forgiving her for trying to abort their baby. And Linn has to learn how to forgive herself for tearing apart Natalie's family. The old adage is true: forgiveness isn't easy. But do you find it easier to forgive others—or yourself? Why? Whom do you need to forgive—and why? For what act(s) should you seek forgiveness? How would forgiving others and yourself make a difference in your life and in your future decisions?

Read the rest of Denise Hunter's New Heights series